Making it Big

Other books by this author

The Rainbow Weaver

Making it Big

Lyndsay Russell

OLDCASTLE BOOKS

First published as FAT CHANCE in 2008 by Oldcastle Books,
P.O. Box 394, Harpenden, Herts, AL5 1XJ
www.oldcastlebooks.co.uk

A CIP catalogue record for this book is available from the British Library.
This is a work of fiction. Names, characters, places, and incidents either are the product of
the author's imagination or are used fictitiously, and any resemblance to actual persons, living
or dead, businesses, companies, events, or locales is entirely coincidental.
While the author has made every effort to provide accurate telephone numbers and Internet
addresses at the time of publication, neither the publisher nor the author assumes
responsibility for errors, or for changes that occur after publication. Further, the publisher
has no control over and assumes no responsibility for author or third-party websites
or their content.

978-1-84243-273-0

2 4 6 8 10 9 7 5 3

Typeset by Avocet Typeset, Chilton, Aylesbury, Bucks in 11.5pt Garamond MT
Printed and bound by CPI Group (UK) Ltd, Croydon, CR0 4YY

*Dedicated to every person who feels that
they are not the 'perfect weight'*

Acknowledgements

It feels a little weird and premature to say all those pompous 'I'd like to thank my editor/agent' bits, because even though I'd love to, who knows if this book will actually be a success? Indeed, with so many novels out there, what are the actual chances of really 'making it big'? So, instead, I thought that maybe I would just share with you a little fantasy that happened to me last night.

I had a dream…

I'm alone on a stage (but for once, not in a 'naked actor' nightmare) and I'm making a speech …

'First, I'd like to thank … Annette Crossland. My eccentric, but utterly brilliant, publisher. Taking chances on new writers is always a gamble. A huge thanks for publishing my first book, and now for having the belief in this one … the second. Ms Crossland is a remarkable woman whose beauty, intelligence, unstinting enthusiasm and love of her job make her a joy to work for – I suspect that any company she chooses to go into partnership with is very, very lucky.'

Publisher smiles warmly, and waves big fat contract for third book.

'I'd also like to thank my team buddy and husband Mike, whose fantastic support, talented mind, critical eye, and editorial suggestions were invaluable. I'd also like to hug our adorable daughter Tippi for her understanding when I was "too busy". By the way, sorry, kiddo – I'm not changing my mind. The "naughty bits" will be blacked out in your edition. And highlighted in my husband's.'

Wild applause and laughter. I pause graciously – smile, and look earnestly towards TV cameras …

'I'd also like to thank my mother, Reeva. Hi, Mum, I know you're watching … Thanks, you've been a terrific help with the book. I'll never forget the "night of the cocktails" at the Petersham, bouncing ideas off you in the rain. Or the day in the pool in Antigua, bouncing ideas off you in the sun. I love you.' *Blow kisses.* 'The same goes for my sister-in-law, Anita – who was there for me when my father was ill and my inspiration flagged. Great suggestions. You are so much more creative than your family give you credit for. I won't name names, but he's my brother … he's a sod. What can I tell you?'

My voice breaks, wavering with emotion …

'At this stage I'd also like to send a big thank-you to Diana at Guards Polo Club for the low-down on Cartier International, (any tickets?), Julie D. on PR, Patty on fashion, Hannah and Hazel, my editors, and Ion, – publishing head honcho and signatory of important monetary contracts. Thank you one and all.'

I wipe a tear as I clutch the Man Booker award to my breast…

'Finally, it's vital that I thank *you*, the press, for supporting a book that tries to correct the sad, twisted notion that ultra skinny is desirable, and that we're all butt-ugly if we're above a size ten. Together, we can address this mess …'

Paparazzi photographers and journalists get to their feet, and applaud. I sob unashamedly and place a steadying hand on lectern.

'But most important of all … Sorry, please – I just need to take a moment.'

Dramatic pause as I swallow deeply …

'Most important of all, I want to thank *you*, the public, for buying a novel that hits back at the celebrity fashionistas. A novel that struggles to correct the model images that have so distorted our minds. A book that fights to give us back … our dignity.'

'Bless you, thank you. This statue means so much to me, I will treasure this moment for ever …'

Uniformed Body Police march on stage. They try to drag me off. I resist, wearing a martyred facial expression. I raise a fist, I cry out:

'Comrades! Sisters! Join forces! Do whatever you can … Fight back! Just remember these words …It's better to light the candle on the double chocolate triple-layered birthday cake than to curse hungrily in the dark.'

One

Poor sad lonely Sharon Plunkett: she had tried every fad, every diet, every exercise and every cream – but like a stain of grease on a pure silk blouse, her rolls of fat refused to budge. Life had never been a bed of roses, just a solitary thorn of despair. A big, fat thorn that constantly pricked her fleshy body, draining every drop of self-confidence.

Blinking away bulbous tears, she savoured the square of milky chocolate, marvelling at the way it melted on her tongue. It veritably oozed. As always, the guilty pleasure hit her taste buds with masochistic force.

As she clutched the giant bar to her bosom, the ridiculously expensive low-calorie salad waiting in front of her seemed deeply unappealing. The mushy grated carrot and sesame seed coleslaw looked like something prised from the cheeks of a hamster, while the black-eyed prawns stared at her reproachfully. Avoiding their accusing gaze, she disdainfully tipped the plastic package into the office bin. There! I've just saved myself a few calories … she reasoned, trying hard not to think of the squandered pounds. Feeling a digging pressure on her waistband, she shifted awkwardly in an effort to ease it.

So what if the other girls hadn't invited her to the wine bar for lunch? She knew why they'd left her out. A tight little coterie of skinny girls obsessed with fashion, they saw themselves as 'cool', and she cramped their style just because she was a bit plump.

Who was she kidding? screamed her inner voice. Size eighteen-to-twenty isn't plump. It's fat, Sharon. FAT, FAT, FAT. The only thing she hated more than her life was the bathroom scales. Had it always been so? Throughout her twenty-one years she couldn't really remember a time when she hadn't felt 'lumpy'.

As a child she had usually been first in the school meal queue, often up for seconds, and always last in the Sports Day run. Nope, there wasn't an age she could remember when what she ate hadn't ruled her day. Now halfway through the chocolate, she had to make the rest last as long as she could. She sipped her tea, dunked a couple of precious squares, and sucked the resulting sticky mess noisily, like a baby finding comfort at a nipple. As it dissolved, so did her resolve. She sighed, and reluctantly let the sad memories of the weekend re-enter her head. The night had started off as usual …

Her 'bestest' friend Debbee had insisted they go to a kitsch country-and-western theme night at Kingston's hottest club, Kool Kat's. Sharon had dressed with care. Well, sort of. She'd applied a splash of blue eye shadow, donned a black A-line tent dress, and half-heartedly curled her long shiny hair in a Tammy Wynette sixties style. But it had started to drizzle. Fearing her damp waves would turn into a frizzy tsunami, Sharon grabbed a spotted scarf she'd picked up in Top Shop and, in an attempt at bandana 'trendy', tied the knot at the back of her neck.

Alas, instead of 'American Cowgirl Chic', the fashion look was more 'Albanian Peasant Crap', and she desperately wanted to change. But as she surveyed the dismal choice in her wardrobe Debbee was honking the car horn, and Sharon knew she hated to be kept waiting.

As expected, Debbee was impatiently clicking her acrylic

French-manicured nails on the steering wheel – a habit that made Sharon grit her teeth.

'What took you so long?' Debbee wanted to know. 'Strap in, kiddo! Yee-haw! Hey, girl, it's time to round 'em up!'

For a split second, Sharon didn't know if she meant the male population of Kingston or her large, spilling breasts. As she struggled to pull the seatbelt over her stomach, she glanced jealously at Debbee's lithe form. It was Saturday night and, as usual, her friend had morphed from trainee suburban beautician, into a sexy, sophisticated wannabe WAG, her perfect, pert breasts displayed in a tight leather waistcoat, her slender hips in a short suede Versace skirt from eBay. Kitten-heeled white cowboy boots completed the look – 'Best Lay at the Chicken Ranch', thought Sharon, though she'd never have had the nerve to say it.

The muscles in Debbee's long, St Tropez fake-tanned leg tautened as she pressed down on the accelerator, Sharon couldn't help admiring how the outside of her smooth thigh hollowed. Like an athlete's. She could feel her own thighs spreading over the plastic front seat, like melting margarine. 'You look fantastic,' she said, hating herself for crawling. But somehow she fell so easily into playing her expected role: to make Debbee feel great.

In response, Debbee preened her blonde Farrah Fawcett mane in the car mirror. 'Do you think so?' she asked, knowing the answer.

'Sure – every man'll drool over you. They always do.'

Debbee smiled at Sharon warmly. 'Actually, that outfit's pretty trendy you're wearing,' she said, awarding Sharon a rare compliment. Sharon smiled back. A tiny glow-worm of confidence lit up inside her.

'Not sure the look is you, though.'

The worm curled up and died.

Totally oblivious, Debbee studied her face lovingly in the car mirror and smoothed her new hair extensions. Applying a slash of crimson Urban Cool lipstick at the next traffic light, she teased, 'I heard Simon's coming tonight, Sharon.'

Sharon's heart did a little two-step as she heard his name. Simon Mercier. Sleek, handsome Simon. Like a shaggy-haired lurcher. A vision in denim. Secret crush of her life for two yearning, burning years of unrequited lust. Something about the way he always looked deep into her eyes made her feel he could see the real her buried under the mounds of massive flesh. His smile made her feel special. Normal.

Last time they'd been to Kat's, he'd even bought her a drink. But not long after they sat down to talk, Debbee had staggered over and said she wanted to leave because she was feeling sick on Sea Breezes. The two girls had made a hasty exit, and Sharon hadn't seen him since then, which she knew was exactly four weeks, six days and twenty-two hours ago.

'I said, I hear Simon is definitely going tonight … really sorry about spoiling it last time. If you see him, use your brains! Offer him a drink or something – and go for it!' Debbee said patronisingly, applying mascara now as she accelerated through the changing lights.

'And you could use your brains to take a PhD in Transit Makeup Application,' quipped Sharon, in an attempt to deflect the comment.

'Don't ignore me – I know you think he's *gorge*. Tonight could be your *big* chance!' Debbee giggled.

'Big' was the operative word, thought Sharon. Big, indeed.

'Simon? Nah, do I look bothered?' she said, with nonchalance so naked her real feelings were completely exposed.

'Yeah, right. Whatever.' Debbee had heard every detail of that famous 'drink' a few times too many.

As she concentrated on crashing the gears of her Clio convertible and cursing the lack of parking spaces, Sharon made occasional clucks of sympathy and let her mind wander back to when she had first met Simon.

He'd walked into her life the moment he stepped through the door of her office to chase up a missing invoice. For the first time since joining top advertising agency Sharpe, Bates and Colt, Sharon was thrilled her job was only junior filing clerk in Accounts. Because it was her he had to talk to.

'Hi, I work for your company as a freelance photographer, and there seems to be a problem with my invoice. The account exec's told me it's been lost,' he'd said, shooting her a sparkling I-floss-twice-a-day smile. As Sharon's heart did a springboard high-jump-double-twist in response, she realised there had been no mix-up at all. The agency had a mean-spirited secret policy to ensure a three-month delay of payment to lesser mortals by any means, fair or foul. The 'sorry, we lost your invoice' schtick was a rite of passage reserved for the absolute newcomer whom they could always replace.

Yes, sirree, SBC hadn't become a successful conglomerate from its advertising talent alone. But Sharon couldn't resist his lazy charm. She dug out his invoice and promised to put it through ASAP. But as she glanced at the address, she caught her breath for the second time that meeting. *He lived in Kingston*! Same suburb as her.

'Ohmigod! We're neighbours!' she blurted.

'Really? You live in Kingston? Whereabouts?'

Sharon began to describe the university area and the flat she owned around the corner. They fell into an easy, laughing conversation about the joys of drinking down by the river and picnicking in Richmond Park.

It turned out Simon had studied photography at the local college and decided to stay because he loved the buzzy little market town and its holiday atmosphere.

'Condé Nast say there's now an open-air coffee bar for every three residents,' joked Sharon.

'Then we must go for a coffee some time,' he said, leaning on the desk towards her.

'Sure, whatever, I'll see you around,' Sharon answered curtly, looking down at the paperwork to hide her reddening face.

He stood back, a bit surprised. 'Oh, okay, then. Another time,' he said slowly, staring at her.

Sharon had done what she always did when anyone showed the slightest bit of interest. She'd come across as cold and dismissive, a protective habit she'd adopted from an early age, even if people were just being friendly. Poor man. Perhaps she'd trapped him into suggesting coffee because she'd waffled on so much about the coffee bars. She'd just wanted to let him off the hook, having to arrange something he couldn't possibly want to do. Silence hung in the air like a frosty mist. She tried to think of a witty icebreaker but her mind was an empty deep freeze. When she looked up again, it was to see him heading towards the door. Politely, he turned and thanked her again for sorting the invoice.

'I'll no doubt bump into you around town,' he called out, with a farewell grin.

For many days after, Sharon would wonder whether he had been making a reference to her mammoth size. If he had, she deserved it.

But the strange thing was, they *had* bumped into each other. Quite a few times. Nearly always at Kat's. And whenever they saw each other, he always stopped and chatted. 'How's Sharke, Bait and Caught?' he'd tease her about the agency – he was wise now to the fact that Sharpe, Bates and Colt was run by a board of heartless bastards.

'Still reeling the clients in,' Sharon would laugh, enjoying their mutual bond.

*

'It's looking *gooood*, girl!' growled Debbee, parking the car and bringing Sharon's attention to the nightclub queue ahead. It was long and, as always, Sharon quaked with nerves that she would be turned away. But, as usual, Debbee had it all under control. Guarding the door, like a pompous pit-bull, her bouncer cousin was playing God with the crowds. Sharon pondered which was thicker – his neck or his head? He was currently arguing with two skinny young teens who, despite the chill night air, insisted on walking around with bare midriffs and indecently fringed micro-minis. 'Are you *sure* you girls are eighteen?' he asked uncertainly.

'*Course* we are.'

Of course they *weren't*, thought Sharon. You could practically see their nappies.

Unceremoniously, Debbee elbowed the kiddies out of the way and after air-kissing the bouncer, like a famous VIP greeting an equally famous VIP, she swanned through the crowd, Sharon waddling in her wake, the perennial ugly duckling.

The club's Denim and Diamonds Country Night was in full swing. The wooden floor was a mangled mob of bobbing cowboy hats and clicking, tripping pointed boots, as the drunken British attempted a display of line dancing.

Blocking the bar, a gaggle of three tarty girls looked like backing singers out to upstage Dolly Parton. Sharon felt like the tour's big, butch roadie as she elbowed through them to the counter.

The barman took her order. 'Okay, I'm just going to have a *Diet* Coke,' she emphasised loudly (and totally unnecessarily, as she was the one getting the drinks).

'Make mine a tequila,' shouted Debbee, over a sea of floating bottle blondes. Turning her back to the bar she stuck her thumbs in her rhinestone belt, flashing her flat midriff, thrust her slim hips forward and struck a raunchy cowgirl pose. Men stared. Women glared.

As Sharon waited for the drinks, she pondered for the zillionth time why someone like Debbee was happy to hang out with her. Fair enough when they were best friends as toddlers – they'd grown up next door to each other, shared nursery toys and gone to primary school together. At secondary, though, the balance had changed. In the same class, they'd stayed mates throughout teenage acne, angst and adolescence – but Sharon had grown in weight and size as Debbee had grown in looks and vanity.

Regardless, Debbee still chose to see her when she was at a loose end. And Sharon was grateful – though a deeply insecure part of her suspected her friend liked to have her around purely because, when they stood next to each other, Debbee knew she appeared even more pretty and petite.

Sharon hated the way those two words went together: pretty and petite. But there was no getting away from it. As Debbee sipped and Sharon slurped their drinks through purple straws, she was painfully aware that they looked like a gazelle and a buffalo sharing the same watering hole.

Together they surveyed the cattle market. Dusty images of *Dallas* sprang to mind, with the dazzlingly tacky outfits more Rodeo Drive than rodeo.

Dirk, the club owner, sat in his usual booth, alone and aloof, eyeing up the women. With an Indian bootlace tie, white hair and a fake moustache, he looked like General Custer surveying the last one-night stand. His wife, Kat, was busy chatting to the DJ, her hair so teased it could have performed its own strip.

'Howdy, gals!' They turned round to see an extremely cute-looking cowboy doffing his hat and directing his white smile totally at Debbee.

'Gee, are you a real cowboy?' she flirted back.

'Course, ladies. I'm Chuck from the States – Tucson, Arizona.'

'Nah, are you *really*?' simpered Debbee, eyes wide. 'Hey, Sharon! He's the real thing! A gen-u-ine cowboy!' She giggled, nudging Sharon so hard her face dipped into her glass and emerged with a frothy Coke moustache.

'Sure am. I'm visiting mah English cousins. We thought this would be a hoot for a night out. Show them mah roots. Ya don't believe me, do ya?'

'Um … no,' said Debbee, suckling her straw and batting her eyelashes, like a newborn colt.

'Okay, lady. D'you know how you can tell a real cowboy?'

Debbee shook her mane of hair and practically neighed.

'First, check out the boots. None of that fancy pointed crap. They've gotta be ropers.' These were round-toed versions, apparently ideal for roping steer.

'Now, check out mah jeans. Wranglers.' He flashed the label, which sat perkily on an even perkier male butt. 'Gives you more room when you're in the saddle,' he whispered suggestively, his accent changing mysteriously mid-flow.

Yeah, right, sniffed Sharon, narrowing her eyes. She reckoned the nearest he'd ever got to a steer was eating steak.

But too late. With a whooping 'YEE-haaw!' from 'Chuck', Debbee was on the dance floor, doing a two-step, and Sharon was alone at the bar. Feeling hungry, she asked for a packet of crisps – barbecue steak flavour. She shrugged – hey, she was just getting into the theme of the evening.

Although Sharon felt painfully self-conscious standing on her own, it was amusing to watch Debbee struggle to keep in step. It was impossible to say whether the toe-crunching was the result of her inept dancing or his adept drinking.

But then, as the music wailed 'Ma Man Gone An' Did Me Wrong', in walked Sharon's ultimate Mr Right.

And Sharon panicked. Had she time to race to the loo to reapply some lippy? Rooted to the spot with indecision, she watched him fall into relaxed chat with some friends and swig beer from the bottle in a very languid, sexy way. He looked so damned cool that Sharon actually moaned.

Wearing his usual faded denim shirt, he resembled a young, laid-back Clint in a Sergio Leone movie. Suddenly, as if sensing he was being watched, he turned his head and squinted through the dark in her direction. That was it. Too late. She was dead. He caught her eye, smiled – then sauntered towards her.

Stuffing the crisps into her bag, Sharon grinned a welcome.

'Hey, how's it going, partner?' he asked, giving her a friendly kiss on the cheek.

'Well, not so great. Debbee's abandoned camp and gone off with an outlaw!' Sharon laughed. Despite her nerves, something about Simon made joking so easy. Normally she would mumble like a moron to any male between sixteen and sixty. But not with him. There was no doubt that he brought out the best in her.

'An outlaw? Which one this time? The Good, the Bad … or the Lousy?' laughed Simon.

'Judging by the way he just stomped on her toe, I'd have to say the Clumsy!'

'Drink?' he offered.

Oh, yes! screamed Sharon's inner voice. 'Er … okay, why not?' she answered serenely, and asked for a spritzer – sophisticated and refreshing, she reckoned, without getting her too light-headed to make conversation. As he turned to order, Sharon spotted Debbee now rowing with the guy on the floor. She pushed him back, and he slapped her bottom, laughing. But Debbee wasn't. She stormed towards them in a furious mood.

'Bastard says I dance like a heifer! He's got a bloody cheek – told me to call him when I'd learned to walk. I'll show him … How dare he?' Seeing Simon, Debbee grabbed his arm. 'Hey, Simon, I need you!'

'No!' whispered Sharon, pleadingly. 'He's getting me a drink!'

Debbee shot her a shucks-too-bad look, and pulled him away from the bar.

'Honey, can you come with me for a while?… I jus' wanna have a little ol' dance with you,' she said huskily, in a tone developed to melt the one male brain cell that controlled 'decency'.

'Um, er … I was just getting dri – Well, okay – sure. Sorry, Sharon … maybe later,' he muttered, as Debbee trailed him on to the floor like a lassoed stallion.

Crestfallen, Sharon watched the couple move to the music. Chuck the cowboy was wrong: Debbee was a great dancer normally, and she took pains to show just how good she was. Her sinewy silhouette snaked sexily against Simon, and as he instinctively moved towards her, she threw back her head with a throaty sigh.

The cowboy watched, amused, from the sidelines, as Sharon stared aghast. The music changed to 'Jolene', and Dolly Parton started trilling how she couldn't compete with her rival's beauty. Oh, the mocking irony, thought Sharon … if blonde, drop-dead gorgeous ol' Dolly could be usurped in love, what bloody hope did she have? Sharon's eyes welled with emotion. She leaned forward to pick up her bag, and a tear plinked on to her ample cleavage – lost like a drop of rain in the Grand Canyon.

What the hell was she thinking? As Mr Blobby's ugly sister, what on earth did she expect? Simon probably didn't even recognise her as female, let alone an attractive mate.

Debbee now draped a loose hand over Simon's shoulder and whispered in his ear. He whispered something back … She twiddled her hair extensions coyly.

Standing there like a plum pudding, Sharon dug her fingers into her pudgy, sweating palm to stop the sobs. Debbee, her closest friend, was moving in on the only man Sharon had ever confessed she wanted. She caught Debbee's eye with a look so plaintive it would have shamed a puppy.

Deliberately ignoring her, Debbee just pulled Simon closer and rested her head against his shoulder. It was a calculated move, as if she was flaunting her power over Sharon.

The country song now twanged on about the 'bitch rival' taking Dolly's man just because she could – the lyrics dangerously egging Sharon's bitterness on. She literally saw red. Painful, red-raw scarlet. Crimson. Blood. She saw his muscular arm brush Debbee's naked shoulder. And with that simple move, he began ripping Sharon's heart out of her body. Moving towards them, unsure what she was going to do, she knew she had to find a way to stop Debbee. Tell her she had a call on her mobile phone … trip her up … blowtorch her smug face off and stamp the scorched flesh into the ground … whatever.

As their lips danced closer and closer, with every gyration from Debbee, Sharon felt as if a loaded gun was pointing at her chest. She had to stop it before it exploded.

Seeing the Ladies behind the pair, she decided to head that way and gently remind them she existed. Pushing past a smooching couple and two girls swaying round a handbag, she found herself in earshot of their conversation.

'So, my place, about eight o'clock, then,' said Simon.

'Sure, I'd love to come. I'll see you then, sounds fun,' said Debbee, breaking free and wiggling her pert arse to the instrumental.

The gun had gone off. Sharon could not deny what she had heard. She was dead. Killed by her best … well, actually her only friend. Slain by the betrayal of her erstwhile 'love' – a man like all the others, weak and stupid, who had fallen for Debbee's quack doctor charms.

Stumbling past them, she headed into the foyer, and the cool night air. If only she could just ride off into the horizon and never be seen again. If only she could disappear. But this wasn't a movie, and she would never have a happy ending.

She hated herself. Every single hundred, thousand, million inches of her fat, fat self.

The phone rang. Sharon sat up at her desk, startled. She had been so immersed in reliving that night, she had almost forgotten where she was.

It was unbearable. She had been a means for Simon to get to Debbee, that was all. A pathetic joke. And as for Debbee – she could have torn her foxy little face to shreds. The bitch. And an affected one, at that. Fancy changing your name to put two 'e's at the end. So pathetic.

Sharon felt desperate. She couldn't bring herself to be friends with Debbee. But as the loneliness of night after night stretched ahead, she was at a complete loss. Sharon stared around the empty office. Time to kill, but she'd already read the morning's paper and had forgotten her book.

Glancing up at the office clock, so cool in design you struggled to read the time, she worked out there were still another twenty minutes before the girls would come back from lunch. The chocolate bar she'd been eking out was now down to a mere three squares and, as usual, she craved more. To take her mind off it, she looked around for something to read. She noticed that Lou-Lou, the daffy blonde in the office gang of six, had a stack of rag mags beside her desk. On the top lay some copies of *Now*, a glossy dedicated to celebrities and their body image. She picked one up and flicked through it, consuming the endless pages of slim Hollywood stars, studying their slender limbs and lithe bodies enviously. Then she looked down at her own reality.

Compared to the celebs, she might have been an alien reject from the planet Heffalump. Miserably she reached for another square of chocolate for comfort. If she was slim, her life would be *so* different …

She reached out for the second issue of *Now*, read the headlines, and nodded, shocked.

98% OF WOMEN ARE UNHAPPY WITH THEIR BODIES! 31% THROW UP AFTER EATING. 62% FEEL UNLOVABLE BECAUSE OF IT!

Opening the pages, she read on, eyes widening at the statistics, yet identifying with each one.

69% WOULD RATHER BE AN UNHEALTHY SIZE 0 THAN A SIZE 16.

How ridiculous, she snorted. Though she knew she would eagerly choose size zero. How the hell had it come to this madness, she wondered. Yet every single statement rang deafeningly loud and true. She tossed the publication back on to the desk.

On a neighbouring chair, she saw a different kind of magazine poking out of a recycled-hemp shopping bag. What's Saffron got in there? thought Sharon. Saffron, hippie child of the office, was the only one who was vaguely pleasant to her … But she was nauseatingly pleasant to everyone, from snotty little kids to Teutonic traffic wardens. She was 'at one' with the universe and always muttering on about *karma*.

Predict was its title. Well, I predict this is a load of old crap, thought Sharon, feeling like a thief as she leafed through its pages.

Guiltily she flicked past the 'I talked to Elvis' article, past the 'My Granny Runs A Coven' exposé, and the 'Do You Have Alien Blood?' quiz.

Her eyes alighted on the small ads at the back of the magazine. Along with 'Half-price Crystal Balls' and 'Navajo Indian Dream Catchers – buy one get one free' nestled three little lines that leaped right out of the page.

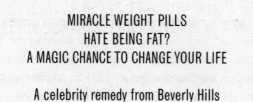

MIRACLE WEIGHT PILLS
HATE BEING FAT?
A MAGIC CHANCE TO CHANGE YOUR LIFE

A celebrity remedy from Beverly Hills
– end of stock offer only £80

There was no telephone number … just an address.

For an appointment write to:
DR MARVEL'S
Miracle Weight Clinic
150 Riversal Road
London W1
Director: Dr Maximus Marvel BSc, DDc, TGIF, ACDC,
Assoc. Hon. Diploma Neuro-nutrition

Sharon studied the advertisement, hooked by the dream, as always. The doctor had so many degrees, titles and diplomas. She didn't recognise the letters after his name but they looked impressive. He must know something others didn't. The advert was tantalisingly simple and to the point. Could it work? Maybe this was the answer to her problem – the 'big one', she thought ironically.

Nah, this was ridiculous. She worked in an advertising agency, for crying out loud. She knew all about false claims and irresistible promises. Every time she looked at the back of shampoo bottles she'd remember not to be fooled. Not since the day she had come across one of the agency's creatives writing copy for a new conditioner.

'*Senses*. Give your hair the scent of fresh air – a touch of silk with the sheen of ice,' read the mock label he wanted to test on her. But when she asked to smell the product to see if it lived up to the claim, the writer laughed arrogantly. He had no idea what it smelled like because the manufacturers hadn't yet produced a drop of it. Production depended entirely on whether the agency could create a brand image to fill a perceived market gap.

The experience served as a warning to Sharon never to believe a single word of packaging descriptions – 99.9 per cent of the time. When it came to slimming, her desperation was such that she'd believe anything. Against all her intelligence, she couldn't help thinking, *Something new!* Feverishly, Sharon copied down the advert and the address. MIRACLE and MAGIC.

The two words missing from her life.

Two

Lonely, the Saturday-morning blues felt just as bad as the Sunday-morning blues, thought Sharon. And in fact, with nothing planned, twice as bad as the Monday-morning blues.

It had been nearly a week since she had posted her request for an appointment at the clinic – a long, miserable week in which Sharon had refused to acknowledge any contact from Debbee. Well, actually there had only been one attempt, on the answerphone. But, to be fair, it was a long, rambling diatribe – and the slaggette did say, 'Sorry,' twice.

'Still, that's not good enough,' huffed Sharon. 'May her Manolo fakes snap, and her highlights turn green,' she cursed, looking in the mirror at her own puffy eyes.

Sharon was not a staunch drinker, and her head felt muzzy from last night's three-quarters finished bottle of Merlot. Also, downing that much on her own made her feel she was spinning out of control and into the depths of alcohol dependency.

'My name is Sharon, and I'm a chocoholic. Er … sorry, wrong meeting,' she practised in the mirror, with a wry smile. She looked so pathetically sad that she put her hand out to the glass to touch her reflection in comfort. The ache in her eyes was always there. The look of a kitten that had been abandoned by its mother. Which was, in effect, what had happened all those years ago. Her mother had been gasp-breakingly beautiful. Gizelle … A glamorous, graceful creature, who had totally suited the gazelle-like nature of her name. A fairylike sprite, who had gently alighted on the arm of her father, never to leave his protective side. Until she'd had to …

'Jeez, I look nothing like her. Maybe we have the same-shaped little finger.' She sighed. Maybe if she hacked off the fat she would see some similarity. She pulled back her cheeks. She did have very high cheekbones, but they were more curved than razor sharp, like her mother's.

Dispassionately, she studied herself and, as always, decided her hair was her best feature. She put her hand to the small of her back and felt it brush softly against her fingers. Long, straight and white-blonde, it had the touch of silk with the sheen of ice – and that had *nothing* to do with conditioner. It was also the one part of her that never changed, whatever she ate.

As for her eyes, no matter that they were large and almond-shaped, they were just too damn tragic. Green. Unusually luminescent in hue, they had a strange tendency to match and reflect whatever shade of green she wore. Her eyes could change from palest duck-egg to rich peacock. But right now they were a delicate shade of puke – tinged with bloodshot red. A charming look, thought Sharon. Matched her blotchy cheeks perfectly. What was to become of her …?

As always the bathroom scales stood waiting; lurking behind the door like a silent assassin, ready to stab her self-esteem. Every morning, before getting on to them, she had a pee, took off every bit of jewellery (including studs) and every item of clothing.

This morning was no different. Standing sideways so she could see past her tummy, she gingerly placed her feet on the surface. It should be okay today, she thought. Mentally she raced through all she had eaten the day before. She'd been good. *VERY* good. Only wholegrain cereal for breakfast. Um, she'd had a little bit of double cream with it, but only two spoons of low-cal sugar to make that lovely, yummy creamy crust. For lunch she'd had a chicken Caesar sandwich, very good for you. And, okay, there were those peanuts, and a bar of chocolate on the way home, but for dinner she'd only had scrambled egg, a couple of low-fat sausages, some fresh bread and butter …

As she stepped on the scales the pointer wavered until '210 lb' swam alarmingly before her eyes. 'Ohmigod! Fifteen stone! This is insane!!' she cried. *Another* pound gained. How could that be? Hitting the fifteen-stone mark for the first time made her heart palpitate with panic. Mentally she calculated, and felt sick. She redid her maths. But there was no getting away from it: 210 pounds divided by fourteen equalled what now felt like fifteen giant slabs of concrete.

Impossible. She'd starved herself yesterday. The scales had to be faulty. She lifted them up and checked the pointer was spot on the centre. She wanted to hurl the hideous mechanical device out of the window, but she contained her pain and put it on the floor again.

She stepped on once more, as lightly as she could, balancing her body by holding on to the towel rail … then gently released her hand. To find it read exactly the same. Despair weighed her down. As tears welled in her eyes, she struggled to understand why on earth she had gone up.

'After a day of being good, I'm not even the same weight,' she wailed. Again, she counted the calories in her mind … cereal … Did she have two Branbix? No … it was three … Oh, and there was a banana as well. She'd forgotten that. The first thing she had consumed, in an attempt to get into eating more fruit.

Then she remembered there had been a mid-morning break. What did she have? The latte … But that was liquid, and didn't really count. She only had two sugars with it, and the spray of cream on top was so light and fluffy, it surely couldn't contain many calories. Not even worth counting. Oh, there had been a slice of pizza too, but the topping of artichoke and pineapple was healthy.

The flapjack she'd had with afternoon tea was full of raisins and oats – good for you, all fibre. In the evening, she remembered, she'd finished off a carton of Stilton soup before it went off. But she had missed pudding with great resolve and just hit the bottle of wine. Liquid *again*, like the soup. No, she just couldn't understand it.

She pulled a fluffy dressing gown around her for comfort, and stuffed her swollen feet into a pair of matching slippers. The bulky wrap added stones to her frame and she looked like a pink, pregnant polar bear. What the hell? It was cosy.

Sharon knew her dress sense was always battling to surface but was daily drowned in sail-sized clothes. Still, at least her surroundings had some style. Her home was her sanctuary, and every penny she earned that didn't go on the odd night out or straight into her mouth went on her studio flat. For the third time that morning, she rearranged the sweet peas in the triangular glass vase from Habitat, polished the glass table and plumped up the deckchair-striped cushions on the soft feather-stuffed sofa.

The colours of the room were peaceful ice-cream pastels. Pale peppermint, pink and duck egg blue. It reminded her of happier, younger days by the seaside ...

She heard the iron garden gate swing open.

Since answering the *Predict* advert, Sharon had watched the post flop through the communal hallway door every morning. The draught swept around her feet as she went downstairs to wait, turning her ankles a fetching shade of purple. Finally a curious pale pink envelope poked its nose through the letterbox. It was addressed to her, marked 'URGENT'.

'A reply!' she squealed. Ripping it open, she found a gold-edged appointment card with the address of the clinic, the date and time of her appointment with Dr Maximus Marvel.

'Ohmigod!' gasped Sharon. It was *that day*, at noon.

She raced back up the stairs, grabbing the banister and heaving herself up two at a time – it was already ten thirty, and she had to get dressed and find the place. London W1. From Kingston to the West End would take at least an hour and a half.

Sharon panicked. Would she have to undress for this appointment? Possibly. The thought filled her with dread. It was a clinic, after all. They might want to measure her or weigh her accurately. As she avoided any activity that involved a communal changing room, and was a thousand light years from having a lover, her underwear drawer held every conceivable shade of grey. Well, at least everything matched and toned. She groaned. Grabbing the only bra that didn't currently cut under her arms, she teamed it with a high pair of knickers, favoured for not creating an extra ridge around her tummy.

Yanking on a caftan top and an elasticised skirt, she picked up her rucksack and headed for the station.

Everyday events made her aware of her size. She always dreaded going through the automatic ticket barrier, squeezing through sideways, terrified she wouldn't clear it in time. Boarding the tube or train meant either squishing into a seat with arms, or spilling over her allotted space and elbowing the poor sod reading the paper next to her, so she usually stood, which made her worry that an unexpected lurch would send her flying, flattening some poor toddler or helpless pensioner.

But more than that, she hated the advertising that surrounded her everywhere. As she waited for the train, she eyed the giant poster showing a new range of lingerie. The model's body was amazing, with a firm, elongated and impossibly tiny waist, metal-smooth stomach and long, slender limbs. She posed provocatively, one knee perched on a velvet boudoir pouffe, flaunting the daintiest, cutest bra and chiffon panties in the world. Edged in running-stitch satin and a frothy chiffon frill, the soft, pleated grey set mocked the dingy nylon undies Sharon was wearing. Well, at least the colour of my knickers is 'in'. She laughed bitterly, sad that she would never wear such glorious confections.

The tube was even worse. The posters running alongside the escalator displayed an endless line of thin girls wearing bras, thin girls advertising makeup, thin girls advertising cars. And today, at the top, the perfect irony, a thin girl clutching a box of beribboned designer chocolates and popping one between moist damson lips.

Yep, thought Sharon, enviously, studying the model's form. No doubt a skinny cow like her *would* have the willpower to stay slim enough to keep the kind of man who could *afford* to spoil you with such luxury. The model was probably like Audrey Hepburn who, legend had it, limited herself to just one chocolate a year, on her birthday. Sharon bristled at the irony of the confectionary campaign, and looked away.

Instead, she decided to concentrate on her favourite game. Time to play 'Who's fatter than me?' Hitting the start of the next escalator, she eyed up her fellow commuters and began counting. On a good day, there would be four or five, which made her feel better. And also worse, because at the same time she would check out the figures of all the other women sailing past in the other direction. Surreptitiously she'd enviously peek at slim, young girls flaunting their bare midriffs and skinny jeans. Or gaze despairingly at older women in their forties, fifties and even sixties who had better bodies than hers. No doubt she would grow old and grey, never knowing what it felt like to wear a mini-skirt.

On the other hand, maybe today her life would finally change. She glanced down at the gold-embossed appointment card in her hand. It was suspicious that his name was Dr Marvel. It made him sound like a real quack. Still, she knew of a dentist called Dr Savage ... and there was an undertaker in Kingston called Fred Paine. Besides, the advertisement had said it was a celebrity remedy from Beverly Hills, and they loved flash names out there. He'd probably changed his surname to fit in, she assumed – chances were it was phoney.

Although she was an intelligent woman, Sharon refused to consider the next logical step: perhaps the miracle remedy she was chasing would be just as fake. But she ignored the possibility because she was so desperate for an instant cure. In her mind, *anything* was worth a gamble, however stacked the odds.

She checked her watch, then scoured the *A–Z* with growing anxiety. Riversal Road? The newspaper vendor she asked had never heard of it. But finally she found the name on the map. It was a little road behind Harley Street, famous for its leading doctors and medical consultancies. Well, that made Dr Marvel seem a lot more bone fide. And if he wasn't such a mega-success, surely he couldn't afford the rent.

Oh, hell, that meant the clinic would be smart, Sharon suddenly thought, apprehensive that the eighty pounds quoted might only cover the initial consultation.

Pushing through the crowds she glanced at her watch again. Only six minutes until she missed her appointment! The hordes thinned as she reached Harley Street and turned into Riversal Road. She spotted a grand house and peered at the number on the gatepost: 2. She was at the wrong end. Number 150 must be miles ahead. She quickened her pace, hurtling down the street, counting house after house. Then she stopped, out of breath and confused. The road had turned from elegant period properties into a series of smart boutiques and shops. The time sifted away like sand through an hourglass.

Scanning the names above the windows for numbers she realised her side of the street jumped from 148 to 152. On the other side they read 147, 149, 151, 153. She crossed the road. She crossed back. Still no sign of 150. A bead of sweat trickled down her neck and her heart was pounding with the unexpected stress. She asked a couple walking past, but they were tourists and didn't even speak English. Turning away, her mind rambled in panic. She was late. She was going to miss the appointment. They would be cross. They would refuse to make another – she would be fat forever.

She steeled herself to look at her watch once more, and let out a breath of relief. Still one minute to go. Casting around helplessly for a traffic warden or someone else to ask, she saw two workmen carrying a heavy horizontal mirror out of a white van. As they crossed the road in front of her, she called out to them: did they know where number 150 was?

'What's that, luv?' answered the older man, straining under the weight of the ornate gold mirror.

'I'm looking for one hundred and fifty Riversal …' Sharon stopped short. There, reflected in the antique-looking glass, was the series of shops right behind her, plus a red Regency door, with a sign above it that read *Dr Marvel's Miracle Weight Clinic*. Good grief, thought Sharon, turning around. There it was – right behind her all the time. She turned back to look at the shops in the mirror.

Something was odd about the reflection, and she paused, trying to put her finger on it. But a nearby clock started its midday chimes and there was no time to think. Something about the lettering? What the hell? She'd found the place and that was the important thing. And she was on time.

Sharon swung around again and rushed towards the door, looking for a bell or buzzer. But there wasn't one, only a gleaming brass plaque beside the door, inscribed with the doctor's name and host of initials. On the door itself there was an impressive brass knocker in the shape of an open-mouthed gorgon. Above it, in gold lettering, the number: 150.

Relieved, she banged down the gorgon's head.

On the last stroke of twelve.

Three

The door swung open of its own accord, and straight ahead of her sat a nurse at a smart chrome and white desk. She was wearing a brilliant white tunic and matching white smile. All the whiteness was dazzling.

'Miss Plunkett? Hi, honey! We're expecting you,' said the nurse, putting down her nail file and standing up to greet her. Sharon tilted her head in surprise. The nurse must have been nearly six and a half feet tall. And every inch of her was stunning. Her impossibly long, slim legs disappeared into the cute pleats of a tiny white skirt that skimmed her thighs like a tennis outfit. She swiftly sashayed round to the front and whipped Sharon's jacket off her shoulders.

'Coffee? Tea? Elderflower cordial? Magazine?' She pouted glossy red lips. On her platinum-blonde, wave-bobbed head perched a ridiculous nurse's hat. She was every hospitalised man's dying dream – a killer blonde who could raise the blood pressure faster than a coronary. 'Take a seat.' She gestured with a nonchalant flourish towards the right.

Tearing her eyes away from the nurse's cartoon beauty, Sharon glanced around and noticed the waiting room was also pure white. So white, in fact, it was hard to see where the floor ended and the walls started.

In the corner there was a back-buttoned, white suede *chaise-longue*. A tinkling sound came from a fountain on the left wall – the plump mouth of a snowy cherub spouting forth water endlessly into a Baroque white basin. Above the tinkling, she could hear the strains of new-age music, a hideous mix of noises that sounded like Celtic harp, Andalusian sand pipes, and possibly mating humpback whales.

If God's waiting room existed, this would be it, thought Sharon, uneasily. She carefully lowered her bulk on to the spindly *chaise-longue* and sat in a prim, knees-together position. The nurse was still waiting for the answer to her offers of refreshment.

'Er, nothing, thank you.'

'No problem, honey,' replied the nurse, in a throaty transatlantic drawl, reminding Sharon of a gangster's moll. 'I'll just go and check on Maximus – Dr Marvel. Tell him you're here.'

She pressed a lever and seemed to disappear through the wall. When it shut, only the faint outline of a door was visible. No handle.

The surreal atmosphere intensified as long moments ticked by. The overwhelming whiteness of the surroundings was disorientating – it was like being in a thin, floaty cloud. As Sharon's head swam with the dreamy sounds, from the corner of her eye she caught a movement. Startled, she could have sworn the cherub winked at her. She was walking over to investigate when the door in the wall flew open again, the tinkling at-one-with-nature Muzak suddenly competing with distant funfair organ music – a noise totally at odds with all the new-age purity.

'This way, sweetheart. The doctor is ready for you,' said the nurse, beckoning Sharon through. The narrow, winding corridor reminded her of an American 1950s Fun House. The wood-panelled walls were lined with distorting mirrors that made their shapes change from skinny to short to fat (in Sharon's case, fatter) to wide to tall (in the nurse's case, taller). Sharon longed to stop at the mirror that made her skinny, but the nurse grabbed her arm to hurry her along.

'This is all – um – unusual for a doctor's clinic,' said Sharon, nervously.

'What is, honey?' asked the nurse, puzzled.

'Well, the décor … and the music,' she added, as the fairground organ got progressively louder.

'That's the "inner child" in Dr Marvel,' sighed the nurse, with fan-like admiration. 'He believes we should never lose it. Wrote a thesis in the *Lancet* about it – won three awards. Here we go,' she said, pushing Sharon through a door before she could ask anything more.

A gold-fringed curtain – more befitting a Victorian vaudeville theatre than a doctor's surgery – hung before her.

'In here.' The nurse drew it back with a flourish and shoved Sharon forward.

A handsome man in his late forties, sporting sleek hair, a black moustache and a charming Hollywood smile, grinned. 'Welcome, welcome, I'm Dr Maximus Marvel.' He talked and looked like a slick American game-show host, complete with an air of insincerity. Still, catching the merry twinkle in his eye, Sharon relaxed. It was as if he was sending himself up, having a private joke with her.

But then she took in the room. It was *so* not what she'd expected. Instead of clinical Beverly Hills it was predominantly pink – and in every possible shade. Pink and fleshy. Dark pink. Pale pink. Rose pink. Deep fuchsia. And almost red-pink. The only other colour was antique gold – beautifully carved filigree wood, which decorated the desk, mirrors and chairs, in the elaborate manner of a steam carousel.

He directed her towards his large, antique desk. 'Yes, yes.' He sighed as he walked around her. 'I can see the problem.' He rubbed his hands, as if he was loving the challenge, and delved into his doctor's coat for a stethoscope. 'Formalities, my dear. Just formalities. A few tests, that's all … Nurse, bring the optimum fat measurer,' he instructed, slapping the nurse's cheeky butt, totally oblivious to Sharon's presence.

'Yes, Doctor.' She giggled, opening a mahogany wall cabinet and handing him a pair of pincers that Sharon thought were more suited to an elephant. Her instinct was to make a bolt for it. But, then, she *was* an elephant. It focused her mind. That was exactly why she was there. And anything – and that meant ANYTHING – was worth a go.

Lifting her caftan, he applied the instrument. Sharon winced at the cold metal. 'Lovely, lovely …' the doctor murmured to himself, jotting down reams of figures and words in illegible handwriting.

The volume of the fairground music seemed to increase as the nurse returned with an empty test tube and a giant V-shaped glass that contained a smoking green liquid. 'Take this, darlin',' she coaxed, sitting on the edge of the desk and crossing her endless legs. 'It's a neutraliser.'

What? Sharon pulled away, nervously.

'Sure, sweetheart. All those nasty little ol' toxins currently swimming around your body, it wipes them out and prepares you for … You wrote and said you wanted the Celebrity Remedy, didn't you?'

'That's right, that's right,' cajoled Dr Marvel, now studying her eyes with a spotlight and a giant magnifying glass, his own enlarged eye looming through it with a mad gleam.

The nurse handed her the glass of swirling green liquid. With no way to escape, Sharon gulped and swallowed, then waited for an explosion of foul taste. Instead, the very sweetest flavour imaginable hit her tongue. Like a juicy mint leaf dipped in sugar and morning dew.

'Well done, darlin'. Now, this way,' said the nurse, wiping Sharon's mouth with a silk handkerchief. But as she tried to stand, things seemed to speed up. Sharon's head felt a little woozy and happy. The carousel music grew even louder.

'I love this tune,' laughed Dr Marvel. 'Reminds me of travelling funfairs. I used to hang out with them all the time when I was a kid. Roll up, roll up!' he barked, like the great Barnum himself. 'Come and let me do some measurements.'

Feeling like the Fat Lady With the Beard, Sharon let him pull her towards a stark, full-length mirror on a far wall, surrounded by bright light bulbs – the kind you'd find in a clown's dressing room.

Out came a tape measure and a lot of 'Ah … huh … uh … huh … um …' from the doctor as he wrapped it round various parts of her anatomy and jotted down yet more figures.

'You're exactly between the classic official measurements of sizes fourteen and sixteen.'

'Really?' said Sharon, delighted.

'That's fourteen to sixteen in *American* sizing … In England, you're a big size eighteen.'

Her joy popped, like a fairground balloon hit by a dart.

In the unforgiving light, Sharon could barely face herself in the mirror. The white bulbs gave a ghostly pallor to her skin. To the side of the mirror was a giant jackpot handle, and without warning the doctor put his clipboard aside and pulled down on it with two strong hands.

Suddenly the lights began to flash in rotation around the edge … and it started to change. Like the mirrors she had passed on the way in, her shape began to distort … but this time, all in one mirror. With a life of its own, the glass rippled and bulged in different places, altering her torso and limbs as it did so. From fat to thin, tall to wide … like a fruit machine window gone wild.

Dizzied by the fast, repetitive movement, Sharon felt her head spin. She closed her eyes and held her hand out – she was going to faint. The doctor slammed the jackpot handle to a standstill. The mirror came to a halt.

'I have the perfect solution for you,' he announced, supporting her elbow.

She opened her eyes and saw her reflection. It was the same as when she had first looked.

'It's the lights, my dear. I do apologise – they tend to make one feel a little strange. Now, there's one final test we have to do, to make sure you're really suitable – the change is very drastic, you know. We have to be absolutely sure. Are you sure?'

'Absolutely certain.' She wavered a little, nervous at what he was planning to do to her. He didn't look convinced. She tried again. 'I'm dying to be slim – please, anything you can do …'

After a long moment's consideration, he nodded to his gorgeous assistant, who jumped to attention.

The nurse steered her to a corner of the room where an old-fashioned giant weighing machine stood waiting. It was red, and a sign on the top said, **'Speak your weight.'**

'Are you serious?' asked Sharon, half laughing, half horrified. This was hardly hi-tech Beverly Hills! The doctor and nurse looked at each other, as if sharing an intimate secret, then smiled. Saying nothing, they ushered her on to the platform.

The machine started to groan and creak. It felt as if it was actually coming to life. The hands on the dial began to swing round and round, faster and faster … Sharon's head swam again as she watched them spin. Above the groans and the organ fairground music a voice from the bowels of the machine growled: 'She is much deserving.'

'What did it say? Deserving of what?' asked Sharon, confused.

'No, darlin'. The machine said, "Too many servings." Here, sit down, take a rest. It's all a bit much to take in, we know.' The nurse helped her to the chair in front of the doctor's desk.

'Please, can somebody explain, what exactly *is* this weight loss course? And how well does it work?' asked Sharon.

'Work? Why, it works *MARVEL-LOUSLY!*' answered Dr Marvel, holding a test-tube of fluid to the light.

'But how quickly will I lose the weight? Will it really make me slim?'

'So many queries, my dear,' he said, patting her knee and winking at his nurse. 'Take the medicine as directed and you'll have the enviable figure of a celebrity – and face, if I'm right,' he replied, cupping her cheeks in his hand so tightly she felt them puff out like a hamster's.

'But the thing is, my dear, read the instructions CAREFULLY. Understand? Very carefully indeed.' He turned to a side-table and began pouring various luminescent liquids and coloured powders into a funnel that led to a small silver machine. 'Now, while I distil the ingredients for you, Nurse will take you outside to wait.'

It was all happening too fast, like being on a rollercoaster with no time to ask questions or get answers. 'But – but what's actually in it?'

The doctor put his fingers to her lips to quieten her. 'Shush.' Leaning confidentially towards her, he whispered, 'It's called a secret remedy because … it's a *secret*!' And he laughed, throwing her another wink. 'Trust me, everything you need to know will be in the instructions.'

The nurse led Sharon out through the corridor, past the mirrors and back into the pure white waiting room. 'It won't take long, honey,' she soothed.

'Er … okay. Let me pay you,' said Sharon, nervously. She had drawn out cash in anticipation and handed eighty pounds to the nurse.

She counted it with her long, glossy red fingernails, licking between notes to check the amount. 'Marvellous, darlin'. We give it to charity. Every donation is really welcome.'

'Which charity?' asked Sharon, surprised.

'Y'know, the Needy. Those who can't have what they want to eat.'

Again, a distinct lack of specifics. Sharon gave up. Whatever. She sat back on the sofa and flicked through a magazine from the rack at her side. It was *Saga*, aimed at the over-fifties. She noticed how the models were older, not silly sixteen-year-olds but *real* women with a few wrinkles. How odd it seemed, compared to normal fashion magazines. She read a few articles, and picked up another *Saga*. Flicking through, she realised how swiftly the older models had begun to look fine in her eyes. It didn't take long to get used to the change. Actually, these women were really attractive, with their elegant, wiser faces and chiselled Garbo cheeks …

'Ready, honey?' trilled the nurse, holding a neat white cardboard box in the palm of her perfectly-manicured hand. It was tied with a delicate pink ribbon. Like a gift.

Good grief, thought Sharon, taken aback.

'Er … *that*'s it? That's my medication?'

'Sure it is,' said the nurse, sounding puzzled at her patient's reaction. 'Take it with any liquid you want – even a milkshake if you like.' She smiled conspiratorially. 'But whatever you do, follow the instructions inside. *Don't* break the rules, or there's no guarantee the remedy will continue to work in the long run. It could change everything for you. And you won't want that once you've enjoyed its success.'

The phone rang, interrupting them, and the nurse turned her attention elsewhere. 'Dr Maximus Marvel's office, how can we help you?' she said.

Sharon thanked her with a wave and left. The door automatically opened, as it had when she had arrived, and closed behind her.

Looking down at her watch, she was startled to see the time. It was only a minute past twelve. She shook it, figuring it must be broken. Then, feeling hungry, she cast around for a café.

Four

The streets around Oxford Circus were swarming with shoppers and workers. After such an extraordinary experience, it struck Sharon as a very ordinary sight. Unnerved but excited, she hunted for somewhere to sit and examine the doctor's package. She wanted a coffee bar with a table outside in the sun. A coffee bar with a table in the sun that also served chocolate and cookie cream milkshake. This, she had decided, should be the drink with which to take her medication. After all, the nurse had practically insisted on it.

She finally spotted a pretty little peppermint and pink café that was busy selling cakes in beribboned French patisserie boxes – a reverence she appreciated. The name on the stripped awning said, 'Your Choice'. Sharon immediately decided it was hers.

While she was queuing to order, she eyed the trays of caramel and chocolate shortbread squares, lemon drizzle slices and crumbly walnut cake with desperate desire. In her rush to get to the appointment, she hadn't even had breakfast. No, she corrected herself. This was going to be a new start. But the queue was long … and against her will she found herself eeny-meeny-miny-mo-ing between the delicious possibilities.

Finally, it was her turn: 'A chocolate and cookie cream milkshake, please … with a little bit of cream on top,' she added at the last second. Then she looked at the package in her hand. 'Can you

ake semi-skimmed? I'll also have a bottle of
a sense of self-righteous control. But then,
ntriloquist's doll, she found herself adding,

, her hand reached out for a fat fairy cake.
, plate, the old-fashioned choice looked
incongruous compared to the *frou-frou* pastries surrounding it. But coated with thick butter icing and topped with a plump glacé cherry, its nostalgic appeal was irresistible. A fairy cake! How magical. She handed over the money. What the hell? She hadn't actually started the course yet, had she? So it wasn't a problem.

Settling down outside, she carefully placed the neat white package in front of her and pulled at the pretty ribbon. Like a music box, the lid sprang open to reveal a bevelled mirror. Dazzling her for a second, it glinted in the sunshine, sending rainbows skittering across the table.

The interior was even more surprising: nestling cosily in a layer of fleshy pink velvet sat a pure white egg. It snuggled there, precious and perfect, like something a golden goose would lay. Except this egg was encased in a net of criss-crossed twine. This was truly bizarre.

Her fingers plucked at the twine. Silver in appearance, it stretched like some kind of weird animal gut. How symbolic, mused Sharon, as she snapped it apart. She was breaking the umbilical cord to her past life of being fat.

She held up the egg to examine it. Made of bone or ivory, it was finely carved with indecipherable swirls and inscriptions. It reminded her of those ancient Chinese puzzles. And of her figure. Spherical. Rotund. She studied the egg and saw that a faint line ran through the centre, but it wouldn't open. Press a lever? Pull a stop?

She stopped and took a gulp of milkshake, contemplating the egg. There were no instructions. She held it in her palm, enjoying the coolness and weight ... and then it slowly opened of its own accord, like the petals of a flower opening towards the morning sun.

Out dropped a single, solitary pill. A large, white and shiny tablet. And with it, a tiny scroll of instruction. Sharon read it again, and again.

But, edged in gold, all it said was:

'AFTER CONSUMPTION, DO NOT EAT FOR TWO HOURS.'

That was it. No side-effects leaflet, no ingredients. She eyed the pill warily. It could be made from Balinese bongo dust for all she knew ... But she also knew that, regardless, she would take it. A lifetime of fat was a bitter pill to swallow. In comparison this could only taste sweet. Please, God, let it work.

But it all looked so exotic. She had expected something clinical. This was more like the latest Bohemian answer from a spaced-out Californian guru. Still, who knew? Maybe it contained some magic ingredient. Imagining herself to be a hippie-chic high priestess holding court in a Beverly Hills yoga centre, she decided the actual swallowing of the pill deserved a certain druid pomp and ceremony: she would have it with the milkshake, but first perhaps she'd get a cream-cheese bagel to eat as a main course before the chocolate fairy cake.

Then she caught sight of her chubby face in the bevelled lid. No, this was her last hope and this time she'd do it right. *This time* she'd do whatever it took. *This time* she'd have the willpower.

She held up the fairy cake. Reluctant to throw it away – she was mindful of waste – she took a token nibble of the icing. It tasted so good. She took another nip. Then another. The chocolate butter topping tasted perfect with the crumbly vanilla. Her tongue scooped a tipful ... Enough! That was it. A new beginning. She wrapped the remainder of the cake carefully in a couple of paper napkins and popped it into her bag, resolving to feed it to the pigeons on her windowsill when she got home.

Ceremoniously, she held up the pill in one hand and the instructions in the other. It was all so simple, she couldn't believe it. No exercise, no starving, no dieting, no grief.

'AFTER CONSUMPTION DO NOT EAT FOR TWO HOURS,' she reread out loud.

Fair enough. That'll be a piece of cake.

She said a silent prayer. No, a mantra. And as she prayed, she opened her mouth to take it …

Five

An hour or so later 'Californian Princess Sharon, priestess of hippie-chic' wandered into an outsize shop still giggling about the yogic mysticism of it all. She was enjoying this so much. Determined the remedy would work, she'd been shopping.

'If I'm going to lose weight, I'm going to need new clothes!' she reasoned. It was time to spoil herself, ready for the new figure she would soon have.

First stop had been Selfridges, and a delicate pair of high-heeled shoes. A soft leather pair in palest beige. They would make her shapely new legs look even longer. Next, she had browsed along the jewellery counters. Jingling the shiny goodies like a naughty magpie, she'd found herself drawn towards the rings. She'd bought a dainty triple one with matching bracelet – slightly tight, but when she lost the weight it would look stunning. Dainty jewellery on dainty little bones. A look she had always coveted.

The weirdest thing was, she hadn't thought about food once. Not once. It was as if the pill was already working, her willpower getting stronger by the second. She thought back to the moment the deed had been done, and smiled again. She'd had a bit of a fright because the huge pill had caught in her throat and almost choked her. Finally, washed down by milkshake, it had slid into her cavernous stomach. The irony of 'death by slimming pill' hit her later, and she hadn't stopped chuckling – she was experiencing a feel-good factor that was making her giddy.

Sharon loved the outsize shops because they were the only places she felt normal. She adored the fact that the assistants were large too, not like the usual skinny bitches who manned changing rooms, or the snooty model types at the till. Sweeping up armfuls of clothes, she headed towards the cubicle, stopping only to check out a beautiful fifties-style yellow dress with a tiny blue cornflower print. Made of crisp cotton, it was so sunny and fresh – like the way she was suddenly feeling. As she struggled to hold all the clothes so she could rummage the rail, she was disappointed she could only find it in a size sixteen.

What were the chances of it fitting? Nil, she thought, aware that its slightly boned waistline made it look an even smaller size than it was. Whatever, she decided, adding it to the pyramid pile in her arms – she would fit into it soon enough!

The shop was hot, and as she waited in the queue, she longed for a cold drink. She hesitated, trying to decide if the wait was really worth the goodies in her hand. It was, she decided, feeling the gorgeous stiff cotton of the yellow dress. For a split second, she wondered what Simon would think of her in it? Then she blanked him from her mind. Simon would think what he must always have thought: by being friendly with the 'fat girl', he would get to Debbee.

As a large woman finally padded out, Sharon told the assistant she had six items and held out her hand for a tag. It never failed to annoy her that the salesgirls liked to double-check even though they could clearly see how many she was helpfully holding out. A pathetic power-trip, they might as well call you a thief to your face. She sighed, getting irritated. Overweight, the heat was beginning to get to her, and she felt her good mood start to evaporate. Her armpits and neck felt sticky and her head hot. Shoving the hangers on to the changing-room hooks she knew she'd picked out too many clothes, but couldn't resist trying them on anyway.

It was always a nightmare finding the right size – she often had to take two or three of the same style in with her to see which worked best. The gamble of which to try on first would depend on whether she was feeling fatter or thinner that particular day. Well, today was a good one, she told herself, trying to keep her mood buoyant.

Undoing the side button on her skirt, she felt her flesh spill out. As she took off her caftan, she ran her finger under her bra strap, and took the opportunity to soothe the deep ruts. This is all going to change, she comforted herself. And, optimistically, she launched into a size sixteen blouse.

Made of a shiny, stretchy red and blue fabric, she was disappointed to see the buttons pulling across – her bosoms looked like two beach balls in a tug of war. Annoyingly, it did the same in a size twenty. The material was too cheap. She progressed to a T-shirt but it puckered in the same place. Worse, in all three sizes the material bulged at the back, showing the deep indentation of her bra.

By now her throat felt cracked. Then she remembered the bottle of water in her bag. A swig later, and she was ready to try the trousers. They zipped up fine, but the material was too tight in the crotch and looked obscene. The larger size was too baggy round the bum. Despite her original happy mood, her shopping trip was evaporating into the usual hell. The heat increased and she felt beads of sweat form on her brow.

But there was still the yellow dress. By habit she always left the best to last. All her hopes were pinned on this creation. The petticoats rustled as she lifted it over her head and gently shimmied it down. Halfway, it stuck. She checked that the zip was undone, and it was. She struggled aimlessly, like a porpoise caught in a fishing net. The tight sleeves had her arms in a vice grip; the bodice was stuck over her breasts. She struggled some more, determined to get it lower, to see how it could look if she lost a bit of weight – when she heard the most terrifying rip.

Tears sprouted at the hopelessness of it all. Trying to backtrack the dress off a shoulder she twisted it inside out, and as the whalebone dug into her rib, she felt like the very same beached creature – stranded and unable to move. Somehow, the more she squirmed, the more her semi-naked body became exposed. The heat and humiliation made her head throb. She couldn't possibly ask for help. Swimming in panic and hopeless despair, she shut her eyes and felt herself almost black out. The ground gave way and she sank to her knees in a dishevelled heap. Her bag spilled open on the floor beside her, contents scattering. Sobbing, with her one free hand she reached out for the cold bottle of water and pressed it to her forehead. Then she saw the napkin containing the remainder of the fairy cake … What sweet comfort it offered in a moment of stress.

Chanting, 'I am not a fat whale, I am not a fat whale,' she took a series of slow, deep breaths. Her panic subsided and logic returned. Arching, she released the pressure on the back of the dress, wrenched it over her head and flung it on to the chair.

There was a knock on the cubicle frame. 'Miss, are you all right in there?' said the assistant.

Sharon didn't answer. The heat of embarrassment burned her face, and her nose ran from hot tears.

'Miss, I've something I think you'd like to try on …' coaxed the shop assistant.

With no option, Sharon opened the curtain a little way and peered out, red-faced, guilty and miserable.

'Don't worry, this is perfect for you,' the woman said.

She was brandishing the most hideous frock Sharon had ever

seen. Yards and yards of garish green fabric overlaid with wavy brown horizontal stripes and dotted with large yellow sunflowers. It looked as if a blind farmer had ploughed a field on LSD.

'I promise it will make you look *really* fat,' smiled the shop assistant, sweetly. At first Sharon thought she'd misheard, but the woman blithely continued: 'Horizontal stripes – they always add pounds, you know. I bet you'll look divine in it.'

Sharon was speechless. How could people be so cruel? Now even an assistant in an outsize shop was making fun of her. Shaking her head, she snapped the curtain shut and withdrew into her cell. Blinking back more shameful tears, she hurried into her own clothes, ready to run out of the shop.

How dare they be so rude? And in *this* shop of all places. She would complain to the manager. But maybe the manager would laugh at her as well. No, she would just get out of there. Tucking her bulging flesh back into her skirt, she yanked on the caftan top. She just wanted to get home, to her pastel ice-cream sanctuary where no one could cause her pain.

With her head held defiantly high, she swept up her handbag and sailed out of the changing room, curtain wafting in her wake. Straight past the assistant, straight out of the shop and straight into the high street. The cooler air hit her ample cheeks and she embraced her freedom from the cell of the changing room, like a prisoner on day release. Taking deep breaths she leaned against a wall to get herself together... But when she finally looked up, she took another deep breath – this time, for an entirely different reason. A reason that caused her to stand stock still, her pupils dilated in shock.

All around her there were fat women. Not twenty, not forty, but hundreds. Roly-poly shoppers waddled up and down the road like Sumo wrestlers on a coffee break. Puzzled, she walked on. Was there a Fat Persons Convention in from Las Vegas? Yet it continued endlessly. Fat girl after fat girl passed her. Occasionally somebody was really slim, but so occasionally she stood out. The cars were full of chubby women. The buses. The taxis … the female traffic wardens, the policewomen. All plus size sixteen. Where had they all come from?

Breaking her golden rule, she glanced at the shop windows to look at her reflection – an action that used to make her cringe in horror. But for the first time in her life, she looked the same as everyone else. And then she noticed something even more amazing.

Unlike the male mannequins, which were normal, the female mannequins were enormous, sporting hammock-sized dresses. Not just in that shop, but also the one after it. And the shop over the road. And the one after that. Two young men in jeans and tattoos walked past her in deep conversation. Then, unexpectedly, one turned, looked her up and down and let out a loud wolf-whistle.

Sharon gasped in bewilderment. She sat on a pavement bench to catch her breath. Her heart palpitated. Was she dreaming? She shut her eyes tight, counted to ten and opened them again. They focused on a mega-large poster on a billboard opposite. She remembered it being there last week: a model was sexily flaunting her skinny butt in a pair of Calvin Klein jeans while she was wrapped around a male with the torso of a retouched Adonis. But what the hell had happened?

Instead of the model with third-degree anorexia, a pretty Beth Ditto lookalike was grinning like a Cheshire cat, squeezing her huge bottom into a pair of denims. Next to her, a semi-naked male model was pressing his toned torso into her back suggestively. The caption read: 'MAXIMISE YOUR CURVES WITH THE CALVIN CUT.'

Shaking her head in confusion, she wandered a few paces down the street. A news-vendor called out. Sharon surveyed his stand. The latest edition of *Hello!* magazine stared back at her. On the cover there was a picture of Oprah Winfrey, fist punching the air in victory, beaming smile on her face, looking happy and bloated. The banner headline underneath her screamed:

'OPRAH OVER THE MOON! 16 stone 6lbs again!'

Next to it sat *Grazia*. On its cover stood a very pretty, very plump girl in a short silver skirt. At her podgy waist she clutched a tiny fluffy dog:

'MILAN SHERATON INVITES YOU INTO HER HOLLYWOOD HOME.'

Further up, *FHM* bore the cover line

'WHO'D LIKE A GO WITH JO?'

And Sharon recognised a famous comedienne known for her keen wit, feminist patter and mega-sized body. But there she posed, grinning shamelessly in a bikini, with the tag line 'Voted older woman we'd most like to sleep with'.

On a lower rack, the most curious of all: Sharon picked up a magazine called *FATTIES* and studied its cover: 'FATTY OF THE YEAR'.

Enough! Head spinning, she hailed a taxi and headed straight for the safety of home.

'Can you see what I see?' she asked the driver.

'What yer talking about, Miss?'

Sharon gestured out of the window. 'All these people. Fat women everywhere. What's happened?'

The driver fell silent. He had the resigned look of a cabbie who had picked up yet another weirdo.

She kept her mouth shut as she avidly watched the endless procession of paunchy, bosomy, busty women swarming the streets. Her heart stirred with fear – and with incredible, undeniable hope.

Sharon entered her flat with relief and swiftly locked the door behind her. She went into her room and sat on the edge of the bed, pulling the pastel quilted eiderdown around her shoulders for security. Then, hand trembling, she dug out the remote control buried under the biscuit tin at the base of her bedside table and switched on the TV.

Maybe there was an explanation on the news. Glancing at the clock, she saw it was coming up to the hour. Perfect timing. She flicked the screen guide on to the BBC News Channel and watched as the familiar icon showed and the signature tune sounded. And then Sharon jumped. Jumped out of her ample skin. Instead of the usual sleek presenter, the newscaster's bulky bosoms filled the entire screen. She was massive. Her chunky jowls delivered the latest disaster with sincere gravitas.

Switching channels, Sharon caught a recipe programme. A gargantuan female chef was gesturing wildly at her newly baked creation. It was the most decadent chocolate cake Sharon had ever seen. It looked like a cocoa-covered Tower of Pisa. 'Now, don't forget,' twinkled the beautiful dark eyes of the mammoth cook, as she licked her fingers. 'Serve the portions to your guests with lashings of cream. And don't cheat, you naughty viewers. I don't mean single cream or, heaven forbid, *crème fraîche*. Make sure it's *double*. And, most important of all, when preparing the icing, make sure to be generous with the sugar.' The celebrity chef tossed her luscious brunette locks, ran her fingers round the bowl, and sucked them seductively.

Sharon felt faint. She started to giggle insanely. There was no doubt about it. She had entered the Twilight Zone. Or should that be the Twiglet Zone? Whatever, it was clear it was a world where it was IN for women to be fat and OUT to be skinny. A world where heaven was a plus size. How had this happened?

Her mind raced back to the advert in *Predict* magazine. Now she really thought about it, the words hadn't actually stated that Dr Marvel's Miracle Weight pill would make you *lose* weight, just that it was a *magical way to change your life*. And, ironically, that had happened when she'd stepped into the changing room. How the pill had worked, she didn't question. Didn't want to. Why question a miracle? She felt her soul surge with joy – joy as free as a bird. An eagle. A wild, soaring creature whose possibilities knew no bounds.

Whooping round the room, she manically switched TV channels. A popular blonde presenter in her late forties called Vanessa was hosting a daytime chat show, and listening attentively to a slim woman sobbing into a handkerchief. 'The truth is, my husband was repulsed by my weight loss. Though personally I blame his unfaithfulness on *her*.'

A picture flashed up of a huge female mud wrestler entitled 'My Husband's Mistress'.

'I was so jealous when they were working together, I just couldn't eat,' continued the sobbing guest. 'Before I knew it, I went the other way. But look at me, why would he want me now?' she cried, indicating her slender frame as the very voluptuous Vanessa sympathetically handed her another tissue.

'Yes! Yes! Yes!' screamed Sharon, frantically pressing the TV buttons again and again.

Next came Slob high-calorie yogurt. An actress in a white track-suit sat on a cushioned white stool. She looked like a fat snail on a puffball mushroom.

'At four hundred calories a pot... can you say "not"?' she chimed, spooning a toffee-flavoured substance into her face.

'Mmm ... and packed with goodness to match your greatness!'

Sharon collapsed on the bed in hysterical giggles. For the first time ever, she thought it could be incredibly fun to be in the world of advertising, instead of despising just about everything it stood for.

Next the screen flashed up the launch of a new family car.

'Enough room for *four* people, including the missus!' boasted a sincere voice-over. Oh, this got better and better! Sharon felt so light-headed she wanted to throw open the window and yell, 'Hallelujah!' She settled for tossing all her pastel cushions into the air, like a juggler at the circus. But it was the final advertisement in the break that really hit home. She turned back to the TV and watched in dumbfounded silence.

A pretty model was smoothing some kind of cream into her wobbly, tree-stump legs. Winking seductively to the camera, she husked, 'Try *Pig Lard*. Just smooth it on your body every morning for three weeks, and you'll see an amazing difference. Apply with our special rubber mitten and, within days, your skin will develop an attractive, bumpy texture. Yes, GUARANTEED CELLULITE! See how my dimples have doubled ...'

Oh, thank you! There *is* a God. Sharon yanked up her skirt and looked at her orange-peel thighs. Oh, far more than orange peel. More like grapefruit. But somehow, and she struggled to comprehend this, it was now considered beautiful. Could it be? Could it *possibly* be?

Calming down, she stretched out on the bed and studied her legs. 'I suppose the bumps do create a sort of interesting pattern ...' She tried to observe herself objectively. The blue veins showed through her soft, translucent skin, twisting like rivers across her mottled, purple blotches. In some places her skin looked goose-bumped. In others it strained, taut and firm. The more she stared, the more her flesh took on a surreal appearance. With a flash of understanding, she gazed at her body again. Like a blind woman seeing for the first time.

The way the dimples on her buttocks popped in and out had a definite cheeky charm ... The variation of texture gave excitement to her skin. No *way* could you call it boring. The soft, sagging skin under her arm crinkled delicately, like finest crêpe silk. In fact, when you looked closely her flesh was fascinating. Like an intricately woven fabric of different-textured threads ... cotton, wool, satin.

Miraculously, the colours didn't look so bad either. For the first time, she noticed how the shades of blues, pinks and purples on her pale skin blended in perfect harmony. Like splashes of a pastel watercolour, she decided. An Impressionist painting! 'My God! I'm a picture. As pretty as a picture!'

Sharon threw back her head and let tears of gratitude cascade down her cheeks.

FLESH! It was the most glorious canvas in the world.

And she had reams of it.

Six

Monday morning, and this time there was NOTHING blue about it. Instead it was a rainbow world of infinite possibilities.

The weekend over, Sharon woke up at six a.m. and, as she had on Sunday morning, flicked on the TV to double-check she hadn't been dreaming.

A mum proudly spooned breakfast cereal on to her plate. 'How many Branbix make you feel great? For a healthy breakfast always eat *eight*,' sang out the advertisement.

No, she laughed, the magic was still working. Dr Maximus Marvel had done just that. He had sold her a marvel, a maximum marvel. She brushed her teeth, and noticed her eyes were sparkling. This was such a fun world. She shook out her long, white-blonde hair, and ran a comb down its glorious length. It hung in a straight line, soft and shimmery, like a Chinese silk wall hanging. For the first time in so, so long, she couldn't wait to get to work.

journey on the tube proved enlightening. Walking through of commuters, she noticed that her figure caused a lot ces and envious side-looks from skinny girls. What hape? Carefully comparing herself to the others she knew she was firm for her size, and her unded, even though they were size 36F. er size better than many, and her legs were proportionately very long. Her neck was graceful, and she noticed she didn't have the squat look that so many people around her now had.

And, of course, she had waist-length blonde hair, which she normally tied up to keep herself inconspicuous. Today she had let it swing free, and it flew up and around her face like angel's wings as the tube trundled into the station.

The trip up the escalator was brilliant. Poster after poster of plump, pretty women lined the walls, their faces sparkling with health and *joie de vivre*. She began to count the fatties as usual, but instead found herself adding up the slims and skinnies. No more than eight.

Tra-la-la-ing, she pushed through the revolving door to Sharpe, Bates and Colt and swept into the lift.

'Morning, Sharon,' said a quiet voice.

She turned to see Samantha, the ringleader in her office. 'Oh, hi,' she replied, clocking her outfit and figure. Now that was odd. Really odd. Samantha looked slightly different. Plumper. Or was it Sharon's imagination? She seemed definitely larger, a spare tyre round her middle. Or had Sharon never noticed that before?

'I love your dress,' Samantha added tentatively. Samantha was the kind of girl who was only friendly when she wanted something. Once she got it, she cut you dead – almost taking pleasure in fooling you. A girl so self-centred she could only relate to a mirror. What was her game?

'Cheers. I bought it this weekend,' answered Sharon, waiting for a bitchy comeback. But there was none.

'It suits you really well,' came a flat, honest response.

She indicated to Sharon to go first, and they walked towards the office. Sharon took her seat in customary silence, just nodding to the others in the room. But in a cacophony of girly voices, they all simpered, 'Hi, Sharon, did you have a nice weekend?'

'Er ... I did. *Really* did,' answered Sharon, aware they were staring at her body and flowing hair.

'Do you want a coffee?' asked Alexi, half-an-hour later. The slimmest of the gang, her slender body suddenly looked like a diary pencil that might easily snap.

'Sure, two sugars – no, make that three,' smiled Sharon, gratefully.

'I wish I had your willpower.' Alexi sighed, as she delivered the coffee and slunk back to her desk. Sharon was confused. What did she mean? Was it because she'd had the extra sugar?

She looked at the stack of invoices on her computer and inwardly groaned. So many. The printer clicked into action. And then out of it. Damn, no ink.

She pushed herself out of her chair, picked up the coffee and walked into the lift to head up to the supplies office. It was crowded, with just six people crammed into it. She didn't recognise anyone else. As nearly all exited, she became aware of a man studying her from behind. Glancing over her shoulder, her eyes locked on to a familiar face. Oh, God, she thought. It was Mr Bates, the chairman.

She smiled shyly. Then she remembered she was holding her coffee and worry flitted across her face. Not only did she look as if she was on a permanent tea break, there was probably something in the blasted health and safety rules that said, 'No coffee in the lift.'

A neatly-dressed, courtly businessman, he was so engrossed in studying the changing expressions of her face that his folder accidentally slipped from under his arm. The contents spilled, and Sharon squished down to her knees to help him sweep up his papers.

'Thank you so much, that's very kind. Do you work for us?' he asked, adjusting his tie as he straightened up.

'Sure. For over three years. I'm in Accounts.'

'Good grief – you're not!' He laughed. 'What's your name?'

'Sh-Sharon,' she stammered.

The man waited for more, gazing into her woodland green eyes like a mesmerised fox.

'Er … Sharon Plunkett,' added Sharon.

Throwing politeness to the wind, he weighed her up silently, from head to toe. 'That's all I needed to know,' he said. 'Good day.' He stepped out of the lift with a curt nod.

Two days later, Sharon was summoned to Human Resources.

'Dolores Drummond has asked you to go and see her straight away,' said Samantha, sympathetically.

That was bad news. Sharon felt sick. It was the coffee incident. Or was it the computer disaster? Okay, the computer had crashed sucking the filing she'd done into the ether and setting her back a whole day's work. But it was hardly her fault. And, conscientiously, she'd worked late to make amends. She had sacrificed her first invitation to go to the West End nightclub Chinawhite with the girls from the office – Saffron and a few of the others wanted to see if they could get in – and had asked her to come. But, in truth, she hadn't wanted to risk being turned away, and since the Denim and Diamonds nightmare, nightclubs had about as much allure as a cowboy's armpit after a week-long cattle drive.

Sharon knocked on the door and Dolores summoned her in.

A large Jamaican woman sat behind a huge desk, paperwork piled around her like termite towers. Taking off her thick pebble glasses to flash a crocodile smile, she beckoned Sharon forward.

'Come in, come in, sweet child.' She grinned, strangely friendly for a woman who usually dismissed her with a disdainful sneer.

'Um, I'm really sorry about the filing system going down … It honestly wasn't my fault. I tried to retrieve it and Frank said it was the software we'd been given ...' mumbled Sharon.

'No, no,' said Dolores, waving away the apology, as if she was swatting an irritating wasp. 'That's not why I've called you in. I've had a visit from our illustrious chairman Mr Bates, whom I believe you bumped into in the lift.'

'Yes, I did. He dropped his papers, and I helped him pick them up,' explained Sharon.

Dolores watched her silently, fingers pressed to her lips. She appeared to be appraising Sharon, as if it was the first time she'd ever seen her – or, worse, like a slave trader checking out damaged goods.

The contemplative silence was broken by Sharon. 'Okay, look, maybe I shouldn't have taken the coffee with me ... I'll never do it again. But it was my break, and I was very careful ...'

Dolores held her hand up, like a lollipop lady stopping traffic in full flow. 'Mr Bates has had a talk with me,' she said, neatly making some quick notes on a piece of paper. Head down, writing, she asked, 'Do you like your job, Sharon?'

Oh, no! She was about to be sacked!

'Um, yes I do.' Sensing this wasn't confirmation of dedication she lied, adding, 'Very much. It means so much to me. Er... I *love* it. Filing is such fun ... A great job.'

'Then that's a real shame,' said Dolores. 'Because you no longer have it.'

Sharon's guts lurched. Her life flashed before her. Well, in truth her lovely little flat and the rent bill unpaid on the kitchen counter.

'However ...' Dolores paused for maximum effect, like a nasty talent-show panellist, and shot her an almost evil smile '... he would like to offer you another.'

'Really? Doing what?' Sharon was now befuddled, her palms sticky and her heart pounding.

'Head receptionist. Front desk. The greeting face of Sharpe,

Bates and Colt. We think your looks and charm are wasted in Accounts.'

Sharon was startled to hear this, and her large green eyes widened with delight. So it was true, then. Her face *was* attractive. Sometimes she had thought it was, but it had been hard to see past her pronounced cheeks. All she ever saw was her body and its bulges.

'Your duties simply involve greeting guests with your beautiful smile and handing them a visitor's badge. Here is your own badge.' Dolores handed Sharon a special gold one, embossed with 'SHARON PLUNKETT'.

Sharon held it in awe, as if she had been given a jewel from Tiffany. The seat behind the magnificent marble console desk in Reception was the most coveted in the company among many of the young female staff. Sure, she'd read *Cosmopolitan*. She knew she should have been insulted. But no way. She was thrilled. She'd spent a lifetime hiding away and now somebody thought she was worthy of being on display.

An agency was judged by its image. And the girl on the desk was always the model of beauty.

'The money is almost double – it includes an extra allowance for dress and hair,' continued Dolores, as if it was a done deal. And, of course, it was. Sharon was elated. Ecstatic. Free from the drudgery of Accounts. Free to smile, laugh, greet, talk on the phone and drink coffee. From now on, the only thing she would be filing was her nails!

By the seventh day in her new job Sharon had spoiled herself in TK Maxx with a tight white suit that showed off more curves than a Mr Whippy ice cream. And, judging by the tongues hanging out, it certainly seemed to whip up the same amount of desire.

It was so strange. From the moment she had started a week ago, men and women had been giving her the once-over every time she stood up from behind her marble front desk. From big butch biker boys to effete corporate clients. Sharon furrowed her brow as she smoothed the pencil skirt over her curvaceous buttocks. It was a style she had never worn before and, as an experiment, she had chosen it in white. Unlike black – her usual colour of choice – made her look even larger than normal. But this appeared to attract men even more, she mused, as a pinstriped businessman approached her with a salacious grin.

'Let me take you for lunch,' said Mr Pinstripe, with all the arrogance of a man expecting an instant 'yes'.

'So sorry, I'd love to, but we're not allowed to date clients,' Sharon apologised sweetly.

'Not even top ones?' he asked, handing her a flash-looking business card stating 'International Brand Manager'.

'Especially the top ones!' she answered, fingering it with a coquettish smile. As he walked off, she casually opened her drawer and tossed it onto a pile of five others.

The idea of dating still frightened her. She had thought of Simon many times, and wondered when he would turn up in front of her. Part of her couldn't wait. The sight of his face ... Would he now find her attractive? But another part of her still reeled from the fact that he'd betrayed her and gone after Debbee.

Deep down, Sharon knew she was being a bit of a drama queen. Simon hadn't actually betrayed her *as such* because he'd never been hers in the first place. To be fair, the poor devil didn't know he'd been 'living with her' for the last two years. Yet that didn't soothe the deep hurt she felt. Irrational, ridiculous. But very real.

Her thoughts were interrupted by the inconvenience of a purring ringtone. 'Sharpe, Bates and Colt,' she trilled, flicking the board with newly manicured acrylic nails. As she switched the person through, she admired her hands. So odd, she pondered, that there was a cachet in the nails being obviously fake. No one had tips that white, or lengths that perfect – the kudos was in the fact that you could afford to have them done.

'It's important you look the part,' echoed Dolores' warning in her head. Fair enough, Sharon conceded. The fabulous entrance to the agency deserved it. The building was 1930s art deco – high ceilings with ornate cornicing, giant aluminium doors with a revolving centre. Mixing old with new, SBC had installed a twenty-foot plasma screen to flash up the latest TV ads from the agency. It was complemented by a massive pure glass coffee-table and matching glass chairs by up-and-coming Italian designer Tino Quaradelgini. Overall, the effect was stunning. Waiting clients seemed to be sitting on pure air. (And, no doubt, full of it too, Sharon often thought, with their painstakingly cool dress, designer bags and goatee beards).

But the best bit was behind her marble and glass console desk. Starting from high above her head, water spilled over a giant steel ball, then disappeared – to reappear from under a long steel track. From there, it tumbled in a backlit waterfall sheet down the white marble wall, breaking in strategic places like splintering glass. It was a masterstroke of design, a dramatic backdrop that took away the breath of even the most jaded art director.

Sharon smiled as in came another cute biker boy, wearing more Lycra than a Romanian circus act. His butt was neat and small, his torso long, lean and firm. She eyed him from head to toe, waiting for a jaunty flirt. But instead he bowed his head and avoided her eyes. Almost embarrassed.

'Hi, can I help you?' she fluttered, flicking her flaxen hair back and dipping her long eyelashes over her brilliant green eyes. He turned bright red, stammered and shoved a package at her.

'For the production office,' he stuttered, casting her a longing glance over his shoulder as he left.

How odd to have this effect on men, she thought, still unsure of her new-found attractions.

But here was the strange thing. Over the next few days, some of the biker boys and cool guys started to look a bit scrawny. A bit weedy. She slowly found herself eyeing up the beefier despatch riders and wider clients. There was something so wonderfully big and bear-like about these men. Men that could match her for size. She booked a lunchtime make-over at Cheeky Chops – a popular new Covent Garden cosmetics boutique – and headed back to work two hours later with a skipload of goodies and the knowledge she would never make the mistake of blue eye-shadow again.

As the attention at the reception desk increased, her confidence grew, and Sharon Plunkett blossomed like a gorgeously puffy pink chrysanthemum.

It was about this time that Simon wandered in. At first he didn't recognise Sharon. She, on the other hand, had spotted him coming at a thousand paces. Time to get used to the pounding of her heart and to look cool.

'My God, Sharon? Is that you?'

'No, my sister died. I'm her beautiful, identical twin,' she shot back, with a confidence that shocked her.

'Haven't seen you around for ages. When did you get this gig?'

'A couple of weeks ago – been fun.'

'You look seriously great …' He whistled.

Yeah, maybe I do, thought Sharon, for the very first time in her life.

'By the way, that awful Denim and Diamonds night at Kat's, where did you go? I looked over and, dear God, you were doing a getaway faster than Billy the Kid.'

'I was meeting someone … picked up by a cowboy in a pick-up truck!' said Sharon, blurting out the first thing to enter her head. Anyway, not that you'd have given a damn, she thought, with your nose nuzzling in Debbee's neck like a tame palomino pony.

'Well, that was a shame, cos' I was asking Debbee to come to my birthday get-together and I was going to ask you too, but you disappeared into the sunset leaving nothing but a dusty trail.'

'Birthday party? Really?'

'Yeah, I had a few friends round. Thought you'd find it fun. Never mind, there's always next year,' he added.

'Sure. I can easily wait that long,' replied Sharon, looking down shyly, wondering if she had the courage to look up again and ask him for coffee. But too late. Yet again her words and actions had come out completely the opposite from how she felt. Like a sarcastic, cool snub. When she did lift her head, she was just in time to see Simon shrug and turn towards the lift.

Holy Moses. He'd only been asking Debbee to a birthday party! Not a date. It still didn't quite explain why Debbee had had her mouth so close to his ear she could have sucked his brains out, but on the other hand she *did* have the knack of wrapping herself around a man quicker than a fur coat around a hooker, she thought charitably.

Whatever, for the second time she had just screwed it up with her ridiculous behaviour.

All afternoon Sharon action-replayed the moment, like a football fan unwilling to accept the final outcome of a game. She had been too offhand. Her mind kept a tight score of the things she shouldn't have said. What she could have said. What she hadn't said.

Amid the remorse, one strange fact niggled. Of course she still adored him, but he looked as if he'd lost weight. The man was definitely a bit too slim. A bit less impressive, maybe, than she had remembered. She had spent so long worshipping him from afar that it was almost blasphemous to think of Simon as less than a perfect god. But she had to concede that with a little more padding around the chest he'd probably look a wee bit better.

'Red alert! They're on their way!' squeaked the junior executive, running past her towards the lifts. 'Sharpe says you've got to be extra charming or you're fired!'

The entourage of Ziegfried and ZaK, the team behind the global brand Z&ZaK, swept into the vast reception area before Sharon had had time to fluff her hair. The assorted coterie of cool fashionistas standing arrogantly in front of her made her feel like a girl from the returns counter at Primark, but she was being paid well to hide her insecurity.

'Good afternoon, we've been looking forward to your arrival,' said Sharon, with her dazzling new smile. 'Please go straight up to the tenth floor. Mr Sharpe and Mr Bates are waiting for you ...'

Ziegfried, the famous designer, stopped dead, giving her a harsh, assessing look. Then, licking his little finger, he smoothed down his hair parting, and clicked his fingers imperiously. 'Zis way, team,' he said in a guttural accent, mincing off towards the lifts. With his mandarin-style coat and floor-length scarf swirling around his portly body, he evoked the image of a half-dressed geisha.

Trailing like a couple of cute kittens, two identical Japanese women dressed as roly-poly Manga schoolgirls, complete with plaid skirts and bobby sox, lowered their orange-dyed hair and followed. The butch bodyguard put his hand to his earpiece and checked the corridor, ahead and behind, as he muttered in a sinister fashion into his mouthpiece. Behind him, stood the cool, impeccably dressed ZaK.

As the entire world knew, ZaK was Ziegfried's lover, and also his brilliant manager. The man epitomised success in his silver grey suit and dove suede tie – a look of colour and texture he had made his own. He checked his platinum Patek Philippe watch impatiently and signalled a brief nod to the three briefcase-carrying executives at his side. As they swept by, the last executive paused, and winked at Sharon. 'Still waiting for your call,' he whispered, with a leer, tapping his fingers on her desk.

Sharon looked at him, puzzled, then realised he had been one of the first to hand her his business card a couple of weeks ago when she had just started the new job.

As they disappeared into the lift, she picked up the pile in the drawer and spread them on the counter like a deck of cards. The coolest one, on the top, stated:

JACK DE WINTER

BRAND MANAGER

ZIEGFRIED & ZAK

NEW YORK. PARIS. LONDON. MILAN

It was a designer work of art in silver, grey and black. The exact shades of ZaK's outfit. Well, thought Sharon, good luck, Sharpe, Bates and Colt. Word was out that they were about to lose the entire ten-million-pound business. It was always a nightmare in advertising. When a new brand manager takes over, they always like to make their own mark. And that usually means dropping the agency in favour of another (usually run by a good golfing buddy). The creative teams had been working for two weeks in sweaty desperation to come up with a pitch to save their sorry arses, and the whole agency had been holding its breath for today's meeting.

She briefly wondered if it would affect her job. Possibly … but SBC was a giant conglomerate and, though heads would roll for sure, chances were it wouldn't really impact on either her or the jets and yachts of the board.

Nonetheless, a feeling of guilt and power crept over her. If she called this man and arranged a date, could she help keep the business? Would she do it for SBC? Should she? A fantasy started to play in her head. The agency in despair. The account dribbling down the plughole. Everyone from the post-boy to the chairman dressed in black, widow's weeds, weeping. Her old colleagues from Accounts standing there, eyes red, heads lowered, bags packed. Sharpe and Bates on their knees in front of her, hands piteously begging. Then she, like the Mother Teresa of Marketing, would smile magnanimously making the sign of the cross, bountifully lift the handset, raise a manicured fingernail, poised to dial the number ... and make the bastards beg.

Two hours later, she realised with deep disappointment that her martyrdom would not be called for. The lift doors shushed open. Sharpe and Bates escorted the same ensemble out with laughs and handshakes, guffaws, jokes and pats on the back. The business was undoubtedly saved.

'It's such a great name,' smiled ZaK, shaking hands. 'The concept is spot on. Well done, gentlemen. But we must launch fast.'

Across his shoulder, Jack De Winter stole a look at Sharon, then turned back, seemingly startled. Sharon saw him whisper into ZaK's ear. He turned to stare directly at her. Then, one by one, so did everyone else, their conversation falling off until they were all silently gazing in her direction.

Following their stares, she glanced over her shoulder, but there was nothing other than the marble wall and the slick, tumbling waterfall cascading down behind her. Deeply uncomfortable, she placed her hand protectively to her neck, surreptitiously checking her buttons weren't undone. 'Sorry, gentlemen, may I help you with something?' she muttered, trying to work out what she'd done wrong.

'You just have,' said ZaK, quietly.

'My God, she looks like a water goddess,' whispered Ziegfried, theatrically.

Sharon wouldn't grasp its importance until much later, but at that precise moment, the sun had come out from behind a cloud and was sending rays of brilliant light through the arched windows of the reception area.

The effect was mesmerising. As the hall unexpectedly illuminated, skittering beams bounced off the cascading waterfall behind her, creating reflections that played and danced around her like silvery sprites. As she stood statue still, they lit her platinum hair like a silver halo, and made her green eyes sparkle like the wild Atlantic Ocean.

Drinking in the scene, the men looked at one another. Finally, breaking the spell, ZaK nodded, and the others shared looks of knowing agreement. Then they slowly turned and went on their way.

'Sharon,' said the voice of Dolores Drummond, a few days later, 'we'd like to see you in Mr Sharpe's office right away. Joanne is coming down to take over.' The phone clicked off before Sharon could ask why.

She had never been inside the hallowed walls of Mr Sharpe's office, or even to the floor it occupied. The tenth level held a mix of fear and awe for all employees. And now she would see it. Applying a quick dab of cheap Boots lip gloss and adjusting her wrap-over dress to hide her cleavage a little more, she stepped out of the glass lift and onto the polished oak floor. Her heels clip-clopped self-consciously down the corridor, until she came to an original art-deco desk, and the striking brunette, with a 1930s bob, who manned it.

'Through there. They're all waiting,' she said, with a tinge of disgust, as if she knew what the meeting was about. Sharon got the distinct impression she was enviously giving her the once-over and not liking what she saw. She gave her a sweet smile to try to break the ice, but it was met with a disinterested glance away.

The other side of the door was a totally different matter.

'Sharon, welcome – do sit down,' smiled Dolores, arms outstretched as if she was a long-lost cousin from Kingston (Jamaica). 'This is Mr Paul Sharpe, our creative head, and I believe you've already met Mr Gerard Bates, our chairman,' she said, indicating the older man on the sofa.

'Drink?' asked Sharpe, pouring himself a Budweiser from a mirrored cabinet straight off a Hollywood set.

'Er, no, thank you – just a glass of water.'

'Sparkling or still?'

Sharon had to bite her tongue not to answer, 'Tap, please.' Instead she replied, 'Sparkling is fine.'

Sharpe settled himself into a leather armchair, leg slung casually over the edge. The perfect 'creative head', he looked like Keith Richards' kid brother – his bad-boy image and rock 'n' roll nonchalance impressed the clients no end and netted the agency millions.

'Sparkling, it is, my dear,' said Bates. 'Just like yourself. A sparkling example of charm and beauty.' Sharon thought at first he was being ridiculously sarcastic. But Gerard Bates was of the old school, perfect manners, to go with his cufflinks, three-piece suit, pocket handkerchief jauntily matching his pink silk tie. It was all so odd. Was she in trouble? The friendly looks on the three faces studying her only served to confuse her.

'The thing is, Sharon – it is Sharon, isn't it?' said Bates, looking to Dolores for confirmation. 'You're a valued employee of ours. Indeed, you have been for …' Again, he looked to Dolores for help.

'More than three years – since she was eighteen,' filled in Dolores.

'Exactly. We gave you your first job,' he guessed.

Sharon nodded. (At this point, she couldn't really see the merit in mentioning her Saturdays spent sweeping the floors at the Cut Above salon in Croydon.)

'Well, we've some incredible news for you. Very exciting. Ziegfried and ZaK are keeping their account with us … you won't have known this, but they were thinking of moving.'

Not know? Sharon smiled. *Per-lease.* How little the management knew about the daily tom-tom drums of gossip that beat around the building. Gossip. The lifeblood of any agency. They could pick their nose in the executive loo, and the post room would already have re-ordered the Kleenex.

'Well, not only have we kept the account, but we're also launching a new perfume for them,' continued Sharpe, straightening his Gucci tie. 'A fantastic product, great name.'

Bates held up his hand to stop Sharpe in mid-flow. 'Please, Sharon. Be aware this is top-secret information. Only a handful of people in the world know about this. The scent is going to be called … Descent,' he announced proudly, as if naming his firstborn at a *Hello!* christening.

'Decent?' repeated Sharon bemused, not at all sure why they were imparting such high-level information to a receptionist.

'No, De*scent*,' repeated Sharpe. 'A perfume for the decadent, the cool, the laid-back. For a woman who's "wild". A "fallen angel". Descent … for a temptress, like Eve. A woman not scared to experiment, a woman who –'

Noticing the growing look of bewilderment on Sharon's face, Bates cut in, 'A woman who is …*YOU.*'

'Me?' squawked Sharon, spilling the water down her front.

'Well, maybe not *you* exactly. But – well, that's how you look,' explained Sharpe, with a 'cheers' raise of his beer glass.

'A woman keen to experiment?' she repeated, mortified. 'Oh,

my gosh, you've got it all wrong. The thing is, I don't normally dress like this …' Sharon blushed as she realised her new style of tighter clothes had been taken the wrong way. No doubt the attention had gone to her head and she'd got stupidly carried away. The thought that she'd let them down in Reception by looking like a tacky trollop made her mortified.

'I'm really sorry, but the thing is, the only experimenting I've ever done was in fourth-year chemistry, and I failed at that. I can easily go back to my old style – but, please, I love the job! I'll change my look back tomorrow.'

'You certainly won't!' snapped Bates.

'Listen, Sharon, this is an amazing opportunity,' put in Dolores, swiftly, like a mother duck nudging her fledgling out of the reeds. 'I'm not sure you understand. We want you to be the face of Descent. A top modelling job – a new career. Our discovery.'

Big pause. Big, long pause.

'You're kidding, right?' Sharon laughed nervously. 'That's funny. That's really funny. This is some kind of reality TV set-up, isn't it?' she said, looking around the room for the inevitable crew to jump out. In fact, she'd felt like that for the whole of the last two weeks, since she had entered what she now called the 'Twiglet Zone'. Her world had turned upside down – but now it was going totally insane.

'We're not. We're seriously not. The contract we want you to sign will show you just how serious we are,' cajoled Bates.

'The fact is, Sharon,' explained Sharpe, 'Jack De Winter, the new brand manager, spotted you in Reception a few days ago. He was right. You have the exact look we've been searching for. We've had three emergency casting sessions over at the photographer's. Hundreds of girls from Milan, New York and London – but none has come close to what we want. You're it. We all thought so when we saw you standing in Reception in front of the waterfall – it knocked all of us for six. Ziegfried and ZaK are wild about you.'

'They want you. We want you,' said Bates, putting a fatherly arm on her shoulders and puffing out his chest with pride.

'Kiddo, trust me, it'll be fun,' said Sharpe. 'You'll do an exotic shoot and get paid shedloads of money. We're planning posters, double-page spreads ...' he continued, in the transatlantic drawl he'd picked up from years of client-paid trips.

'But I've never modelled before!' said Sharon, terrified of the attention it would entail.

'But that's exactly what's going to be so great about it,' enthused Sharpe, clearly the creative force of the agency. 'You'll be a completely new face, discovered by accident – innocent, sweet, shy ... Succulent and perfect. Like a young Eve ... a ripe apple, ready to fall ... into Descent! The press and PR will go f—ing wild!'

'How much is the contract for?' asked Sharon, in a daze.

'Five hundred thousand pounds,' said Bates.

Sharon was so shocked she just shook her head in utter disbelief.

'Well, of course, if you're not happy with that amount, we can up it a bit ...' he added nervously. De Winter had sent a fax that morning. This was the girl they all demanded. And Bates had to deliver. Retaining the account depended on it.

'That's just for the editorial. We'll add a further hundred K for the posters and, of course, if they agree to a TV campaign, there'll be all the commercial repeats. You'll need an agent, of course. We'll find you one. Don't you worry your pretty little head about the figures. Just sign the agreement in principle and celebrate!' Bates pushed Sharon's chair towards the desk where a contract lay waiting. Then, standing back, he handed her a Mont Blanc pen.

All eyes were on Sharon, and what she intended to do.

'Sign here, my dear,' said Bates, mopping his brow with his silk handkerchief. Then he gave her one of his famous client-charming smiles. 'The perfume may be called Descent but you, my girl, are definitely – *definitely* – on your way up.'

Seven

'Muss the hair a bit more – and, Gilly, she needs gloss. Add more lippy …' The photographer was in full swing, directing the minions and multitudes buzzing around Sharon like extras in a Cecil B. DeMille film.

Sharon looked at the palm trees and exotic flowers on the bank ahead of her. The heat was intoxicating, and the spray from the waterfall tumbling down beside her a blessed relief. The makeup artist had spent nearly two hours experimenting, plucking, smoothing and polishing her face. When she had finally steeled herself to look in the mirror, she was shocked. With Velvet Moss Mac eye-shadow smudged artfully underneath and lashings of mascara and eyeliner layered on top, her green eyes looked mysterious and mesmerising. Like iridescent pools of petrol on water.

The magic the blusher had worked on her cheeks was startling too. They looked elegant and high-boned. And her lips … Some product had been smeared on to plump them up, and they pouted of their own accord, like two pretty pink pillows blowing bubbles.

Sharon felt this was a dream. A weird, never-ending dream. She tried to remember if she had polished off a whole slab of Cheddar earlier in the day and this was the result. To check, she pinched her flesh. Nope, it was all there. Especially around her tummy. But so were all the people crowding around her, making appreciative noises and fussing with her hair, face and body.

Except one.

'The thing is, she's too sodding small. Doesn't fit the sample sizes. She's an eighteen, they're all size twenty-two – you know what the designers are like. They love BIG,' bitched the fat stylist, loudly, holding up one gossamer top against Sharon then another. 'Anyway, I don't know why they picked an amateur. She needs to fill out more. Needs to put on a few pounds.'

Sharpe looked furious, and pulled the woman a couple of feet away from the bewildered Sharon. 'We picked her 'cos she's bloody gorgeous,' he snapped. 'The wind machine will puff out the caftan a bit, but after one look at her face, no one will care. Stop moaning and do your job.'

Too small! An unfamiliar emotion swept through her. Confidence. So this was what it felt like. She looked at her curves with new pride. If this was small, what the hell was she worrying about?

Holding a green apple, Sharon was posed leaning back against a rock, hair tumbling down behind her, while a live snake twisted round a branch just above her head. The spray had made her cotton caftan almost see-through, and she was only too aware of her nakedness underneath. The cold water made her creamy-milk skin glow, and her nipples stand out like tempting chocolate buttons. A horrifying thought furrowed her brow. What would her father say when he saw the posters?

'Okay, Shaz, now listen to me. Gently bite into the apple again, then lick your lips – but *don't* smudge the lipstick on the apple.'

By the time she bit into the umpteenth apple, the taste was beginning to give her acid reflux. Still, imagining she was biting into a giant doughnut, and thinking of Simon, she let herself give a wicked little smile as she held the apple to her mouth.

'Perfect! Perfect!' cried the Mockney photographer. 'What a doll!

Magic, darlin'. Jus' as you are … again. Hold it, hold it. Eyes to me. Stick yer bum out more, arch yer back to balance … Okay, that's it. Done. Relax. Over.'

The room burst into spontaneous applause and an assistant raced over to wrap her in a warmed towel. Sharpe swaggered over, beer bottle in hand. 'Gorgeous, darling. Bloody gorgeous. D'ya wanna go out and celebrate?'

But before he could say any more, Jack De Winter interrupted frostily: 'Sharon, there's someone I want you to meet. Jules D of Jules D Creatives. Our PR lady. She needs to get some info on you, and she's there to help you if you need her. Hurry up and get changed.'

Glancing over to the catering truck, Sharon saw a smartly dressed woman in her late thirties, with short brown spiky hair. The thing that struck Sharon was the neatness of the woman's figure. About size eighteen, she was perfectly proportioned and toned. Wearing enormous black designer shades, she currently had her pretty ear glued to a mobile phone.

Sharon disappeared into the dressing room to peel off the wet caftan, and emerged in a sweatshirt and jeans, hair pulled back in a ponytail. No makeup.

'Hello, darling,' said Jules D, kissing her on both cheeks. 'Are you having fun? Or are they being mean to you?' The woman's eyes twinkled with fun as she linked arms with Sharon. 'Tell me, I hear you were just a receptionist, and my dear employers Ziegfried and ZaK plucked you from behind the desk of depression and raised you to the heights of glamour. Now, you can tell me the truth. And you always need to. Is that story really true?'

'Er, well, yes. It is, actually.'

'*Marvellous*, darling. Mar-vell-ous. What a story.'

'Except the desk was hardly depressing,' said Sharon.

'Yes, it was, darling. Very. The press will love that.'

'But it wasn't. I loved my job.'

'No, you didn't, sweetheart. You *didn't*. You dreamed of escape.'

'But that's not exactly true.'

'Listen to me, Sharon – you can trust me.' Jules D lowered her voice, 'I'm an *ex*-journalist!' She chuckled. 'Look, I'm sure this whole thing is totally overwhelming for you. But don't be afraid, I'm here to help you. In fact, I can help you far more than you realise right now. I have a feeling about you …' She hugged Sharon's arm tightly, sat her down and ordered a glass of milk for her.

Milk? thought Sharon. She really wanted a glass of wine now the shoot was over.

'Milk, darling. So good for you. All that calcium to build lovely big strong bones. Okay? Now then, back to your history. It says here that you're originally from Bournemouth, and you're an orphan.' She was flicking through a file.

'Not exactly. That's an exaggeration.' Sharon wondered just how much private info on her file Dolores had divulged. 'My mother died of leukaemia when I was ten. My father remarried.'

'Well, that sounds good, okay?' said Jules, making furious notes.

'What – my mother dying or my father remarrying?'

Unabashed, Jules D laughed. 'Both, darling. The former is good for the press, the latter for you, dear heart.'

'Well, no … not exactly,' said Sharon, her emotions surprisingly thawed by the warmth of this woman. 'Not exactly "good",' she clarified.

'Why not? What was she like?' asked Jules D, pausing in her note-writing to study Sharon's face.

Sharon hesitated. Then she told the truth. 'He tried to rebuild the family too fast and ended up marrying a woman who had two daughters of her own. She threw me out as soon as she could, when I had just turned sixteen. That was how I ended up in

London. Never actually chose to live here.'

'Oh, no, how dreadful,' said Jules D, looking genuinely sad. Perhaps she had seen the pain in Sharon's eyes because she changed the subject. 'Now listen to this. We're going to run a full PR campaign alongside the advertising. That means press and radio interviews, okay?'

'Sure,' said Sharon, totally unsure.

'Now, boyfriends … got any? Had many? Who was your first?' asked Jules D, matter-of-factly.

'Um …' Blank. Sharon somehow doubted that a quick schoolgirl snog in a game of Spin the Bottle would count as a relationship. Likewise, the tapas waiter, and their drunken dawn tumble on a beach in Ibiza. But it seemed so lame to say, 'No,' to both questions.

Could she mention Simon? No, that would be a big, big lie. She finally shook her head, a little ashamed.

'None at all?' asked Jules D, kindly. 'I find that hard to believe …' Sharon looked at her, puzzled. This world was really going to take some getting used to. Sensing her embarrassment, Jules D changed tack.

'This is good. Mar-vell-ous. We'll paint you as still an angel, about to fall,… okay? Maybe that's an even better angle. Leave it to me … I'm going to work on the press release tonight … Speak to you very soon. Hugs bye-bye. Miss you already.' And with a kiss on both cheeks, Jules D waved a farewell and headed off the set.

It was nearly deserted. Sharon slowly collected her things, reluctant to leave the magic she'd recently experienced. But around her, the lights were being disassembled, the fake grass torn up and the plastic flowers dumped in a truck. The water pump was turned off. And the waterfall dried. Sharon shuddered. The strange new world she had entered seemed as surreal as this set. An illusion that could dissipate at any moment.

'How about that drink now?' said Jack De Winter, offering her a plastic flower. 'I think you owe me one,' he murmured suggestively.

Sharon looked into his eyes. Ultra-trendy with a tyre-mark goatee running down his plump chin and slicked-back hair, he was so not her type.

'It was me that pointed you out to ZaK, you know. He wouldn't have noticed you otherwise.' He placed a hand on her shoulder, twisting her to face him. 'At the very least, I deserve a kiss …' His lips puckered wetly, and he placed a proprietory hand firmly on her breast. Shocked, Sharon looked around for an escape.

'Tut tut, darling. Not a good idea to do that. I don't think Z&ZaK would be too impressed to think you pushed her forward just because she's your girlfriend,' said Jules D, nonchalantly picking up a folder as she re-entered the studio. 'Sharon, sweetheart, would you like a lift home? I live in Richmond, not far from you. We can share a cab, and I can take a few more notes.'

Sharon bolted for the door, giving Jack a shy apologetic shrug.

'Night, Jack. We'll see you soon,' said Jules D.

Jack laughed, resigned. 'Jules D … if you weren't so bloody good at your job …'

'But I am, darling. I *so* am.' She smiled, blowing him a kiss.

'Hi, darling, it's your publicist here. We have you sorted.'

Two days later, Sharon stood in the reception of Glacé Inc., the world's leading model agency. Jules D had made a few calls, and they were keen to meet her. The walls were plastered with huge girls in various poses, but no matter if they were wearing evening gowns or swimming costumes, they all looked incredibly womanly. Very feminine, with strong, beautiful faces that stared at the camera with a defiant, Amazonian attitude. Sharon found herself thinking that actually, despite any bulgy bits, they all looked pretty cool.

'Hi, I'm Kristen Saint-Donis,' drawled a woman in her late

forties. She had the kind of elegance that would have made Jackie O feel like a spotty adolescent.

Jules D introduced Sharon to Glacé Inc.'s famous boss. An ex-model, her hair and face were pure Grace Kelly and, despite her age, she was still stunningly beautiful. Her full figure was encased in a loose, *écru*-coloured robe that ebbed and flowed over her considerable shape, like poured cream.

'Jules D says there's a contract in the post for us. We take twenty per cent of everything. Are you cool with that?' Matching her exclusive style, the woman's voice was frosty, with a tinge of boredom.

'Okay, sure,' said Sharon, trying to work out how much she was going to be giving away – and why.

As if reading her mind, Kristen answered, 'If you do as we say, and that's a big if, I'll quadruple those earnings in a year. If I sound unimpressed, it's because we see a lot of girls in here. Hundreds. All with their dreams of becoming the next supermodel. There's only ever been five. Six, if you count the scrawny one with a drug problem.'

She pressed a silver-manicured fingernail on the intercom. 'Coffee, Zara.' There was no 'please', no 'thank you'. Then she launched into a long speech, without a pause for reaction.

'Fact is, this is a tough, tough business. Z&ZaK think you've got what it takes to be a high-end model. But, if that's true, you're going to need to catch up fast. To be frank, you're already old for a newcomer.' The insults just kept on coming.

'To be a Glacé girl, you need to work on your butt. Build it up a bit. Add a few more pounds. As I suspect you already know, Glacé Inc is world famous for its girls – all sumptuous cherries. The icing on the cake. Indeed, you could say we ruthlessly cherry-pick the best. It's true.'

'In your case, you've somehow got a big contract – and you've been assigned a top publicist, who believes you're really going places. Personally, I have my doubts.'

Zara came into the room and placed a cafetière of coffee and a slice of cherry cheesecake on the table. Kristen indicated her dismissal, and the girl walked backwards, as if in the presence of the Queen.

As Sharon stood there, feeling lost and forlorn, Kristen raised one of her beautifully arched eyebrows and studied her, like an artist about to mould a piece of lumpen clay. 'On the other hand …' she added, sucking thoughtfully on a gold pencil, then using it to punch the phone '…there is something vulnerable there. Something fresh. Something undeniably sexy. Whatever, I can't send you on go-sees looking like that.'

Sharon was hurt. She had worn her best dress from Wallis, a wrap-over in small print, with a pair of beige court shoes.

Kristen pressed her pencil on speed dial and picked up the handset. 'Mario, I have a new girl. Do your job.'

Sharon was on her way to her eighth go-see that week. On the advice of the agency's freelance stylist, she had pulled her hair high, in a glossy fall that swished behind her like a circus pony's tail, and wore a plain black Miu Miu shirt with a simple white Abercrombie and Fitch T-shirt underneath. Her trousers were low slung and flared, a perfect fit, hugging her thighs and bottom like a second skin. Over her shoulder she hooked a supple leather vintage jacket that matched the soft portfolio in her hand perfectly. At her throat lay a flat silver Tiffany heart.

The whole ensemble was Mario's idea. And it was working. Of the eight meetings, two had booked her, and three had pencilled her in for a recall.

As she walked down Regent Street she hummed to herself … This world was perfect. She felt perfect. For the first time in her entire life. She sashayed along, this time daring to look at her reflection in the windows. As always, they made her look even larger, the dark shadows highlighting her curves. BUT NOW IT DIDN'T MATTER! There were hundreds around her size, but few had her height, and now it seemed she had a pretty face. Which gave her an edge. Her mind wandered to Simon … She'd love to see him again. This time she'd make a move. Ask him for coffee.

Or, better yet, coffee and *cake*. How great it would be to bump into him. It would be a dream. She turned the corner. And stopped dead. Her breath caught in her throat. Ahead, she could hardly believe what she saw.

Eight

People were standing, staring. Pointing, talking. Sharon followed their gaze. High on a billboard overlooking the swarming streets, there was an image so arresting it was stopping passers-by in their tracks.

Everyone was looking at a giant forty-eight-sheet poster of a lush tropical waterfall. Lit by strands of sunlight, the cascade served as a backdrop to the most gorgeous blonde model imaginable. Her lustrous hair was haloed like an angel's, her face innocent – but the wet strands that tangled down her breasts gave her a wanton, dishevelled look. Her huge almond eyes were smudged, as if she'd been up all night, but they danced with reflected sunlight, their striking green colour echoing the glinting pool of water. In her hand, a juicy apple, her mouth tantalisingly close in a wicked, lazy smile. But the most breathtaking thing of all was her body – enclosed in a soaked pink caftan that opened to her waist, yet clung seductively to her ample shape. Nipples clearly outlined.

She looked amazing. Firm, buxom, pale-skinned and all-woman. But more than anything, as wanted by Ziegfried and ZaK, she looked just like man's original Eve eating the apple. A fallen angel. A naughty cherub who was about to practise fellatio for the first time. The line underneath made her want to die: 'Descent. Get wild, go down…'

No question, it had a decadent, inescapable double meaning.

As Sharon stared at herself in shock, waves of disbelief and horror swept over her. She was proud of her face and body but wanted to run up and cover her erect nipples, and tear the line off the poster – anything to lessen its unbelievable impact. In turmoil she scrabbled in her bag for her phone. The only person she knew to call was Jules.

'Jules, it's me! Ohmigod. Have you seen the posters?' asked Sharon, aghast.

'Mar-vell-ous darling. Fab-ul-ous. Leaves you speechless. The phones haven't stopped ringing.'

'But it's disgusting – I don't even look like that.'

'But, sweetie, who else do you think it is? Stop being so modest. Or maybe you need to take a good long look at yourself, darling. Maybe you need a spot of self-esteem therapy. I know this marvellous man, runs a mind and body course – I'll email you his details. Hell-*o* … Just a moment …'

Sharon could hear Jules D chatting on another of her phones to a newspaper: 'She's a find, darling. A one-off. Practically an orphan … discovered in a boring receptionist job, wasted. I know … I know … Stunning. Her name?' Jules D paused. Inspiration hit. 'Her name is Shaz. Interview? Of course … Sorry, just a minute …'

'Sharon, can I call you back?' The phone went dead. Sharon looked at her useless, silent mobile, then back up at the billboard. It was so huge. *So* in your face. A few young men were staring up at it too. Then one glanced at her. Then at the billboard. Then back at her.

'Hey, it's *you*!' they chorused, tongues hanging out like excited puppies.

'You look great!' one shouted appreciatively.

'How about an autograph?' asked another.

Sharon shook her head, terrified they thought she was up for a blowjob, and ran towards the tube, and the safety of her little pastel ice-cream-decorated flat and a comforting tub of Ben & Jerry's.

But the journey home was anything but comforting. Her poster seemed to be up everywhere in all sorts of different sizes. Down the escalator, on the tube platform, in the magazine of the girl next to her …

There was no escape. No exit. It was even there on The Way Out.

The next week was a smorgasbord of emotional highs and lows. By the end of it, Sharon had been interviewed by five radio stations, three national newspapers and two magazines.

As predicted by Ziegfried and ZaK, the perfume campaign had created an instant and outrageous publicity storm. People demonstrated outside the Advertising Standards Authority demanding it be removed. Church heads railed, talk shows talked, and tabloid sub-editors had a creative field day:

'DESCENT – advertising standards drop to new low.'

Of course, sales didn't: they zoomed sky high.

Women everywhere bought it to show they were cool, decadent and 'up for it' while men everywhere were buying it for their women … in the vain hope they might be. Within days, the glass bottle in the shape of an apple sat on the dressing table of thousands of women. However it got there, all wanted to capture the essence of 'Shaz's' angelic, devilish appeal.

'Shaz, listen to me, darling,' said Jules D, pouring her a glass of champagne. 'This is a turning point in your life. Grab it with two hands, savour it, and enjoy.'

Easier said than done. They had just watched her featured on the six o'clock news – and protesters had branded her a shocking example to young girls. 'Jules, you don't understand, do you? I'm nothing like this creature.' She was still trying to adjust to her new nickname, no matter the image.

'Oh, come on, sweetheart – it's fun, isn't it? Look on the bright side, you may come across as a bit of a goer, but you've got buckets in the bank, international modelling offers flooding in and me as your friend. Okay?'

Sharon laughed. Jules was right. The woman had the precious knack of making everything seem okay, no matter how bad.

And, actually, she was right. Her life was magical, really. She'd had an enormous bouquet of lilies from Ziegfried and ZaK, a giant, triple-layered gold box of Godiva chocolates from Sharpe, Bates and Colt, and at least five phone calls from an excitedly rambling Debbee, congratulating 'Shaz' on her startling success.

What was more, on her last visit to the offices of Glacé Inc., Kristen had treated her with sudden respect. Sharon suspected this generosity of character was solely due to the castings and contracts that Zara, her appointed booker, was now juggling on her behalf. However, during the mid-morning meeting, Kristen had actually ordered a minion to pop out and get Sharon a double chocolate milkshake and some blueberry cheesecake.

'Now, as for the love life, let's see what we can conjure up, shall we?' continued Jules D, while she waited for someone to pick up the phone at the other end of the mobile held to her ear. 'We need to get you out more. You should be seen around. Good for publicity. Tonight, take a cab to – Oh, hello, Don, did you get the papers today? Great piece on your brilliance…' Jules D chatted brightly to another client, a famous cosmetic surgeon, while Sharon sipped her drink and took time to reflect on the way her life had changed.

Jules D was right. What was she worried about? The only person whose approval she regularly sought was Debbee's, and they weren't talking. Besides, judging from the host of phone messages she'd left on Sharon's answerphone, she clearly thought the whole thing was a hoot.

The girls at the office were long gone. In fact, thinking about it, there were only two people in the world whose reactions she worried about: Simon, who was a photographer and, let's face it, knew how advertising campaigns worked; and her father. The latter was a totally different matter. But he was getting old now, seventy-seven. So short-sighted he probably wouldn't see a billboard if it smacked him in the face.

On the other hand, if he did, he'd have a massive stroke.

Maybe she should call him. But, as always, the thought of speaking to her stepmother to get through to him filled her with sickening dread. So rude, Carolyn always snapped, 'I'll get your father,' before Sharon had even had a chance to finish the word 'hello'. Regardless, she'd call him tomorrow, just to warn him about the posters. She suddenly felt really peckish, which was amusing, considering the next conversation.

'Right, all sorted,' said Jules D, putting down her mobile phones. '*Grazia* want to run a story on you. Particularly your diet. They'll be asking you questions like "How do you stay so fat?", "What are your eating habits?" , "Favourite recipes?", "How do you avoid exercise?" You know, the usual.'

Sharon giggled quietly to herself. This upside-down world just blew her away! But every time she tried to ask anyone, 'How the hell did this reversal happen? When did big women suddenly become so desirable, and why?' they just looked at her blankly, with pity – as if she was a little crazy.

And maybe she was, because five weeks on, saturated every day with magazines, commercials and adverts, it was beginning to seem normal to be a big woman. She had learned that it was better to say nothing to anyone. In fact, she was beginning to think she'd imagined a world where it was once in to be thin. Perhaps *that* was the dream and *this* was reality.

'So, what was I saying?' asked Jules D, popping her notebook into her Prada briefcase. 'I know – your love life. Let's hit the town tonight. How about we head to the Sugar Cube? One of my clients is the owner – a guarantee of champagne and VIP pampering all night. Plus, the truth is he'd love to have you in his club. Adores having the latest models hang around. Kudos. So it's up to you.'

Sharon liked her honesty. It would never have occurred to her that Jules D would win points for bringing her to the club. 'Sure. Why not? Especially if it helps you.' Sharon smiled sweetly. A night out. Hadn't done that since the Denim and Diamonds Debbee Débâcle, as she liked to refer to it.

A few hours later, they met at the silver VIP door of the Sugar Cube. Sharon had donned a cute geometric sixties tunic she'd bought from Mario, while Jules D was her usual sophisticated self in sharp, tailored trousers and short Chanel jacket.

Burly bouncers nodded, and they swept past the glamorous West End crowd outside. The girl on the desk air-kissed Jules D, then gestured them in a direction away from the coat-checking crowds. 'Straight up the stairs, champagne's on ice.'

Jules D took Sharon's arm and steered her up an underlit purple glass staircase and through a heavy mirrored door.

The noise crashed into them, like a wave, and as Sharon adjusted her eyes, she saw they had entered a three-walled mirrored room that overlooked a packed dance floor. Potted palms, chrome armchairs, purple cocktails. Sharon thought she was in Beverly Hills – it made the Kool Kat in Kingston look like a half-drowned, three-legged moggie.

The VIP area wasn't full. But that was the point of it. No shoving your way to the bar in this joint. The image of Betty Boop, a dark-haired girl dressed in titanium shorts with long, shapely tree-trunk legs, balanced sexily on strappy white heels while she took their order.

The Mojito cocktail Jules suggested she try was amazing. It cooled Sharon's throat with its delicious minty tingle. The crowds below looked up at her enviously. People pointed, some even took pictures with their mobile phones. She smiled for them. Waved. This was such fun.

Jules D seemed to know everyone. And everyone knew her. Visitor after visitor kissed her cheek, then shook Sharon's hand. Chat, chat, chat ... Sharon mentally drifted off as they talked to her PR lady.

The female guests in the club had uniformity. Streaked blonde hair, long extensions, white French-manicured fake nails, Gucci belts, Chanel gags ... Fake or not, who could tell in this light? Sharon glanced around for Betty Boop, keen to have another Mojito, when the man at the bar caught her eye.

Strikingly handsome. Straight dark hair, chiselled cheeks, tall. He raised a glass to her, then downed it in one. His tight white T-shirt outlined his powerful shoulders. She clocked his arms, muscular and strong. For the first time since Simon, Sharon felt a tightening in her stomach. A definite lurch. He smiled. The most gorgeous smile of perfect white teeth. When he turned his head, she could see that his nose was slightly dented. But it was a cute dent. Looked like the result of a bar fight he had won single-handed.

Betty Boop placed a Mojito in front of her. Sharon was surprised – 'I was just about to ask you for another. You read my mind.'

'Not me ... He did.' She winked, indicating the stranger at the bar.

Sharon tossed her waist-length ponytail over her shoulder and raised her glass to him in thanks. He smiled, and walked over. 'Dean,' he said, offering his hand.

'Sharon … I mean Shaz,' said Sharon, tripping over her new 'cool' identity.

'You're everywhere, babe. We're all crazy 'bout you …' he said, in a strong Essex accent. Sharon blushed: the poster line, 'Get wild … go down', and its double meaning was probably on his mind.

But he was so hot he veritably smoked. What the hell? For the first time in her life, she suddenly *felt* like *getting wild*. As if he knew, he pulled her to her feet and led her over to the corner of the room. The music pounded, but he moved slowly, gently placing his hands on her hips and moving them towards him in a slow, painfully slow, dance.

'So, what do you do?' asked Sharon, raising her voice above the music to make some kind of communication through the sexual steam. It sounded so naff: she hated the sentence as she uttered it. But he didn't seem to notice its ordinariness.

'Footballer. I'm a striker for Manchester … You didn't know?' he asked, surprised. Sharon had never liked the game, considered it a pansy's choice compared to rugby. No, she truthfully hadn't had a clue, though she did recognise Manchester as a leading club.

'I'm Dean Brockton.' *Ohmigod*, thought Sharon, the penny dropping. It was Dean, better known as 'Hurricane Dean' for his force on the field – and off. Recently she'd seen him spread over the pages of the nationals for three different reasons. His amazing skill at footie. His amazing style in clothes. And his amazing success with women. And now she was in his arms. She turned, panicking, to see Jules D staring at her, in shock, concern and … yes, amusement. After all, her new friend had only turned her back to chat for a second, and there was her client in the arms of a famous hunk when only hours ago she'd insisted she wasn't that kind of girl. ' Ah, well, people change.

Sharon excused herself from his embrace, and walked back to Jules D, who was busy pouring herself a glass of delicate pink champagne.

'Okay, Jules D. What are you thinking?'

'I'm thinking, it's okay,' laughed Jules. 'Go for it. Why not? I would. Forget I'm here. Go and enjoy. Children,' she said, raising her glass, 'you have my blessing.'

Sharon gave her a grateful smile and walked back. Dean took her in his arms as if they'd been a couple for years. It felt natural. Normal. He brushed a strand of hair from her face, then ran his index finger softly over her lips. The tingle she felt was far greater than anything a barrel of Mojito could have conjured. 'Gorgeous. I just had to touch them …'

His dark brown eyes flirted with Sharon's as he tilted her chin. 'Look at your beautiful cheeks … like plump, delicious plums,' he murmured, kissing her face softly. 'I could eat you up …'

By the time his lips brushed hers, she had melted faster than a double nut sundae on an August bank holiday, desire making her body shake with anticipation.

'Hey, Dean! Put her down!' Five or six mates came over to slap him on the back, and get a closer look at his prey. Sharon smiled at them shyly.

'Holy shit! It's her!' said one of his team mates.

'Hello, darlin', you don' wanna waste your time on that loser.'

'Yeah, waste it on *this* loser,' interrupted another, jostling to pole position in front of the gang. 'Can I get you a drink?' He laughed drunkenly, taking a macho swig from his bottle. 'How about an Appletise. Or should that be *apple teaser*?'

They guffawed.

'Guys, guys, please. Give us some space. This lady is special. Go and play elsewhere …'

'Aw, Dean, dear boy, you've gone turtle,' said the closest to her, touching her hair.

'Turtle dove, in love – aaah …' said a mate behind him.

'We'll just leave you two to get *down* to it!' joked a third, heading off to the bar with winks and thumbs up to Dean.

'Oh, God. I'm so sorry, Shaz, I really am. What a bunch of absolute pricks. A total embarrassment. Trouble is, they're my team mates. Have to get on with them for the sake of the club.' He looked so upset for her that Sharon was touched.

Dean took her hand firmly. 'Let's get out of here.' They headed down the stairs, out of the club doors and into the fresh air.

It was then that a thousand flashguns went off. Shocked and dazzled, Sharon shielded her eyes, confused by the fireworks.

'SHAZ, over here! DEAN, give us a smile!'

The bank of paparazzi hadn't been there when either of them had gone in, but someone had tipped them off. Complete strangers were calling her name, pleading with her to give them a look. Sharon couldn't believe the attention. It was unexpected, but amazing. Like being an old-fashioned movie star. Dean looked pretty happy to be photographed with her too, and drew her close to him.

She was overwhelmed by the praise being shouted from all directions: it was her first big taste of celebrity fame, and it was intoxicating.

'Beautiful, Shaz – look this way!'

'Give us a smile! Great, really gorgeous!'

She replied to their incessant requests with 'Sure! Another smile? Is that enough?' The gentlemen of the press loved her. And she liked their love.

Dean opened the door of a limo and they piled in, giggling. 'Fun, isn't it? We should hang around a lot more together.' His voice deepened. 'A lot, lot more …' He pulled her close to his chest, and ran his fingers down her back. For a second, Sharon stiffened as they reached the bulge at her hips caused by her pants elastic. She straightened to lessen the bump, but Dean just groaned, 'My God, your body is to die for. I've never felt anything like it.'

As Sharon gingerly ran her fingers over *his* taut, tanned athlete's chest, she sighed with bliss, and had to agree.

Dean's Chelsea Harbour penthouse was a schoolboy's wet dream. Giant plasma screen, black leather sofa, white rugs, sound system as expensive as a NASA console desk. The bedroom echoed the monochrome décor with a zebra-skin rug. On the bed, black and white suede pillows nestled on crisp Egyptian cotton sheets monogrammed in grey, 'DB'.

The headboard on one side had a chrome panel with a series of shiny buttons, which monitored everything from the under-floor heating to the overhead planter's fan.

On the far wall a grubby blue T-shirt encased in a black frame was inscribed with the signatures of the '66 World Cup winners. By his bed, a giant silver football stood on a plinth. Next to it, incongruously, sat a plastic green Teasmade.

'From me mum,' grinned Dean, patting its vile Formica top, and pressing a couple of buttons above it. The lights went down, and the blinds went up. Sharon gasped at the view. A marina of expensive yachts swayed in the moonlight, edged by a city of twinkling lights.

Dean came up behind her and unzipped her tunic. Slipping it off, he lifted her bra strap and kissed her flesh where it had cut in. Slowly, slowly he removed more clothes, ordering her to stand still. He couldn't take his eyes off her. It felt like he was worshipping her.

And, indeed, he was. Finally naked, she stood in the moonlight like a celestial fertility statue. Her shiny hair tumbled down her body in a silver stream of light. To Dean, her rounded belly and full breasts were the symbol of femininity from thousands of years ago.

Sharon smiled to herself. Her life was perfect. This was perfect. She … was perfect.

Nine

Humming merrily to herself she unlocked her front door, put on the kettle, and headed to the bedroom to change into fresh underwear. Watching her milky breasts plop firmly into her bra, she ran her palms over her mountainous regions of flesh, and found tender miles of delicately dipping hills and vales.

Such a variety of shape and contour, texture and colour. Then she thought how much had changed. As well as the contract and a model agency, she now had a lover. She was finally like any other normal girl. Well, not quite. Her life was better.

Over the next few days she learned that being a WAG was a hoot.

Out of the blue, the crabby old manageress of The Cut Above salon in Croydon was on the phone full of smarmy charm and tales of how much fun it had been when 'her favourite trainee' had worked there. The woman was obviously suffering from false memory syndrome, thought Sharon, especially when she cut to the crunch with an offer of unlimited free nail, eyelash and hair extensions – as 'a sign of our esteem'. How ironic, thought Sharon, that the last time she'd heard from her, it was to cancel the extension of her Saturday contract.

There was another turning point. The first freebie arrived almost as soon as the tabloids ran the pictures of her and Dean together. A delivery boy handed her a box containing a soft velvet gym bag embossed with the gold lettering of Gucci. From inside, she withdrew a duck-egg blue buckle bag in kid leather. It smelled divine and, being large, balanced well with her figure. She was photographed swinging it around town the very next day, along with the tag, which said it cost a thousand pounds.

'WAGS WATCH OUT!' screamed the headlines.

Cooler, younger, prettier … overnight, 'Shazza and Dean' were the new darlings of the tabloids. Jules D was on the phone every other hour with requests for quotes. *Loaded* magazine had rung fifteen times that morning, trying to persuade Sharon to pose in her undies. The money was good. She was tempted. But her model agency had bigger ideas and firmly took control.

On the instructions of Kristen, Zara had asked Sharon how she felt about New York Fashion Week. The idea seemed thrilling, but terrifying. Tottering in heels down the catwalk in front of *Vogue*, *Tatler* and the rest was a far cry from a stills shoot.

It was about this time that she had another message on her answerphone from Debbee: 'Shaz, Shazza or Sharon. Don't know what I should be calling my ol' mate any more. Anyway, Sharon, give me a call, can you? I doubt you're interested now, but just to let you know, I bumped into Simon a couple of days ago, and he asked me for your number … If you want to hear the gossip, speak soon – yeah? Please call …'

Simon. Sharon hadn't had time to think about him for days. Hey, she was Dean's girlfriend now. A celeb. She didn't need him. Still, she wondered what he'd said to Debbee.

A day later, she decided to drop in and find out.

Getting ready to meet her ex-mate was an interesting exercise.

Which dress to wear? Opening her wardrobe, Sharon smoothed the silk of her taffeta blue smock with the big green spots, and then the white flowing number. The white. Sharon grinned. It was *so* fattening.

Debbee cautiously opened the door. She looked abysmal – and was clearly shocked to find Sharon on her doorstep. Her normally slick blonde mane of extensions had matted into dull Rastafarian clumps that swamped her gaunt little face. Wrapped in a frayed greying dressing gown, she stared gratefully at Sharon 'I'm so glad you came,' she gushed, thrusting her skinny body into Sharon's plump, comforting arms. Sharon winced at her friend's frailty, Debbee's bones grating on her. It had been a mistake to come.

Seeing Sharon's reaction, Debbee wasted no time in smalltalk: she went straight for the full grovel. 'I feel really awful about that night at Kat's. Such a heel,' said Debbee, mournfully. 'I just wanted to make that cowboy jealous, and poor Simon happened to be there.'

Sharon pulled away.

Debbee pleaded on: 'I never meant to hurt you – you must know that. You know me, a stupid little flirt … Anyway, all he did was ask us to his party. *Both* of us. I turned round to catch your eye and tell you, but all I saw was the back of you bolting towards the exit. Please forgive me. I'm so disgusted with myself. I know you were crazy about him. But, please, Sharon … I care about you far too much to lose you as a friend. Forgive me?' Debbee approached her for another hug.

Sharon started to feel magnanimous – and, after all, the way her life was going she could afford to. But she'd let Debbee grovel just a little, no, a *lot* more.

As Debbee clung, Sharon remained unresponsive, carefully untangling herself from the thin, daddy-long-legs arms. 'The thing is, Debbee, I just don't understand why it was necessary to stick your tongue in his ear.'

For a moment, Debbee was startled at the confrontation. This wasn't the easily-pliable Sharon she was used to manipulating. 'Well, the main thing is, it's not *me* he's interested in. It's you,' she said, attempting a side-step with more skill than she'd ever shown on the dance floor. 'As I've been trying to tell you, the last time I saw him all he did was ask me for *your* number. I bet he's cray-zee about you,' continued Debbee, trying out flattery as a defence. 'He asked if I thought you'd be interested in posing for a shoot with him.'

Sharon laughed, and looked up at the gods. This had been her fantasy ever since she'd entered her magical new world. And now it was happening. Dr Marvel's Miracle just never seemed to stop. 'That could be fun. Maybe,' she answered, with a casual shrug.

'Glad you said that, because I already gave him your number. Mind you, I don't know what you see in him. You're far too attractive and famous,' said Debbee, ingratiatingly.

Sharon paused to mull that over. Casting her mind back, she pictured Simon objectively. There he stood in Reception. Tousle-haired, and wolf-like. Lean, mean and hungry. Actually, did Debbee now have a point? What *had* she seen in him? He could certainly do with a little feeding up.

Nowadays she found she liked a real man, like Dean. A man who could wrap his arms around her (all the way) and hold her tight. A man – nay, an athlete – whose magnificently muscled body could shelter her, make her feel feminine, safe and warm. 'Know what, Debbee? You're so right. Forgive and forget. How about a cup of coffee?'

Debbee did a little clap of glee. 'Sure! Anything! In fact, I can even make us a hot chocolate. Jam doughnuts? Or orange cheesecake?'

'Glad you're trying to eat sensibly,' said Sharon, admiringly. 'You don't want to let yourself go.'

Debbee cast her eyes downward, and puffed out her tatty dressing gown to try to make herself look larger. 'I've put on a few pounds by forcing myself to eat, but I'm not sure it shows. What do you think?'

Sharon was so tempted to be cruel. But that wasn't her nature, so she stopped herself. 'Course it does. You're definitely filling out.' Then she added, for good measure, 'Have you seen your bum? It looks much bigger.'

Debbee's sad eyes brightened. 'Really? Do you think so?' But as she twisted herself to look in the mirror her brightness faded, as if someone had pressed a dimmer switch. 'You're just saying that to be kind. Next to you, I look disgusting. But thanks, anyway.'

Defeated, Debbee slunk onto the sofa, sipping her hot chocolate and dunking a doughnut, her slim legs underneath her. Sharon looked at them with new eyes. They were plain. Uninteresting. Straight. Breakable. She questioned why the hell she had ever wanted a pair like them. She must have been delusional.

'Oh, Sharon, I'm so desperately sorry,' wept Debbee, unexpectedly. 'My life is hell. I've been so lonely.'

Sharon plopped a plump, comforting arm around her shoulders. 'You've got so much going for you, how can you say that?'

Debbee snivelled a silvery line of snot across her hand and let forth a giant sob. 'LOOK AT ME! I'm a nothing. A … slim … tiny … nothing! I'm not even petite. Let's face it, Sharon, I'm – I'm skinny! A hideous size eight! Probably even a six!'

'Let's not exaggerate, Debbee. Anyway, lots of men find your kind of figure sexy.'

'Really? Name one,' wailed Debbee, in despair. 'That cowboy couldn't wait to get away from me, and your Simon – he just wanted to get to you, through talking to me.'

Oh, God, this was so weird, thought Sharon. At what point did Debbee remember the old world? 'But *you* always used to be the gorgeous one,' said Sharon, curious and confused.

Debbee shot her a hurt and angry look, as if she was teasing her, and pulled away. 'Don't be cruel, Sharon. You're mocking me. You never used to be mean …'

Sharon sighed in puzzled defeat. 'Fine. Look, all you've go to do is try harder. Y'know, eat more, exercise less.'

'It's okay for you to say that,' sulked Debbee, curling up like a whiny whippet. 'You're naturally fat.'

'Wrong. I have to work at it,' replied Sharon, with generosity, cheesecake crumbs making a white moustache round her mouth.

'Well, I've tried everything, and I just give up. I'll never be like you,' moaned Debbee.

Sharon noticed a copy of *In Vogue Beauty* on the table. She flicked through it until she came to the page she'd read that morning. 'Good article in here – have you read it?' she asked nonchalantly.

Debbee sighed. 'I bet I know the one you mean. Is it:

HOW TO HIGHLIGHT YOUR STRETCHMARKS?

Sharon nodded.

'Forget it. I bought the pen yesterday. Cost sixty quid! And all it does is leave something that resembles a snail's deposit on your skin. A total con.' Debbee picked up the magazine in dismay. 'Make your cheekbones chubbier,' she read out. 'I can guarantee another bloody useless article.'

As if to prove the point, she puffed out her cheeks, eyes crossed, like a demented blowfish, and counted to ten on her fingers. 'Phew – and they tell us we've got to do this a hundred times a day! It's hell. I'd rather have one of those bottom grafts.'

As Debbee reached for her coffee cup, Sharon noticed how the angular shape of her elbow stuck out, the gristle between the arm muscles showing like two lines of a suspension bridge. She could even see the ugly big bump of her wrist bone.

Poor Debbee, thought Sharon, with a wry little smile. There's really no hope for her. 'By the way, Debbee, I hope you won't be offended, but can I suggest something?'

'Sure,' said Debbee, looking very, very unsure.

'Why don't you spell your name like you used to? The double *e* is so affected.' Debbee was totally stunned. For a moment or two, she looked as though she was going to hit Sharon. Then she regained her composure, bit her tongue and lowered her eyes. 'Do you really think so?' she asked meekly.

Sharon nodded imperiously, her final revenge on the Simon matter now taken.

'Well, if you think so, Sharon, maybe you're right,' she agreed.

'Shazza and Dean' dined out and clubbed most nights, trailed by a posse of hungry photographers. They revelled in the media attention. She slept over at his flat, not sure how an Essex footballer would take to her mini-palace of peppermint cushions and pink throws. He never really challenged her intellectually, but he was thrilling in bed. His strong body and athletic build were delicious, edible and yummy. All was fine in that department. Except one niggly little thing. He loved her going down on him, a new and unnerving practice for Sharon, who had less experience than a novice nun.

Worse, he wanted her to do it as often as possible, and usually in dangerous situations. In a lift, in a taxi, behind his wheel … No wonder they called him Hurricane Dean, thought Sharon wryly. He really loved blowjobs. It sometimes worried her that he wanted her to act like the poster girl – or was he attracted to the poster girl because of his penchant?

Whatever. Fact was, he was really fun to be with, kind to her, and she was falling for his boyish charms. It wasn't long before she started to imagine a mansion in Chingford and a wedding in *Hello!*. And Dean was proud to be seen with her. He was hot, she was cool. Or was it the other way round? It didn't matter: they looked good together and every tabloid said so. But four weeks into their

'Hurricane Affair', as the *Sun* repeatedly and proudly referred to it, the summer approached and Dean was called up for pre-season training.

It was on one of his visits back to London that he cooed, 'I'm missing you, babe,' seductively putting a finger into her mouth. 'Maybe me an' you should think about getting serious. Y'know, come up and live with me. We could get a flat in Manchester together.'

Sharon looked into his molten-brown, lash-laden eyes and nodded. No one had asked her such a thing before. She'd always assumed she would end up dead in a stinky flat with five smelly cats. It was major. To LIVE with him! The next step would be marriage. To Sharon, that meant the end of loneliness. No more empty Sundays – well, empty Saturdays too, for that matter. And, come to think of it, Friday nights.

'We're kicking around at a practice pitch in Nottingham next week to get us into playing away. Join me Friday night – they're putting me an' the boys up at the Hilton. Think of it – plasma screen, Jacuzzi, you, me, champagne on tap… If you're coming, I'll get a suite.'

Sharon sighed. 'I'd love to, but I've got a three-day hair shoot commercial booked in Italy until Sunday. That's a real drag.' Actually, it wasn't a drag at all. It was truly amazing. Sharon was thrilled to be the new Herbal Freedom girl, and the location was a glorious beach in Sardinia. However, having met a few top models at the agency, she knew the most successful always acted nonplussed and jaded.

'Never mind, babe. Come up the week after and meet me in Manchester. I've rented a big pad there – nothing special, but you'll like it … See how you feel about the city.' He slowly kissed her neck, moving down her throat, licking the top of her ample cleavage. Lower, lower, lower. Mmm … thought Sharon. This striker certainly knew how to score.

*

The following weekend the hair shoot went incredibly well. She gave the director exactly what he wanted. Innocence and wildness. In the strong Italian sun, her polished locks shone more brightly than a newly sprayed Ferrari.

During a long afternoon break, she shopped in the little designer boutiques and was photographed, by the Italian paparazzi, laden with pretty little parcels and bags, tottering down the cobbled streets in the shortest skirts and highest heels she could manage. A gossip mag's dream cover.

In fact, she was also amazingly good as a model, twisting, turning, posing and pouting like a seasoned pro. By Saturday night, the director had pronounced, '*Mamma mia*! Naturally *bellissima*,' and the shoot was over early, with hugs, air kisses and '*Ciao, bella*' all round. After farewell drinks, Sharon found herself alone, sitting in her sumptuous beachfront bedroom, missing Dean more than she could have imagined possible.

He would have loved it here, she mulled. Twenty minutes of mulling later, she was heading on to a late-night charter plane to East Midlands airport. Their last conversation played over and over again in her head. He wanted to live with her. *He* wanted to live with *her*! She could have kissed every muscled inch of his powerful body.

Childishly, she even played a wedding scene in her head…

She'd ask her father to walk her down the aisle, she'd throw her bouquet to Jules D and the waiting crowds, wave to the paparazzi, and ride off with her footballer in the back of a white vintage Rolls-Royce.

As the taxi roared up at the hotel, she raced into Reception. It was two a.m. She would sneak into his room and curl up next to his body. The male receptionist recognised her immediately.

'Dean Brockton's room, please,' she said sweetly. 'Do you have a spare key?'

'Of course, ma'am. Delighted to have you stay with us. Room three oh seven,' he said, giving her a shy, appreciative look.

Sharon rewarded him with a dazzling smile, then headed up the stairs, too excited to take the lift, and gently placed the key card in the lock.

It wouldn't work. She tried again, turning it around. After three frustrating goes, the door finally opened, and she headed towards the bed, groping in the dark. As her hand touched the tight, neat cover, she realised it was empty. Damn, she thought. He must still be in the bar.

Then a better idea struck her. Rummaging through her bag, she quietly got undressed and put on a classic Janet Reger négligée that showed off her every curve with gossamer glee.

After flossing, plucking and brushing in the bright mirror of the limestone bathroom, she slipped between the cool cotton sheets, fighting exhaustion and excitement in equal measures.

Just as she dozed off, she heard a crash, gales of male laughter from next door, and Dean's voice.

Oh, no, he was with his mates, she realised, disappointed. Not wishing to brave the gang, but keen to see her babe, she wrapped herself in his dressing gown and ventured outside. The drunken cacophony increased as she knocked loudly on the neighbouring door.

'You go!' cried someone. 'No, after you!'

Come on, boys, she thought, irritated. Just one of you open the door. She knocked again. But this time there was silence.

The door eventually opened and Sharon marched in, ready to handle them all. There they were, the core gang of idiots. Dean's team-mates, grinning, tottering, swigging and spilling beer. And there was Dean. He looked at her in shock and disbelief. A soppy grin split his handsome face. 'Shaz! Babe! What a surprise!'

Sharon was touched to see such obvious joy, and stepped towards him.

He twisted towards her, arms outstretched, but unfortunately, something was holding him back.

It was his cock. Still rammed into another woman's body.

'Oh, my God, babe, this is not what it seems!' he blurted out helplessly.

'Yeah, Dean. The bitch has *you* tied to the bed!' snarled one of his cronies, with a cruel laugh.

'Fancy a roastin', darlin'?' shouted another, beckoning Sharon into the room with a lecherous leer.

'Or how about givin' us all a blowjob? Yeah, Dean says you give them all the time!'

Sharon felt shock, shame, anger and hurt. She parted her famous, pouty lips to speak – then turned and ran.

Ten

'I'm here, darling! Open the door!'

Sharon wrapped her old furry dressing gown around her tummy, rubbed the mascara grit from her eyes, and slowly opened the door of her flat.

Jules D was shocked by her dishevelled appearance. 'Dear God, Shaz – you look like Chi-Chi the panda after a three-night bender!'

Sharon let out a giant sob, and collapsed into Jules' expansive arms. They retreated to the squashy sofa, and Sharon blew her nose into a giant hanky. 'How could he do this to me? I TRUSTED him.'

'Big, big mistake, darling. Never trust a man who plays with balls for a living. Here, let me pour you some champagne, and we'll add a little peach juice, okay?' Out of her enormous bag, Jules D produced a bag of freshly baked chocolate croissants. Her version of chicken soup.

'Now, first thing you need is some media training – you're a celebrity now, and when your world crashes and burns, you must play the fiddle faster than Nero, okay? Happy, happy, happy.'

As she spoke her silver phone began to tinkle the tune of *Mission Impossible*. 'Oh, it's my trouble-shooting phone … Yes, yes …' pause 'No. No. He did *not* dump Shaz. She's sitting here with me now, we're having champagne brunch and she's fine. Just got bored with him … I mean, let's be honest, he's a footballer, for God's sake!'

Jules D scribbled something on a piece of paper and shoved it over to Sharon. 'LAUGH,' it ordered. She banged the point of her pen down on the word.

Sharon forced out a sound that sounded more like a croak. She tried again, from further in the background. It worked better.

'Yes, yes! As I said, she's absolutely fine,' said Jules D, in clipped, no-nonsense tones. 'The Hurricane has blown itself out. Totally. You can quote that.' She snapped the phone shut.

'Champagne?' She poured, as she continued explaining: 'Damage control, darling. We don't want that prick reaching the press before we do. In fact ...' Jules D dialled again, flicking through her BlackBerry with stern concentration. 'Gerry, yes, hi, it's me. Get hold of your man and tell him that Shaz has called it a day – she's bored, and he's heartbroken. And if one little word against Shaz is leaked by that scuzbag Dean, the whole story – and I do mean the WHOLE story – gets out. You can remind your boy that the only balls he'll be holding are his own, in a cell, trying to protect them from a horny thirty-stone Romanian drug dealer. Okay?' She cut the call with a flip of the phone's lid. 'More champagne?'

'I'm not sure? I'll get my people to call your people.' Sharon grinned.

The next few days were a paparazzi blur. Zara had told Sharon that 'paparazzi' apparently means 'annoying bug' – and, for the first time, she felt stung by them.

Jules D had warned her to show absolutely no emotion, to laugh, smile and toss her magnificent blonde mane in the wind. But it was as if they were holding their breath and waiting for her to break down, to show the slightest sign of upset. She would walk along the street, and as she lifted her hand to her face, all the cameras would train on her, even if it was only to scratch her nose, rather than wipe her eyes.

The good news was that her public standing wasn't damaged. She was painted as a *femme fatale* heartbreaker – a woman even more desirable than before – and the sales of Descent perfume went up.

Z&ZaK were rubbing their hands in glee, and Jules D got a bonus for her handling of the affair.

As for Sharon, she kept replaying their imagined wedding scene in her head …

She'd asked her father to walk her down the aisle, she'd thrown her bouquet to Jules D and the waiting crowds, waved to the paparazzi, and ridden off with her footballer in a white vintage Rolls-Royce. It had swept around the corner, and stopped to pick up a female hitchhiker and his ten team-mates …

But the odd thing was that a few days later the hurt had stopped. Was it just the image of being with a top footballer she had loved? Sharon tried to recall moments and conversations they'd had but, apart from the first great sex in her life, it had all revolved around ducking cameras, having a laugh, being seen, and drinking with his mates.

In a down moment, she'd invited Debbie (formerly Debbee) for coffee and they'd struck up the old rapport. There was a difference, though – and Sharon could definitely feel a shift in weight, so to speak. She was now the top dog, and Debbie, dwarfed by her flamboyant size and fame, was happy to trot along at her heels like a yappy toy poodle.

She'd also had a call from Simon. But it hadn't been quite as she had envisaged. She had wanted to sound his equal and full of confidence, but he'd got her when she was feeling like plain old dumpy Sharon again. He'd sweetly asked, and she'd agreed to do a shoot for peanuts – a friend of his was a new designer and had come up with an amazing collection.

All the way through the conversation a little voice buzzed in her head, urging her to say, 'Meet me for a drink,' but she felt way too vulnerable for another rejection. Sadly, with a barrage of whirling thoughts, she couldn't concentrate, and when he awkwardly asked if she needed to meet and chat in person about the shoot he was organising, she didn't want to sound like some difficult diva. So instead she murmured that she'd be happy with whatever he wanted to sort – and would see him there on the day.

Stupid, stupid girl. Later she kicked herself.

That Sunday, Jules D asked her to 'Come and watch ponies pootling,' at Cowdray Park. It was the British Open, and to soothe her broken heart, Pimm's, polo and a picnic sounded bliss.

But what to wear? Jeans seemed too casual. A dress looked like she was trying too hard to be an English lady. Digging in the pit of her wardrobe, she finally emerged with a pair of fashion jodhpurs she'd picked up in a charity shop three years ago. They fitted well, her voluptuous shape emphasised by the massive, sensual curve of her thighs. She added a pair of Ravel riding boots, pulled on a tight white T-shirt and tied her hair back in a bouncy ponytail, with fringe. Without even trying, the look was '*Vogue* Stable Girl'.

'Hell-*o*, darling, you look fab. Absolutely fab,' said Jules D, greeting her with three kisses in the air and a glass of bubbly pink Veuve Clicquot. 'This way, sweetie,' she said, steering her towards the bar. 'You'll get the best view from here …'

Sharon looked puzzled. 'But the pitch is out there,' she said, pointing out of the window towards the galloping ponies.

'True, darling, but it's far more spectacular from where I'm sitting.' Jules smiled, raising her glass to the perfect rear end of a tall Argentinian player clad in tight white breeches and polished riding boots. He and his compatriots stood in clusters around the bar, soiled, sweaty but utterly irresistible. Curls of black hair, like fetlocks, framing handsome, dark-eyed faces. What was the collective term for a group of polo players, wondered Sharon. 'A posse of polo players'? 'A herd of hunks'? 'A stable of studs'? Or maybe it was 'a thrashing of thighs', she imagined wickedly.

Before long, the managing director of the drinks company sponsoring the day joined Jules D. Naturally, he was a client. Excusing herself, Sharon wandered out into the dazzling sunshine, and over to the barrier to watch the play.

'Beautiful, aren't they?' husked a voice from a heavenly hunk, who swung a boot on to the chair next to her, and casually adjusted the strap.

'Absolutely,' said Sharon, taken with the most dazzling white teeth she'd ever seen. The South American accent emanating from the most delicious mouth that owned them was so seductive that she shivered.

'Zey are even better to ride … I love zees sport so very much. It ees my life …'

Unsure what to do with this dramatic statement, Sharon replied, 'I know what you mean.'

'Do you? Really?' he asked, his eyes catching hers in recognition of a soul-mate.

'Er. Yes. I totally understand,' she lied. The last time she'd been on a pony it had been at the St Michael's School Fête, and the poor beast had barely made it once round the playground.

'So whose team are you with?' he asked, curiously.

'Team?' Oh, God. Her jodhpurs had been a bad, bad mistake. 'Well, I'm not exactly with a team, so to speak.'

'But you ride, do you not?' he asked, puzzled. 'You are wearing the jodhpurs?'

Sharon hadn't got a clue about the etiquette surrounding polo matches, but she now had a suspicion that the wearing of jodhpurs when you couldn't ride a rocking horse was probably not the done thing. 'Er … yes. I do. Love it,' she lied again.

'I knew you were being modest. Your figure is fantastic. The seat of … 'ow you say? An 'orsewoman.' Sharon guzzled up every smooth word, noting how Dean's Essex vowels suddenly seemed as coarse as pork pâté.

A furious player beckoned. 'Juan Carlos! What the hell are you doing in the bar? We're playing in a bloody minute, you arrogant sod. Come on, we need you, damn it.'

Damn it, so do I, thought Sharon, as he took her hand and slowly kissed it.

'Will you be 'ere when I finish?' he asked, picking up his mallet and giving it a practice swing.

'If you'd like me to be …' she answered, batting her eyelashes like My Little Pony, and hoping he'd pat her on the head.

'Of course … Perhaps you will honour me with a chance to see you away from all this.' He indicated the scene with Latin disdain, as if his soul was born for better things than entertaining the wealthy with his polo prowess.

'No probs,' said Sharon, thrilled. He looked confused. 'I mean, I'd be delighted.'

As the man strode off masterfully to find his mount, Sharon raced inside to tell Jules D all.

'Darling, I see you've been hobnobbing with Juan Carlos Garcia.'

'Don't tell me you know him too?' cried Sharon, exasperated and deeply impressed.

'His father owns a magnificent vineyard, along with half of Argentina. One of the foremost names in the country. Related to the Peróns. Good choice, darling.'

Sharon was stunned. 'I just assumed he was a paid rider.'

'Paid, certainly. Probably hundreds of thousands,' answered Jules D, filling a flute for Sharon and handing her a plate of cashew nuts. 'Eat up, darling, nuts are good for you. Nice and fattening too.'

For a split second, Sharon was too excited to eat, and more so when the speakers blasted out his name, describing him as one of the best players in the world. A ten goal. Whatever that meant.

She watched the top sportsman fly over the grass, his pony kicking up the turf as it turned and swung round again and again. Like a winged centaur, they hounded the ball, and shot goal after goal.

In position two, he was the key player – his pony swerved and turned as he swung and leaned, weaving in and out of their opponents with desultory, effortless ease.

The heat beat down and the game intensified. But regardless, during every break between chukkas, he remembered to smile in her direction. She lifted her glass in a return salute.

At the end of the match, he handed his last horse to a young female groom, who simpered at him pathetically. He totally ignored her, and headed straight to Sharon, stripping off his soaked polo shirt.

His body was unbelievable. A firm six-pack narrowed at his waist, perfectly balanced by broad, olive shoulders. He was smooth-skinned, apart from a sexy dark line leading into his jodhpurs. Further, his insouciance to club house rules of decorum only served to make him more glitteringly attractive. Wiping his forehead with his shirt, he reached down into his saddlebag and pulled out a clean one.

'Congratulations – you won,' said Sharon.

'I always do,' he replied slowly and deliberately, sultry eyes flashing a challenge. He left a dangerous pause.

'Do you like England?' squeaked Sharon.

He laughed and shook his head.

'You Engleesh girls … so sweet.' He leaned forward to brush a blonde strand off her cheek, and somewhere in the distance a camera clicked.

119

'Juan Carlos, come on.' His team was gathered around a manager, and what looked like a cluster of sponsors. A corporate gathering keen to get their money's worth.

'Unfortunately I have a cup to collect. Give me your name and number ... We go out, yes?' Sharon scrawled on a Pimm's coaster and, after twice crossing out and correcting what she had written, handed it to him.

'Until we meet again...' He kissed the back of her hand once more, his lips hovering teasingly before they touched the pale, plump skin.

Sharon felt scorched. And it had nothing whatsoever to do with the blisteringly hot summer's day.

'Shaz, darlin', let me at least see you to explain–'
BEEP.
'Babe, it's me again. I know you're pissed off–'
BEEP.
'How can I make it up to you...?'
BEEP.
'You're being a silly bitch, now–'
BEEP.
With relish, Sharon deleted message after message from Dean. Though it had been six days and still nothing from Juan Carlos, she was still thrilled that the day after the polo one of the leading tabloids had run a stunning front-page sun-dappled photo of her and 'Juan to know you', as she liked to call him. And it was no doubt niggling Dean that she was so over him so fast. And so publicly. Revenge is a dish best served full in the face. She giggled.

But, better than that, there was a message confirmed by Glacé Inc. that Ziegfried and ZaK wanted her to open their New York show. Zara at the model agency filled her in on the gossip. Apparently, breaking with tradition, the show was being held *five weeks* before the start of the official September Fashion Week, and was creating an almighty industry furore.

The world's top designers were livid: a couture show standing on its own was destined to steal mega-column inches. Worse, designers often followed the advice of the 'mood theme experts' at the trade cloth and trimming shows, whose job was to predict the season's lengths and colours. That was the simple reason why all the designers suddenly went for orange and silver one year, purple and green the next. The gurus dispense advice on behalf of the cloth industry to all who ask, and it ends up giving a cohesive look to the season. But if Z&ZaK showed first, it would seem to any outsiders that all the other names were simply following their lead a few weeks later.

Ziegfried and ZaK were outrageously blasé. They explained it was because they were 'so tired of being ripped off by other designers' that they wanted to show first. Basically, they were being naughty rebels, and sticking two little pinkies up at the competition.

As for Sharon, she didn't care about the politics – they were flying her out BA First Class the week after next.

'A fashion show – in the Big Doughnut!' cried Debbie, when she rang her. Sharon was knocked out too, and couldn't be bothered to pretend otherwise. 'Ohmigod! Can I come as your assistant? I'll pay my own way,' begged Debbie.

'Well, in that case I don't see why not … I know others have their own entourages. Maybe I should play the game too,' agreed Sharon.

Debbie squealed at the other end of the phone. 'We'll have such fun! You'll see … like the old days.' Sharon doubted that anything would ever be like the old days. Thank the Lord.

She had to ring Simon to cancel his shoot as it clashed with New York – a phone call she was dreading. Not only did she have to speak to him, but she was also letting him down. Mind you, the fear of the former was a little diluted by the fact that Juan Carlos had asked for her number. (She tried to dismiss the fact that he hadn't actually called.)

'Simon, hi – it's me, Sharon.' She deliberately used her old name to put them both at ease.

'Sharon, hi – everything okay?' She loved the sound of his voice, deep, warm and beautifully spoken.

'Well, not exactly. I'm so, so sorry but I've just been booked for Z&ZaK's New York fashion show and it clashes with your shoot.'

As Sharon spoke, the surreal nature of saying this to Simon hit her. Sometimes she got caught out, and the old Sharon crept back in. When it did, it was like a mirror shaking, and she felt momentarily split in half, like being two different people. Before Pill and After Pill. BP and AP, as she secretly referred to it.

'Right … um … what a pain. But that's okay … totally understand. Thousands of dollars walking down a catwalk for the world's top designer, or a couple of hundred squid posing for a loser like me … no brainer.' He laughed.

Sharon fell silent. She felt so bad that she wanted to cancel New York – but Kristen would be hacked off and not likely to forgive.

Simon misinterpreted the silence. 'Look, you don't have to do the shoot if you don't want to.'

'Of course I do – we're old mates,' said Sharon, worried he'd cancel.

'Of course we are. Old mates,' he repeated.

Did Sharon detect a faint trace of disappointment in the word 'mates'? Why had she referred to them as mates? But before she could say anything, she had a call waiting. The incessant beeping addled her brain even more than it already was. 'Oh, there's a call coming in. Can I just take it?' She needed time to think how to turn this round.

'No worries, I'm heading out – and the call's probably important.

Ring me when you get back from New York. Let me know how it goes, and we'll fix another date.'

The phone went dead before Sharon could say anything to counteract the fact that New York was days away. Mind you, he probably knew that, she thought sadly, and didn't care. To top it all, the call waiting was just a nuisance sales pitch for a timeshare holiday. She fell back on the fat sofa, and started to munch her way through a deluxe box of champagne and strawberry cream chocolates. On the table sat a stack of celebrity supermarket magazines.

Milana Sheraton was on two covers, clutching different toy dogs and looking more vacant than an M&S car park on Christmas Day. But Sharon was amazed to see herself inside three different magazines. Full pages, describing what she was going through, what she was wearing, and how she kept her full and fabulous rococo figure. Each had made a full-page story over a single tiny quote she'd given them. Unbelievable. Actually, even more so when you considered that the quote had really come from Jules D.

'I love my life, and don't need a man,' said the headline in *Grazia*, with an image of Sharon, head thrown back, laughing as she downed a glass of pink champagne.

'White is so fattening! It's my favourite colour,' revealed *Closer*.

'The best way to stay fat is to eat late at night,' ran *Hot*.

The phone suddenly rang. ''Ello, ees thees Shaz? Thees ees Juan Carlos.'

'Hi, Juan – how are you?' purred Sharon, casually. (She'd been practising saying 'Juan' with a silent sexy Spanish J for days.)

'Keen to see you. Do you have Saturday off? I have a surprise for you.'

'I think so, let me check my planner …' Sharon rustled the magazines. From the way he handled his horses, she figured this man liked total control, and she was determined not to be taken for an easy ride. 'Yes, I can clear a couple of things. That would be fine.'

He took her address, they flirted about the surprise, and Juan Carlos said he had to go – he was phoning her from the Hamptons, and the team was about to leave the hotel.

His last words were: 'Oh, just one theeng … wear what you wore when we met. You were … 'ow you say? Really ideal.'

Sharon smiled: she had made an impression on one of the most fabulous men on earth. How was that for a fat girl from Accounts Filing?

Eleven

Humming merrily to herself, Sharon heaved her rolling body out of bed. With pride, she watched her creamy smooth breasts flop gently into place. As she shifted her weight, she watched her mountainous regions undulate exquisitely, like butterfly wings. The quiver of her stomach: sheer poetry in motion.

It was Saturday morning, so she brushed out her shower of hair and put on her freshly washed jodhpurs with a crisp sleeveless blouse. The curve of her buttocks and huge breasts emphasised her relatively small, curvy waistline. She knew Glacé Inc. wanted her to put on a few pounds before New York – the models out there were so disciplined – so she added extra double cream to her cereal and three spoonfuls of sugar. It tasted like heaven.

Her mother had often made it for her like this when she was a little kid …

She came down to earth. The one person she hadn't spoken to for far too long was her father. But she kept hoping he would call of his own accord. See her in the papers, realise how well she was doing and pick up the phone.

But he didn't. So, she steeled herself to ring, dreading the curt tone of her stepmother, Carolyn.

'Hi, it's me. Is–'

'I'll get your father,' Carolyn interrupted.

The routine was like this *every* time she phoned. Sometimes the woman's deliberate rudeness made her laugh. At others it cut her to the quick.

'Hello, my darling, what have you been up to?' said a whiskery old man's voice.

'Loads, Dad. Loads. Can you believe it? I've started modelling. *Me!* Like Mum. I've been doing an advertising campaign for perfume,' although she really hoped he hadn't seen it, 'and a shampoo commercial. Plus I've been dating a footballer.'

'A footballer? Anyone I would know?'

'Have you heard of Hurricane Dean?'

'Harry who, dear?'

'Not Harry. Hurricane. Hurricane Dean.'

'Harry Candean?'

'Oh, never mind, Dad,' said Sharon, sadly. He was really beginning to show his age.

'Sorry, dear, I've not been feeling too well, having some tests …' said her father.

Sharon felt a slight panic, but her dad was always having tests of some sort.

'Nothing to worry about, darling … Got a sore throat, that's all,' he added.

'I was thinking of coming down to Bournemouth to see you,' said Sharon, brightly.

'That would be nice. But you know we don't have anywhere to put you up, and it's so expensive to stay in a hotel.'

Sharon grimaced. Their house had four bedrooms, but Carolyn always made it plain she wasn't welcome to stay. 'Well, I can afford a hotel now – I'm famous!'

'What? Are you? For what?'

'Dad, for being … well, for being beautiful.' She choked on the words.

'Like your mother?' he asked proudly. 'She was stunning. I

remember the time she turned all the heads when she walked into –'

'Joe! Tea's ready!' came Carolyn's shrill, bossy voice in the distance. She'd probably been eavesdropping on the extension as usual. Any mention of his past life set her off in a dreadful strop. Sharon had worked out this was probably why the woman had been so mean when she was just a little kid.

'Got to go, darling, ring me again soon,' said her dad sadly, and the line went dead.

Carolyn bullied him, but this was a fate *he* had chosen, and Sharon's sympathy was measured. Feeling hungry, she headed to the fridge for a glass of milk and the packet of Oreo cookies she'd stashed away that morning. As she dipped the biscuits into the milk and licked off the filling, she thought back to when she was just eleven years old.

Her daddy had been attracted to the woman's young, but icy beauty, and the fact that she had two daughters. Instant mother and sisters for Sharon, he had thought. She knew he had been missing her mother badly, often hearing him cry in the night.

But why had he picked Carolyn? Sharon suspected that his broken heart was why she had snared him so easily. She knew he was desperate to replace the loving home he'd lost, and he'd remarried way too fast in a sorry attempt to make a new family. Well, they say men hate to be alone. Sharon suspected it was tragically true. Unfortunately, he hadn't got to know his new wife properly until it was too late – once the woman had a giant diamond ring on her finger.

Sharon recalled how she had changed almost overnight, revealing a vile, vitriolic temper that had terrified her and, at times, even cowed her father. Then she shuddered as she remembered her stepmother's face: the first time she had shown her true colours, it had literally darkened and changed, contorting like that of a woman possessed. Sharon gave a dry laugh: her dear stepmother made Jekyll and Hyde seem like Sooty and Sweep.

She loved her dad dearly, but he was so weak. What had he done at those times? Nothing, thought Sharon, contemplating another cookie. She never knew if he had been unable or just unwilling to protect her from Carolyn's rages. Whatever, she did know he preferred to keep the peace with his young wife at all costs. And that included his daughter.

Years later, when he was visiting Sharon's new flat in Kingston, he'd confessed that maybe he'd ended up marrying the wrong woman. The bottle of wine had loosened his tongue, and he told her that rushing into his second marriage was one of his biggest regrets. But he felt too old and too ashamed to divorce and start again. And Sharon had already left home. It was too late. Certainly way too late for the eleven-year-old child who had hidden under the covers of her bed, sobbing.

Now, just the sound of Carolyn's voice resonated with a dark, sad time in her life – and hearing her curt tone on the phone was enough to make her feel like a frightened little kid again.

Then the doorbell of her flat rang. And Sharon the fully-grown woman bounced down the stairs, to the open-topped silver Porsche below. She glanced round, hoping the neighbours were taking this all in, and settled into the leather bucket seat.

Juan Carlos drove his cars as forcefully as he rode his ponies, the gear stick handled with a firm Italian leather glove. She fantasised about the same gloved hand holding her hair so that he could force a kiss on her lips …

As they sped into the countryside, Sharon wondered where the surprise destination was. A cosy pub lunch, maybe – or perhaps a seaside marina stroll.

Finally Juan swung the car sharply into a magnificent driveway that sprawled towards a stately home. 'No, ees not mine!' laughed

Juan Carlos, watching her green eyes open wide. 'I use their stables. Zey like me to exercise their horses.'

'What a fab place. You must love riding around here…'

'Zat ees why I come …' He smiled, patting her thigh.

Oh, no! The penny suddenly dropped. More like a whole sack of them. Heavily. On her head. He had asked her to wear her jodhpurs. She felt sick. Panicked. Sweaty. Her mind raced with excuses. Blank. The only one she could think of was 'the wrong time of the month', but that hadn't even got her out of school gymnastics – and it certainly wasn't going to work now.

Maybe she could step out of the Porsche and 'twist her ankle'. But the car was so fashionably low slung that even a vertically challenged pixie would have a hard time using that one with conviction.

They walked towards the immaculate stables, he purposefully, whip in hand, Sharon dragging her feet, like a terrified toddler.

'Fantastic to see you, Juan Carlos,' said a tall, striking woman with black hair pulled into a tight Spanish bun.

'Lady Annabel.' Juan Carlos bowed over her hand.

'Take your pick…' she offered generously.

The exquisite thoroughbreds snorting and tossing their heads over the stable doors bore as much resemblance to an ordinary hack animal as Pegasus to Dobbin the Donkey. Sharon paled, her firm legs shaking in their boots.

'Is there any chance you'd take Lightning out?' asked a senior stablehand, leaning on his shovel. 'He's been giving us so much trouble – he needs a firm grip.'

'When did you last have him out?' Juan Carlos enquired, soothing the creature on the nose. In response, it bared its teeth angrily.

'Been about four days. Even threw Lady Annabel off. Since then, he won't let us near him.'

'No problem. Come on, my beauty.' Juan held the beast's head steady while a nervous stable girl put its tack on; Sharon watched from a safe distance.

Then Lady Annabel reappeared. 'Which one would you like to ride?' she asked, walking over to Sharon. Her handsome, perfect features gave her an aristocratic air of a bygone age, helped by her smart black hacking jacket and side-saddle skirt. A highly bred, elegant creature, who looked much better standing next to Juan Carlos than Sharon suspected she ever would. The bitch had no doubt been born clutching a silver spoon in one hand, and a Pony Club rosette in the other.

'Which horse? Um … I'm not sure. I'm feeling a bit queasy from a late night. Perhaps I shouldn't…' she whispered.

'In that case, you want Fireball,' said her ladyship, matter-of-factly.

No, no, I don't! I want a Shetland pony called Slugbug, or Snailtrail! screamed a voice in Sharon's head. But it was Fireball they brought out. An autumn-coloured horse that loomed much larger than it had first looked in its shed as they led it towards her. The saddle was high up, and Sharon's cotton jodhpurs were a fashion item – as luck would have it, the only fashion item in the Western world *not* made from stretch Lycra.

There was no way she could lift her foot into the stirrup, never mind swing her body aboard.

'Um … can I use the execution block?' she asked, indicating the concrete mounting block by the gate. 'It's been a very long time,' she explained, as two hands attempted to heave her butt on to the skittering creature for the third time. As she finally settled into the saddle, the animal's back legs buckled a little under her weight. The hard-hat strap dug into her neck, and fear made her hands sticky as she grasped the reins.

'You hold polo-pony reins differently,' called Juan Carlos, kindly, mounting Lightning in one sleek move and cantering over to her side.

He took her hand and put both straps into it. 'The other is free for the mallet. Come, we'll play around in the field over there.'

Frozen with terror, Sharon let her pony follow. Why was it called a pony? She wondered. A misnomer of the sport. It was a bloody great hoofing horse. She caught Lady Annabel looking at her smugly as they trotted past. Fireball? Oh, God, the bitch had deliberately set her up.

The good news was that the field was enclosed. The bad news was that she hadn't a fucking clue how to ride.

'Always let the beast know you are the boss,' said Juan Carlos, his horse rearing and kicking out. 'Never show fear.'

Too late, thought Sharon. It knew exactly who the boss was. And she was fully prepared to call it 'Master'.

The pony trotted in a straight line, Sharon's buttocks slapping the saddle.

'Rise in the stirrups and indicate right with your rein!' called Juan Carlos.

Sharon pulled very gently to the right, and the horse responded instantaneously, wheeling around violently, almost tipping her off as it circled.

'Zey're like Ferraris, are zey not?' laughed Juan Carlos, cantering closer. 'Gently. You have to use ze faintest touch. Zey are like … how you say? Finely tuned. Magnificent. Try again. Zis time just wiz your knees – push it towards ze direction you want it to go.'

Sharon pressed ever so carefully against the pony's silky belly … and it moved graciously in the direction she had indicated. The relief was tangible. Only an hour or so to go, she thought bitterly.

'Shaz, now try ze ozzer knee.' She did. And once again, the horse responded as she wished.

'Try a fast stop!' shouted Juan Carlos, from the other end of the field.

Sharon pulled very lightly on the rein. And it stopped short, sending her pert nose on a collision course with its head. As she straightened, it waited patiently for the next instruction. It didn't bolt, it didn't buck. It just stood stock still.

Relieved, Sharon's confidence grew. The horse was so perfectly trained, her fear slowed to mere panic. Then, as the pony took her round the field at a gentle trot, she felt the dawning of a little curiosity on how to control it. Finally, as it responded again and again, she felt a tiny thrill.

The fact that they were enclosed removed the terrifying prospect of a bolting mount. Half an hour later, she was cantering behind Juan Carlos round the paddock, her own blonde mane streaming behind her, green eyes flashing with excitement, cheeks flushed with exertion.

A couple of times an icy fear would re-grab her, especially when Juan Carlos's black mount continued to rear, eyes wild like the Horse of the Baskervilles. In response, he laid his whip to its flank, and the creature snorted in fury. But each time it had a tantrum, Garcia the Beast Master won.

An hour or so later, she and Fireball were in love. Sharon was ready to bundle her into the car and have her sleep on a blanket in the kitchen. She kissed the creature on the nose as she handed the reins gratefully to Lady Annabel – she suddenly felt like hugging her.

By the time Juan and Sharon were nursing brandies in the pretty local pub, the adrenalin withdrawal and relief of finding all her limbs unbroken made her feel relaxed and fuzzy. She found herself confessing the truth to Juan Carlos.

'Fashion jodhpurs?' He roared with laughter until he almost cried. And by the time she added she'd only ever been on a pony for a led ride around a playground, he was not only holding his sides, but suitably impressed. 'You are special! Very brave. Fireball responded to your every whim.' His eyes darkened. 'And so do I … my leetle *enchalata*!' Sharon wasn't sure if this meant 'little one who enchants me', or something you eat in a Taco Bell. Whatever. The way he spoke it sounded so romantic. She was his little *enchalata* …

As he leaned across the bar for a couple of Pimm's, Sharon imagined life with this man. Well, actually, nothing that deep. Just the wedding day.

She'd ask her father to walk her down the aisle; she'd throw her bouquet to Jules D and the waiting crowds, wave to the paparazzi, and ride off into the sunset behind Juan Carlos, masterfully handling a white stallion.

'What are you smiling about, leetle one?' he asked, stroking her thigh lazily.

'Just wondered if you'd tell me a little more about polo. It's so fascinating,' she fibbed perfectly.

'Eet ees the game of kings. It was first played in Persia, as long ago as the sixth century BC, with as many as a hundred a side …' Sharon bathed in his accent and attention as he told tales of old kingdoms lost in time. '… and the word "chukka" comes from ancient Sanskrit, *cakra*, meaning circle or wheel.'

Amazing, she thought. This man could make a game of eight grown-up blokes chasing a plastic ball around a field sound like a ride on a magic carpet.

Day turned into night – and dinner at La Corpulent, an elegant restaurant, so trendy you normally had to put your name down for a table at birth. A call from Juan to his manager, and they were in.

Sharon loaded her plate with three helpings of starters. Fresh buffalo mozzarella sprinkled with bacon and avocado shavings, delicate pasta shells in oyster sauce, and a rich lobster pâté with toasted almond and walnut bread.

'Eet ees so good to see a girl take care of her figure,' said Juan Carlos, approvingly. She held his dark eyes and saw her desire mirrored in them. Leaning forward, he offered her a large asparagus tip. Warm butter dripped off its juicy head.

'You will be at the Cartier International next week?' he asked, dropping her off outside her flat and walking her to the door.

'Of course,' said Sharon, with not a clue how one got tickets.

As his hand wound round her waist, instead of wincing and breathing in, Sharon poked out her already full tummy as far as she could.

It was too much for Juan Carlos.

'Can I come up?' he asked, voice breaking. 'I'd like to stay.'

'Gosh, but we've only just met,' said Sharon, aware she had sounded like a prudish pupil of Miss Jean Brodie.

In response, he kissed her passionately, pushing her hard against the cold wall and thrusting his jodhpur-clad leg between her thighs. His lips were firm, his tongue searching. Then he broke off and walked away.

Sharon couldn't breathe. He was so dashing. This was such fun. And, again, a camera flashed somewhere in the dark.

Over the next few days Sharon bubbled permanently with pleasure, like a fountain of champagne. 'You look better and better, darling,' she announced to herself one morning, clutching the customary croissants in a bag.

Indeed, Sharon did. Her new life had given her confidence, wit and style. Ready for New York, Glacé Inc had sent her off to get her hair cut at Pudding Basin, the most fashionable salon in London. The result was that her waist-length hair became even more platinum than blonde, with a cool spiky fringe. She'd also enjoyed the attention of the makeup artists whenever she did a shoot. As they experimented with different looks, she had picked up every trick, from elongating her almond-shaped eyes to maxi-plumping her perfect, petal-soft lips.

To add to all this, the royalties from her hair commercial were proving astounding. For the two-day stint she had done in Ibiza she was receiving thousands of pounds every time it was aired on television. And it was on daily.

Meanwhile, photos of her and Juan Carlos had boosted her public profile. Though it had to be said that the shot of Juan pressing her against the wall with the tabloid screamer '… UP THE JUNTA!' had been more than a tad humiliating.

Nonetheless, the daily diet of glamour was turning into a Bacchanalian feast. And Sharon Plunkett was gobbling up every marvellous millisecond.

Debbie (that's with an 'ie') had latched on as her assistant, and was a good little gofer. Sharon noticed her friend had finally managed to put on a little bit of weight. She might even be a size ten. Whatever. At least it was a start.

It was fun to have Debbie at her beck and call, easy company when Sharon felt like it after a long day. And after years of having it the other way round, Sharon just *lurved* the way her mate whined, 'I'm so desperately jealous.' Scraggy little thing, Sharon would think. And, with smug superiority, she'd force Debbie to eat a full box of chocolates, and make her view the latest get-fat-fast celebrity DVD from the States. Together, the girls would often curl up on the sofa to watch.

'My regime is simple,' said Jo-Jo, an American actress and singer famous for skimpy showgirl outfits and sexy toy boys. 'Every morning I get up slowly and eat three pure cocoa-bean chocolate bars before breakfast. Make sure you stuff them in fast. That way they can't digest quickly.'

The woman looked terrific for her age, thought Sharon. A real icon. Jo-Jo's G-string sequined costume revealed a bare navel completely hidden by mounds of excess skin. They viewed the rest of the tape transfixed, Debbie shifting uncomfortably as the celebrity downed plateful after plateful faster than a pelican.

'And finally,' gushed the dark-haired beauty, 'the most important thing of all is to have a full dinner as late as possible.'

'Hey, that's my favourite tip too!' grinned Sharon.

Jo-Jo was served a massive portion of cheesecake by a semi-naked youth. With a salacious lick of her fingers, she continued, 'Yes, ideally eat just before going to bed. After all, you don't want to burn off any excess calories, girls, do you? Good night. And sweet, sweet, very sweet dreams!'

From the corner of her eye, Sharon watched Debbie turn from the TV despondently, shoving away the tray of chocolates.

Sharon leaned over to pop another into her mouth, and as the taste hit her eager, trained buds, she couldn't stop the corners of her pretty mouth tilting upwards into a tiny smile.

Jules D had come up trumps. Like a magician, she always had the right tickets up her sleeve, and producing two for the Cartier International was easier than falling off a polo pony.

'How did you organise that?' asked Sharon, as Jules D flashed a smart envelope under her nose.

Jules D laughed, as if she was withholding a secret. 'Actually, one came for you, anyway,' she said, tossing a heavy gold-embossed invitation into Sharon's lap.

'What? Who from? Juan Carlos?' asked Sharon breathlessly.

'No, darling, from the chairman of Cartier. Special invitation to his closest six hundred celebrities! We're invited into their marquee for lunch. Best one to be seen in, sweetie, okay?'

Sharon learned it certainly was.

On the day, she dressed in a cream floaty chiffon number sent over from New York by Ziegfried and ZaK. Topped with a wide-brimmed sun hat, it looked as deliciously *frou-frou* as a *mille-feuille*. Jules D was as smart as ever in a tailored navy and white Dior suit that heavily emphasised the size of her hips.

On arrival at the prestigious Guards Polo Ground, the chauffeur heaved Sharon elegantly out of the back seat of the complimentary limo, and the two women tottered towards the Smith's Lawn enclosure and its temporary city of white hospitality tents.

The undulating crowd of visitors were all exquisitely dressed. On the lawn, celebrities milled with celebrities, the aristocracy with the aristocracy, and the royals with nobody.

As they approached the famous flag-flying Cartier marquee, Sharon looked at the topiary arch spelling out 'CARTIER' in awe. She wandered underneath and into the tent. Her first impressions were overwhelming.

'Every year they pick a top interior designer to decorate,' explained Jules D, quietly. And this year whoever it was had no doubt been inspired by peacocks, Paradise … and possibly a bongful of seventies pot. The tent was stuffed with birds in cages, ostrich feathers in long gold vases, peacock chairs and lava lamps.

'So very retro, darling,' oozed Jules D, to a giant man poncing about in velvet flares and smoking jacket.

'Shaz, dear heart, have you met Nicky Houselman? A *roué* of extraordinary talent, and designer of the crazy emporium we see before us. A triumph, darling. Love it.'

Sharon held out her hand, and he ignored it, heading for a camp three-cheek air kiss instead.

The food was also divine. Tucking into a giant starter plate of Norwegian gravadlax edged with fresh king prawns, Sharon counted three celebrities at her table, and an outcast from *Big Brother*, who, she noticed, from the wrong name on their Cartier name tag, had snuck in on someone else's.

She looked at the name on hers, dangling casually from her cream silk bag, and smiled. Sharon Plunkett, you lucky ol' thing. Near her sat three top models, and a Hollywood starlet. Further away, a famous rock star, his wife and model daughter. The place was gleaming with glitz on an unprecedented scale. And she was part of it. People were surreptitiously looking at *her* too. She tried to eat normally, but dropped her bread roll on the floor. Thinking quickly, she gave it a swift kick with the side of her shoe, and disposed of it between the legs of a man at someone else's table. A private polo goal of her own. She giggled.

Three champagne flutes later, with spiky heels that sank into the ground, Sharon and Jules D found the journey across the grass to the grandstands deeply treacherous. They broke into fits of hysterics over their stupid choice of footwear, and clung to each other like drunken ladettes.

Managing to straighten up just before they passed the bank of paparazzi, Sharon proudly flashed her Cartier swing tag at the steward, who let them through to the Blue Grandstand for Cartier guests and privileged members. Further away the Red Grandstand was for the day's 'ordinary members'. And on the other side of the ground, there were seats for the lesser-mortal non-members. Twenty-five thousand spectators, all knowing their pecking order. The sport of kings – or a game of keeping the peasants in their places.

Sharon proudly took her place among the 'chosen few' with aplomb, squeezing past the knees of those already sitting – much to the delight of the many males in the row.

But most exciting of all for Sharon was recognising the distant tall figure of Juan Carlos Garcia in the pony line. As the July sun streamed down, the Pony Club Polo Players' Parade trotted past, followed by packs of hounds and their red-coated Masters.

Then the commentator introduced the players. The distant crowds roared, while those around her clapped politely. But, ignoring convention, she cheered very loudly when she heard: 'In the number-two position, the star ten-goal player from Argentina, Juan Carlos Garcia. Highest ranking rider of the day.'

He tipped his helmet, raised his mallet in salute, and cantered masterfully into place.

The game was a blur of balls, hoofs and falls. Fun to watch, vicious and fast. At one point, she recognised Fireball – *her baby*! He performed magnificently, turning complete circles like a whirling dervish, and warding off horses far heavier with his brave little heart.

At half-time the spectators were invited on to the pitch to tread down the turf – a wonderful tradition during which everyone milled around the grass chatting about the weather while replacing the cut-up tufts. Unfortunately, with their heels Sharon and Jules D seemed to be having the totally opposite effect. As they walked, they noticed that people behind them were angrily covering their 'plough tracks'. Tipsily racing off the grass in disgrace, they giggled even more.

The second half was even more aggressive. This was supposed to be a friendly game, Argentina invited to play England's finest, but judging by the intensity and fury on the pitch, it could have been the battle for the Falklands, with Mrs Thatcher cheering on 'our boys'.

The result in the end was a humiliating defeat for the England squad who, naturally, took it on the chin.

Sharon watched with bursting pride as, on behalf of his team, Juan Carlos received the Coronation Cup from the Queen. What was that famous rhyme? 'I've danced with a man, who's danced with a girl who's danced with the Prince of Wales'? Well, she'd snogged a man who was currently getting a long, friendly handshake from The Queen. Top that!

The prize-giving ended with another surprising high, when Fireball was announced the best pony of the day. Sharon jumped up and clapped with joy, then watched with ridiculous pride, a tear in her eye, as his owner stepped over to receive the Cadenza Trophy.

'What a great day!' sighed Sharon, giving Jules D a giant bear hug. 'Shall I go over to see him now?'

'Um … I'd give him a chance to cool down, pose with the press and talk to the sponsors. Be laid back. Let's head over to Chinawhite's tent for drinks, with a wee stop in the retail village *en route*.'

The row upon row of tented shopping cubicles held a bazaar of designer goodies: shopping heaven. There was everything a spoilt, rich débutante could want, from mink-lined dog baskets to thick leather gaucho belts. Sharon held the latter in her hand, feeling the supple hide. Then, smiling, she handed it back to the stallholder. When it came to gauchos, she had the real McCoy to wrap around *her* hips!

Later, laden with bags, they headed back to the first tent for a much-needed cream tea, with scones and chocolate éclairs, then went over to Chinawhite's marquee. The exclusive nightclub regularly took a marquee at the event, offering its London members a chance to boogie with the players, aristocrats, celebs, royals and luvvies involved in the polo scene – and as dusk turned into night, what a scene it was: dishevelled girls, shoulder straps slipping over plump, pretty shoulders, men, shirts unbuttoned, ties askew, champagne flowing faster than the Nile. Amid the mêlée, Sharon spotted her man.

'Juan.' She waved.

He disengaged himself from a buxom brunette and headed over to her. '*Enchalata*,' he whispered, sweeping her into his arms for a deep, delicious kiss.

Sharon's emotions soared. Could the day ever be more perfect?

Crushed and moulded together on the dance floor, she could feel his heat. Or was it hers? Every few seconds someone would come over and slap him heartily on the back, or slosh a flute of champagne over them. The music pounded, and the night threw a dark, muffling cloak over the field. All life pulsated in the tent. All life existed there.

Unfortunately, all manner of top totty existed there too. A blonde called Stephanie, with a voice so plummy you could barely recognise a word, whispered something very rude into Juan Carlos' ear about what they had done in Houston. Alas, judging by his wicked smile, he understood every syllable.

Sharon noted bitterly that the blonde had far chubbier, even more succulent legs than she had. Moments later, another aristocratic beauty with enormous hips (again, Sharon noted enviously, a little larger than hers) sidled over and slipped her number into his palm, bemoaning the fact they'd missed each other in the Hamptons. It was a scene Sharon felt totally outside of. They all knew each other intimately. And continued to, it seemed, all over the world.

One glass too many, and Sharon's head began to float. She tapped Juan Carlos on the shoulder and asked him to take her outside. Excusing himself from the circle around him, he led her through the throng, a docile filly on a leading rein, into the cool night air, towards the dark corner of the grandstand.

Without a word, he spun her around and pinned her back. Finding herself pushed up against a hard wall, she tried to protest as he placed his hands roughly on her breasts. God, it felt good. But also bad. Really, really bad. This was not what she wanted. Way too fast. They had hardly talked all night. She could have been anybody, and she wanted him to value her. He bit at her neck and she shivered in anticipation, trying hard to remember her resolve. As his hand slid up her chiffon skirt and pulled urgently at her silk panties, she struggled to stop him going further. He took little notice. Which made it even more hot and hard to stop him. But she *had* to. 'Oh. Juan, this is – this is – Oh, God.' By now, he'd unbuckled his breeches with his other hand and pulled out the most massive throbbing cock. 'Oh, my God –'

Shaking her head, she tried to dispel the lust between them and say 'no' at the same time. It wasn't working, so with one giant effort, she pushed him back with both hands.

He looked down at her – shocked and startled. And totally, totally confused.

'I'm so sorry, Juan! I think you're – you're incredibly attractive. This is great but, please, just give me time. Give us time.'

'Time for what?' he asked, genuinely puzzled.

'Time for you to get to know me better. For me to get to know you'. There was an awful silence. Then Juan Carlos started to tuck his shirt in, laughing. As if he was enjoying some hilarious private joke.

'What's so funny?' said Sharon, nervously, not sure if she should be laughing with him.

'*You* are, my little *enchalata*. You are.' Sharon relaxed: she'd made him smile.

But his next words weren't what she'd expected.

'Why should I wait, hey? You are talking to Juan Carlos Garcia, the best player in the world. I 'ave my choice of ze most beautiful women in every country. Hundreds of zem. Sportswomen, models, actresses. Why should I waste my time waiting for *any* woman? Including you,' he finished, with a disdainful sneer.

Sharon felt as if she'd been slapped across the face. The shock was so numbing, she could only stammer, 'B-but – but the day we had … the fun …' Her voice trailed off.

He answered with an aloof shrug, and suddenly looked exactly what he was: an appallingly spoilt, rich, arrogant prick.

As he stalked off, she sank to her knees and cradled her body, the drink making her head swim faster than any Olympic medallist could. Through pained eyes, she watched him swagger back to the party tent, clearly thinking he was the coolest, most desirable man on the planet.

Sharon pushed her way back into the crowd, to see Jules holding court, clinking glasses with a group of fawning executives. She was having a 'mar-vell-ous' time, and Sharon couldn't bear to burden her with her latest romantic disaster. She forced her face into a rictus smile, waved she would call tomorrow and gave Jules a thumbs-up. Jules shot her a delighted look, thinking she was leaving with Juan and gave a double thumbs-up in return. Sharon sighed. This time, it would take a skipload of croissants *chez* Jules to make her feel better.

As she slipped away from the scene in a taxi, only one thing stopped her bursting into tears. It was the last sight she had of him: he was gyrating on the dance podium, bathing in the stares of the in crowd below – totally unaware that his flies were still undone.

Twelve

She'd asked her father to walk her down the aisle; she'd thrown her bouquet to Jules D and the waiting crowds, waved to the paparazzi, and ridden off into the sunset behind her polo player, masterfully handling a white stallion – then the miserable beast reared up and tossed her to the ground.

'Thank God you didn't let him go any further, darling – what a horror. Here, eat another croissant,' offered Jules D, pouring pomegranate juice into the pink champagne. 'I do so like a healthy breakfast,' she said, without irony.

'He was just so damn beautiful. Every girl's dream,' sighed Sharon, dipping a croissant corner into the jam pot.

'Bloody nightmare more like, darling. Can you imagine marrying someone like him?'

Sharon was way too ashamed to say she had.

Jules D continued, without a pause, 'No, this is perfect. We'll just say you're JGF.'

'JGF?' asked Sharon.

'Just … good … friends,' explained Jules, between bites of her croissant.

'But there was that shot of us snogging against the door!'

'Exactly my point. Keeps the intrigue going. Are they or are they not? Column inches, darling, column inches.' She reached for her mobile phones.

As always, Jules D was right. A couple of newspapers and two or three weekly gossip magazines ran short photo-caption stories, ending with the comment that Sharon had left the Cartier International early and without him, supposedly 'feeling exhausted from too much work. Close sources say, 'They are just good friends.'

The first-class flight to New York left Sharon flying high. Having only ever experienced easyJet charters to the Costa del Crappos, the size of the reclining seats was an education. Just two in each row.

She arrived in the 'Big Doughnut' pampered by the hostesses, fattened by the non-stop mid-air banquet, ready and rested for her first-ever fashion-show fitting. Debbie, on the other hand, had been squashed into economy and arrived exhausted, struggling to organise all of Sharon's bags. But she was happy because Sharon had actually got her on the official pay roll as 'assistant', with Z&Zak agreeing to cover her accommodation at a Travelodge hotel.

At the other end of the scale, so to speak, there was Boho House, the boutique hotel they had booked Sharon into, an ultra-chic sanctuary for the rich and famous. Quite exquisite. It nestled in the Meatpacking District, the west-side warehouse neighbourhood that had shed its poverty to become a munching Mecca of trendy cafés and restaurants.

Heavenly, thought Sharon, as she sank onto the puffy cotton duvet of her ornate French bed. In the same room, a large oval mirror stood over a thick-rimmed free-standing egg-shaped bath that waited for her to dip in her toes. A bath run by her own room butler.

A little later, as she hummed and scrubbed her body, she thought of her little flat in Kingston. Maybe it was time to kiss goodbye to the 'pastel palace' and buy something new. As she shifted her weight, nearly sending a tsunami on to the polished wood floor, the water ran in rivulets down her sides, bubbles pasting themselves to her private bits – like a cheeky burlesque dancer. She giggled.

Singing 'I Wanna Be Loved By You', she jiggled her beautiful, bulbous 36F breasts to the 'Boo-boo-be-do' and laughed, looking at herself in the mirror and loving what she saw.

It was a good thing she had this confidence because it was about to be seriously tested.

International fashion shows are not for the faint-hearted model. Every insecurity is multiplied and magnified by the competition. Ziegfried and ZaK chose only the best for their line-up.

When Sharon visited their workshops with a host of other models, it was announced that she was to open, *and* close the show. The other girls politely clapped. To those in the know (and Sharon had only just qualified when she overheard a loud, bitchy voice saying, 'Why *her*?'), either 'opening' or 'closing' was the biggest honour a catwalk babe could have. Hair extensions and fake nails had been pulled out for far less. That Z&ZaK had picked this newcomer to do *both* made her the envy of all. It was also guaranteed to get her coveted consumer and trade press attention.

Sharon was filled in on the growing practice of the pre-Fashion Week show, in which many designers offer their choicest key items to a chosen audience a couple of months before the official Fashion Week. Many complained these shows raised the stakes hideously, with some designers having to churn out eight collections a year.

But Z&ZaK's huge in-your-face pre-show was going to be far bigger than that. It was the full all-singing, all-dancing number. The world's press were being alerted. Stars were being invited. The boys were deliberately pushing the boat out – and taking no survivors.

Not only were their rivals now panicked to hysterical hissy-fit-screeching-point that they should do something similar to compete, fashionista harpies were terrified they would spend a fortune on something in the official Fashion Week that was already considered *passé* by those who had seen it on the catwalks of Z&ZaK. The rivalry was rabid.

Thus, the dogfight to attend and be ahead of the game made these events the hottest tickets in town. Unfortunately for Sharon, it made her a nervous mound of pink jelly.

'You can do it!' whispered Debbie, encouragingly, as Sharon faced walking down a mock runway for the first time.

Sharon looked at Debbie's skinny frame, and immediately felt better. *I'm big, I'm bold, I'm beautiful*, she thought, repeating the mantra for the four-hundredth time that morning.

'Walk with more confidence,' barked the artistic director, as she wobbled down the showroom in stilettos. 'You're stunning – show it!' he ordered tersely.

Luckily, she had only two outfits to wear: a caftan to open the show and a bridal dress to close. Sounded simple enough. She hadn't seen either yet – the styles were under wraps. There'd been a shocking number of high street rip-offs appearing within minutes of the shows recently (not to mention a certain amount of idea-pilfering between designers). For secrecy's sake her 'key' pieces had been fitted on a tailor's dummy matching her measurements perfectly and would be altered on her if necessary.

It suited Sharon fine. She sat munching a bag of crisps, watching the other models being pinned, pricked and generally ordered around. Many were bigger than her, a few a little smaller. But she felt she measured up. There had been a lot of talk in the papers recently about how big was 'too big'. In fact, some cities had taken the step of banning any girl over size twenty-four.

'Hey, girl, what size are you?' asked a magnificently large Russian kid of about seventeen.

'Er, twenty,' said Sharon, knowing she was really somewhere between a British eighteen and a twenty.

'Mmm, do you think twenty-four's a bad thing?' she asked, lowering her stunning brown eyes thoughtfully.

Sharon weighed her answer carefully. 'Maybe. Though I can easily see how you'd get to that size.'

The kid seemed momentarily puzzled, and answered Sharon sharply, 'Sister, that may be okay for you, but there are times I *so* crave a fresh salad or crisp apple instead of a cake … I don't know how some of those girls do it.'

Sharon knew that, according to the recent papers, many experts believed size twenty-four was dangerously big, but it didn't stop young, impressionable models gorging themselves to attain this dress size. Designers were being blamed for encouraging this dilemma. The bigger the girl on the runway, the greater the impact. Oh, how they loved to see yards and yards of their glorious materials floating down the catwalk.

Of course, the more cloth, beads, sequins and work involved, the more they could justify the outrageous price tags. But it wasn't just the designers' fault: the model agencies encouraged their girls to beef up so that they'd get the jobs. And some models would eat so much they were regularly sick. Probably true, thought Sharon. She had noticed there was always a faint smell of vomit in the loos at Glacé Inc.

There was no doubt that, for models, the pressure was on. The sample sizes looked huge on the rails. The idea of filling some of them was daunting. Unlike the consumer sizes in the shops that were made smaller to flatter, these really were size eighteen to twenty-four. Anxiously, Sharon asked Debbie to run and buy her another bag of crisps.

She turned back to the kid she'd been talking to and looked over her shoulder at the magazine she was reading. And knew the responsibility lay there too. Every page was stuffed with stories of how so-and-so celebrity had gained their fifteen-stone body to die for. Columns were devoted to 'gain weight' and 'how to look fatter' tips. Proud, buxom, buffed bodies dwarfed sad grainy shots of skinny-thighed actresses caught out on the beach with their concave tummies and sticking-out hip-bones.

And there was another sick twist to these magazines, one that screwed up the psyche, for sure. As one story paraded the joys of so-and-so's enviable weight gain, it was counteracted by a snide, cruel tale about so-and-so's ugly weight loss. Yo-yo signals with the yo-yo diets that told women the perfect weight was only safe by a couple of pounds' margin up or down. The Body Police, beating up the female mind on a daily basis.

But right at that moment, Sharon was absolutely thrilled to be one of the fat girls – relieved she never had to worry about being too skinny. She was naturally fat. Some people found that hard to believe. Girls now envied her for it. There wasn't an interview she'd given when the reporter hadn't asked her for some diet tips on how she maintained her enviable weight.

The other practice she'd noticed was that a few short models – no more than five foot two – were getting catwalk jobs. Some avant-garde designers, including Z&ZaK, chose these girls deliberately because they gave the clothes a more rotund, ball-like quality. Personally, Sharon didn't think people were fooled by this, and she was pleased she was nearly six feet tall. With her exuberant curves, the impact on others when she walked into a room was almost palpable.

Bauble and Bangle, the top salon in the area, arrived to discuss hair. Tingay, their top art director, spread out Sharon's blonde locks like a mermaid's tail, and examined their quality. 'Superb!'

she cried. 'We cut this here –'

Sharon gasped in horror.

'No, darling, not her. The others,' interrupted Ziegfried, bursting through the doors with his usual entourage of Manga twins, bodyguards *et al.* He waved his hand like a queen reprieving a subject from execution. 'Away with the scissors. We love this darling girl exactly as she is. So do the public.'

'Now, Sharon, my lovely cherub, I need to have a private word with you,' he said courteously, taking her hand in his plump palm and gently stroking it. 'We've got this *marvellous* idea for the opening …'

That evening, when Sharon got back to Boho House she was stunned to find a massive bouquet of snowy lilies waiting for her, and a tinkling Tiffany bracelet. All from a man she'd never met.

'The model hunters,' Zara had warned. Some disreputable managers and staff at agencies would secretly send out pictures of the new girls arriving in town to the playboys and sleazebags with loads of dosh who helped 'support' the agency bosses. They were a spoilt breed of beauty-obsessed lowlife that inhabited the nightlife of the city. They would circle like hungry lions waiting to gobble up a little lamb.

The very young girls, especially the Baltic beauties, often fell prey to them. Sharon just smiled, tore up the card inviting her downstairs for dinner and ordered room service. Tomorrow was a big day.

The show was due to start at eleven thirty a.m., so at nine Sharon stood shivering with fourteen other freezing girls in the unheated back rooms of a meatpacker's warehouse. The tables were laden with piles of doughnuts, cinnamon buns and pretty iced fairy cakes.

Copious amounts of hot chocolate were being poured, along with the choice of three vintage champagnes.

Three people were working on Sharon as she tried to calm her nerves. Her hair was being crimped out like a holy angel effigy … and a pair of white feather wings were waiting to be fitted on to her back. She tried to remember what the director had told her, and she knew only too well what they expected her to do.

'It's high fashion darling … Couture. You'll be fine.' Okay for them! They didn't have to do it. Her stomach churned, like ten ferrets bouncing inside a space-hopper. The world would be watching. She couldn't go through with it.

'Here we go,' said her dresser, producing the most fantastic green silk caftan imaginable. It was sheer, but beaded in all the strategic places – a modesty map, with little islands of mother-of-pearl and shells. To finish off the ensemble, they placed a delicate shell and seaweed circlet on her head, creating an innocent, Pre-Raphaelite look to her beauty. She was to walk barefoot.

The crowd filled the seats. Press jostled in the pit, and celebs made their well-timed last-minute entrances. Finally, the editor of *Vogue* arrived, and with her, the signal to start.

Music blared in the cavernous warehouse, and Sharon recognised her cue as she heard the cult reggae song '96 Degrees In The Shade'. Like the song, it was real hot … really hot. Clammy with fear, she was anything but. There was no turning back. A shove from Debbie, and a deep breath.

She stepped out, spun hair ablaze in the lighting, feathery wings framed behind, conch shell in her hand, like a castaway, and faced the sea of darkness ahead. Light bulbs flashed like a thousand firecrackers, and she heard appreciative clapping as she tossed her incredible blonde mane and sauntered slowly down the runway. Reaching the end safely, she turned, lifted her curtain of hair high with her hands and, crossing one leg sexily behind the other, slowly and deliberately walked back along the runway, swerving at the last moment to the left where a tropical waterfall was pouring. Either side of the stage, they had created a magnificent set of Paradise, just like the advertisement for Descent.

Shafts of fake sunlight filtered down around Sharon as the rest of the lights lowered throughout the vast auditorium. Under the stage lights, the colour of the silk made Sharon's eyes light up like the sheen of a dragonfly. Turning to the water and looking at the audience over her provocative shoulder, she smiled a wicked smile, then, as directed, stepped into the cascading water. The audience gasped in shock. As did Sharon – it was bloody cold. But as the water drenched her hair, she acted as if she was in the throes of native ecstasy.

The waterfall undulated down her caftan, turning it into a clinging, see-through gossamer shift. And there she stood, side on to the crowd, water streaming down her face, hair soaked, wings dripping. Then she turned her back to them and held her arms up, worshipping the waterfall, water spilling off her upturned palms. It made the curve of her long, graceful back carve down like an S to massive, rounded buttocks high and taut as the Venus de Milo's. It was one step further than the billboard. A wild, naked angel in front of the entire world's press.

The audience roared. And the lights went out.

For the moment, Sharon's work was done. The show continued, with the other models illustrating a Faustian Descent into Hell via the seven deadly sins …

Sharon was fascinated by the backstage scene breaking around her, and felt like a romantic heroine trapped in a Georgian brothel. Rouged faces, backcombed tangled hair – she was surrounded by glorious painted creatures in various stages of undress, as if they'd just stepped straight out of a sumptuous painting.

She heard the audience gasp once more when it got to 'Sloth' and horned satyrs dragged a Titan-sized model standing in a wheeled golden cornucopia down the catwalk. There was a hum of anger too – she had to be at least size twenty-six, way too big to *walk* the distance in time to the music. Z&ZaK were deliberately stirring up controversy on a debate that was already boiling. And although the garment hung fantastically and she looked like a magnificent, multi-coloured butterfly, many felt this was going one big fat waddling step too far.

As the girls filed on and off the stage, and panic continually broke out all around her, Sharon was being blow-dried and primped for her dramatic finale. The 'wedding dress' was finally produced for her to put on. She was astounded. Two assistants carried over an enormous scarlet taffeta and velvet creation. Once on, it swathed her body firmly, emphasising her opulent proportions, then kicked out with a saucy mermaid's tail. Embroidered with gold leaf, garnets and tiger's eye along the raised tulle hem, the jewels rose up her calves like licking flames. The robe was designed to sit off the shoulders, the whole effect crowned by a magnificent feathered headdress decorated with rubies. A work of camp genius, the plush red bodice and the red veil were delicately 'singed' as if the wings of a moth had got too close to a flame.

As the dresser sewed her in at the back, three frenetic assistants all working at the same time applied crimson lipstick to her face, red talon fakes to her fingernails, and piled up her hair, letting tendrils snake down. Green shimmery eye-shadow and coal black liner were smudged to give a decadent look … and a live snake placed around her, like a living pashmina. The green of its iridescent scales and the reflective colour of Sharon's mesmerising eyes set off the vermilion dress perfectly: it flared brightly in its own hellish decadence.

'Oh, God, does it bite?' She squirmed as the snake eyed her warily.

'No worries, Sheila,' said the Australian animal trainer. 'I've just fed her. She may like to give you a little squeeze, though, but then, who wouldn't?' He laughed.

The music changed to the retro beat of Arthur Brown's 'FIRE!' Out stepped Sharon again, her heart racing with the thrill, four men dressed as demon ushers leading her to the front of the stage. The audience took an audible deep breath. Their angel had fallen into Hell, and turned into a demon's playmate.

Then out leaped her groom, in a red mushroom cloud of smoke. She was marrying the devil incarnate. Or, more accurately, a sensational seven-foot bare-chested model, his face and body dramatically painted red. Swirling a magnificent peacock-feather cloak, he stalked down the aisle towards her, ruby-studded horns, pitchfork blazing with real fire. Lights dimmed. The Paradise set exploded, and flames leaped along the walkway as the Prince of Darkness passed. The world had blackened into Hell. They stalked hand in hand down the catwalk to the front of the stage. Music pounding he reached out to claim his dazzling, virginal, decadent bride, spun her round, kissed her forcefully on the lips ... then lifted a dagger, ripped her bodice open, and plunged it into her heart.

Women screamed.

The lights went out.

The audience went wild.

By the time the lights went on, two thousand people were giving a standing ovation. As Sharon curtsied, and Ziegfried and ZaK bounded on to the stage to present her with a bouquet of specially dyed red lilies, tears filled her eyes. Nothing could have prepared her for such an adrenalin high.

Back in the dressing rooms, TV crews, radio reporters and press photographers clamoured around her. She couldn't believe the casual nudity of her fellow models, the nonchalance with which they stripped off around her, totally ignoring the media scrum, and enviously looking in her direction. But then she thought of what she'd just done. It was worse – but wickedly good fun. The microphones were thrust towards her.

'How did it feel to open the show?' asked CNN.

'Amazing. Incredible.'

'What do you think of Ziegfried's clothes?' asked the BBC.

'Incredible, amazing.'

'What was it like to close the show in that way?' asked NBC.

'Amazing, incredible.' Sharon realised she was sounding like an autistic parrot, but she was truly at a loss for words.

'It's been such an honour to work for Z&ZaK. It's the best designer label in the world,' whispered Jules D, from behind her.

'It's been such an honour to work for …' Sharon repeated Jules' speech, laughing at the ludicrous idea of being fed the words – but at the same time deeply grateful for her friend's support.

At that point, there was a hushed parting of the waves. A very plump woman with sleek bobbed hair and dark glasses came towards them. Wrapped shamelessly in black and white fur, she looked like a very elegant puffin. Then Debbie made a *faux pas*: she accidentally crossed the woman's path as she hurried to give Sharon a glass of water. She stumbled out of the way, muttering, 'Ohmigod,' in recognition – the only one around making a sound.

The 'puffin' didn't introduce herself. No need. Everyone knew she was the editor of New York *Vogue*. Cupping Sharon's chin in her hand, she announced, 'I'd like you to do our next cover.'

That was it. No intro, no exit line. She just walked on past, towards Ziegfried, who greeted her, arms outstretched, triple air kisses at the ready.

*

That night, Sharon, Debbie and Jules D drank Mojitos and pink champagne in the bar at Boho House. It was an incredible night. They stayed up until dawn, flirting with a host of talent scouts, agency bookers, media luvvies and model hunters. Finally shaking off the hangers-on, they grabbed smoked salmon and cream cheese bagels from Frank's Deli, and headed over to the news-stands. Sure enough, Sharon had made the front pages of nearly every single daily. 'Dear God! I'm famous!' she squealed, gathering them all up and handing a wad of dollars to the amused vendor. 'Really, really famous.'

'Darling,' laughed Jules D, 'it's just the start.'

Thirteen

And it was. It seemed that Sharon had the indefinable 'something' that the camera, the media and the public just loved. The Diana factor.

Knocking a top Hollywood actress off the next cover, New York *Vogue* organised an emergency shoot for their forthcoming issue.

The unscheduled session had been a blast. Mauro Testostero, the hottest celebrity photographer in the world, was so endearing and easy-going that Sharon relaxed from the moment she met him. Although the studio was vast and teemed with assistants, his crinkly-eyed charm and warm humour brought out the very best in her, and she was desperate to please him. In the end, he shot her with her hair in pigtails, green eyes twinkling, head cocked. She looked unbelievably cute in a green low-cut hemp tunic that showed her ample curves. Arms crossed protectively, she looked like a little pixie trying to hold on to a pair of puppies that were struggling to escape.

Where *Vogue* led, others naturally followed. Zara from Glacé Inc. was calling Sharon's mobile in New York at least three times a day with castings, spread and cover offers.

Sharon also found it fascinating how the supermarket magazines had increased the status of their pleas. Two weeks ago, they were asking her to pose for a couple of pages. Now they were pleading for a solo cover. Meanwhile, the glossies were offering minimum four-page fashion spreads. In the fame game, she was definitely on the way up.

She was told by her agency to stop off in Paris for the cover shoot of *Elle*.

Appointing herself international travel co-ordinator, Debbie persuaded Sharon to employ her temporarily, insisting she had done a lot more travelling than her friend and, unlike Sharon, knew how to handle it all (she argued that, as well as their holiday in Ibiza, she'd done a disco cruise on the Channel ferry, been to Amsterdam for a weekend, and had undergone a student exchange with a girl from Bordeaux).

Whatever. Sharon was happy to go along with it. Suddenly earning skiploads, she was just delighted that Debbie organised the hotel and bags, and took charge of the ticket pick-ups and check-ins.

When they arrived exhausted at the Hôtel de Crillon, Debbie ordered late-night room service in their suite, while Sharon popped on to the canopied bed, a pooped-out princess. 'This isn't a hotel, it's a palace,' she sighed, fingering the heavily woven drapery. The room was astounding in its graciousness.

Framing the Place de la Concorde with its long line of Grecian pillars, the view from their room was possibly the most elegant in the world. The famous Needle pointed up to the cloudless night sky, a few steps away, the floodlit promenade of the Champs-Élysées.

'Boy, I can *so* see why the citizens revolted,' laughed Debbie, sticking an oyster vol-au-vent in her mouth and washing it down with a peach Bellini.

Sharon laughed decadently, like Marie Antoinette, kicked off her kitten heels and felt the plush carpet between her toes. In the dark distance, the Eiffel Tower twinkled like a giant magic wand. It couldn't get any better, thought Sharon. Could it?

*

The session with *Elle* was only one day but, in a subtle manoeuvre to raise Sharon's worth, Glacé Inc. had insisted their rising star had a night of unparalleled luxury so she would look her best for the magazine. *Elle* had balked, bitched, and bridled, then finally broken. The five-star hotel suite was on them. It set a status precedent that all would have to follow.

For this cover, Sharon was neatly jacketed in Dior. Glossy red plumped-up lips, and a chic black hat perched on her head, saucily decorated with a luscious pile of ripe cherries. The art director figured the use of strong red would remind the readers of her outrageous Z&ZaK catwalk finale.

Inside, the pages would show her lounging in a bath of profiteroles and cream. It was stylised, rather like a Doris Day movie: she was posed with a giant pink powder puff in her hand, flowered bath cap on her head, fluffy fur mules at the edge of the roll-top bath, and legs kicked in the air.

It was so funny to be lying in her favourite food, with all the people fussing around her, that she laughed all day, popping a profiterole into her mouth whenever she felt like it, and driving the poor makeup girl to distraction.

As it turned out, it wasn't for a fashion spread. It was one better: an interview about being one of the world's most in-demand models. After an excited quickie phone-call to Jules D, she fielded the questions expertly, declaring Dean still a close confidant (the bastard) and Juan Carlos a treasured friend (the fuckhead).

Finally, at eleven o'clock that night, she arrived at home in England, alone, tired and ready for bed. The light flashed on her answerphone, and she pressed the button sleepily.

'Beep. Hello, darling, how are you? D'you know? I think I saw you in the papers. Are you modelling or something? Maybe it was just somebody who looked like you. Anyway, it would be lovely to talk to you. Need to tell you something. Give me a call. Thinking of you … lots of love, Dad.' Her father always signed off his messages like a letter. Sharon figured it was an old-person thing. These days he just seemed to forget everything she told him. It was sad: she so wanted him to be proud of her, to understand how well she was doing.

Hungry, she grabbed a packet of crisps as she listened to the calls.

The next two beeps were from the model agency and her old advertising agency. The girls from Accounts had left a communal message of congratulations, asking when she was coming round to say hello and have lunch. Yeah, in your dreams, thought Sharon, pressing delete, with deep satisfaction.

The last message was from Simon. Sharon felt as though a hand had reached inside her ribcage, grabbed her heart and squeezed it.

'Hi, Sharon, wow. You're doing so well! I doubt you're going to have time to do our shoot now. Really hope you can, but totally understand if not. Either way, can you just let me know? The designer's on tenterhooks …'

His voice sounded wonderful, a familiar tone, from the days before the madness. Of course she'd do the shoot. No way would she let him down. She started to dial the number – and caught sight of the clock. So late. She'd ring him first thing in the morning.

That night, Simon filled her thoughts. She'd missed him, and she enjoyed the luxury of remembering. His smile, his eyes… his laugh.

Next day, her agency rang first thing. Could she meet an advertising agency team in the West End to discuss a possible global makeup contract for a hip, happening brand? They were sending a car for her at ten. The fees they were talking were insane. She was never good at maths, but even Sharon could work out she'd be earning something like twenty thousand pounds an hour for pouting at a lens four times a year. It was obscene, she grinned, brushing out her hair and pulling on a low-cut Z&ZaK jumper. She couldn't possibly accept it, she smiled, stepping into a flowing skirt. It was too much! She laughed, working out all the wonderful things she'd buy.

Applying her face in the limo, she marvelled at how she'd mastered the art of makeup so quickly. Was this really the same girl of a few weeks ago? Cat-like eyes perfectly emphasised with liquid liner, edged with a slash of cobalt green. Mascaraed eyelashes colt-like in their amazing length. Full lips 'natural, delicately lined and polished with a clear gloss'. Skin flawless with the aid of a camouflage stick and a speck of foundation.

Apart from the nights out in Kingston, she had never, ever bothered with makeup before. Her cosmetics bag had consisted of a crumbling brown Rimmel eye-shadow, dry old Maybelline mascara, a bland Nivea lip balm and a mucky tin of Vaseline. If she got this job, the irony of becoming the 'face' of Urban Cool was just too much!

Swinging through the Covent Garden doors of De La Guarde Advertising, she was shown straight up to the boardroom. Oddly, she had no nerves. None at all. She tried to work out why, and then realised that so much was going on that she didn't care whether she got the job or not. She was already a success. Nothing to prove. It was a confidence that *no* training could buy, and it explained more clearly than any books, or any course, exactly why success breeds success.

Seven men and women stared at Sharon inscrutably. She smiled brightly, helping herself from the plate of cookies on the table with relish. They asked questions about her past and current makeup choices, and she told them the blunt truth about the murky secrets of her makeup bag before her recent cannon-shot to fame. Warmed by her honesty, they laughed. She was so unpretentious that she was achingly cool. She landed the contract before their shoulders had finished shaking.

Leaving in the same limo, she asked the driver, on impulse, to drop her off near Riversal Road. Part of her still felt she was walking in a fluffy marshmallow dream … Dr Marvel's clinic had irrevocably changed her life, and she wanted to thank them with flowers and gifts – and get some answers as to how the miracle had happened.

She passed the coffee bar where she'd taken the magic pill. The place was still there, exactly as she remembered. Feeling peckish, she went in and queued for a chocolate and cookie cream milkshake. Then, just to confirm that the snack selection was the same, she bought a fairy cake. No, it was only her entire life that was different. She was having such fun! As the sun shone on her happy face, she flipped out her phone to call Simon.

'Hi, it's Sharon, I'm back.'

'Hey, great! Are you still up for it?' he asked. Up for it with Simon? She certainly was. Sharon paused, desperately trying to think of a witty answer that wouldn't come out smutty … Too late.

'Sharon, are you there?'

'I'm definitely up for it. When do you want to do it with me?'

Oh. God, thought Sharon, mortified. It was coming out all wrong. *Not* witty, Sharon, *so* not witty.

'Well, what are you up to now? The designer will be back by lunchtime – we could set something up right away! Now I've got you, I don't want to lose you!'

Was he flirting? *Was* he flirting? Sharon's mind raced. 'You've got me, Simon. You always had. Give me the address. I'm on my way.' Phew. She sounded decisive, flirtatious and professional.

Clipping the phone shut, she looked at the studio address she had just written down. The Coal Face, next to the Steam Museum, Kew. Curious, she sipped her milkshake and finished the crumbs on her plate. Thank heaven she was already looking good from the agency meeting she'd had earlier. She glanced in the direction of Riversal Road. Finding the clinic would have to wait. She was on a confidence roll: this was definitely the right time to face him.

Getting out of the taxi, she looked at the imposing Victorian red-brick building in front of her. White carved-masonry lintels topped the windows, and above the panelled mahogany door a large polished brass plate proclaimed, 'The Coal Face'.

She pressed the buzzer that said 'Mercier Photography' and Simon answered cheerfully.

Third floor up, she pushed open a red fire door, and walked along the corridor. All the way along, various-sized open cubicles were buzzing with activity. Artists, iron welders, mosaic makers, fabric weavers …

At the far end, she found Simon's studio. Large doors opened into a bright white room.

He kissed her on both cheeks, then held her at arms' length to study her. He whistled. 'My God, you look great! Sit down, sit down. Can I get you a coffee? Or a tea?'

Sharon savoured the way Simon looked too. Confident, relaxed and totally at home in his surroundings. It struck her that it was the first time she'd not been offered champagne at a shoot or show. 'Tea would be marvellous, two – no, three sugars, please.'

As Simon headed over to the far side of the room and the makeshift kitchen, she had a chance to take in the large photos running along one wall. They were stunning, a line of arresting portraits, from a battered, bleeding boxer wiping his forehead with a soiled towel to a sad old Spanish matador, holding his hat forlornly against his chest.

'My series entry for the Academy of World Arts,' said Simon, who had noticed that Sharon was now walking along the row, studying the images one by one.

'God, they're amazing … they all look so, so …'

'*Defeated*. That's the title of the collection.'

'When's the competition?'

'It's just been.'

'Oh, shame. And, tell me, were *you* defeated?' she asked, pleased with her Lauren Bacall-style delivery.

'No, not at all – I won. The finalists' exhibition is next week. You can come, if you like?' he added hesitantly.

Before she could answer, a pretty girl with a purple fringe popped her head into the room. 'Simon, don't forget to give me your invites. I'm sure I can get a few creatives from Saatchi's to come.'

'Cheers, Darcy. By the way – love the new pottery. Great colours, much better than your usual grey crap! Let me know if you need some press shots.'

The girl laughed, totally unoffended, and disappeared.

'Right, Sharon, let me show you what we're shooting. It's something special by a terrific new designer called Max Du Pré.' Simon walked over to a clothes rail, flicked through a few items and pulled out a large, chalk white garment.

'Wow, that's a great tent dress!' said Sharon, amused.

'It is, isn't it?' said Simon, laughing.

And it was. Exactly that. A tent dress. A brilliantly designed 'A' line frock made from hand-stitched canvas, complete with punkish trimmings of metal tag rings and guy ropes. Sharon was eager to try it on.

She changed behind a simple black curtain, then stepped out. Simon folded his hands and leaned back against the white Victorian radiator. 'It looks so cool … just bloody marvellous.'

On Sharon, it hung perfectly. Scooped around the neckline, it fell in a straight A-line, but as she walked it flowed, giving it a sexy sixties swing. Although it looked as if it was made of canvas, the material was actually soft, like a silk parachute. The whole design was fun, mad, modern. And a wonderful play on the idea.

'How are you going to shoot this?'

'*Voilà!*' Simon produced a huge fifties silver fan, lowered slatted blinds behind her, and handed her a pair of white patent seven-inch stiletto heels. 'Can you handle those?'

'I can handle anything you give me.' She winked.

Simon laughed, and brushed her hair off her face with his finger. The gesture felt laced with electricity. 'I think I want your hair wild and free. After all, it's your trademark.'

There was no makeup artist, so Sharon retouched her own face while Simon played with the lights. He switched the fan on, and the dress billowed. Sharon tried to hold it down with her hands, giggling, her legs splayed like Marilyn Monroe's over the air vent. Her waist-length hair flew up and out, and as she tossed her head against the wind, it fanned out, like a stormy sea of platinum satin.

He clicked on a hi-fi, and the Eurythmics blasted out of four speakers. The hot electric beat was perfect. Sharon slowly and self-consciously started to move – but, as the sounds pulsated through her, she loosened like a wild cat. As Annie Lennox sang, 'Sweet Dreams Are Made Of This' Sharon thought they truly were. Flash after flash exploded in time to the music, and as she sucked her bottom lip, pouting and tossing her hair, the atmosphere in the Coal Face turned steamy, steamy … steamy. And then white hot. A few times their eyes locked above the camera for many seconds longer than necessary.

And as Simon looked through the lens and gave orders, she drowned in the beauty of the moment. She would have done whatever he wanted. Anything.

'Beautiful … Great! Stunning … This way … Look down … to the left … Gorgeous …'

Sharon was loving it. Simon was fixating on her – her fantasy come true. She had his full attention, and he was acting as though she looked amazing.

At times, the dream was briefly interrupted.

'Hey, man,' said a large guy with a goatee and short sideburns. 'Mike's finishing the CD copy now. Are you joining us for the brainstorm later?'

'Yeah, yeah, I'll be there,' answered Simon, not taking his eye off the camera. 'Keep that up, Sharon, place your legs wider …'

Minutes later, they were interrupted again. 'Hi, Si! Guys, that looks fab! Great work!' called a girl as she passed the door.

Sharon just had time to note she was a cute size eighteen, in swirly seventies top and fuchsia hair. 'What *is* this place?' she asked, feeling like an outsider with a very, very hip gang.

'It's the nature of the Coal Face. Anyone who takes space here has to be in a creative field. Look at me, eyes down. Y'know, no solicitors or accountants. Makes us a sort of co-operative of talent. A kind of creative hotchpotch. Works really well. Okay, eyes looking past my shoulder, smoulder … That's it! Max designs in a studio below, Darcy's two along. We all help each other in any way we can. Don't smile, look mean … horny … Mike's a musician – his band's just finishing their first album, and he wants me to shoot the cover. If it's a hit, I get a shit-load of dosh.'

She so wished she was a 'creative'. She envied his lifestyle, and felt, once more, insecure. They stopped as Simon adjusted the lighting.

'What about this job? Are you doing it for free?' asked Sharon.

'Yep. I know this designer's going to be huge. Okay, turn your back to me, look over your shoulder and give me a sexy wink … Fabulous – that's it. Hold it … But the most Max can afford to pay you right now is the amount I mentioned – three hundred pounds. We're giving it all to you. I know your rate's probably a lot higher so we really appreciate it.'

'No problem. Glad to help out,' she said, knowing he'd be disconcerted if he knew just how much higher her rate was. But she was equally disconcerted at the use of the word 'we'. How much of a 'we' were they? Oh, no! Was Simon bisexual? She'd heard a lot of photographers were ... 'Well, I think the designer's a genius! I want to meet him – where is he?' she said, with false brightness.

'He's a she, actually,' said a smoky voice at the door. 'And I'm right here.'

They stopped and looked towards a stunning brunette with a cigarette holder in one hand, trench coat draped over her shoulder. She sported a short, unbelievably sleek, shiny bob, and was wearing a sophisticated black shift dress. Typically French, thought Sharon, uneasily.

'Sharon, meet Maxine Du Pré ... Max, meet Sharon.'

Sharon winced at the ordinariness of her name. This creature looked as if she should be sitting in a café in a French *film noir*. 'You can call me Shaz,' she said, embarrassed as she said it. Why the hell was she using her press nickname? The woman just made her feel inadequate. She wasn't even as big as Sharon, but something about the way she carried herself made for a similar impact.

'You look exceptional,' Maxine purred. 'Darling Simon, you were right. No other woman would look as good in this.'

Sharon was both mortified and pleased by this. Delighted that Simon had said such a thing, but sickened at the way Max was so familiar with him. They must be lovers, she reasoned bitterly.

The rest of the shoot didn't go so well. Sharon's sparkle had dimmed, and Simon sensed it. 'Let's call it a day. We got some fantastic shots earlier.'

Maxine's hauteur had cooled the room like ice in a hot bath.

As Sharon changed, she heard them talk in hushed voices.

'No, Maxine, don't you dare. Not here. Don't even think about it …'

A low, throaty laugh emanated from the French beauty. 'Tut, if you insist. You know I always do as you say, darling …'

Sharon felt broken. She had been right. It took her a few minutes to compose herself before she pulled back the black curtain. 'Okay, guys,' she trilled brightly. 'I'd better be off. Great dress, Maxine. Love it.'

'Keep it, angel. You deserve it.'

'We're releasing the photos to the press in a couple of days, so can you just sign the form?' asked Simon, becoming business-like as he handed Sharon a model release, which would allow the shots to be used anywhere, along with an envelope of money.

'So …' said Sharon, awkwardly.

'So …' said Simon, awkwardly.

'So … are you coming to his show?' said Maxine, smoothly.

'Er … yes, if you want me to?'

'Of *course* we do,' said Maxine, using the bloody we-word again.

Simon picked up one of the invitations that lay on the table. A smart black and white card announced that the Academy of World Arts was holding this year's show at the Serpentine.

'One or *two*?' he asked pointedly.

It was a leading question that she didn't know how to handle. 'Two, please,' she replied mysteriously (but knowing full well that the other would be for either Jules D or Debbie). Cheek kissing, Sharon said she'd see them there, and left with a deep sense of anticlimax that stayed with her the whole way home.

Sharon made a concentrated effort to put Simon and Maxine out of her mind, and the next few days passed in a flurry of go-sees and agency talks. So it was with surprise that she walked into the newsagent for a pint of milk and saw herself on the cover of a major weekly gossip mag wearing the tent dress. The shot was fantastic. The silver fan and shadows from the blinds gave it an iconic fifties feel, as her hair and dress billowed about her. She looked like a younger, sexier Marilyn, all big curves and boobs. She also had poutier lips, higher cheekbones and gorgeous green eyes.

The same shot was in the *Evening Standard*, and the *Daily Mail*. But, to Sharon, the copy was even more amazing than the photo – 'LOOKING SHAZULOUS!' said one headline. 'SHAZERIFIC!' howled another – and they all hailed her as a trendsetter! A fashion leader, able to spot new talent a mile away.

Taken aback, Sharon couldn't believe they were talking about her – a girl who used to think 'cutting edge' meant a pair of scissors: 'Shaz shows the way … Discovering new designer Maxine Du Pré, she wears one of her witty creations, the Tent Dress.'

Within days the dress was a massive hit, and Maxine Du Pré sold hundreds to the department stores in navy, red and white. Its popularity was all encompassing: big girls looked even bigger, skinny girls could hide their lack of curves. The silky canvas made it feminine, yet sporty. Tough, yet girly. Over the weeks to come, it was a style that sold in thousands – inevitably ripped off, variations appearing in every boutique and discount chain across the nation. And Sharon had started it.

Then something else happened to set her above the other models for good, and establish her as '*The* Fad Queen to Follow'. A total accident…

Fourteen

What to wear? What to wear?

As Simon's exhibition loomed, Sharon learned that being a fashion icon was fraught with worries. Suddenly, nothing in her wardrobe seemed trendy enough – or, worse, too trendy. She had sauntered down Portobello Road last weekend and picked up a few things. High on the possibility list was a vintage gown that skimmed the floor. It was alabaster silk, which scored points because the event was a celebration of black and white photography. But was it too dressy? The tiny lines of covered buttons running along the wrists and down the long back were so delicate and feminine, likewise the pinprick ruching under the bust, which gave it an elegant empire line. It was probably perfect.

The problem was, Sharon could only think of Simon's cool crowd. She couldn't imagine any of the women there being seen dead in it. She thought of Darcy, and Maxine, and Fifi, or whoever … They'd all be clad in grungy trench coats, with spiky hair, like existentialist extras in a Jean-Paul Sartre documentary.

'Darling, I'm outside. Taxi's waiting,' cooed Jules D, on Sharon's mobile.

As they swept down the drive to the elegant, columned Serpentine Gallery, Jules D smoothed the strands off Sharon's face. For once, she'd tied her hair into a high, loose bun, and it suited her, emphasising her long neck, ample Regency bosom, high cheekbones and neat retroussé nose.

'Oh, my God, what's that?' asked Sharon. This year the gallery had commissioned a Japanese artist by the unpronounceable name of Yoki Yamiharata to build the temporary pavilion, an architectural installation erected on the lawns in front of the traditional building.

Always acclaimed as the very height of innovation and design, the invitation to create the building was an internationally craved honour. This year's result looked like a giant white egg surrounded by spilt yolk. As they got out of the car, they realised the yolk was actually a moat reflecting the setting sun, on which swam stately white swans from the Serpentine, with a couple of black swans imported just for the night.

'Black and white? How apt,' said Jules D, noticing the detail. She was referring to the theme of the exhibition – 'A World Celebration of Black and White Photography'.

They crossed the moat and stepped through the 'cracked egg' opening, past a spot-lit plaque explaining Yamiharata's architecture:

THIS YEAR'S PAVILION REPRESENTS THE HARMONIOUS RE-BIRTH OF CREATIVITY, SOLIDIFYING THE TWO PRIMAL OPPOSING, YET COMPLEMENTARY, PRINCIPLES FOUND IN YIN-YANG.

'Hey, I was just going to say that!' giggled Sharon to Jules D.

The scene was exactly as they had expected: the bold, the beautiful, the famous and the *über*-cool, all floating in a bubble of tinkling glasses and laughter. Sharon stood and chatted politely to a few people who introduced themselves and asked her about her experiences at Fashion Week, or about the 'Tent Dress' they'd seen in the *Daily Mail*.

Excusing herself, she caught the eye of a waitress and snaffled a black and white sushi off a glass chessboard. Designer delicious, she thought, helping herself to three more, leaving a checkmate position on the waitress' board.

No sign of Simon, but she could see his work prominently displayed on the main large wall, spotlights to either side. His images were also being projected one by one on to a giant plasma screen. She felt proud, and even Jules D had to admit his work was really arresting.

A fading actress made a beeline for them with the intention of asking Jules D Creatives to relaunch her non-existent career. For a while, they were cornered mercilessly. After the woman's fifteenth sentence beginning with 'I', Sharon excused herself from the humiliating situation and sidled off, leaving Jules D to let the woman down gently and discreetly.

The other finalists' work adorned the other walls, and Sharon walked along, pretending to study the photos, which protected her from talking to anyone and also gave her an intellectual air. The theme was sport – right across the world. Weighed down by their own worthiness, the entries seemed to cover everything from cock fighting in Vietnam to toe fighting in Tibet. '*Jockeys in their Jockies*,' read one card, alongside images of skinny white men in their Y-fronts. '*Stripped bare, the riders show their fragile association with nature and beast ... Influenced by the post-expressionist movement ...*' Blah, blah, blah. Sharon chuckled at the pretentiousness.

Another series of photos – the third prizewinner – showed an Indian weightlifter hoisting another man into the air: '*Günter Andderton's unique series investigates the symbiotic relationship between resistance and force, pushing to the limits the thresholds of pain ... a secret and subversive narrative of society's oppression, etc., etc., etc.*'

Sharon snickered into her cocktail glass.

'I love the way he captures the essence of angst by highlighting

172

the uselessness of man, don't you?' said a deadly serious voice behind her.

She turned, and looked straight into the blue-grey eyes of Simon. They were crinkled with amusement in contrast to his tone. They both started to laugh.

'It's a pretentious load of ol' crap, isn't it? Sorry, Sharon – had I known it'd be like this, I wouldn't have invited you.'

'Don't be ridiculous! This is great,' she said, sweeping her arm in the direction of the whole room. 'Pretentious it may be but, Simon, it's incredibly prestigious and I'm so proud of you.'

'Really?' he said, pleased.

'Yes, really. Your work stands out as … um … deeply authentic.' She started to laugh at her own words. 'And, er … arrestingly modernist.'

'And worthy – don't forget "meaningful and worthy",' he said.

Then they rejoiced in the game of who could find the most conceited description on the walls, finally wandering towards the canapé table to admire the ice sculpture of a swan on a black river of caviar. As Simon downed a pint of black-and-white Guinness, and Sharon took a mouthful of caviar, they enjoyed watching the arriving scene together. One gay couple turned up draped in monochrome kimonos, but they were trumped by a woman in a fifties black and white polka-dot cocktail dress, with two Dalmatians on a checked lead.

Heading straight towards her, entourage in tow, Sharon recognised Paul Sharpe from her old advertising agency. Black leather jacket, black leather jeans, black shirt, silver earring and black cowboy string tie. 'Shaz, kiddo! The girl's done good,' he schmoozed, swigging a beer in his usual rock 'n' roll fashion, and planting wet kisses on her cheeks. He turned to the people with him. 'I remember the moment we knew we had a star in our presence. There she was, a lowly receptionist, when the sun came out and made a halo around her … God, it was one of those electric moments you never forget …'

As he went on to describe the waterfall and how it had influenced the final poster for Descent, Sharon smiled, embarrassed, and edged away to stand with Simon, who was watching her curiously. 'Simon, I haven't had a chance to tell you how much I love your photo of the Tent Dress. Amazing – it's been in a lot of papers.'

'I know. That's cos you looked so good in it – it was easy to take a great shot. I owe you one. The phone hasn't stopped ringing with job offers.'

'Not at all! You're now in the presence of a style icon, thanks to you.'

Simon looked at her seriously for a moment, locking eyes with her. 'This is all a far cry from the Kool Kat, isn't it? Do you remember that last time we were there? It was you I really wanted to dance with, not Debbie.'

Tingles shot up her arms. Sharon tried hard to listen, but was uncomfortably aware that people glanced at her all the time, making it hard for her to concentrate and relax. Photographers circled, snapping the two of them standing together, but they carried on talking, as if they hadn't noticed.

Simon was the first to break the pretence between them. 'Okay, there's one to your left. Run your fingers through your hair, and give me your best model smile,' he said, through gritted teeth, smiling back.

'Another swooping in at three o'clock. Take a sip and look passionate about your work,' countered Sharon. They were having such fun … until Maxine Du Pré tapped Simon on the shoulder. He turned, and automatically gave her a kiss on the cheek …

'Have you missed me, darling?' she asked coquettishly.

At that point someone tapped a microphone, and a pompous

man in a dinner jacket made a speech. 'Fantastic to have entries from all over the globe … blah, blah, blah … Nikon … Kodak … sponsors …'

Sharon noticed Simon looked a little edgy. Was it because Max had slipped her arms through both of theirs as they listened?

'And our fantastic winner, Simon Mercier, really captures the essence of man's ability to … blah, blah, blah,' said the host.

The room broke out in applause, and Simon walked forward to the podium. 'I am really, really pleased to get this award. It means a lot to me. I've always loved black and white photography …' He hesitated.

Sharon noticed that something had caught his eye above the crowds, and she saw a subtle, almost imperceptible smile play at the edge of his lips. She doubted anyone else had ever studied his mouth like she had, and doubted even more that they could see what she could. So, as everyone looked at him in rapture, she followed his eye-line …

Oh, no! She turned back to him with the biggest beam ever on her face. He grinned.

Alongside his work, a bright banner announcing the awards hung all the way down the wall. The same banner also hung in various places horizontally. But it was the vertical wall banners that made her gasp. She and Simon hadn't noticed it before. It would appear nobody had. Certainly not the graphic designers who had designed the vertical version from the horizontal. But it clearly said:

ACADEMY OF
WORLD
ARTS THIS YEAR SPONSORED BY
NIKON AND
KODAK

Simon seemed to hesitate. He looked at his notes, as if he wanted to change his planned speech. He looked again at Sharon. She knew the acronym was irresistible and, sure enough, Simon rose to it, like a man with Tourette's.

'Indeed, I'm somewhat overwhelmed at the entries this evening.' He screwed up the paper. 'When mine was submitted to the committee, I never expected to get this,' he lifted the trophy, 'a W-A-N-K from the Academy.' He said the letters swiftly, so it was hard to tell if anyone actually had realised what they spelled. Regardless, Simon continued: 'And I can see tonight that there are many finalists out there who have earned this experience far more than I have. What can I say? I'm enjoying this moment. I feel ecstatic. And I truly thank you – the organisers – for giving it to me in front of all of you ...' He just managed to finish, disguising his collapse into hysterics with the sudden development of a heavy coughing fit.

The sponsors slapped him on the back and handed him a cheque for twenty-five thousand pounds. He struggled with his composure, posed for more photos, then slipped off towards Sharon and Max.

When he reached Sharon, he let out a guffaw, and they both creased up, holding on to each other as they shook. Max looked on, puzzled, in that petulant, sexy way only the French can pull off. She finally caught the joke, and smiled. 'Cute, darling, very cute,' she said, squeezing Simon's cheek.

At that point, a tray of drinks went floating past, and Sharon twisted round to take one. She heard an almighty rip. As buttons pinged off the back of her dress, the blood drained from her face. A huge tear now ran from the centre of her back to under her arm. The fragile material around the rip disintegrated and frayed. She stepped back, catching her satin Louboutin heel in the long hem as she did so. Tottering dangerously close to the ice swan, she made another twisting manoeuvre to avoid falling face first into the caviar. She heard another rip as the bottom half of the skirt split apart.

She looked at Simon, horrified. He looked at her, mock-horrified. Jules D ran over to help.

'Get me out of here! Help!' whispered Sharon, trying to hide behind her. Photographers were circling like sharks about to eat a juicy morsel of photo-gossip.

'Listen to me. Stay calm. Stay absolutely calm. Don't let them see a single sign of worry while I fix this. Give them a little laugh, go on. That's it. Now, let's see … Thank God your bra's really pretty …'

Then they were laughing. Such a stuffy, pretentious crowd – it was the worst thing that could possibly happen to a celebrity. It was also the funniest. Sharon knew her bra was showing, but it was new, edged with pretty chiffon and very clean! As for her dress …

'Darling, just tie it up or something …' said Jules D, taking control. Sharon did, in a knot at the side, like a sarong. It looked pretty good. The frayed areas had a cobweb quality, and her vintage full-length gown had been transformed into a chic little number. She kicked off her shoes, which now looked ridiculously high, and let her hair half down. Barefoot and beach-babe leggy, the effect was very, very Bohemian.

When they had recovered enough to mingle, their little circle moved around the room. People stared enviously in admiration at the in gang. Max, however, was now acting in a very predatory manner, coming physically between Sharon and Simon at every opportunity.

Jules D took Sharon aside. 'Darling, I'd give up tonight. She's never going to leave you alone with him. Come on, sweetie, let's head off. Never good to be the dreg at any party. Call him tomorrow, and say you're sorry you had to leave. Gives you a chance to speak to him alone. Maybe he'll suggest meeting up or something.'

'You're right. What's the point?' Sharon sighed. 'She's got her perfect French-manicured nails into him. I don't want to share. Or fight.'

They walked out into the hot August night, and as Jules D disappeared in search of a taxi, Sharon sat at the edge of the moonlit moat and dangled her bare feet in the water. It was cool and refreshing. As she watched a serene swan sail silently past on the silvery water, it reminded her of a rubber swan she'd once had. She'd floated it on the Bourne stream in Bournemouth Pleasure Gardens when she was about five years old. It had sailed out of reach, under the bridge, past the pavilion and eventually to the big bad sea. She'd been devastated. Her mother had tried in vain to comfort her, but all she could think of was her poor little swan, lost and alone in the vast ocean. Just like her now.

'There you are! Why are you going? Something I said?' asked Simon, settling down beside her.

'Not at all. I just thought you were busy.' Sharon wanted to add 'with Max', but she knew she wouldn't be able to hide the jealousy in her tone, and it would be such a humiliating giveaway.

'No, I'm not. I'm all yours …' He gazed at her intently. The words hung in the air. They both said nothing, just slowly moved their faces closer and closer. Feeling an uncontrollable force of gravity, Sharon couldn't resist the overwhelming pull of her lips towards his. She so, so wanted to feel his touch hers that they actually ached. Their faces were only a fraction apart. She could smell his cologne … feel his cool breath on her cheek …

But the fear of rejection kicked in. 'What about Max? You're with her.' Her voice cracked.

Simon made a last-minute swerve, brushing his lips against her cheek. It broke the moment. 'Max? Good God, no! Why the hell would you think *that*?'

Sharon didn't know how much to say so she started with little things. 'Well, she – she calls you "darling".'

'Maxine calls *everyone* "darling", including the tax man!'

'Okay, well, um, when we were doing the shoot, I heard her come on to you, and you were laughing and said, "Don't you dare! Not here!"'

Simon started to laugh, his shoulders shaking. 'Go on. What else?'

'Well, she doesn't leave us alone – she's been squeezing between you and me all night.'

'Oh, Sharon. This is *so* funny – you have no idea.'

'Funny? Not to me it isn't,' said Sharon, perplexed.

'Oh, it is, believe me. It *is*. Sharon, I don't know how to tell you this, but … Maxine is *gay*. G-A-Y! She's had the hots for you for ages!'

'WHAT?'

'You were her muse for that dress. She has cuttings of you from Fashion Week up in her room! I knew what she was up to the minute she came slinking into my studio. She wanted to make a pass at *you*, and you're right – I said, "*No way! Don't you dare… not here!*" Actually, I was really cross with her, because I wanted to go out for a drink with you after, and I think she knew it.'

Now it all made sense – Max always squeezing between her and Simon, getting physically closer to her. And, now she thought of it, it had been *Maxine* who had insisted she came to the exhibition. How could Sharon have been so blind? She started to laugh uncontrollably, both flattered and relieved.

'Taxi, Sharon! Come on!' They looked up to see Jules D in a black cab.

'Oh, no, now I've got to go.'

'Stay a bit longer,' said Simon, placing his hand over her wrist.

'Ah, there's our boy!' cried a suited organiser, leading a posse of photographers and sponsors behind him.

As the two were reluctantly pulled in different directions, Simon called out to her, 'Damn! Sharon, I'm off to Los Angeles for two weeks' work. I'm leaving tomorrow – I'll call you when I get back, okay?'

'Okay, do that!' she shouted back, as she stepped reluctantly into the meter-ticking taxi.

Looking out of the back window, the last thing Sharon saw were two fighting swans, and a soaking gaggle of Academy organisers trying to pull them apart before guests and press realised the anthropological error of mixing the black and white birds together.

Fifteen

Sunday brunch: Debbie and Sharon sat in Jules D's stylish slate-topped kitchen, drinking Buck's Fizz and guzzling endless croissants.

'Which ones next? Chocolate, almond or plain?' called Jules D, pulling out a tray from her Smeg oven. The scent of baking wafted through the air, bringing with it dreams of smoky French bistros and Gauloises cigarettes.

'Well, I just can't believe you didn't realise she was after you,' said Debbie, giggling, as she topped up her flute.

'No idea. And I'm sure he was going to kiss me! If only I'd kept my mouth shut.'

'Yes, for once that would have helped,' said Jules D, settling at the counter with a stack of Sunday newspapers and a frothy, machine-made cappuccino.

'Now he's off for ages – I can't bear it!'

'LA, did you say? What's he doing there?'

'Absolutely no idea – photographing something or other.'

'Here's a good piece,' interrupted Jules D, as she worked her way through the papers with a yellow highlighter. She held up a spread on the Egg Pavilion, and there, largest picture on the double page, was Sharon, moonlit hair tumbling down, dress suggestively ripped along her shoulder line, the hem tied up saucily at the corner. She was sitting by the moat, one foot paddling in the water, other knee up to her chin, showing an indecent amount of ample thigh. She looked like a naughty water-baby about to do a skinny-dip.

The copy trilled:

Shaz does it again – is she the coolest babe on the planet? A night out at the Academy for World Arts, her vintage Chanel dress tore, but did she run home crying? No, not this model. A nip and a tuck was all it took to transform her glam gown into a hot little mini.

'Coolest babe on the planet? As if! And where did they get the idea it was vintage Chanel? I just picked it up off a tatty old market stall.'

'Makes good copy, darling – who's going to contradict? Not you. Certainly not Chanel,' explained Jules D.

'Hey, let me see the other photos.' Amid the pictures was a small one of Simon and the organisers. He looked calm, confident and handsome – if perhaps a tad too slim compared to the bear-like men around him, thought Sharon. 'Can I keep this copy?' she said, tracing her finger over his face.

'You'll want this one too, then,' said Debbie, handing over a broadsheet showing a picture of the two of them laughing together.

This time the text concentrated on Simon.

Up and coming advertising and fashion photographer Simon Mercier, winner of this year's Academy of World Arts trophy, beat fierce international competition with a striking series of black and white images depicting sportsmen at the end of their game. His recent picture of Shaz in the Tent Dress by Maxine Du Pré has started a new fashion craze – the garment sold out in Harvey Nichols last week within an hour of opening, and the names on the waiting list are said to be in the hundreds.

Now Britain's newest supermodel may have started yet another craze when her dress ripped. Tying up the tattered hem, she kicked off her shoes and carried on partying. Chances are this season's new look will be 'tatters'.

'Wow. Very, very good. Two things in that copy have just earned me a nice fat bonus from Ziegfried and ZaK.' Jules D grinned, popping a buttered morsel into her mouth.

'What things?' asked Sharon and Debbie in unison.

'The fact a *broadsheet* is now referring to you as a single name is a mega-sign of your celebrity status. Tabloid or otherwise.'

'Really? I'm just relieved. I've always hated "Plunkett". What's the second thing?'

'The fact they describe you as a supermodel. Horribly cliché, I know – but it does put you firmly in the big league. Kristen owes me one huge fuck-off favour, the stuck-up bitch. Now she can eat her words along with her cheesecake every morning.'

'Everybody owes you a big favour, me included!' said Sharon, getting up to give her a giant hug. 'I was ready to run and hide. It's insane how something like a ripped dress can create such media interest. I was mortified that I'd stuffed myself so much I split the back – the humiliation was awful.'

Both Jules D and Debbie looked at her, puzzled.

'You just don't understand, do you? You see, the world used to worship skinny women … before I took the magic pill.'

Debbie sighed. 'This again. Sharon, I'm really worried about you. Maybe it's just the pressure you're under, but sometimes you say mad stuff and I can't help thinking you should see a doctor or a psychiatrist or something.'

Jules D nodded. 'I agree, darling. Or if you want to, say it to us, but please, please, don't ever repeat that kind of crap to a journalist. Remember how they crucified Cruise?'

Sharon stayed quiet, defeated – and reached for another croissant.

'Good girl. Try the kiwi jam. It's full of nutrients and pure sugar,' urged Jules D, a walking encyclopedia on healthy living.

As the papers launched the 'tatters' look, and Sharon ripped the sleeves off a few old T-shirts to feed the press more fodder, she was surprised to receive a hand-delivered invitation from the States. Screen-printed on silk and mounted on papyrus it said:

Koo Ranjani and Alex Avalon
request your presence at their wedding
in Las Vegas, Jaipur, London and Reykjavik

With it, there was a handwritten note from Koo:

Shaz, I'd love you to join us at any of the venues – and I'd be deeply honoured if you'd agree to be my bridesmaid. Call me ...

Koo was a massive Bollywood star turned chart-topping singer, and Alex her good-looking US producer/Svengali. She re-read the note. Sharon would have been deeply honoured too. Except that she'd never met the woman.

'Look at this! Why would they ask me to do such a thing?' said Sharon, showing off the invitation the next time her little gang of three got together.

Debbie was agog. Jules D just yawned. 'Well, it's kudos for them, darling. You'd be adding a few thousand to their *Hello!* deal, I suspect. Having said that, you should do it, of course. It's a very clear two-way street. Publicity for them. Publicity for you.'

Debbie felt otherwise. 'Well, I think it's appalling, asking a complete stranger to be a bridesmaid.' She sniffed. 'And look at the itinerary – it's very last-minute. The first service is in less than a couple of weeks.'

'Oh, so I gather you won't be going with Sharon, then?' asked Jules D.

'I didn't say that. I just think it's in bad taste. But, then, I *love* bad taste. Sharon, we should go!'

'But it's crazy … a non-stop marathon. Just look at the venues and dates. London, Las Vegas, India and Rejkjavik – isn't that Iceland? Why the hell Iceland, Jules?'

'I suspect it'll be in one of those ice hotels, and then they'll be called the coolest couple on earth. My guess is their PR will already have been seeding that headline with the chosen hacks. Anyway, say yes, darling, and I'll give their people a call. Maybe we can get to design some of the bridal party outfits. Ziegfried would love that – yards and yards of sequins and saris, baubles, bangles and beads.'

'How many bridesmaids do you think Koo's actually asked?'

'However many Liza had, double it. I'll check out who they are first. You don't want to be ending up in a line-up with any of those losers from her days on that *X Factor* show.'

Jules D was referring to the fact Koo had started out as a hairdresser from Hounslow. She'd made it to the top in a tacky 'Find a Bollywood Star' reality competition and then shot, like a comet, to the highest reaches of the celebrity cosmos.

'Fifteen,' said Debbie.

'Fifteen what?' asked Jules and Sharon.

'Fifteen bridesmaids. Liza Minnelli had fifteen. And two maids of honour – Elizabeth Taylor and Marisa Berenson.'

Jules D and Sharon looked at her pityingly.

'What?' She shrugged defensively. 'Years of devouring *Hello!* – what can I say?'

'Well, that's useful to know, Debbie. Well done,' said Sharon kindly.

Debbie looked pleased to have contributed something worthwhile, and the three went back to discussing how good or bad Sharon would look in a sari.

As it turned out, with Vegas the *numero uno* on the whistle-stop wedding tour, she had to look good in Gigi Versale first. Ten days later, the knock on the door of her suite at the six-star Menagerie Hotel told her the bridesmaid's dress had arrived. It came complete with a camp male dresser from the designer, who explained that it was 'Kong's Fay Ray meets Vegas Show Girl'.

Made of bright yellow satin, it clung like a condom-tight sheath, then flared and split at the side as if it had been torn. 'That last touch has just been added, and was inspired by you,' said the dresser, placing his hand to his mouth in a feminine flutter. 'We love the tatters look, sweetpea, so *in* right now.'

Sharon hated the hideous frock. Worse still, the spaghetti straps and plunging neckline created a massive headache in bosom leverage. Sharon's 36 Fs were pretty good at defying gravity, but this dress had so little support she could have done with a pair of space helmets. Copious reams of boob tape later, they had made two giant steps for mankind. And it looked surprisingly good. Although the crazy choice of colour played havoc with Sharon's complexion, it did make her green eyes glint like a dangerous lynx's.

There was another knock at the door and Debbie ran to open it. A distinguished elderly man, silver-haired, in green livery, entered with a box of jewels. 'Please, take your pick,' he said, holding open the case with pride. 'They're on loan to Koo and her bridesmaids, compliments of Deia Jewels.'

Sitting down at the marble coffee-table to study the contents, Sharon felt in awe as she handled the precious trinkets from the famous jeweller. The multi-coloured stones gleamed in the bright lights of the room, like baby fireworks.

'For the actual wedding service today, may I suggest yellow diamonds? These earrings go so well with the bracelet and choker,' said the man, politely.

'You can suggest anything you want!' laughed Sharon, holding up a heavy chain dripping with sparklies.

'How exactly "Deia", are they?' gasped Debbie, agog.

'Oh, to the nearest hundred thousand? About two million.'

'Fine. I'll take three – one in each colour!' teased Sharon. 'Trust me, I'll keep them Deia to my heart!'

At that point, the man's mobile began to chime prettily. 'Yes? … Yes … oh dear. Okay. All right, I'm on my way.' He looked crestfallen. 'I'm terribly sorry, ladies, it seems the bride is unhappy with her choice and wants to look at everything we've sent over. I've got to go right now. But I'll be back as soon as I can.'

He swept up the entire pile displayed on the black velvet cushion and raced out of the room, looking harried.

'That was fun while it lasted,' said Sharon, staring at the empty table, like a child robbed of its sweeties.

An hour and a half later, as the sun set on the Strip, she was in the lobby with twenty other bridesmaids, lining up for the walk into the hotel's wedding wing. The Menagerie was the latest outrageous Vegas construction, a glitzy over-the-top theme palace based on a zoo. Which, quite frankly, was exactly what Sharon found she had got herself into.

From the concierge desk to the bellhops, staff were dressed as safari guides, the boys in tight-butt shorts and butch khaki flap jackets, the girls in mini box-pleated khaki skirts and crisp cotton shirts, rolled down wool socks and ankle-laced tracker boots. Since 90 per cent of the girls had legs as long as a giraffe's anyway, the effect was surprisingly sexy. The massive real palm trees growing in the centre of the foyer reached up to four floors high. At the top mechanical monkeys leaped from branch to branch. Below, at ten-minute intervals, a herd of elephants would wiggle their ears, trumpet, then dip their trunks into a pool and spray water into the air, like a ten-spout fountain. The entrance to the wedding wing was along a rope bridge, through the splayed legs of a giant giraffe sporting a massive diamond collar.

Watching the unruly commotion outside, Sharon could see the press corps was out in full. As fashionably late guests squeezed through the mêlée, the helicopters came buzzing down like angry wasps desperate to taste the celebrity jam. On the ground, black-suited bodyguards were holding surging crowds in check, all talking importantly into their earpieces, trying to look like stars in a CIA movie.

Sharon glanced along the line at her fellow bridesmaids and gave them friendly nods. Nearly all were recognisable, some far more so than others. Behind her was Tricia Trendall, a stunning fifty-year-old international soap star, so perfectly preserved she shamed the embalmers of Tutankhamen. In front of her, sashaying her big high arse, was Batista, a street-tough Cuban singer renowned for her latest mega-hit single, 'Beat You Up, Bitch', which was a slight improvement on her previous release, 'I'll Fuckin' Have You!'

Sharon made a mental note not to tread on her hem.

The bridesmaids were all dressed the same and it was interesting to note how some of the beautiful women in the line-up looked like scrawny little birds in the canary yellow frocks. You certainly had to be big to carry the look off. But something else united them all. A sickly pallor of green.

Koo must have spent days researching the worst shade of yellow, thought Sharon, irritated. How clever. What better way to make yourself look famously fabulous than to line yourself up against the world competition, and nobble it?

Alas, it also seemed the doddery silver-haired footman had found the time to visit all the girls except her. In true Vegas style, all the bridesmaids dripped dazzling diamonds. Sharon noted that there was enough bloody 'ice' around to save the polar bear. No worries, she thought bravely. Feeling somewhat intimidated by the amount of fame around her, she was happy to be underdressed.

As they waited in the anteroom for the appearance of Koo Ranjani, they were handed pretty bouquets of yellow and white jungle lilies, with trails of creeper twining down.

Finally, the bride arrived: a pure white lace-covered bodice encased her ample, curvaceous body, teamed with a Victorian organza skirt, bustled at the back with large yellow orchids. To maximise her girth and impact, she had draped a long chiffon wrap encrusted with pearls and diamonds over her shoulders, which rested elegantly on her arms. Arms she held gently outstretched either side like the Holy Madonna. The chiffon trailed effectively along the floor as she swished towards them, making the idea of a head veil and train seem immediately old-fashioned. In the surrounding jungle décor, the overall effect was brilliant. Smouldering sexuality underneath a prim exterior, she looked like a voluptuous Victorian Jane, about to meet Tarzan.

Her entourage of 'closest girlfriends' on the other hand, looked like a bunch of bananas for the apes.

The bridesmaids warmly air-kissed the bride. As Koo worked her way down the line, Sharon felt nervous. What was she supposed to say? 'Nice to meet you?'

But, being a practised ol' pro, when Koo got to Sharon, she simply exclaimed: 'Shaz! How are you? I'm so, so glad you could make it, I really am.' She gave Sharon an emotional hug, eyes closed, as if they were twins who had been torn apart at birth. Then she moved swiftly on.

Jungle drums beat out a rhythm as the bridesmaids led the way in, entering under a jungle ruin into the next hall. A fake stream ran down the main aisle, and the wedding party had to negotiate stepping-stones all the way up to the altar. The room had more foliage than the Amazon Basin, with gay birds of Paradise tweeting mechanically from the high branches of the plastic mango trees.

Either side, sitting uncomfortably on rocks and trunks and stumps, sat the glitterati. Celebrities, authors, rock stars, artists, all dressed in bright tropical colours. Ahead, looking impossibly LA with a deep tan and sparkling white smile, Alex Avalon was waiting for his bride. His hair was swept back and shaggy, and his collarless white shirt was undone to reveal a bronze, hairless (probably waxed) body-builder's chest. Sharon was sure he winked salaciously at her, which was a little disconcerting since he was about to be betrothed to his beloved in the eyes of the Lord. Well, sort of.

A large minister, with a necklace of ancient symbols, asked everyone to stand as he 'smudged' the air with incense.

In Sharon's mind there was no doubt the ceremony was pure hocus-pocus as the couple recited saccharine vows, exchanged wooden tribal drinking bowls, pinned exotic flowers in each other's hair and ended with an embarrassingly long public snog to make everyone aware of their uncontrollable passion for each other.

The photo line-up afterwards seemed to take hours, as the 'chosen one' did his photos for the magazine that had bid the highest for the exclusive rights to record this holy event for prosperity. The security was unbelievable. She had been frisked once and asked twice if she was concealing a camera, though in this outfit she dreaded to think where they thought she might have hidden it. As the bridal party were asked to pose again and again, she realised this was pay-back time for the free flights, hotel and banana dress.

Suddenly a TV reporter, who had been staring intently at her, walked briskly over and, in a clipped New York accent, asked, 'How come you're the only bridesmaid not wearing bling? I hear Deia Jewels loaned out their top collection.'

Sharon was taken aback. It had been noticed. Sharon felt herself blush as she tried to focus on what Jules D would say. And then it came to her: 'I never wear anything I can't afford to buy,' she bluffed, with an arrogant shrug. She softened it with a smile, and wrinkled her pretty little nose. Hard to say if she was joking or not.

The newswoman lit up with unexpected joy. 'Great soundbite, Shaz, thanks.'

The wedding breakfast was so gargantuan it could have passed for a two-weeks-all-inclusive. Laid out on a 150-foot table that had been made to look like a ledge of rock, the buffet of lobster, prawns and crab claws was piled higher than Kilimanjaro. But the room's centrepiece was a giant open fire, with a spit-roast choice of pork, lamb and, in keeping with the theme, antelope.

As for pudding, a chocolate fountain was never going to be enough. Instead, Koo and Alex had a nine-foot-high chocolate waterfall that poured gooey mocha into a tropical pool. Sweet-toothed guests could scoop it up in freshly cut coconut shells.

The roof had been retracted to show a vast, darkening Vegas sky. Vines and creepers, festooned with flowers and fruit, hung down the ballroom walls. Real parrots flapped around the edges on gnarled wood perches, and in the far corner a safari guide handled snakes, tarantulas and two-foot centipedes, entertaining the spoilt brats of the rich and famous.

Koo had now swapped her corseted bustle and bodice for a becoming Victorian chiffon chemise and a tangled hair wreath of ivy and flowers. She looked as if she'd been carried off to the treetops and ravished by her newly married gorilla.

For a couple who had a daydream life, the official wedding list had been a nightmare for someone of Sharon's new celebrity status. The last time she had chosen something from a wedding list, it had been a toss-up between a sandwich toaster and a bread bin for her cousin Barry. But not so here. The choice was terrifying. Amid the demand for a Lalique crystal goblet set of fifty and a sack of gold and platinum golf clubs rested the sanctimonious suggestion that a donation to their favourite charity would also be acceptable.

The dilemma of being (a) an honoured bridesmaid, but (b) a complete stranger made the amount she should spend on the happy couple completely unfathomable. Add to this the fact she was now famous and therefore supposedly rich … She was at a loss.

In the end, as she was still waiting for a shed-load of money to come through from the agency's accounts department, she had plumped for a five-hundred-pound donation to the couple's pet project – the Poor Children in the Orphanage of Rahdipur. Now, considering the opulence of the occasion, she wondered if she had been expected to donate more. On the other hand, it irked her that by cutting out just *one* of the wedding ceremonies, the happy couple could probably have rebuilt the entire village, complete with plasma screens in every five-bedroom house.

Taking a healthy portion of skewered meat and sweet potato, she sat on one of the tree trunks near the fire and concentrated on not overturning her plate.

'So, what do you think of all this?' said a deep male voice. Sharon looked up into one of the most famous faces in the music biz. It was Jaz, a laconic, laid-back naughty lad, who had made his name by escaping a boy band into mega-stardom. She couldn't believe he was actually talking to her. 'Move that beautiful butt over,' he said, settling himself down next to her on the tree trunk. 'How do you know the happy couple?'

Sharon blushed. She was a bridesmaid – a woman who had sold her soul for the freebie trip and the publicity circus. 'I don't,' she answered honestly. 'Never met them before in my life.'

'So what did you do? Grab a giant banana, skin it and gate-crash?' asked Jaz, highly amused.

'They asked me and I said yes. Sounded fun,' she explained, a little embarrassed.

'And why not? So did I,' smiled the star, with a twinkle.

'You don't know them either?'

'Depends on interpretation. I did meet Alex in the toilets once, and he lent me a rolled-up fiver, so in this business, I guess you could say we're bosom buddies.'

Sharon was shocked at his open reference to cocaine, but amused by him, too.

At that point, Koo and Alex could be seen kissing in front of them through a haze of barbecue smoke. 'They look so right together, I wish them days of happiness,' quipped Jaz. They looked up – and were startled to see a microphone dangling over their heads. They laughed. No doubt the video of the event would have a curious mute moment.

God, he was cute, thought Sharon, glancing at his childlike blue eyes, edged with dark, spiky lashes. She noted how strong his arms looked in his white vest, very manly and covered with tattoos. He was so rock 'n' roll. If only Debbie and Jules D could see her now.

Sharon talked easily with Jaz as they ate, and her excitement doubled when he told her to stay there while he got them some rum punch. Three rounds later, the lights went off and they found themselves surrounded by forty Amazonian fire-dancers, flames blowing at them from all directions.

This was followed by bridesmaid Batiste performing especially for her 'good friends' the loving couple – for an undisclosed fee. She was sensational. By the third number her sizzling mix of salsa/Caribbean beat had the revellers screaming, 'Bo-Bo, shake your booty!' a chant the enchantress was well known for, and more than happy to oblige.

As she shimmied her massive arse off the stage, African native drummers belted out a hypnotic rhythm from the tops of four jungle tree houses nestled in each corner of the room.

And then an air of decadence broke out. The heat, the bright clothing, the abundance of drink and food made a heady mix. The jungle atmosphere came alive with the light of a hundred flaming torches. With the added arrival of maidens scantily clad in zebra skins, bearing platters of cocktails, Sharon was reminded of an old Hollywood movie – was it *The Fall of Babel? Sodom and Gomorrah?*

As for the great gathering of the rich and famous, fully aware the press were being held at bay, they gleefully loosened their proverbial ties and ripped off their inhibitions.

Despite being who he was, Jaz didn't seem to want to leave her side. They gyrated to the beat, lost in the heat of the night, pushed close by the pressing crowds. In the firelight, her eyes glowed even more like a lynx's, her sleek blonde hair wild and tangled as the sounds swept over her.

This was surely a dream … Sharon closed her eyes to the beat, then opened them. No, the rock idol was still there, staring at her with a cheeky smile that said, 'Let's get naked.' Pulling her behind a palm tree, he gave her a spliff, and Sharon took her first ever puff of weed. It made her cough. So did the second puff. But by the third, mellow happiness was drifting through her, lifted by the incessant, throbbing beat.

At around midnight, there was a terrifying crash of thunder – then a blue flash of lightning. The sky ripped apart and rain sheeted down, drenching the dancing guests in a torrential shower. Regardless, the frantic pounding of the African drums increased, and hedonistic pagan madness, heightened by the forces of nature, galvanised the throng. As the storm increased, everyone danced with wild abandon. Soaked to the skin, clothes clinging to their bodies, Jaz pulled her to him and crushed his mouth on hers, his hands and lips devouring her like a lion that hadn't eaten for months.

As the water poured down her face and between their lips, her head swam, her ears burst. She was in heaven. She was in hell. She was in Descent. She no longer looked like the girl in the poster, she *was* the girl in the poster.

And she was loving every *fucking* second of it.

Sixteen

She was drowning, she tried helplessly to float, but wave after wave after wave kept hitting her, rocking her from side to side … She was sinking… she was going under. She was …

Sharon found herself lolling in a giant, oval-shaped waterbed, and shifting next to her, the toned, rock-hard, rock-solid, rock-on body of a rock star. She almost squealed with delight, then shuddered. What had she done with him? Her mind was a blank. Well, sort of.

The passion had been crazy, insane. But she thought she'd passed out before they'd reached 'last base', as it were. She sincerely hoped so, because she had a gut feeling that the only way she'd hold on to this boy was to play a little hard to get. He was a kid at heart, and she reckoned he played games.

Jaz sleepily opened his famous blue eyes, propped himself up precariously on one elbow, and ruffled his hair. It gave him a rakish look that emphasised his high cheekbones and enormous eyes. 'That was a hell of a night … Now, be a good girl and get me a coffee,' he croaked.

Indignant that he thought she was some kind of waitress, Sharon lifted her considerable hips and dropped them back on to the waterbed. They sent a mini-tidal wave his way, dislodging his elbows and causing him to collapse and convulse with laughter. 'Whatta girl!' He leaned over to kiss her, and the heat reignited.

But Sharon swiftly turned it down. 'Hey, let's get up and do Vegas!' she suggested, flinging back the hotel's blackout curtains, and staring out at the only city in the world that twinkled in daylight.

Four days later, they were still doing it. Vegas, that was. Like two kids in an all-night candy bar, they gorged on everything the Sin City had to offer. Bouncing like shiny bright pinballs from street to street, they experienced every theme going, from pyramids in the Hotel Luxor, to the gondolas in Venice. They went to every over-the-top bar, every eccentric eatery, every feather-fanned show, every far-out attraction ... It was fabulous fun, from the Mardi Gras in the Masquerade Village to the M&Ms World of Chocolate.

As they spent every single hour together, their friendship grew into something real. Jaz was really funny and affectionate but, most importantly, despite his fame, he had a warm heart. Sharon watched him smile and joke with his fans and sign autograph after autograph. It wasn't an act. He genuinely loved people, and made time to chat with them all. He was also generous. Everyone got a great fat tip, from the chambermaid to the doorman.

'What the hell? I was once broke,' he said to her, after handing a polite taxi driver a hundred-dollar bill for a ten-minute ride.

The paragon even helped old ladies cross the street. Well, not exactly. In fact, he went one better. They enjoyed the people-watching possibilities of Vegas and one night were fascinated by the pensioners pouring dollars into the hungry one-armed bandits – heartless mechanical outlaws that held them prisoner with false hope, and robbed them blind.

An old bird hefted money into the Giant Jackpot for thirty minutes straight, until she was down to her last nickel. She lost and started to cry. Jaz walked up to her, and poured all his winnings into the cup at the bottom of her machine. About five hundred dollars. He walked away without a word. The woman looked as if she'd just seen Jesus Christ.

With so much to do together, they found themselves on a spinning fairground ride that never stopped. And Jaz was always up for the next thrill. They delayed their flights home three times, but by the fourth night, Sharon was shattered.

Jaz, on the other hand, had enough energy for the two of them. It dawned on her that was probably related to the white powder he sometimes sniffed. He was generous, always offering to share, but Sharon remained wary. It scared her because it was classed as dangerous and illegal, but she didn't like him taking it because she wanted him to be high on her. On the other hand, she was aware from the gossip mags that it was part of the rock 'n' roll scene. Who was she to stop him?

As for the sex, she tried her damnedest to keep him at bay. Indeed, she often thought of Simon and wondered whether she was breaking an unspoken bond – perhaps that was just wishful thinking on her part. Simon hadn't even kissed her. Anyway, she was with a ROCK STAR! Yes, she was shallower than a rock pool, but the looks the other girls gave her were priceless.

When Sharon finally caved in, on day four, it was hot, horny and dangerous in a back alleyway. Leather jacket, leather jeans – he knew exactly how to turn her on, and she adored the way he felt against her. She also loved his boundless energy and enthusiasm. Caressing her in the limo on the way back to the hotel, he was like a puppy with a new toy.

'Why did you make me wait so long, babe?'

'Because you would never have got to know me.'

'Not true. I knew you the moment I laid eyes on you. Come here, you luscious lump of lurve.'

Sharon sighed with contentment. Although she chided herself she'd only held out for four days, she reasoned they'd been together non-stop for the equivalent of twenty dates. And in rock-star groupie terms, four days was probably equivalent to the chastity of a born-again Christian.

By the time she jetted home, with promises to come to his next music festival, she had no idea the British papers had been covering her non-stop from the day of the wedding.

Jules D and Debbie met her for lunch, armed with stacks of magazines and papers. Sharon was astounded. The headlines had quoted her, wrongly, as saying,

'I WON'T WEAR FREEBIES!'

and the copy stated:

> *Shaz sets a new standard in* über-*cool as she refuses the freebie jewels offered by Deia Jewels. While the other bridesmaids decked themselves out in borrowed bling, one supermodel stuck to her principles.*
>
> *'I never wear anything I can't afford to buy,' says Shaz. No question, her understated look set her apart from the rest of the spoiled beauties in the bridesmaid line-up. A refreshing change to the usual greedy grabbing, and other celebrities would be wise to follow ...*

The accompanying photos showed Sharon serene, laid-back and natural, unlike her usual green-eyed wild-child look.

'Oh, my God,' said Debbie, excited. 'Now you're leading the celebrities!'

Sharon couldn't believe it. 'I hate the expression "*über*". It's trying so hard to be cool. This is an *über*-load of cobblers.'

'Darling, well done! I can't believe you turned down all those freebies.' Jules D hugged her.

'It didn't exactly happen like that, did it, Debs?'

Debbie had been a little miffed with Sharon for running off with a rock star, and had caught the plane home from Vegas the next day. On the other hand, she'd also met the rock star's manager at the airport: he was, in her view, 'a real hunk'. With so much in common to bitch about, the two employees had bonded in the VIP lounge. As a result, she, too, had been invited to go to Jaz's next concert. So, she was on a big high, and her best pal Sharon could do no wrong. 'Yes, it did. Well, sort of. Whatever, you had the brains to spin the situation,' she said admiringly.

But when Jules D heard the whole truth from Sharon, she let out peals of laughter. 'Good girl! I'm so proud of you. On the other hand, don't expect an invitation to the rest of the wedding ceremonies ... The clip of you, smiling like Mona Lisa and saying, 'I never wear anything I can't afford to buy,' was on TV stations all over the world. It's on YouTube as one of the biggest hits. I just *love* what you said, and the way you said it. Leaves one wondering if it's a wind-up or not – a real classic on the lines of that ol' chestnut "I don't get out of bed for less than ten thousand dollars." But the thing is, darling, as big as Koo is, she won't like being overshadowed. I'd expect a cancellation call to the other ceremonies any moment now.'

She showed Sharon the *HIYA!* marriage spreads, which gave equal billing next to Koo of 'Shaz' simply dressed (in the banana). Worse, in a couple of the downmarket weeklies, her picture featured twice the size of the bride and groom's. But who cared? Sharon's star was still on a dizzying ascendant.

Amid the recent newspaper cuttings and photos, the glossier magazines that took longer to print were concurrently running shots of her in the Tent Dress, or the Tattered Dress, and finally – in undoubted confirmation of her trend-setting ability – spreads of other models in the Tattered Look.

But it was that morning's Sunday papers that made her smile and panic at the same time. A front-page screamer shrieked, 'SHAZ

AND JAZ!' and there they were, sharing a giant candyfloss, holding hands. The days with Jaz had felt like a holiday romance – that surreal Limbo Land where whatever you do, so far away from home, doesn't count. She had never expected her exploits to be blazoned across her home papers for friends, family, and – yes – Simon – to see. Naïve, really. Someone was bound to recognise them out there, despite dark glasses, fake beards and hats. (Well, the fake beards were just for an hour – Jaz had dared her to put hers on and walk into a beauty salon.) On the other hand, she was glad it was 'out there', although she didn't know if Jaz saw the relationship as 'going anywhere'. They did look good together – and she was learning fast that it could only help her career.

'It's great. Footballer, polo player, rock star ... Good girl. So "on the way up".' Jules D was dreaming of her next bonus from Z&ZaK.

'But what if it doesn't work out? What will people think? Where do I go from here? And Simon ... what about him?' Neither of her friends could answer that. Instead, to change the subject, they brought over a plate of cookies and ice cream.

After the news of the Jaz relationship broke, the paparazzi seemed to be camped outside Sharon's door permanently. Even trips to the shops became a hazard, and in truth a bit of a pain. She had to slap on makeup just to nip out for a pint of milk, and it became abundantly clear that she would have to move from her flat for security reasons.

Three estate agents came round, and she took the middle quote, looking for a fast sale. In return, glossy brochures featuring bijou mews houses and riverside penthouses were sent to her home, and between modelling go-sees and assignments, she began looking for a new place to live. As she struggled daily past the intrusive lenses from her car to her door, gated entrances and protective porters seemed deeply appealing.

Meanwhile, although Simon flitted in and out of her mind, there was no denying she was dating one of Brit Rock's hottest icons. It was an incredible high. She reasoned there was no guarantee that Simon would call or, indeed, that he was particularly interested. Better a bird in the hand – especially when it was a fab-looking famous songbird, who guaranteed unlimited press coverage.

Confirming her status as his 'babe', she'd been receiving intimate texts from Jaz saying exactly what he'd like to do with her – and she couldn't wait for the weekend. He was tied up recording for the next few days, but the Big Alternative Festival was looming.

The rock-chick look was a tough one for Sharon. Her 'man' was headlining Saturday night – which, Jules D told her, was a very, very good thing. The old Sharon had only ever been into folk music and Abba, and had dressed in whatever she had found to fit. For her, the new abundance of clothes for women her size was overwhelming. Designers pandered to the bigger shape, and the choice in the stores had quadrupled.

Aware that the press were featuring her every move, from toenail colour to choice of lip-gloss, Sharon's dilemma wasn't aided by the fact that she and Jaz were going for the whole weekend, it was bound to rain, and they were staying in a teepee. On the other hand, with the growing influx of press stories, freebies were arriving daily – designers wanted the kudos of having one of their products photographed on an icon who chose to 'buy her own'. Soon, her little flat began to resemble a car boot sale of stolen goods, with piles of designer handbags, shoes, sunglasses, skirts and tops building up in every corner of every room. But it wasn't accessories that were a problem. It was the whole look. Finally, after a quick call to Mario from Glacé, she was sorted.

It was a strange experience to go into a famous designer shop and be told to take whatever she wanted. All she had to do was let them have the stuff back when she'd finished with it. And not even take it back. Just ring a number, and they'd send a car. Oh, indeedy, life as a celebrity was a blast!

She selected a large soft suede weekend bag, and packed into it her vintage leather jacket, a new floppy sun hat, a pink wool beanie and matching scarf from Gucci, a baby pink cashmere jumper and grey angora hoodie from Chanel, flower-patterned wellies from Cath Kidston, two pairs of wonderfully faded, fattening jeans from Diesel and a black chiffon kimono from Agent Provocateur. Just for good measure, she also stuffed in her old fluffy pink dressing gown. She reluctantly refrained from taking her bunny hot-water bottle – it was *so* not rock 'n' roll. Then she thought, Why not? Who says what's cool? It seemed that *she* did. And so she chucked it in.

Running short on space, she only took one bag from the designer pile with her, a supple leather tote with Indian fringing. Very Glastonbury, she reckoned.

Jaz said he didn't want her there for the build-up as he needed to concentrate on his act, so the Big Alternative Festival was in full swing by the time the manager's white limo dropped her and Debbie off. Sharon noted her assistant was looking better, these days, filling out to a more acceptable size twelve. However, she'd chosen to wear white cowboy boots and a very short white leather skirt, topped with a tight white T-shirt and cropped leather bomber. Hair messily backcombed, lips stained red, and makeup deliberately smudged, the look was porn-star-groupie-meets-group-for-group-gang-bang. Still, it was rock 'n' roll so maybe Debbie had got it bang-on, so to speak.

The grounds were bursting with people, colour, tents, stalls and noise. Very, very loud noise. A massive stage with banks and banks of speakers at either side dominated the skyline. Handed 'Access All Area' tags by an assistant as they arrived, they were whisked through a back-door maze of corridors and curtained areas.

'Debs, there you are, babes!' said the manager, sweeping her away from Sharon and crushing her to him in a giant bear hug.

He wasn't what Sharon had expected at all. Wearing a suit, he could have been a City boy. But his face was fun, round and jolly … and Debbie looked smitten as he chucked her under the chin.

'Shaz, your man's in there,' he said to Sharon, with a friendly smile. 'But I have to warn you he gets really uptight before a show. Go easy on him, okay? Keep him cool.'

Feeling nervous – she hadn't seen Jaz since Vegas – she popped her head around the door. The room was a mess of guitars, ashtrays and beer bottles. In the corner, yelling at a girl holding a black sparkly jacket, was Jaz, his face tense and angry. 'Why do you think I'd wear that? For fuck's sake – what kind of prick do you think I am?'

'I thought you said this was the one you wanted to wear today – don't you remember? I spoke to you about it yesterday morning.'

'Well, that was yesterday. You should have checked with me today, stupid cow. What else have you brought?'

The girl opened a suitcase and pulled out a striking blue silk shirt. 'It's so great – I thought you'd love it. It'll match your eyes, and catch the wind when you dance around.' She swirled it to demonstrate.

Jaz's eyes softened as he took in the beautiful garment. He sighed, resigned. 'I wanted the white silk, but since you've fucked up, this'll have to do.'

Sharon coughed, shocked at what she saw but determined not to show it. Maybe rock 'n' roll stars always acted like monsters to their staff. Maybe it was acceptable – normal, even.

'Shaz! At last! Welcome to the house of hell! Come here! Great to see you!' From a spoilt bully he had changed into an adorable little boy. All big eyes and winning smiles. Looking every inch the mega-star, he swept her into a delicious snog, but as he held her close, she felt his hands trembling on her back.

'Are you okay?' she asked him gently. Imperceptibly he shook his head, then turned to the poor girl, who was backing into the corner, unsure what to do or where to look.

'It's okay, Dee. Sorry about that … You can go. Shirt's fine.' He waited until the girl had left the room, then cleared the mess of magazines and cans off the sofa, and sat down, pulling Sharon close to him. 'No, Shaz, I'm not okay. I hate this bit. The nerves. I can't stand it. I don't know why I'm in this business. Hate it. I'm such a fuckin' loser. People just don't see it.' He ran his fingers helplessly though his hair, and sat dejected, elbows on knees.

Sharon forgave the monster, and melted protectively over him, pulling him into the safety of her luscious curves. He let out an enormous slow breath, and she rocked him back and forth. He murmured, lost in the delicious-smelling, enveloping comfort of her body. 'Jeez, I wish I could stay here like this for ever – you're so soft, warm, soft … soft …' He swallowed a sob.

'Jaz, you're great. The best. Everyone loves you. You'll go on stage, and be fantastic. Magic. And I'll be in the wings, watching,' soothed Sharon, her heart breaking for him.

'Will you? I'm really glad you're here. I think you're the greatest.' He squeezed her hand, then got up and walked over to the dressing table. A little cellophane packet was tucked next to a tissue box. 'Back in a sec.' He winked, and disappeared into the WC.

Sharon figured he was getting some chemical help. But who was she to criticise? After all, she wasn't going outside to face two hundred thousand screaming people.

There was a tentative knock on the door. 'How's my boy doing?' asked the manager. 'Are you ready for it?'

Jaz emerged from the WC with a big grin and high fives to everyone. He ripped off his T-shirt and pulled on the silk shirt, staring at himself in a bare-light-bulb stage mirror as he buttoned it up. 'Shaz, come here. What d'you think?'

Sharon walked over and stood just behind him, looking at the two of them in the glass. Her heart lurched as she suddenly remembered the mirror in Dr Marvel's clinic. Now here she was, the girlfriend of one of the biggest stars in the country, and he was asking for her opinion on his stage outfit. Would he have given a damn what she thought in the old world? No way. She wouldn't even have got an autograph from his roadie. Pushing away the negative vibes, she answered, 'I love it. Fab colour on you.' Jaz turned, pecked her on the cheek, and simply said, 'See you later. It's showtime!' He slapped his manager on the back. The two men left the room. Unsure what to do or where they were supposed to stand, Sharon and Debbie trailed behind, flashing their Access All Areas tags at all and sundry. They parked themselves in the wings beside a mammoth speaker.

The lion roar of the audience was so strong it was physical. Jaz was blown a few steps back. Then he came forward and bowed. The band opened with the deafening decibels of 'I'm Just A Jester', his first solo number one, and he illuminated the world around him. Electrifying charisma shot off him as if he was a superhero. He only had to look at them for the crowds to scream. With a cheeky wink here, a saucy bum pose there, he was conquering the universe.

Shaz was entranced. Blown away. Had the lost little boy in the dressing room really been the confident entertainer straddling the stage like a Colossus?

As his silk shirt floated in the breeze, and the lights bathed him in a golden glow, she watched the fans surge forward, time and time again, desperate for a touch of his hand. She smiled secretly, knowing exactly where that hand had been, and where it was probably going to be that night. It was an unbelievable thrill to know he was hers. As he turned and blew a kiss to her just before his fourth single, a hit ballad entitled 'Cup Cakes', Sharon exploded with euphoria. He glanced to the side of the stage at least four times during the song, and she knew he was singing it to her.

Unfortunately, when he trilled, 'You're the one for me, we have to be, I need you to see...' she realised something. 'Debs, I'm desperate. Where can I go for a wee?'

Debbie leaned against the manager and whispered in his ear. Not taking his eyes off the stage, he indicated to go down some stairs and turn right. Sharon raced off, determined to miss nothing.

On her return to the wings, she heard the packed fields clamouring for an encore. Two songs later he had revved them up so much that some fans were burning and crashing, being carried over the heads of security guards to the safety of the perimeter fence.

'Goodnight, God bless, and be GREAT!' yelled Jaz, ripping off his blue shirt. He waved it above his head in a farewell salute and flung it into the audience, his incredibly fit torso gleaming with sweat. Screams went up as it was torn from hand to hand, the lights went out, and Jaz raced off, a hundred backstage assistants clapping him on the shoulders, shaking his hands, all wanting to touch the glistening, golden god.

'Let's go!' was all he said to Sharon, and she dutifully followed the entourage back to his dressing room.

'Man, you were smokin', man.'

'Wow, awesome.'

'Coolest ever.'

'Vibe's amazing, man.'

The accolades poured in faster than the booze was poured, as band members, camera crews, record bosses and other stars surrounded Jaz in a galaxy of worship. Sharon hung back, waiting for him to signal whatever he wanted to do next.

Joints came out, and were passed around, little packets changed hands, and bottles of Jack Daniel's were swigged. Debbie looked at home in the corner of the room, fag in hand, beer bottle in the other. Sharon felt awkward, and wished she and Jaz were alone.

Finally, pulling on a clean T-shirt, Jaz walked over to her. 'We're outta here.' He picked up a duffel bag and a bottle of whiskey, stuffed bottle into bag, and grasped Sharon's hand. 'Thank you and goodnight…. Jaz has fucked off and left the building!'

Everyone laughed and clapped, and he saluted them in farewell.

They pushed their way past major stars, who were either leaving or getting ready to go on stage. The same exchanges passed from artist to artist to artist.

'Hey, man, you missed the after show.'

'Yeah, I bailed, man.'

'You missed it, man, it was all happening.'

'Have a good one, man.'

'Cheers, dude.'

'Fuck off, cunt.'

It was the rock 'n' roll banter that clearly said, 'We're all in the same Fame Club.'

As they hit the cooling night air, Jaz led Sharon to a private performers' area. Fires were lit, and yurts and teepees glowed in the dark. They came to a white cone, with Indian drawings on the roof, and he flipped open the entrance flap to lead her inside.

Moroccan glass lamps edged the walls, and in the centre a real fire was burning. Thick Persian rugs covered the ground, scattered with sheepskins, and in the far corner, a raised pallet strewn with fur throws and silk beaded cushions was lit by Gothic candles. Tribal hangings decorated the walls, and a pot of melted chocolate stood on a rock by the fire with a bowl of pink and white marshmallows. It was Nirvana.

Sharon dropped her bag and sank down by the fire. 'You were fantastic.' She smiled, holding out her hand to him. 'Amazing.'

'Really?' he said coldly. 'If I was that amazing, why did you leave halfway through?'

Sharon was completely taken aback. 'Crikey, I'm stunned you even noticed. God–'

'Of course I noticed. But you haven't answered me. If I was that amazing, why did you fuck off?'

'I didn't "fuck off". I went off to find a loo – I was desperate.'

'I think you were bored,' he said icily.

'*What?* I was bursting, if you must know – so excited, I just had to go. What's got into you?'

'I'm pissed because you missed the best bit. The first encore.'

'For me, the best bit was when you sang to me.' She tried to placate him.

'Fucking don't know why I bothered,' he said petulantly.

Sharon was lost for an answer.

He silently rolled a big fat joint, and took a big fat drag. As he blew the smoke up towards the fire hole in the roof, he pursed his lips, making a blowing noise. She watched, hurt, unsure what to say as his eyes closed in meditation.

After a while, he seemed to calm down, and handed her the joint. Sharon was far more interested in the chocolate and marshmallows, but she took a puff to show solidarity. She tried to forgive him – after all, it had been a tough night.

When he opened his eyes, they were sad and infinitely softer.

Two joints later, he had totally transformed. 'Sorry, babe, it was great to have you there. Come here.' They curled up beside the fire and fed each other chocolate-dipped marshmallows that they had toasted in the flames. As Sharon and Jaz talked through the night, she learned more about him and what made him the way he was. They had so much in common. As she heard about his weak mother and drunken, abusive dad, she related easily to the loneliness he must have felt. The more she related to him, the more he opened up. And the more she learned, the more she forgave him everything.

At times she held him in her arms, at times he cradled her. Two lost souls trying to find their way home. As they took turns to share their pain, the night wrapped the teepee in a protective blanket. Safe inside, they swapped tales of wicked stepmothers and cold fathers until the grey morning mist broke over the sea of tents, swirling in the fresh breath of a new day.

Seventeen

The festival atmosphere was infectious, and Sharon loved it. Venturing from the teepee for fresh coffee and muffins, she and Jaz wandered through the throng towards the hippie hip-hop stalls. Likewise, hundreds emerged, blinking sleepily, into the daylight, many dressed in crazy colours and second-hand clothes. In this festival world, anything went with everything. Feather boas with leather bondage bodices, fairy dresses with biker boots. She even passed a man who was naked except for a tutu and flip-flops.

Apart from the snap of an occasional press photographer or the click of a mobile phone by a friendly fan, they were left alone to enjoy themselves. Luckily, there were many other stars to watch on stage and, besides, a laid-back atmosphere was the nature of the festival.

Set in the hills not far from the stone circle of Avebury, the event was divided into sections: the Performance Zone, the Healing Zone, the Meditation Zone, the Experimental Zone, and Sharon's spiritual favourite, the Shopping Zone. Well, it wasn't actually called that, but there was no doubt in the hearts of the hordes that swarmed over the stalls that it was a dream retail park for hippies.

Browsing lazily along the exotic stands, she picked up shiny bangles made of sweetie wrappers, a shaggy Indonesian bag made of wool and rags, two silk shawls beaded with mother-of-pearl, and – a present from Jaz – a silver circlet that swept down on to the forehead in a point decorated with a small turquoise, like an Indian *bindi*. He placed it on her flaxen head, and stood back to admire her. She looked like a mythical warrior princess.

In the Healing Zone, Jaz was up for a session of personal growth, and Sharon stood by, amused. He was torn between two tents: an hour of reiki, practised by a descendant of Red Bull, or a shiatsu massage, given by an Aboriginal with hot stones. Finally, he chose a third tent, offering High Touch Jin Shin Acupressure, which, according to the chalkboard outside, was known as 'The Art of the Compassionate Being'.

'Hey, Shaz – it says this is a seven-thousand-year-old treatment from Japan! Cool,' he enthused.

As he allowed himself to be led by a kimono-clad healer into a bunting-covered yurt, Sharon sat down in the tent next door and let an Indian woman work intricate henna flowers up her curvy, plump arm. An hour later they emerged into the throng, Jaz with his soul realigned, and Sharon with a pattern she'd smudged into a psychiatrist's ink blot – it would take weeks to wash off.

'That was awesome,' said Jaz. 'The theoretical framework is the Chinese five-elements system – earth, metal, wood, water and fire. They correlate to the physical, mental, emotional and spiritual levels. God, I'm starving … Fancy a kebab?'

They laughed their way around the festival and back to the cosy, rug-strewn intimacy of their teepee. It was Paradise.

'How about coming with me to Bali?' asked Jaz, later that night, passing her a big spliff. 'We could get our union blessed by a Hindu priest. Be fun.' He was serious about her, and he was trying to show it. Sharon looked into his baby blue eyes, and drifted into a wedding finale daydream.

She'd ask her father to walk her down the aisle, she'd throw her bouquet to Jules D and the waiting crowds, wave to the paparazzi, and ride off with her rock star on the back of a big black Harley.

'Sure, why not? I haven't got much lined up. I could go in a couple of weeks. Just got to do a commercial for Urban Cool and a couple of shoots for Ziegfried.'

Actually, by the time she got back from La La Land and returned her booker's calls, the line-up was all the way round the corner and along three blocks: now that she was firmly linked with Jaz, she was dominating the gossip columns and showbiz rags.

The press attention was so intense, from snaps of the laughing pair in Vegas to shots of them eating burgers in the Vegan Zone – she was the golden goose who kept laying double-page spreads.

'Darling, there's nothing to fear, okay?' soothed Jules D. 'You just go on the show and chat. It's a *chat* show, okay? The man is paid a fucking fortune to make you feel relaxed. That's his job.' But it was live. No matter how Jules D dressed it up, Sharon knew she'd feel stark naked on the show.

This particular host was witty and cutting. She'd always loved watching him tease the hell out of his guests. But to be on the other side? Insecurity and terror gripped her in equal measure.

With Glacé Inc. ringing non-stop, offers from all directions were coming in fast and furious. Even emptying the rubbish became a 'Shaz Sets Style Sensation'. All she'd done was drag out a smelly black bin-liner, dressed in a tight black T-shirt, ankle-length old black skirt, bare feet, a black headscarf to hide her unwashed hair and a big pair of black sunglasses to hide the fact that she was wearing no makeup. Overnight 'The Greek Widow Look' was gracing the front pages of a dozen publications, with Sharon compared to a grieving Jackie O.

Later that week, on seeing the press coverage it had provoked,

Debbie, Jules D and Sharon howled until their giggly girly tears diluted the contents of their flutes from pink bubbly to white. The funniest comments of all were from female journalists moaning that this head-to-toe widow look slimmed figures too much, and only big women like Shaz could get away with wearing it. Accused of causing misery to any girl smaller than size twelve, Sharon was even castigated by one columnist who felt that, as a supermodel, she should take some responsibility and stop flaunting her fabulous full figure.

Whatever. The press fever meant the level of attention rose higher and higher, reflected by the increasing worth of the freebie handbags and shoes that arrived. The latest monstrosity from Pucci was a giant doctor's bag made of silver snakeskin and gold studs. The PR blurb pointed out that it cost a mere seven thousand pounds retail. Sharon boggled at the idea that any woman could be foolish enough or brainwashed enough to spend more than a couple of hundred. But she was also aware that, as a celeb, she was expected to look the part – and play her part in fuelling public envy and aspiration, resulting in designer label sales. It was a symbiotic relationship that she struggled to resist.

Her relationship with Jaz went from strength to strength. The papers seemed to adore the rhyme 'Shaz and Jaz', repeating it *ad nauseam*.

Deeply attracted to him, *she* adored the fact that he needed her. That he was mad about her was obvious from the frequent texts and emails that punctuated her days. His dependency grew. But he had a mysterious trick of disappearing faster than Houdini, only to reappear three days later as if nothing had happened. It wasn't just Sharon who got this treatment. Debbie's man, the band manager, rang Sharon regularly to find out if she knew where the hell Jaz was. It seemed he was always late for a photo shoot or missing a radio interview. If ever she managed to pass the message on to Jaz, he'd act paranoid: 'The bastard won't leave me alone. I swear to God he's having me followed. I saw this guy in black the other day, trailing behind me like a spy.'

'He might have been a fan?' suggested Sharon.

'Nah, it's someone the fucker's hired. He thinks I'm going to sign a fucking deal behind his back, arsehole.'

When Jaz stood her up – which he did regularly – poor Sharon didn't know how to handle it. Afraid to make a scene in case he thought her 'too heavy', she'd say nothing – and Jaz would fly into a furious rage because she hadn't even noticed he'd been gone. Either way, she would begin to fret that she was in a lose-lose situation.

And then he'd do something to surprise her. Take the night she finally had to appear on Nathan Boss' chat show: Jaz turned up, drove her there, and sat in the green room holding her hand. He told her time and time again how amazing, witty and clever she was, and how she'd be the perfect guest. It was the confidence and support she needed.

As it happened, he was right. As she stepped out to the studio applause and the band of singers welcoming her on to the show, she smiled. It was fun! The nerves disappeared as Nathan kissed her warmly on both cheeks and led her to the sofa.

'Would you like something to eat? An apple, maybe?' he opened, cheekily offering her the fruit bowl on the table.

The audience roared at the reference to Descent.

Sharon shook her blonde locks. 'No thanks, I ate earlier.' She glanced up at a screen that showed Jaz in the green room.

The audience roared again at the unintentional double-entendre. Sharon picked up the cue, licked her finger and winked. That was it. From then on, Nathan and the nation were putty in her paws.

By the time the floppy-haired charmer had schmoozed her off the stage, he was already begging her to come back in a few weeks.

She stepped into the green room flushed and excited. It had been an amazing high.

'Let's celebrate,' suggested Jaz, sweeping her off in the car to the West End. 'I know just the place. Do you realise we've been together exactly a month? It's perfect.'

They ended up at Waikiki's, a tackily decorated Hawaiian nightclub more renowned for young royals, Sloanes and aristocrats than rock stars. But that made it fun for Jaz. He was approached time and time again with 'Jolly well loved your last CD, ol' man,' and the two of them practically drowned in the crazy array of coconut cocktails thrust at them by all and sundry.

As they slow-danced, Sharon caught the eye of a young prince staring longingly at her. She shook her long hair and gave a throaty laugh. How had all of this happened? The Easter Head spewing steam in the tropical pool beside them had no answer. As she and Jaz shared a jungle-green concoction and pinned flowers behind each other's ears, they recalled the night they had met, in equally ridiculous tropical surroundings.

'Oh, how I miss that banana dress,' moaned Jaz, teasingly.

'You're dreaming of peeling me!' Sharon flirted back.

Later that night he teased her in a far more merciless way, and afterwards they fell asleep, content and warm in each other's arms.

Until cool air hit Sharon's bare flank.

Eighteen

Chilled, she stretched out sleepily to find Jaz's warm body. But it wasn't there. She opened one eye to see the light under the bathroom door, like the ray from a spaceship. She lay there a while, looking at the bachelor pad of a rock star. It was messy. Black walls, cans of beer, discarded T-shirts. It was reminiscent of the backstage dressing rooms he frequented.

In the kitchen, washing-up was piled on the draining-board, while cigarette butts and teabags had left brown stains on the aluminium sink. On the wall hung a giant Andy Warhol painting of Keith Richards, Jaz's ultimate hero. The bookshelves brimmed with rock 'n' roll memorabilia, and the floor was strewn with Tibetan rugs and leather pouffes.

A mess, but nothing she couldn't sort out in an afternoon, she thought. Jaz was taking quite a while, and Sharon suddenly had the urge to pee. Well, just in case he came back and wanted to have her again.

Throwing on his collarless white shirt, as she knew it gave her a sexy 'girlfriend of boyfriend' look, she padded over to the bathroom, and pressed the door handle.

'No! Not now. Just – go away,' he said, and moaned.

'Jaz? What's wrong?' She pushed the door open a little, worried he'd hurt himself, but it wouldn't budge, held in place by something spongy. Peering through the crack, she could see it was his foot. 'What's going on? Are you hurt?'

'I said, FUCK OFF! I mean it – don't come in.'

'Don't be daft!' said Sharon. Fears of something 'not right' flooded her mind. She still reeled occasionally from when she'd stood at a door and discovered her man in the middle of a gang-bang. With that image in mind, she gave the door an extra hard shove and Jaz let out an angry yowl.

Sharon stood in the doorway, looking at him sprawled on the floor. Between his legs lay a couple of plastic-topped vials and, next to them, some little cubes of beige soap. Or was it sugar? Sharon bent down to see what he was doing. That was when she noticed he was awkwardly holding his hand behind his back.

'What are you hiding?' she asked. He looked like a guilty toddler caught with a packet of sweeties. Then, suddenly, he didn't.

His face contorted into an ugly sneer. 'Aw, what the fuck? You were bound to find out soon enough. Fair cop.' He held up a glass instrument. Then Sharon saw the long lighter in his other hand. A sick feeling churned her stomach. It was drugs. *Serious* drugs.

Jaz kept flicking the little lumps across the floor, as if he was playing tiddlywinks. 'Rocks … sugar … ice … twinkie … It's called getting your rocks off. After all, baby, it's *rock 'n' roll*!' He laughed hollowly.

Sharon slumped down, her heart racing. 'It's cocaine, isn't it?'

'Crack. Crack cocaine, darlin'. The best.'

Crack? Surely that was the drug of gangsters and yardies. Quietly, in shock, she asked, 'How long have you been taking it?'

'Um … let me see … Well, I guess it's got to be pretty much full on from my first smoke … er, three or four months, I guess. Who knows?'

'We've got to get you help! You can't keep taking it. It'll kill you.'

He looked at her, bemused. Ignoring her, he lit the burner in his hand and took a hit. She felt totally out of her depth. The closest experience she'd had of drug dependency was a packet of Panadol for period pain.

She sat on the cold floor watching him, speechless. It all slowly made sense. At the beginning, feeling daring, she'd joined him in a spliff or two, and accepted that he snorted the odd line, which she had been hoping to tackle him about once they were even more 'established'. But *this*? It explained so much. His mood swings, his aggression … and even the weird little burn marks on his fingers that he had joked were down to him being a lousy cook.

It scared her so much. This abuse was way out of control. As the drug hit his brain, Jaz laid his head against the toilet and closed his eyes. He had gone somewhere else.

A minute later, Sharon decided she had to do the same. And left.

This time it hurt. It really hurt. Sharon went into her own depression. Not even the chocolate doughnuts or crispy croissants from Jules D could lift the dank despair. It was tinged with the awful urge to 'do' something about it. To help him in any way she could, even though she had read enough articles to know 'addicts have to help themselves'.

Debbie was deeply worried for Sharon, and rang her from Jaz's manager's pad three or four times a day.

Jules D was already working on a damage limitation break-up story, even though Sharon had told her she was going to stand by him.

As for Jaz, he was silent for two whole mysterious days. Then he started emailing, texting and ringing every hour, on the hour. Sharon took his first call, and asked him if he would get help. He agreed. In his next call he said he'd changed his mind, and told her to fuck off. In the third, he cried for forgiveness. In the fourth, he begged her to come over. In the fifth, he swore at her because she hadn't come, and called her a whore. As for the sixth, she hung up the second she heard his voice.

'He's so, so lost. Like a little boy. I can't abandon him, can I?' sobbed Sharon, to Jules D and Debbie. They just looked at each other helplessly, with pity in their eyes.

Sharon found herself in Hell. Loving, talented and fun, the man was like a drug himself. They were both famous, both successful. Mutual experiences and low self-esteem bound them to each other tighter than an addict's tourniquet. Oh, God, he was *her* crack cocaine! Sharon hugged herself to sleep in a foetal position of anguish. And indeed he was. Her moods would alter, like a condor's flight through a canyon – up and down, up and down, riding the very air he breathed. He could change the current in a flash of crack: one moment she was soaring high, only to be sucked back into the deep abyss of despair. Sharon tried to focus on work, but found she was sleepwalking through important castings and forgetting to return calls.

Her head told her to get out now before she got too involved. But instead she spent hours scouring the Internet, trying to find out the success rate for coming off crack. It didn't look good. Apparently it was 'harder to crack than heroin'. Maybe that was why they called it crack, she thought miserably.

He went silent again for another two days. When the phone rang at one a.m. and she heard Jaz crying and pleading with her to pick up the phone, she had no choice. He sounded so desperate. Completely out of it.

'Babe … oh, God, I need you. Please, please, come and get me. I – I love you. God, I love you so much. I can't do without you. Please, I'll give it all up, I promise. Just come and get me.' She knew she had to go. She tried to work out the rambling address he'd given her on the street map as Debbie drove her down Hackney High Road. His manager wanted to collect him, but Jaz had *insisted* he stayed away.

It was down to Sharon to go – with Debbie for moral support.

'I'm going to stick by him,' announced Sharon, as her friend screeched round the corners, like a demented bat. 'No one else ever has, and I'm going to show him I will.' Her resolve was strengthened by the fact he had used the love-word for the first time. Admittedly, it hadn't been in quite the Mills & Boon setting she had hoped for, but he obviously cared. The hard fact was that she'd missed him badly – and, needing her own fix, couldn't wait to see him again. But now the two girls were terrified. Following his garbled instructions, they found that the streets got more and more deserted, and the area shabby and destitute.

'Oh, God, it's here.' They looked at each other, wide-eyed and fearful. The wet street shone in the nicotine-yellow lamplight. Iron staircases and soggy cardboard boxes slumped against graffitied brick walls. A drunken tramp eyed them suspiciously as they got out of the car – Debbie ridiculous in a pair of red Manolo stilettos, Sharon ready to run in a pair of old trainers.

Sharon pressed the dirty buzzer. No one answered. But the latch on the door was broken, so they pushed it open and walked up the concrete stairs. The smell of urine and vomit assaulted their nostrils. A pile of soiled nappies lay on the landing, while the staircases were littered with used condoms and a scattering of syringes. They picked their way up to the second floor and walked into Flat 2B.

There must have been about seven people lying around the squalid room. A couple were holding a lighter flame under a spoon as they sat on a springless sofa, so badly stained it was more brown than its original orange. As it was dark it was hard to tell if the shapes in the room were all people: two or three were so skeletal they looked like a pile of discarded clothes.

'Babe, you made it,' croaked a voice from a corner. And there he was, dazed and smiling, like Dopey in *Snow White*. The kitchen door opened and a tattooed Korean in combat gear emerged with a thick-set African heavy in tow.

'Hey, bitch, who the hell let you in here?' said the Korean, pulling out a knife.

'Cool it, man. She's my girl,' said Jaz, proudly, as if he was introducing Sharon to the in-laws. He staggered to his feet, like Bambi on ice. Indeed, as he stood up, Sharon could see he clearly was 'on ice'. And something else, even worse. A syringe slipped off his lap and clattered to the filthy floor. Disney? This was pure Tarantino.

'My God! Jaz! What have you been doing to yourself?'

'He's been havin' a fun time with the Cotton Brothers,' laughed the African guy. 'Dynamite, man – like you, Shaz.'

Sharon felt sick just to hear him say her name. That was the real price of household fame.

'Have you got any cash?' asked Jaz, lamely. 'My friends want me to give them some.'

Stricken, the girls looked at each other. The Korean walked over and put his grubby finger under Sharon's chin. He tilted it up to his pockmarked face and smiled. A whoosh of foul breath escaped his blackened, rotting teeth. 'Your boy's been criss-crossing the line, ladies, and owes us a ton,' he hissed, like a snake.

'Criss-crossing?' repeated Sharon, confused.

'He's a regular speedball artist. Hey, Jaz – you been keeping secrets from your lady? How'd you 'spect to form a relationship?' He snorted with laughter, and ran his eye over Sharon's body. 'Hey, you're that fuckin' fancy model, aren't you? Jackson, where's your manners, man? The least we can do is explain to the lovely lady …' He turned and slapped the African guy on the back; he joined in the fun. Like a teacher with a pupil, he spelled out the facts.

'Okay, baby, lesson one. You've just busted into a one and one.

That means a house that serves its honoured guests heroin *and* crack.

'Lesson two. Your boy here likes both. It's called speedballing.'

'He's injecting *heroin*?' Sharon gasped, desperate to be told she was making a big mistake.

'That's right, sweet cheeks. The candy brings you up, and the smack mellows you out. Up and down ... quite a ride. Ever tried?'

'Inject, smoke, smoke, inject, what the hell?' groaned Jaz, groggily. 'Shaz, please just give the man the fuckin' dosh.'

Sharon looked at her boyfriend, his lank, greasy hair, vomit-soiled clothes, the cesspit surroundings, the paraphernalia of death. She helped him to his feet and handed her bag to the Korean.

'Hey, what the fuck's this shit? I want money. Two hundred quid. *Now.*'

'That's worth seven grand,' she replied coldly. 'I'm sure you'll get ten times what he owes you on the black market.'

The men grinned in delight.

'Nice doin' business with you, honey. Fancy a takeaway?' asked the Korean, offering her a grimy cellophane packet. 'It's on the house.' They cackled like a pair of happy hyenas as they held up her bag to the single bare light bulb, to check out its designer label.

Dragging Jaz between them, the girls staggered down the fetid stairwell and into the cool night air. The putrid smell continued to fill their nostrils as Sharon shoved Jaz into the back seat. The stench of his vomit and shit killed any hope of a future relationship. To be hooked on crack was a living nightmare. To be hooked on heroin was the road to hell. But to be hooked on both? Rehab was a daydream. The man was too far gone ever to make it home.

He knew it. And she knew it.

Nineteen

She'd asked her father to walk her down the aisle; she'd thrown her bouquet to Jules D and the waiting crowds, waved to the paparazzi and ridden off with her rock star on the back of a big black Harley. Then there was the scream of police sirens. They were pulled over by the cops, and strip-searched.

It was a strange phenomenon. With every downturn of her love life, the higher her working life soared. As the tabloids spluttered with speculation about the demise of 'Shaz and Jaz', the invitations and offers kept tumbling in.

The shoot for Urban Cool took two days in Manchester. The buzz of a new city and the glamour of the impossibly trendy shoot, full of incredibly beautiful people, cleared her mind of the fetid scenes she'd witnessed. She returned to her London flat exhausted and found messages from Debbie. Jaz had booked into the Priory. But Sharon felt leaden. With such a cocktail of addiction, she knew the odds of him staying the course were less than a one-legged mule winning the Grand National. Make that a blind one-legged mule. No, a blind, pregnant one-legged mule with attitude. She turned her attention to the letters and emails that were pouring in.

One amused her more than most. It was a plea from a student at Central St Martins College of Art and Design who had sent Sharon illustrations and photos of her end-of-year collection – a cute range of clothes with an iconic cowboy theme. The student begged Sharon to design her own bag to accessorise the show.

She was flattered. What the hell did she know about design? But then, glancing at some of the freebie monstrosities piled in the corner of the living room, she smiled mischievously. A couple of bags had even come with matching purses full of money – not-so-subtle bribes for her to wear them. No question, the whole celebrity bag thing had been created to fool the public into parting with huge sums of money. And to think that she had once been on the other side, envying the women who could afford such luxuries! Luxuries that probably only cost a hundredth of their retail price to make. Suddenly she felt like mooning the designers. The 'buttock' bag! That's what I want to make. She studied her behind in the mirror. Two very large creamy globes, with deep dimples at the small of her back.

She scrawled her design on a piece of paper, and posted it back to the student.

Five days later, with a letter asking for her approval, Sharon opened a parcel and pulled out a soft, supple leather bag in the rounded W shape of a curvaceous bottom. It was a peachy tan suede with two stitched circles at the top where she'd made the dimple marks. The long adjustable strap meant you could wear it across your body or on your arm. It reminded her of a well-worn saddlebag and smelt deliciously of saddle soap. She *loved* it. A handmade one-off, it looked amazing, and she wore it out that night with a pair of riding boots and an Australian bush hat. By morning, it was in every paper.

SHAZ GIVES JAZ THE BUM'S RUSH!
BOTTOMS UP SHAZ!
BUTTOCK BAG GIVES STUDENT LEG-UP

and so on …

With the Tent Dress, the Tattered Look and the Greek Widow fad still all the rage, the addition of the Buttock Bag prompted a surprise request through Glacé Inc. for lunch with Michael Grey, the entrepreneur behind Bessie B's, a chain found in every British high street.

'The thing is, Shaz,' he said, pouring her a third glass of Château Latour, 'you've got that undeniable It thing going. Kids love you. They want to be you. I'd like to bottle it.'

Sharon wasn't sure where he was going with this, but as he waffled on, she tucked heartily into her Scottish fillet steak on nutmeg mash and caramelised shallots. With all the stress over Jaz, she hadn't eaten for a few hours, and now she was making up for it with gusto. By the time she'd finished her maple syrup and clotted cream tart and polished off coffee and petits eights, the smooth talker had produced a contract for her to 'think about'.

She eyed it curiously. It was the offer of a range of clothes bearing *her* name. It seemed so simple. All she had to do was give the designs the 'once- over' and agree to model the collections four times a year. The amount for this 'exclusive designing' was awesome. The repetitive zeros on the last line looked like his PA had got her fingernail stuck in the keyboard.

'But I've got to be honest, Mr Grey. I'm just a model. I know nothing about design.'

'What about your Buttock Bag?'

'That was a joke! The student wanted something to focus press attention on her show. A one-off. I had no idea it would look so good.'

'A joke, eh? You cheeky, *cheeky* girl!' He snorted, even more pleased with his own. 'I think you underestimate yourself, young lady. Anyway, design, schmesign! Who cares? It's how you wear the

226

clothes that counts, Shaz. It's what you stand for. Just a model? So sweet.'

'Don't you worry your pretty little head. We'll do all the hard work.' Then he winked conspiratorially. 'All I want you to do is tell us your favourite looks *before* you get photographed in them, that sort of thing. Keep us ahead of the game, y'know.'

Actually, Sharon didn't know. She hadn't a clue. How the hell could she have guessed the ripped dress would cause such a storm? Or the back-of-the-wardrobe pile of black crap she'd worn to take out the rubbish? But she nodded back with a confidential wink of her stunning, long-lashed green eye, and the steel heart of Mr Grey turned molten. The deal was done.

Later, as she was sitting at an outside table in Soho's Bar Italia, telling Debbie and Jules D about the meeting, she realised what good friends they'd all become. Laughter tinkled in the air, as Jules joshed Debbie for having a fruit salad instead of a Danish pastry. 'Darling girl, you've been doing so well! Don't weaken. You're going to fade back into a size eight or something. Sharon, the girl has *no* willpower to eat. And I envy her!'

'I am what I am. I've always been slim,' smiled Debbie, 'and luckily my man likes it that way.'

Jules D eyed her fruit salad enviously. 'Mmm, that pineapple looks good. I really fancy the fresh taste ... Can I just have a spoonful? Just a teensy one?'

'Anyway, Debs, how's it going with ... er ... ?' Sharon was embarrassed that she didn't even know the name of Debbie's manager boyfriend. She'd only known him as 'that bastard' or 'the fucker', thanks to Jaz's paranoia.

'His name is Jack Delany,' said Debbie, hurt.

Sharon apologised, with a quip about early-onset Alzheimer's, but she caught a look from Jules D that warned her she was falling into the celebrity trap of self-absorption. It was an easy thing to do. As a celeb, everybody asked about *you* all the time. How do you feel? What do you think? What are you doing next? And the awful truth was that when your life was more colourful than an opium butterfly everyone else's news was pretty mundane in comparison. Generally speaking, the barbecue at the brother-in-law's or the boss's bad habits didn't make for natural conversation after questions about dating movie stars or filming in Hollywood. It was easier for the famous not to ask. And once they stopped taking an interest in others, the more self-centred they became – and the more the world revolved around their brilliant, shining sun. But Sharon knew that was wrong.

Besides, she did care about Debbie, and she was keen to hear (now she had time) what was going on.

'Well, the biggest news is that he's asked me to meet his parents!' The girls squealed in delight for her. It was so un-rock-'n'-roll it was hysterical, and they fell about, imagining his folks were either going to be like Sharon and Ozzy Osbourne, or the Waltons.

Then Debbie went quiet. 'The other news is … not good. And I don't know how to tell you this, Sharon.'

Sharon indicated that she should go on.

'I'm so sorry, but Jack told me that Jaz has done a bunk. He's disappeared from the Priory. It'll probably be in the papers by tomorrow, if they can't find him.'

Sharon's shoulders slumped. She'd known this would happen, but, even so, when he'd entered the rehab clinic he'd lit a tiny matchstick of hope in her; a small glimmering flame that, against all the odds, just maybe he'd stick it out. Clean up his act. With this latest news, the flame blew out – the dark trail left behind symbolic of their relationship finally going up in smoke.

'There is ab-so-lute-ly nothing you can do for him, okay? It's his journey. Rock 'n' roll is all very well, darling, but let's be frank –

you don't want to be seen hanging around with a junkie,' said Jules D, with stark honesty.

Sharon winced at the word 'junkie', but knew its truth.

Jules took a sip of strong coffee, and continued, 'You could lose contracts worth millions – he could just drag you down. I'm not sure I could even stop Z&ZaK from cancelling. I mean, it's not like you're in too deep. Get out now. Onward and upward, okay?' Finishing her speech, she patted Sharon's hand in comfort.

'Anyway, changing the subject before you can cry, this'll bring a smile to your gorgeous face …' She handed Sharon an envelope. As she pulled out a thick invitation, crystals spilled over the table like tiny tears.

Seeing Sharon's sadness, Jules D snatched it from her. 'Right, listen to this. You're invited to the Crystal Ball Gala! Hollywood's biggest charity do. Glamour! Film Stars! Directors! Producers! Everybody will be there – and get *this*. You're not just going as a guest, you're going as a prize in the charity auction!'

'I'm going as a *what*?' said Sharon, choking on her éclair. 'The prize, darling.'

'The prize is a kiss from *you*!' Debbie interrupted. 'Jules said you had the option of a kiss or a date, and I figured a kiss was safer. God knows who might end up boring you all night otherwise. I thought you'd prefer just giving a kiss.'

'Guys, how do you know I'd prefer doing *anything*? You should have *asked* me first.'

Jules D looked affronted. 'But I know your diary, you're free, and it's going to be such FUN. Besides, it's for a good cause.'

'Yes, think of the charity! Hands Across America or something!' interrupted Debbie, again.

'No, it's Reaching Home,' corrected Jules D. 'Helping runaway kids call home. The ball is always amazing, darling – biggest event of the year. It's so fab that even I can't wait!'

'Well, I'm glad you two are so excited, while I get auctioned off like some kind of fat cow.'

They looked at her, startled. 'What's the matter? What's wrong?' 'I just don't want to do it, okay? You should have asked me first.'

The three fell silent. Jules D signalled to the waiter to bring another round of drinks. 'Darling, what's wrong? Explain the problem.'

Sharon looked pained. 'Have either of you considered the hideously embarrassing possibility that nobody will bid for me?'

Now they looked at her as if she was totally insane.

'You are kidding us, aren't you?' said Jules D, puzzled.

Sharon wasn't. Beneath the veneer of success, her childlike insecurity meant that a part of her still believed she was plain old Sharon Plunkett, from Accounts.

'For a top model, you sometimes say the stupidest things,' said Debbie, as if she was stating the obvious.

'Now, your dress,' continued Jules D, dismissing Sharon's fears as clearly the ramblings of a mad woman. 'Ziegfried has told me he's going to create something utterly sensational just for you – he wants you to be the belle of the ball. Which isn't easy, considering we're talking Hollywood and mega-competition.'

'Let me guess, this is all happening because another of your clients is organising the event?' said Sharon, relaxing a little, their enthusiasm allaying her doubts.

'Naturally,' said Jules D, shamelessly, as if insulted it should be any other way.

'Your network web would shame a Black Widow!' laughed Sharon, her mood lifting. 'Okay, when do we leave?'

The days leading up to the ball were pretty busy. Sharon signed the contract on a chi-chi little mews house in Chelsea and, to the delight of Glacé Inc., concentrated on her castings and bookings.

For a girl who once thought the height of travel was a ride on a Ferris wheel, she was rarely off a plane. Now that Debbie was working full time as her PA, the trips were far more fun than they had been when she was travelling on her own, and the whirl around her continued to swirl.

The papers broke the story of Jaz, who had been found comatose in a gutter by a prostitute. Everyone sympathised with Shaz, and totally understood why she had walked. Now that it was clear the relationship was over and she was exonerated, she even had the courage to call Simon (though painfully aware she was publicly in 'break up' mode again). He said nothing about Jaz, instead, he just invited her for a drink at the Pissed Piggy, a cosy pub that served good food and real beer, and had a roaring fire lit nearly all year round. Sharon turned up in black, straight jeans, crisp shirt, waistcoat, and deliberately put on pointed boots, which she knew added a few pounds to her thighs.

Simon looked as cool as ever: straight, sandy hair flopping over his eyes, black leather jacket, soft, faded blue jeans. As always, she felt immediately comfortable with him. They took seats by the fire, and sat chatting about the ridiculous Vegas wedding, his trip to LA, her commercials and adverts. But any discussion that could lead to their love-lives was pointedly avoided.

'Well, well, well! Is that the famous Buttock Bag?' He'd noticed it hanging on the back of her chair after they'd downed a couple more drinks. 'Can I stroke it?'

Sharon offered it to him, smiling in the flickering light, her hair a pinky red in the glow – which was a good thing, as she knew she was blushing scarlet.

As he ran his hands over the suede, he looked at her, his eyes narrowing. They fell silent – shocked as they suddenly imagined him doing it to the real thing. Sharon felt her stomach contract, and her throat go dry. She stared at the perfect shape of his lips, and couldn't speak.

'Why did you go off with him?' asked Simon, huskily.

Sharon didn't know what to say, gulping back her spritzer to buy time. 'I was flattered. He was – he was so keen.' She carefully avoided adding 'and gorgeous'.

'And world famous.' Simon sighed.

'Well, there was that.' Sharon broke into a grin. They both started to laugh, then pushed and prodded each other, teasing.

'Fame hag!' Simon jeered.

'Better than being a worthy drag!' Sharon threw back.

The evening was fantastic. A night full of banter and fun. But Sharon noticed he was acting like a big brother or a great mate. Slinging his arm around her shoulders, he insisted on buying her dinner, but was not intimate again – the intense moment with the Buttock Bag had been a one-off.

It also worried her that when they talked about her success he spoke as if she was somehow out of his league. What could she say to counteract that without sounding conceited? The words never came, and when he dropped her off and kissed her cheek, she felt at a loss.

The other important phone call she made was to her father. He had left a message way back saying he wanted her to ring, but every time she'd called, she'd either got the answerphone or Carolyn saying he was asleep. She decided to drive down to Bournemouth and tried one more call to say she was coming.

'Hello, can I speak to–'

'I'll get your father,' Carolyn said, colder than the Ice Queen.

'Hello, darling,' said her dad, in his whispery old man's voice. 'I hear you're doing well. As your agent, where's my cut? I only want 80 per cent – I'm not greedy,' he jested, voice fading with the effort. It had been their long-standing joke ever since she'd started her ten-pounds-a-day Saturday job in the hair salon.

'Cheque's in the post, Dad,' she joked back, knowing he was probably unaware she had a real agent, who was now getting thousands.

'Darling, I hate to mention this, but I didn't get the keys to the new Ferrari – the post's been really bad. Best to bring the cheque down with you.'

He seemed on form, and Sharon smiled, pleased he'd mentioned her coming to Bournemouth. 'That's what I was ringing about. Thought I'd pop down this weekend.'

'Okay.' Big pause. 'Just a minute. I'd better check with Carolyn.' She heard him put his hand over the receiver. 'Carolyn, can Sharon come down this weekend?' Sharon hated the way he always had to ask her stepmother if he could see his daughter. It was his right, as her father.

'No, Joe. We've got my family coming, remember?'

'When did you organise that?'

'Well, I was going to do it this afternoon.'

Sharon bristled, knowing her dad didn't realise she could hear.

'Hello, darling, it's a little difficult this weekend, though I'd love to see you.'

'Right. I'm coming *now*,' said Sharon. 'I'll see you in a couple of hours.'

'Oh, lovely,' said her father, a little confused, but obviously delighted he would see his daughter so soon.

Alas, the traffic down to Bournemouth was appalling. The weather had turned nasty and rain made the visibility almost nil. Exacerbated by road works, jams from the Southampton junction onwards made progress excruciatingly slow. As hailstones bounced off her new silver BMW (on loan via a client of Jules D), she wondered what her father would make of her success. Her mother had always made him proud. Now maybe she would.

Five hours later, she was in tears. The road had seized up tighter than a rusty lid of homemade pickles, and her car was sandwiched between lanes with no way off. She rang her dad to apologise.

'Don't worry, darling. I can't wait to see you. I'll wait up.'

But by the time she walked up to the door of her father's crumbling Victorian house she was drained, hungry and tired, and it was nearly nine o'clock in the evening. Carolyn's sour face as she opened the door made Sharon's heart plummet.

'Hi, Dad,' she called brightly, seeing a shape coming up behind her stepmother.

Her father hobbled towards the door, leaning heavily on his brass dog-head walking stick. Sharon was shocked by how frail and skinny he had become since she had last seen him, but was careful to hide her reaction.

'Darling, I've been so worried about you. I thought you were coming straight down,' he said.

'Oh, God, Dad. You wouldn't believe the traffic. Horrendous. I got here as fast as I could.'

'Well, that's strange,' said her father. 'Carolyn told me her friend drove down this afternoon and the roads were clear. No problems.'

What? Sharon felt her temper flare and fought to control her tongue. Oh, there were problems, all right: Carolyn was up to her usual manipulative mind games. More lies to make Sharon out to be the 'bad daughter'. 'Dad, believe me – I've just spent hours in a bloody awful traffic jam down the A3. It got even worse after Ringwood. I tried every single side road to get down here but they were all blocked.'

'That's so odd. Carolyn …' He turned to her. But she had disappeared.

'So, Dad, what's been happening?' asked Sharon, a little later. They were sitting at the kitchen table and chatting as Carolyn placed some cold meat in front of them.

'I'm sure it's not as good as the kind of food you're used to having now you're a "famous" model – but then, if you're exposing so much of your flesh to the public, I suppose you need to eat more.'

Ah, thought Sharon – the predictable bitchy dig. She refused to rise to the bait. Instead, she gently questioned her father. It wasn't long before he reluctantly confessed he'd been booked in for some serious tests. He was losing weight. He didn't know why. Worried, Sharon gave him a hug, and was appalled to discover he was skin and bone. Where was the man who used to pick her up and toss her into the air?

She had hoped they would retire to the antique-stuffed living room for a cosy bedtime drink, but instead her father apologised. 'Darling, I'm so tired, do you mind if I go to bed?' he asked, and gave her a kiss on the forehead. 'I believe Carolyn's got the room made up for you.' Sharon turned to his wife and saw a wicked glint in her eye.

'Joe, I really don't want to touch the guest bedroom as I'll have to do it all over again when the family arrive. I've put a camp bed up in the office.'

Sharon knew it was a deliberate snub and her father was either too gutless to counter it or too insensitive to see it. Either way, he said nothing and tottered off towards his own room. Smug with her little victory, Carolyn led Sharon past the pretty pink guest room to the cold office. In it, next to the filing cabinet, was a single camp bed on iron pull-out legs.

Later, she tried to convince herself that her father was simply too naïve to see through his wife's clever little games. She remembered the first time he'd brought Carolyn and her children home. Haughty, high-cheekboned and heavily made-up, she had looked like the wicked stepmother from a Disney movie.

Nevertheless, it had started so well. Originally her new-mother-to-be had been a paragon of kindness, fussing over her and her own two girls, doing motherly things like taking them shopping together. Sharon remembered the time Carolyn had offered to style her hair. The flick fringe did nothing for her, but she had agreed happily to it – behaving like a puppy seeking praise and affection. With her own mother gone, she had felt so alone and abandoned and had badly wanted Carolyn to love her.

She knew her father was keen to make a new family home for everyone, especially his precious child – he had told her so. And what did he do? He got engaged within six months, and married within a year. But the day he had put the ring on Carolyn's finger, he had unwittingly tied a rope around Sharon's neck. Secure in the marriage, Carolyn swiftly revealed her true colours. And they were all darker than black.

Sharon shuddered. She called that period the Change. The atmosphere in the house had altered dramatically. Her stepmother's sudden coldness towards her, coupled with a truly vicious temper, was a shock. Feeling there must be something deeply unlovable about herself, Sharon had tried everything to win her over. She'd even agonised for days about how to give her a Mother's Day card that meant something but wouldn't betray the memory of her own mother. Eventually she settled on 'Dear Ma' because she thought it would show Carolyn that she cared and wanted to be loved as a daughter. She had fervently hoped the woman would show her some warmth.

Excited, Sharon remembered how she had come into their bedroom that morning and tentatively placed the card on the silk eiderdown. Carolyn had picked it up with her daughters' cards. But Sharon had made a terrible mistake: when her stepmother had read it, she had frowned, torn up the card and shouted at her for calling her 'Ma' – it was 'common', she spat. Her name was 'Carolyn'. And that was what she wanted to be called.

As Sharon had lain sobbing, clutching her pillow like a lifebelt, her father had stroked her hair and confided something that only made the matter worse. His new wife had confessed after their first date that her dream was to be with him and her own daughters on a desert island. Foolishly he had thought this information would help. He told his little girl it wasn't her fault: she had never been included in Carolyn's picture, and therefore she shouldn't take the rejection personally. But she was only twelve. Too young to understand. How could she? She felt more unwanted than ever. The feeling had stayed with her ever since …

It was turning into a bad night. Sharon tossed and turned, plumping up the thin pillow as best she could. But the memories were hard to blot out.

When she was fourteen, Uncle Albert, a lovely man who'd been her dad's friend for years, had taken her aside one day. It seemed the real trouble was clear to all of her father's old friends who had watched sadly from the sidelines. 'Listen, little one, you have to be grown-up and try to understand. Your father's wife is more insecure than a tin-pot dictator.'

Sharon had asked him to explain.

'Your dad adored your mum. Let's face it, she was a very special lady, a hard act for anyone to follow, and Carolyn is only too aware of that.'

Sharon recalled how Albert looked around him nervously, knowing he was speaking out of turn. 'Please, go on,' she had begged, keen to understand what she was doing wrong.

'Your only fault is you look like your mother. She's jealous, Sharon. Jealous of Joe's love for your mother. I know your dad well, and I don't think he's ever got over her. Carolyn knows this, of course. She knows she can never compete. The whole of Bournemouth knows it. Unfortunately for you, little one, you're the spitting image of your mother. I think it's driving the woman mad.'

Uncle Albert was right. Carolyn took it out on her with a vicious temper that would flare over the slightest thing. Leave a jumper on the chintz sofa, drop a spoon on the wooden floor – Sharon learned to walk on eggshells, but often missed her step simply through nerves. Every time, the result was a shattering telling-off.

The bedsprings dug into her shoulder-blades, like blunt knives. But they were not as sharp as the pain she felt as she allowed herself to remember the past.

And the grand finale had been Carolyn's giving away Beau, Sharon's little dog. Sharon had been on a school trip, and had returned to find him gone. No warning, no words. Beau had been her companion since she was seven, the only tie left to her past family life. She had cuddled him when her mother died and he had licked away her tears. She still missed him.

With Beau gone, and her older stepsisters determined to make her feel like an outsider, life for Sharon became a living hell. It was compounded two years later when Carolyn triumphantly announced she was pregnant and threw Sharon out as soon as she turned sixteen.

The memory of those days caused a night of pain far deeper than the cold metal of the hard camp bed.

The next morning Sharon rose stiffly at eight o'clock, and left for London.

Twenty

A week later, Sharon, Jules D and Debbie stretched out on the green and white striped lounge chairs and felt the Californian sun warming their skin.

'Be careful, darlings – I think we might end up getting a tan. So unflattering.' Jules D clicked her fingers to summon a pool boy, and in seconds, a white canopy was erected to protect them from the rays.

Sharon sat up. 'Oh, come on, Jules, that's hardly necessary. It's September!'

The weather was sunny, but the air whispered with a cool breeze, and the three women couldn't resist lounging around and posing like movie stars. With its azure blue pool, sculpted bushes and towering palm trees set majestically against the walls, the art-deco beauty of the Beverly Hills Hotel – known locally as the Pink Palace – was breathtaking. Even its evocative location on Sunset Boulevard was a thrill. Since the 1930s it had been the scene of a thousand stills, films and commercials. Set amid twelve acres of lush tropical gardens, it was in this setting that Gregory Peck had wooed Lauren Bacall, the original Brat Pack had played cards, and Gloria Swanson had swanned around.

Now Sharon and her team were there; dolled-up in dark glasses, scarves and floppy hats, sipping cocktails and eating canapés in the same holy spot, like pilgrims paying homage to a bygone age of glamour.

Debbie sounded like a stuck thirties record: 'I can't believe we're here. I can't believe we're here. Really, I can't believe we're here.' The mantra was finally broken: '*Looooook!*'

A famous power couple, often hailed as Hollywood royalty, were taking seats on the other side of the pool. The man stopped to invite some obviously big players to join them, while his much younger wife dropped her peach chiffon beach robe.

'Mmm – since the last baby, she's managed to keep the extra pounds,' muttered Jules D, jealously.

The dark-haired beauty flaunted the tiniest bikini, her body no doubt stretched, plumped and honed by personal trainers 24/7.

As one, all three glanced down self-consciously at themselves to see how they measured up next to the female star.

Debbie had chosen a green fat-striped tankini, desperate to look bigger. Alarmingly, it seemed to match the lounger. Did she look like the staff? Or, worse, like a long skinny peppermint? She panicked and hid her body with a thick towelling robe.

Jules D, on the other hand, looked full and fab for her age. She knew it, and had the confidence to stop comparing.

As for Sharon, she was wearing a white cut-away swimsuit with a pearlescent sheen. She noticed when she stood up that the man's eyes strayed in her direction. Amused, Sharon deliberately stretched her hands above her head in a sensual yawn, shook her long platinum hair loose from her headscarf, and combed her fingers through it.

Every man around the pool swivelled to stare. Her rounded belly curved outwards like a beautiful full moon, her magnificent breasts two perfect orbs that rested in its orbit. Jules D just sat back, smiling at the effect she knew her protégée was having on the producers and directors dotted around the sundeck.

Tonight, she suspected, the effect would be even better.

'"All expenses paid". How I love that expression!' laughed Sharon, dancing round the luxurious living room of her suite.

She'd just returned from the hotel spa after a pedicure, manicure and full body massage with enough free products to launch her own salon. Jules D was sipping champagne by the fireplace, and Debbie was tinkling 'Chopsticks' on the white baby grand piano. The textures and furnishings of the surroundings were in distinct Beverly Hills accents of greens, pinks, apricots and yellows, all elegantly subdued into a palette that splashed the word 'success' across every wall. A pink Grecian marble and Italian granite bathroom completed the picture of the deluxe suite.

'What time did you say the hair *artiste* is due to arrive?' giggled Sharon, emphasising the pretentiousness of his LA title with glee.

'Just after the makeup *artiste* – and before the nail *artiste*!' laughed Jules, replacing the bottle in the ice bucket.

'Is that before or after the doing-up-the-zip *artiste*?' shrieked Debbie, mincing around the room like a camp stylist. She was planning to wear a loose white empire-line gown that did much to hide her lack of curves, while Jules D had opted for a classic Dior satin crossover in ice blue. This time the bling was on full beam. They draped and dripped themselves in as much crystal and diamond glitter as a woman could take. Which, actually, was quite a lot.

'Diamonds are my New Best Friend,' trilled Sharon, in a breathy Monroe voice, admiring a delicate diamond ring sent over by Tiffany's. As for her rule about not wearing anything she couldn't afford, well, now she could. And she slipped it on to her finger. 'Did you know that in Japan models are sacked by agencies if the rings on their fingers slip off?' she asked her friends.

'What the hell are you talking about?' asked Debbie.

'Honestly,' said Sharon. 'I met this model at Fashion Week who'd just got back from a stint out there. She told me they're all given rings by the agency when they arrive. If they make the sinful mistake of losing weight, it shows by the looseness of the ring. The girl is dropped.'

'That's tough on the young kids,' commented Jules.

'It's the most depressing thing I've heard,' sighed Debbie. 'If it were me, I'd go straight out and find a friendly jeweller for regular resizing.'

Waiting for her dress to arrive from Z&ZaK, Sharon was padding around the room in a thick terry-towelling robe and slippers, holding a martini like a fifties starlet. Nervous of the evening ahead, she jumped subjects like a cat on a hot tin roof.

'Oh, wow! It says Monroe stayed here many times too!' she said, flicking through the room information folder.

'Which room? One like this? Or even this one, maybe? Is it this one? Tell us!' demanded Debbie, star-struck as ever.

'Apparently one of the bungalows,' replied Sharon, nose buried in the *History of the Hotel* leaflet. 'Oh, and get this! Marlene Dietrich too! She walked into the Polo Lounge in slacks and got them to change the rules about women having to wear skirts. What a woman.'

Engrossed in the conversation, all three jumped when someone knocked at the door. In walked a bellboy pulling an elegant thirties trolley from which hung a covered ballgown.

'Delivery from Z&ZaK for Miss Plunkett,' he announced theatrically.

Crowding around, the girls saw there were two dresses. The first was white velvet and chiffon, with a slim white velvet shawl. It was exquisitely elegant. Straight, low-cut and Grecian in style. The second was protected by cellophane. They carefully peeled it off, and gasped.

*

Snow fell gently from the sky and settled like soft icing on the white magnolia trees and marble statues of the Crystal Garden. Only in Hollywood could it snow at that time of year. Nothing, of course, to do with freak weather, just the special-effects machine making real snowflakes from its hidden spot on the hotel roof.

No question, the illustrious Crystal Ballroom in the Beverly Hills Hotel was the perfect place to hold the Crystal Ball. For this auspicious, eight-thousand-dollars-a-ticket occasion, the hotel had even agreed to paint the apricot ballroom a cool winter white. White church candles glowed from silver candlesticks on every table and in every corner. The massive chandeliers overhead added a frosted glow, as did the magnificent white velvet drapes and glass icicles dripping from the pelmets. Outside, a thousand tea-light lanterns lit up the bushes and flowers in the scented gardens, sending silvery rays through the fallen snow.

On every table, giant arrays of white crystallised branches were set in sculpted ice blocks and hung with sugared almonds. Dainty gypsophila garlanded the tablecloths, and the centre was further adorned with lilies, their stamens carefully removed and supplanted with swaying crystals. The table settings gleamed with the finest silver cutlery, embellished with Venetian crystal napkin rings threaded with glazed snowdrops.

As a final touch, all the tabletops were scattered with Swarovski crystals, which caught and reflected the light like tiny twinkling stars. It was as if the Snow Queen had waved her frosty wand and turned the land into Narnia. It was a scene so full of fairy magic that you'd only ever find it in a child's dreams. Or, of course, in a Disney movie.

The place was packed. Everyone who was anyone, and anyone who thought they were someone, was there.

Looking divine in her white Grecian gown, Sharon sashayed

through the throng like an Athenian statue that had climbed down from the Acropolis to walk amid the mortals. As she mingled with the guests, famous movie actresses glided around her, like swans on a lake – large, languid and serene. Most gowns were body-con, suggestively revealing, designed to show every capacious curve and catch the eye of a top producer.

Sharon noticed the male actors seemed bigger than she'd expected, taller and heavier built – they had to be, to match the glorious race of Amazons on celluloid.

Quelling any feeling of intimidation with a creamy Snowball cocktail, she took her place near Jules D at a table for ten, while Debbie was assigned organisational duties off-stage. The charity the ball supported had been highly fashionable since a powerful director's child had run away from home, and many famous faces were present. Sharon sent secret nods and winks to Jules D every time she spotted another star. At her own table, she watched Maria hold court. Once she had been the undoubted queen of pop, and Sharon remembered her from a different world. She still looked amazing for her age. But all trace of her past hardness had gone. As she moved her arms expressively, her beautiful bingo wings flapped like delicate butterflies, and the fullness of her face made her seem kind and gentle. Very like the Virgin, in fact. Beside her sat hospital soap star turned matinée idol George Spencer, more handsome in real life, more suave and sophisticated than photographs of him ever revealed.

Every time she caught his eye, Sharon would lose courage and swiftly look away, unable to play the flirt at such a high stakes level. But she was kept busy anyway because immediately to her left the hot young producer, Quinton Selsick chatted animatedly about his up-and-coming casting for *The Banquet*, a sci-fi movie set in a world where food was short, and the rich were growing crops of brainless people to eat.

Sharon paled as he ploughed on with the gruesome plot, but it didn't put her off the feast set before her by white-liveried waiters wearing snow-white gloves. Served on crystal platters, the food was themed shades of white. To start, there was the flesh of baked lobster, and crab pâté on balls of white rice, which Sharon savoured with every morsel she devoured. The second dish was described as *pousses en claire, huître surprise* – one of many courses engraved on the mother-of-pearl menu adorning each table.

She was about to wave hers away, convinced there was no way she could actually swallow an oyster, when she realised from Jules D's expression what the *surprise* bit was. A little unladylike, Sharon grabbed the waiter by the sleeve and pulled him back. There, on the open shell of the crustacean, sat a glistening pearl! Delighted, she fingered its smoothness, and for a second she was reminded of the single magical pill she had taken. How long ago now? She worked it out in her head and realised, with the time difference, it was exactly 150 days at that very moment. How weird, she thought, then turned her attention to the Russian vodka sorbet that had been placed in front of her. The main course of wild chicken in a white truffle sauce was only just surpassed by the dessert of white Belgian chocolate profiteroles with Chantilly cream.

Just as Quinton was asking if she was interested in doing a screen test for *The Banquet*, Debbie came up to her and whispered, 'it's time…'. Sharon's stomach flipped with nerves (and it has to be said, the second helping of profiteroles) as she rose to follow her PA out of the room.

All the men stood up politely with her, and she was startled at the unexpected attention.

'Good luck,' mouthed Jules D, raising her champagne flute in a private toast.

Heart pounding, Sharon stood backstage while hair and makeup assistants fussed around her. By the time she was attired in the second ball gown, the auction was in full swing. It had started with a set of four Venetian brandy glasses that fetched ten thousand dollars. The highest since then was a skiing weekend in Vermont that raised nearly a hundred thousand. Nearly, because just as the auctioneer was about to slam down his hammer, he mischievously announced that he had forgotten to mention it was Spielberger's chalet, and that the great man himself would do the cooking and cleaning for the purchaser. The audience roared, and the bidding shot up to half a million dollars.

At this point, the celebrity host reiterated the reasons for the auction. The image of two forefingers touching in the manner of E.T. was beamed up on the screen behind him. 'Phone home,' said an alien voice over the PA system. Something about the auctioneer reminded Sharon of someone – his smooth patter, false game-show smile … Then the man hit his stride: 'Reaching Out sends teams of people into the heart of the ghettos, the cold streets, the brothels and the bars to look for our lost ones. Posters, advertisements, leaflets, all ask the children – our children – to "Phone home". Please, I ask you, as one American citizen to others, I beg you to dig deep into your pockets … into your hearts.'

Sharon now felt sick. And it wasn't because of the soppy sentimental speech he was churning out. It was nerves. What if no one bid for her?

'I ask you to turn to the person next to you and touch fingers,…' urged the auctioneer. Damn, thought Sharon, trying to take her mind off the moment ahead.

If only she was back at the table and next to George Spencer.

It was nearly her time. She took the fifth and last peppermint from Debbie, who almost had to shove her, shaking, into position. Finally, she was ready to go out there, her new dress arranged carefully around her, headdress adjusted into final position.

'Next, because this is Hollywood and our lives are all about magic and fairytales, we're offering a pair of glass slippers by Louboutin!'

A silver-liveried footman brought out a cushion bearing a sparkling pair of transparent stilettos.

'You can actually wear them, though they look just as stunning in a glass case. Who will give me a thousand dollars?'

Shoes, women, wine and showing-off resulted in a staggering final bid of fifty thousand.

'That's it,' panicked Sharon. 'Debbie, get me outta here! No one's got any money left! I'll be going for a fiver, if I'm lucky!'

'Now, honoured Hollywood royalty, you can't have a glass slipper without Cinderella …' As the lights dimmed, the host turned to the wings, hand outstretched to welcome Sharon with a big smile. He winked.

'Oh, my God, it's Dr Marvel! He reminds me of Dr Marvel!' squeaked Sharon, as she jerked towards the stage.

The audible 'Wow' from the audience gave her an unexpected surge of confidence.

There she sat, in a giant glass pumpkin pulled by two tiny white-plumed ponies. When a footman opened the door, she emerged from the carriage in a fabulous ball gown made entirely of edible sugar crystals. The tiny icicles formed a giant bell skirt, with sugar-glazed roses garlanding her from shoulder to hip. On her head she wore a glass tiara tinkling with crystals. With her Nordic hair crimped and fanned out like a fairy queen's and her ice cool emerald eyes, she looked as close to a fairy princess as it was possible to imagine.

'Of course, we need to find a Prince Charming to kiss the fair maiden.' The auctioneer took her hand and paraded her across the stage. She walked with her practised model's sway, and smiled prettily at the blur of faces scrutinising her face and figure. Inside, she was dying of embarrassment and fear.

'A kiss from the striking ... the stunning ... the intriguing international supermodel SHAZ! Ladies and gentlemen, who will start the bidding?'

There was complete silence.

She was right! No one wanted to pay for such a ridiculous thing.

But, actually, it seemed no one had a clue where to start. Even the host, thrown by how stunning Sharon looked, felt the original reserve was too low, and perhaps insulting. He thought it best to leave it up to the audience. But maybe not ...

The silence was finally broken. 'Twenty thousand dollars!' cried Quinton Selsick.

Sharon was so grateful she would have slept with him for less. Relieved that the ordeal was over, she smiled at him welcomingly and took a step in his direction.

'Thirty thousand,' said another voice. Startled, Sharon looked across to the other side of the room. A portly gentleman in white tie and tails was waving a catalogue at the host.

'Forty-five thousand,' cried another, 'for my wife!' His wife happened to be one of the most beautiful women in Hollywood, and the fantasies of every man in the room were fuelled by the Sapphic thought.

The bidding grew faster. Sharon couldn't believe what was happening. Suddenly she was enjoying it.

'Walk around again, sweetheart,' urged the auctioneer, loving every minute of it. 'Blow them a kiss!'

Like a naughty Queen Titania, she pouted her shell-pink lips as she blew – adding a slow, seductive wink for fun. The men groaned. She threw back her flaxen head, giggling, exposing a perfect alabaster neck.

'A hundred thousand,' said a deep voice from the back. Sharon recognised it almost at once, and put a shocked hand to her mouth.

All heads swivelled to see Brett Stone lounging on his chair, casually tilting a catalogue a couple of centimetres.

Sharon couldn't believe it. The A-list actor, voted Sexiest Man on the Planet, had bid to kiss *her*! More than that, he was actually willing to *pay a fortune* to kiss her. Not in her wildest, craziest fantasies could she have dreamed up this insane moment. Brett had been the subject of avid fanzine stories recently. Since his split from one of Hollywood's most stunning actresses, they had tried to link him with various hot babes. But it seemed he preferred to hang out with his gang of A-list single mates. He was free … and raising his finger to bid again!

The portly gentleman bid against him. 'One hundred and twenty five to Mr Krogenheimer,' said the host.

Sharon recognised that name too. He was a top producer, known for his hard-hitting violent movies.

'One fifty,' countered Stone, coolly.

It was becoming a macho battle, and the room fell silent in lurid fascination.

'One seventy!' shouted Krogenheimer. Sharon wondered if she could offer a free consolation prize to Stone if he lost.

'Two hundred thousand,' said Stone, unemotionally.

Krogenheimer hesitated, and looked ready to pull out.

Sensing an end, the auctioneer clearly had a brainwave on how to get a little more out of the situation. 'Gentlemen, it is for a good cause. Shaz, how would you feel about kissing *both* of your bidders for a hundred and twenty-five thousand dollars each?'

'Er … sure. Um … of course. Reaching Out is a very good cause,' she murmured, unable to think of anything other than reaching out for Brett Stone.

'Gentlemen?' he asked, inviting them to reply to the idea.

'Sounds good to me!' Krogenheimer wiped his mouth with a napkin and rose from his seat. Everyone applauded enthusiastically.

But Stone raised his hand, silencing the crowd. 'Two hundred and fifty-five thousand dollars. And I don't share.' The audience roared its approval. Flash bulbs popped and hands clapped even louder. Krogenheimer sat down again, shaking his head and shrugging in smiling, magnanimous defeat.

'Well, Brett, we all know you're good for the money. You'd better come up here and claim your prize!' The orchestra struck up the hot, soulful song 'Sealed With A Kiss', and Brett picked up his glass of wine, casually finished it, then walked towards the stage, the audience's eyes darting between him and Sharon.

Sharon froze as her idol came nearer and nearer. His perfect features were just as handsome as they were on the screen, wicked blue eyes, sensual mouth and blond hair swept back – a lock fallen nonchalantly over one eye. Even taller and more muscular in real life, his shirt collar and black tie loosened, he stepped on to the stage. The room held its breath. Like a scene from a movie, he walked over, put his hand under her chin and tilted up her exquisite mouth. They locked eyes. Then he turned his back to the audience, swinging her round to shield her, and let his lips touch hers. A warmth spread through every nerve in her body as she swooned with the knowledge that his lips were actually on hers. Lightly teasing at first. Then firmly. She felt her mouth soften and open, and let his tongue enter. Her body went limp, and his arm tightened to support her. Feeling her relax, he gave her a long, hard, slow, deeply passionate kiss. Then he deliberately breathed in, taking her breath with his in an unbelievably sexy, intimate moment.

Somewhere in the far distance, she heard the host saying,

'Enough, kids! Break it up! We're going to have to charge another hundred thousand at this rate! And that's just for watching!'

Everyone roared and clapped, as Brett bowed slightly to her, kissed her hand and left the stage. Curtsying coyly in return, Sharon was led off in the other direction by the footman. Debbie was in the wings, jumping and squealing, like a four-year-old on a sugar-rush.

'Ohmigod! Ohmigod! He's a god! What was it like? What was it *like*?'

'Heaven!' said Sharon, dreamily, truly dazed. 'Like tasting … ambrosia.'

Twenty-one

Climbing out of the sugar creation, which was actually shedding its icicles faster than an igloo in August, Sharon relaxed back into the Grecian goddess number and tried to take in the experience.

Debbie was busy fluffing out her hair and pinning some strands up in the mode of Juno. 'I can't believe what I saw! Shaz, he *paid* for it! Two hundred and fifty-five thousand dollars!'

Jules D rushed in. 'Darling, what a coup! You'll be on every cover, every front page! You mark my words! The press will go crazy!' She snapped off a sugar icicle and gave it a curious lick.

The press coverage was the last thing on Sharon's mind. All she could think of was the Kiss. 'What the hell do I say to him if I bump into him? How do you do? My name's Sharon, nice to snog you.'

She was handed a mirror as the makeup artist reapplied her lipstick. She gazed at her lips. Did they look the same? How had they seemed to him? They were perfectly curved, equally full, top and bottom, with a neat bow shape. Okay, kissable. Definitely kissable.

By the time Jules D and Sharon returned to the ballroom, people had started to gather outside the white-pillared gazebo for a nightcap. As they walked through them, guests raised their glasses and smiled at her, while jokes about her doing so much for charity abounded. Sharon bubbled with the attention.

Above, in the night sky, Cirque de la Craze trapeze artists were performing a heart-stopping act. Dressed in ivory corsets with white ostrich plumes, they sailed against the starry backdrop like Arctic birds of Paradise.

A big band played inside, and through the french windows Sharon could see the revellers dancing. Keen to get her bearings and decide how to greet Mr Stone, should she get the chance, she headed for the outskirts of the group. She couldn't see him anywhere. Debbie was still sorting out dress and travel, and Jules was chatting to a potential client.

Sharon wandered past a white dovecote deeper into the garden foliage. There, amid the swinging lanterns that peeped through snowy branches, she saw a little white and silver tent, the entrance lit by two flickering candelabra. It was small, round and medieval in style. Curious, she strolled over, and peered inside. A gypsy woman was sitting at a little table with a crystal ball. Gloriously attired in veils and silks, she sat amid the lush draperies with a gold-toothed smile. How apt for a Crystal Ball!

'Come in, come in. Be my first lady of the night,' said the gypsy.

Sharon sat down on a silk-cushioned stool, placed her hands on the table, and stared into the shiny globe. She fought a childish urge to shake it in the hope of seeing snowflakes.

The gypsy lit another candle, then followed her gaze, looking first into the ball and then at Sharon's expectant face.

'You've had a very unhappy past, but recently there has been an unbelievable amount of magic and mystery in your life. It has changed your world beyond all recognition.'

'True. Go on!' urged Sharon, astounded.

The woman caressed the ball with her long, spidery fingers. 'Success gave you its calling card – and you picked it up. But now you are looking for love. You will find it. I see a man involved in "pictures". A tall man – talented, witty, handsome … He's very keen to know you much better.'

'And he's standing right behind you!' said Brett Stone, handing the gypsy a thick wad of dollar bills and taking Sharon's hand to lead her out.

'Oh, my God!' She laughed. 'Hi, again!'

'I've been looking for you everywhere.'

'Really? Why?' asked Sharon, unsure what to say to this amazing news, and finally – finally – feeling truly confident of her beauty.

'It was some kiss – thank you,' he said gallantly.

'Well, that's a relief. I thought you were going to ask for your money back!'

He was clearly surprised to discover that a gorgeous woman might have a sense of humour. 'Cute.' He broke into a broad grin. 'Beautiful *and* funny. I like that. Where do you live?'

'Kingston.' It seemed a ludicrous place to name here in Hollywood.

'Jamaica?'

'Err, not exactly.' A vision of the grey streets, shopping mall and local pubs flashed into and just as hastily out of her mind. 'What about you? LA?' she asked, sensing that Brett's level of celebrity meant he would love nothing more than to talk about himself.

'Tonight, right here. The Beverly Hills Hotel. The Presidential Suite.'

'You're kidding! Is that where Kennedy stayed?'

'The very same room.'

'What's it like?'

'Want to see?'

'Yeah! Absolutely – I mean, no. Er, not yet. Er, no … not at all.' She'd just agreed to go to his room and had tried to back-pedal. It was all coming out wrong – as if she'd intended to be there eventually. 'Not at all,' she repeated primly. 'But I'm sure it must be fascinating.'

'Absolutely,' he mimicked. 'Not every day you get to sleep in the bed where he screwed Marilyn Monroe.' It was the way he slowly said the adjective as he looked into her eyes that made Sharon aware he was deliberately playing with her. As he probably did with every single woman he met.

Fine, she thought. I can play too.

'It's chilly out here. I'm heading back for a drink,' she said, and walked off, interested to find out if he would follow. He did. Inwardly, she was screaming, Yes! Yes! Yes!

The man voted the world's most desirable movie star had just paid $255,000 dollars to kiss *her*. He had then hunted her down, told her he'd been looking everywhere for her, and was now following wherever she might go, like a tame wolf! Things just couldn't get any better, could they?

She stopped at an ice-cream stand set up in another corner of the garden, and as he came up behind her, she felt his breath on her neck. He asked if he could share a spoonful of her four-scoop coconut sundae.

They sat on a white stone bench feeding each other with it until the heavenly concoction was demolished. Then, together, they rejoined the main party, chatting, drinking and dancing. Marking his new territory, he never left her side. The studio fat cats were particularly impressed by his obvious attention to Shaz, trying to assess if she had the staying power to become a GOS – Girlfriend of Star. If she did, they all knew that the ensuing publicity could make her a potential Hollywood player. History had shown it happening so many times before.

But was it likely? Was it worth the effort of going over to say hello?

Either way, press cameras flashed, and smiles were thrown at them from all directions as Hollywood's latest 'beautiful couple' stared deep into each other's eyes. Amid the bubble, Sharon also felt the sharp prick of drop-dead glances from three or four starlets. Judging by their killer stares, she got the impression Brett had probably pissed them off in the past. Maybe with a one-night stand.

Looking at his wicked, playful smile and feeling his strong arm around her, she could easily guess how that would make them feel – and sent a silent prayer to the goddess Aphrodite that this gorgeous god wouldn't do the same to her.

As they slow-danced seductively, they were aware of the sensation they were creating. They talked quietly as they swayed to the rhythm, and she forgot the circus around them. Despite her first impression of him as a Hollywood movie star, he was more normal than she'd thought. It turned out that they loved the same music. Who'd have believed he liked traditional Irish folk? But then, from an immigrant family, he had strong ties with Ireland and was proud of them.

Fascinated by Hollywood, Sharon encouraged him to tell her about his life. He talked about his new film, *The Descendant* – a serious script the studios had finally allowed him to make. He was starring and, for the first time, also directing. It was his shot to do something 'real'. He was passionate about the story – a quiet, unassuming man believes he is a direct descendant of the Prophet Muhammad, and is mercilessly persecuted by the CIA. Brett wanted to 'make a difference'.

As they danced closer, Sharon became very aware again that they were being scrutinised by press, producers, directors, waiters, starlets, actors and writers. It was fame at its highest, most giddying level.

'Let's head out of here, have a quiet drink in the Presidential Suite. It's pretty impressive – it has its own pool.'

Hot night, movie star, private pool … no-brainer. It seemed a wonderful idea for two reasons:

(a) She was curious to see exactly *what* would impress a world-famous movie star;

(b) She wanted to see the look on the faces of Jules D and Debbie as they left. But she knew he might take her acquiescence in going to his room in totally the wrong way. 'Okay, I'll come. But only because I'm interested in American political history.'

As Brett unlocked the door to the Presidential Suite, the luxurious Bungalow Five, Sharon had misgivings. She was feeling uncomfortably like a push-over. But twenty minutes later, as their bodies embraced in the spotlighted art-deco lap pool, she was ready to roll over and die. It was surreal – like being in an old movie – and for Sharon, a case of 'Frankly, my dear, I don't give a damn.'

Against the silhouetted palm trees, the inky sky and the mottled white moon, Brett's face wavered in front of hers. Surely she was swimming in an oasis and he was just a mirage. But when she touched his flesh, it was warm. She could hardly believe that the perfect features she'd idolised on a twenty-foot screen were hers to touch, caress and kiss. The thrill was indescribable.

Sharon had the impression that Brett was just as smitten. He confessed he'd seen her face on billboards, and wondered many times how her succulent lips would feel to kiss. How they would feel on his body. As her eyes echoed the pool's deep aquamarine, both were enamoured with each other's image. It was a hot combination, which reached boiling point when he touched between her thighs. She felt her legs part as he pressed her against the poolside wall, and the image of what he would feel like inside her actually made her ache. She lifted her hands to his neck, then ran them down his broad, muscular back to his slim waist. His chest was unbelievably smooth and hard – leading to the taut stomach, the finely tuned six-pack she'd seen in countless films. Now it was all hers to stroke.

In turn, he ran his hands over her shoulders and down to her waist, tracing every curve, mound and dimple with his long, manicured fingers. 'You're unbelievable. Beautiful … bewitching. I bet you're a real handful. Maybe two handfuls,' he added softly, cupping his hand on each breast. 'I've got to have you,' he whispered in her ear, the tickly tingling sensation spreading all the way down to her tippy-toes.

With an admirable amount of mega-willpower, Sharon ducked under his arm and emerged from the water a few feet away. 'I think we need to cool off.' She laughed, wiping the drops from her face. 'So, can you imagine? Marilyn Monroe and Jack Kennedy, where do you think they did it?'

'And you're trying to cool me off!?' grinned Brett. He duck-dived, and pulled her down to join him in an underwater snog.

Actually, Sharon had still to get her Primary Width Swimming Certificate, and this wasn't a good move. She surfaced, spluttering and struggling, like a victim in *Jaws 3*.

'Shit! Sorry,' said Brett, genuinely surprised. The pool culture was so ingrained in LA, he just assumed that everyone in Hollywood was a good swimmer. She coughed and coughed, blindly reaching for the steps.

He followed her, then tenderly wrapped her in giant towels and led her to a chair. As her fit subsided, he sheepishly confessed that the pool had been built in the early nineties, and that Jack and Marilyn had probably got together in her bungalow, somewhere else in the grounds. He apologised for getting her to his room under false pretences, and she relaxed at his honesty. Sipping freshly squeezed mango juice, they curled up on the lounger together, looked at the stars peeping through the palm trees and talked until dawn chased them away with a turquoise hue.

She learned a lot that night, mentally ticking a list as he talked. Brett hated drugs – which was a major relief, after Jaz. He had been born into the Beverly Hills scene, both his parents had been abusers, and he'd seen more than enough directors, actors and producers unable to walk on set unless they'd had enough 'ice' to create a private rink.

He also believed in fidelity. Well, he seemed to dislike the regular LA orgy scene, which was good enough. Another box ticked.

And he was cool with the idea of waiting for the right girl. Hollywood had spoilt him, and he'd 'stuffed himself at the candy box for far too long'. Plus he mentioned something about a religious group he was interested in. They had some neat ideas about monogamy, which resonated with his feeling of isolation at the top of the movie tree.

All of this vital data she recounted at a scrumptious brunch with Debbie and Jules D, who hung on her every word like baby bats at a feeding fest.

'So, how are you going to play it?' asked Jules D.

'I don't know … day by day. Every girl wants him. I think I need to be different.'

'Be cool! Be really cool!' suggested Debbie.

'Be yourself,' insisted Jules D, confidently.

'How do you know that's the right thing?'

'Experience, darling.' Sharon and Debbie were intrigued. Jules never talked about her love life, preferring instead to advise them on theirs.

'I just wondered, have you ever been in love? Really in love?' asked Sharon, cautiously, dying to know more.

'Have you ever been married?' blurted Debbie, far less cautious.

'Of course, darling. It was, er, fun. Interesting.'

'Would you do it again? Have you ever been tempted?' asked Sharon.

'No, darling. I've been there, done that, read the book and got the T-shirt.' She said it in a tone that suggested the book was now firmly shut, and the T-shirt returned for a refund.

The girls were itching to know more, but they didn't get the chance to ask. Jules neatly avoided the subject when her mobile phone rang for the tenth time that morning.

It was, naturally, the press – and, as always, Sharon's PR friend was right. That day, front pages all over the globe carried photos of 'The Kiss'. This time the headlines didn't shout. They screamed. 'Verkdentdkit!!' and '   ' and EÆµnnvlµktµ which roughly translated meant:

SHAZ MELTS HEART OF STONE!

STONE THROWS £255,000 FOR A KISS!

STONE KNOCKED OVER!

$255,000 A SNOG? STONE THE CROWS!

And back in Blighty, the Sun's Man Booker Prize-winning effort:

SHAZ'S SEXY SMACKEROONY!

With a few days free before returning home, Shaz was delighted to take up Brett's offer of lunch in Rodeo Drive, and asked the girls what they thought she should wear. LA was so casual that it had a uniform all of its own. Khakis, chinos, tassel flats … Finally she decided on a pair of classic linen trousers from Prada, but as she pulled them up she was surprised to find the waistband slightly loose. Surprised, because they had been tailored to her measurements for a recent shoot.

Humming to herself, she stepped on the glass scales parked neatly at the side of the sumptuous sage granite bathtub. She tried to work out the kilograms in her head. She'd lost about three pounds. Odd – she'd been eating as much as normal, if not a whole lot more. Well, that was cool: she'd just enjoy a really large meal with Brett. Such joy!

The three blocks of Rodeo Drive were an experience. Just like the scenes in *Pretty Woman*, she flounced in and out of the luxury stores, attended to like royalty, while Brett watched. As a gift, he insisted on buying her First in Van Cleef & Arpels – a sophisticated perfume that made her feel she was his number one.

Unsure what to expect when they had started the expedition, Sharon was amused that the most ostentatious part of the famous shopping district in the world looked like Disney Main Street – fake boulevard with fountains, wrought-iron balconies and cobbled streets. But it was enchanting in a movie-set kind of way, and amid the Coco Chanel, Christian Dior, Valentino and Tiffany, there wasn't a Primark or New Look to be seen. Sharon dipped in and out of the stores soaking it all up, like a *biscotto* in frothy coffee.

In those designer boutiques, they were used to serving only the kind of woman who truly pampered and looked after herself – and that tended to be the rich, famous and élite. There was one very easy way you could tell: the items were straight from the international catwalks. That meant the size eighteen really was a size eighteen: high-street stores copied the lines and often called a size fourteen or sixteen an eighteen to flatter the customer.

As Brett waited patiently, Sharon marvelled at the choice and quality, but most of all she enjoyed the displays. On every rail and on every stand, the large, flamboyant sizes were up front, the clothes diminishing until at the very back, the odd, embarrassed American size two or size zero dress hung, for the customer who had more money than chic. So hard for skinnies to find designer stuff. She grinned.

Not her problem. Two cashmere sweaters, a Valentino skirt and a pair of Cartier earrings later, Brett steered her towards the

Mediterranean-style entrance of Bijan, a men's boutique so exclusive that customers had to make an appointment in advance. Naturally, Brett hadn't – but one charmingly famous smile through the window later, they secretly let him in. He loved the look on Sharon's face when he bought a couple of pairs of silk socks for a hundred dollars each – and she was even more horrified when he explained that the average customer tended to spend in the neighbourhood of a hundred grand.

They had lunch on the terrace at Spago, Beverly Hills. A boyish and spiky-haired gentleman, introduced as Wolfgang Puck, came to say hello personally, kissing Brett and Sharon as if they were close family. His name meant nothing to Sharon, but Brett explained he was a master chef *extraordinaire*, and owner of Spago. He'd been meeting, greeting and feeding the good, the great and the dissolute of Hollywood since the early eighties – the likes of Jack Nicholson, Sean Connery and Clint Eastwood had regularly rolled up at his ramshackle restaurant on Sunset Boulevard. The new eatery in the exclusive postcode of Beverly Hills had now replaced the original, and was even more select – away from Les Touristitos. Bookings had to be made a month in advance, and if you weren't famous, you needn't even bother to try for a table between seven and nine p.m.

'Spago?' Sharon vaguely recognised the name from Oscar Night – the parties were always held there. As they sat on the pretty patio, the tall pepper trees shaded their faces from the hot Californian sun. A fountain tinkled merrily – prompting Sharon occasionally to nip to the loo – and she knew she was sitting in one of the most romantic settings in the world, opposite one of the most romantic faces. She glanced around, and noted the famous faces all around her. Meryl, Leonardo, Whoopi, Oprah … They were returning her smiles with friendly, acknowledging nods.

'You should come over for a while. They love English girls here,' said Brett, pouring a cool glass of crisp Californian wine. 'And you'd love Hollywood. It's a great neighbourhood,' he added, as if he was talking about the joys of living in Surbiton.

Over a lunch of Austrian white asparagus with brown butter sauce, followed by roasted *filet mignon* and Maine lobster with celeriac purée, he told her about his dream of running his own studio. 'I know I can do it … I've got these ideas … I had a meeting with … I so want to make this work.' It was fascinating watching his beautiful lips move, and his eyes light up, but by the time they reached the mocha-macadamia-nut-chocolate-cookie-ice-cream sandwiches, she realised he hadn't asked her a single question about herself.

But she was nit-picking, wasn't she? In fact, it was refreshing. As a celeb in her own right, used to being asked about herself all the time, it was quite a change. It wasn't her ego that was worried, it was something else. She had put her finger on it by the time she was halfway through the main course. She feared she could have been any girl right now, as she listened to him chatter on. Unless he had a chance to discover her likes and dislikes, hopes and dreams, how the hell would he ever get to know her? Perhaps he just wanted a pretty ornament – but she wanted to be a lot more than that. As he went on to describe why he had dropped his last agent, she suddenly thought of Simon, how they bantered together, taking turns to listen, laughing at each other's foibles.

She cleared her mind to concentrate on Brett – which was no hardship, she grinned privately, drinking in his sculpted cheeks and dimpled smile.

It was early days, and it really was a minor worry because they spent the rest of the day in a haze of film-star glamour. When Sharon looked back on her time with the footballer at the Sugar Cube, she saw how naïve she'd been to think it even resembled the glorious reality of Hollywood. Forget palm trees in plastic tubs, now she was relishing the *real* world – tea at the Beverly Wilshire Hotel *a là Pretty Woman*, swimming in the Pink Palace pool, and cocktails at the Polo Lounge.

All the time, Brett was shaking hands with friends, producers and agents. Always introducing Sharon proudly, as if they were together. Later that night, as they walked through the gardens of the hotel, he mentioned his film *The Descendant* again. Would she like to be his date for the première? Sharon was astounded, and deeply flattered. That was like announcing to the world they were a couple. When they reached his bungalow, she fell into his arms and tumbled into bed.

As they roughly pulled each other's clothes off, the attraction was sizzling. He was divine in every department, and she discovered that he was a 'Long-standing Member of the Academy'. He certainly knew how to give an Oscar performance: he left Sharon feeling as if she'd just been handed the Lifetime Achievement Award.

Later, as she spooned her body around his magnificent form, and tenderly held his 'Supporting Roll', she knew that if any woman were sleazy enough to do a 'kiss and tell' that featured him, it would only help his career.

Twenty-two

She'd ask her father to walk her down the aisle; she'd throw her bouquet to Jules D and the waiting crowds, wave to the paparazzi, and sail off with her actor in a golden hot-air balloon …

The farewells next morning were worthy of Romeo and Juliet, the star-crossed lovers torn apart by their rival entourages.

'We're going to miss the plane!' huffed Debbie, guiding Sharon towards the white limo.

Sharon blew a final kiss to Brett, who was heading off to his home in Arizona to chill out before mounting the publicity treadmill leading up to his film première. 'I always find that spending time at the ranch helps me cope with all the horseshit around here,' he joked. 'Come with me, you'll love it,' he added, with a dazzling white smile. Tanned and muscular, casually dressed in a checked flannel shirt, faded jeans and worn cowboy boots, he looked like a hot, horny ranch-hand. For a second he reminded her of Simon. No doubt she had a thing about cowboys – but it was high noon and time to leave town: she was a cowgirl, and needed to return for a shoot with Luxury Leather Wear, and a showdown with Kristen over foreign commission.

However, she was in for a tougher ride than she'd bargained for.

Arriving home, the photographic crush at the airport took her off

265

guard: the news of her relationship with Brett meant that all hell had broken loose. Worse waited at the flat. She could barely see the door for the number of paps lining the street. The group had grown, and the mood had darkened. As the price on her head had tripled, so had the photographers' determination to bag an 'exclusive'.

They now looked so intimidating, hooded and rough that when she got out of the taxi she kept her head down and headed straight for the door. When she didn't glance in the direction of a couple of new faces, she was shocked by their attitude and language.

'Look this way, slag!'

'Oi, you fuckin' bitch!'

Horrified, she turned to them – and they got the shot they wanted.

As she finally shut the door on the mêleé, and went through her phone messages, she was thrilled to see she'd exchanged on the Chelsea mews house. One month and she'd be out of here. There was also a message from her dad. For some reason, his whispery voice sounded as if it was fading on the wind. She had to call him back.

But first, desperate for a soak, she ran a bath and went through her mail. Bills had mounted up, and a quick glance at her credit-card statement made her realise she was spending quite a bit. No problem: she had at least a million in the bank, and plenty more to come, but still, it was surprising where it all went. Taxis, limos, champagne and, of course, clothes. One cannot live by freebies alone. The trouble was, she reasoned, once you were at a certain celebrity level, you couldn't do ordinary things without looking 'cheap'. Travelling by tube was out of the question now, as was shopping in Asda. She'd replaced both with taxis and limos, visits to Harrods and a delivery account with her local delicatessen. And she would buy clothes from a chain store at her peril. She swiftly glanced through the stack of cuttings the agency had sent over to her. The last one, dated yesterday, showed her wearing a smock top she'd recently bought from H&H. One of the tabloids – the one she'd refused an interview – had taken a photo and called her 'SHAZ – QUEEN OF SCHMUTTER'. It was her first negative piece, and Sharon was deeply upset. She rang Jules D, who told her that all publicity was good publicity. 'Par for the course, darling. Rise above it – and get a good night's sleep, okay?'

A week later, Sharon was feeling more relaxed and refreshed. The meeting with Glacé Inc had gone well, and she'd negotiated a good rate for future work. Michael Grey wanted her to look at some designs next Thursday, and there'd even been a surprise phone call from a company in France, keen to discuss the launch of her own fragrance. She suspected her contract with Descent would put a stop to that, but there was no harm in talking.

For once she had a relatively short list of things to do – first, try her dad again: he hadn't returned her calls. Other than that, she had to find a removals firm and source something fab to wear for Brett's première.

Munching an apple she'd picked up at the deli, she pulled out her drawers, mulling over what to wear. Suddenly feeling creative, she wanted to mix and match what she had – see if Michael Grey was right: could she conjure up a combination that would generate column inches whenever she felt like it?

As she adjusted her bra, she noticed the cups looked a little loose. Strange, she thought. It wasn't a cheap one – surely the elastic hadn't gone already. Opening her wardrobe, she picked out a bronze blouse. Mmm … would a metallic look work? She fingered the silver pleated Valentino skirt she'd bought that wonderful day in Rodeo Drive – a crazy spend but, hey, she was dating Hollywood royalty. She could team it with bronze and silver bangles. Why not?

Adding a slip over her silk cami-knickers for extra bulk, she smoothed the silver skirt down over her head. That's odd, she thought. The waistband was a touch loose. She checked that the button wasn't coming off and felt a teensy wave of panic. She was surely imagining it. She puffed out her belly. No … she wasn't. The skirt was definitely a little loose. Just around the top. She made a mental note to eat even more than usual, every day for a week.

'Well, I suppose I could make it,' sighed Sharon, caught unawares, like a trapped hare, when Debbie had phoned later that day. Debbie, unexpectedly free because her boyfriend had had to rush out of town to sign a hot new group, kindly offered to cook Sharon a special gourmet supper. But there was a little problem with the cooking: Debbie couldn't do it. No wonder she was thin, thought Sharon, uncharitably, a seasoned sufferer of Debbie's Dinner Specials.

'So, tell me, how's the love life?' asked Debbie that evening, when she'd told Sharon how Jack's parents had turned out to be just like Richard and Judy (not the Osbournes *or* the Waltons).

'Brill!' said Sharon, between mouthfuls of yellow rubber on charcoal, which had started out hopefully in life as scrambled eggs on toast. She had just had a phone call from Brett: he was flying to Europe via Heathrow, just so he could stop over and see her.

'We're going out for dinner tomorrow at Trotters.' It was one of those fingers-down-your-throat, so-trendy eat-all-you-can restaurants, whose tables required either a month's booking in advance, celebrity connections or Russian Mafia money.

'Good idea – looks like you're losing a bit of weight,' said Debbie, innocently.

Sharon blanched. 'What?' she demanded, through a mouthful of rubberised egg, which splattered Debbie and bounced off her face.

Debbie looked deeply uncomfortable. 'Er, sorry – I didn't mean to upset you. Forget I said it.'

Sharon fluffed up her pink angora jumper and stuck out her chest. 'Where? Where have I lost weight? *Tell me!*' Her voice rose in growing panic.

Debbie hesitated, like a lemming about to fling itself off a cliff. 'Well … um, I think perhaps all over.'

Sharon leaped up defensively. 'You're just being bitchy. You haven't changed, Debbie. You love making me feel bad.'

'How can you say that to me? I'd give anything to have your figure,' Debbie responded angrily.

Sharon pointed haughtily to the bathroom. 'Bring me your scales. We'll soon see if you're right.'

Like a dog in an obedience class, Debbie fetched her blue bathroom scales and reverently set them at Sharon's feet.

Surreptitiously Sharon picked up her wool cardigan and tied it round her waist.

'I saw that! That's cheating,' said Debbie. 'Anyway,' she added quietly, 'you're only fooling yourself.'

Ignoring her, Sharon placed her feet firmly on the machine. The needle landed squarely on 193 pounds, or thirteen and a half stone. She had lost well over a stone since the ball.

'These scales can't be right!' said Sharon. 'They *can't* be. Since I went on those scales in Beverly Hills, I've been eating more than ever!'

'Well, you must be doing something wrong,' commiserated Debbie, trying hard to hide the hint of triumph in her eyes. 'Maybe you're exercising more than you used to.'

Sharon looked away. Maybe sex burned off more than she knew. A headline she'd read recently in Debbie's pile of supermarket mags had said: '68% of Women Would Rather Eat Chocolate Than Have Sex.' Would she? Sorry – when the sex in question was with

Brett Stone, the answer was no: she'd rather have the sex.

The following night, her date with him was preceded by a nerve-racking mirror session before she left the flat for his hotel. Which outfit made her look biggest? She rushed out of her room, leaving the bed strewn with a heap of rejections. She began to hate every single item in her wardrobe. What on earth was she going to take with her for the première next week?

'Darling, you ought to try and exercise a little less control,' said Brett, as they lay entwined in each other's arms much later that night. 'I'm not sure, but I think I can feel a rib.'

Ashamed, Sharon flopped onto her belly.

'Don't be hurt, babe – I'm worried about you.'

Sharon felt sick: she'd just eaten a gargantuan meal, yet her stomach seemed deflated. 'I bet you wouldn't love me if I was slim,' she found herself saying before she could stop the words spilling out.

'I never said I did love you,' he replied coolly. But seeing her huge, iridescent eyes, Brett softened, and kissed her forehead. 'Who knows? Maybe I will someday soon. But, let's face it, sweetheart, I live in Hollywood, and nobody loves a thin girl.'

Sharon smiled weakly, then laughed. But her emotions tumbled like size-zero dresses in a dryer. *He's going to leave me. I know he's going to leave me*, screamed a voice inside her skull.

She lay against him all night, unable to sleep. She was determined to gain weight and keep the perfect creature she was curled up next to.

The following morning there was a knock on the door, and in came a French waiter bearing breakfast. Silver domes wafted wonderful smells. Sizzling crispy bacon, fluffy scrambled eggs embellished with dainty slivers of smoked salmon, plates of cured meat, five flavours of home-made jam. As the linen tabletop filled, a pile of freshly baked baguettes fought for room against iced cinnamon buns doused with dripping clover honey.

Sharon sat up, her breasts tumbling over the duvet. Suddenly conscious of her body's new imperfection, she leaned over to the chair and swiftly hooked up her silk blouse. Slipping it on, she glanced at the pyramid of food. For an instant, she felt nauseous. It's just nerves, she reasoned.

Her hand shaking, she dipped the silver knife into the curled creamy butter and spread it on a baguette. A tiny dollop plopped on to her shirt. Sharon gave a sad sigh. A grease stain on a pure silk blouse. Almost impossible to budge.

Twenty-three

As soon as Sharon got home after her night with Brett, she dragged out her old scales from the broom cupboard, dusted them off and eyed them warily. She hadn't stepped on them for more than three months. Like a prisoner who had shaken off her jailer she was reluctant to go anywhere near them. But she was losing weight in a world where it was 'in' to be a plus size and, like the old days before she'd swallowed the Pill, the daily treadmill began once again.

It became a ritual. Every day her weight changed, often dramatically. Occasionally up a pound – she was happy. Down three pounds – she was depressed. Slowly, slowly, like a helpless junkie, her life began once more to revolve around 'the needle'. Any special occasion or casting involved ripping her wardrobe apart like a frenzied burglar.

Another week later, a niggling feeling pervaded her as she gazed at the unexpected apple in her hand. Had something happened the night of the Crystal Ball to change the magic? She stepped on to the scales and, after a night of bingeing, looked down. The needle wavered, then fixed on 177 pounds. A little less than twelve and a half stone. Sharon looked at it uncomprehendingly. Two pounds less after a full night of eating, making another sixteen pounds in total!

Impossible! There *must* be something wrong with the scales. Sharon kicked them back into the corner. Panicking, she pulled on the tightest jeans she could find in her wardrobe. They hung baggy around her bottom, like a loose nappy. Weird, confused emotions coursed through her shaking body. Years of conditioning meant she'd felt an initial elation at finding the clothes loose, but it was misplaced, and seconds later she was hit by a wave of fear. As a bountiful star in this world of Botticelli beauty, she didn't want to be slim. It was insipid. Not only that, she was well aware that if she should lose much more, the agency would kick her out – and Z&ZaK would be furious. How could she have let it get so out of control, for God's sake? Looking good was her job. Her business. Her life.

She speed-dialled Debbie, who listened in horror and came racing over to Sharon's flat. On first inspection, Debbie thought Sharon was looking far lighter, but this time, she couched it carefully so she didn't offend her friend and celebrity boss. 'Well, I can see a little difference – but you can easily hide it with your height,' she said. She had arrived with a dozen Krispy Kreme doughnuts, but for some reason, probably anxiety, Sharon couldn't face the sticky, sugary softness she normally craved.

Together they examined her wardrobe, and after she'd tried on a couple more outfits, they scooted past the paparazzi, and snuck into the lingerie department of M&S, disguised in dark glasses and hats.

The 'push-out' pants and 'tummy release' vest their expert suggested seemed a comforting answer. Now padded and moulded to emphasise her bumps, Sharon relaxed a little. But she knew the truth, and so did Debbie. Shaz the Supermodel had gone down to size fourteen.

She called an emergency meeting with Jules D, who kindly put her weight loss down to all the emotional turmoil she'd been going through with her love life. But Sharon knew it wasn't that. In truth, she'd been having marvellous fun, each time meeting a more fabulous man to take her mind swiftly off the last.

Changing the subject, she asked Jules D for advice on her immediate dilemma: what to wear for the forthcoming première? Could her brilliant PR conjure up a fabulous dress?

Not sure how Z&ZaK would react to being asked to create a high-media-profile dress for a celebrity with a weight problem and, more importantly, not wanting to alert them to the change, Jules D diplomatically thought she would try elsewhere, whipping out her BlackBerry before you could say 'Google' – but the choice was unexpectedly solved by a timely call from Maxine Du Pré, who had learned from Simon of how Sharon had misread her advances at his exhibition. Ever the egoist, and convinced that all women had a secret desire for Sapphic assignations, she had decided to ring Sharon and make herself very, very clear. After Sharon had declined coffee, lunch, dinner and breakfast in bed, Maxine husked exasperatedly, 'Is there *anything* I can do for you?'

Sharon asked her what she had in red-carpet frocks, and Maxine veritably purred with pleasure. 'Darling, if I can't take your dress off you, let me drape one on you! I have the perfect creation.'

That afternoon she turned up with a black crêpe dress that crossed in the front with large satin panels. Its most distinguishing feature, though, was a giant bow perched on the shoulder. 'It's divine on you darling,' muttered Max, through a mouthful of pins. Sharon wasn't convinced, but the fact she'd already had a 'successful dress' with Max, and that the designer was prepared to take this one in to fit her perfectly, made it a more attractive option. To be frank, she didn't fancy contacting any of the PRs and asking them to send two sizes smaller than 'sample' – you just couldn't trust anyone not to leak the story.

'I think I'll just add some tulle around the hem to fill out the effect, and, of course, you also have the stole,' purred Maxine, sucking her cigarette holder dramatically.

Even with the special underwear, Sharon noticed she looked somewhat slimmer. Was it really wise to wear black? It was so slimming. Still, the stole was great for hiding all sins … and she still had a whole week to go on a crash binge.

Her relationship with Brett was going brilliantly – in the virtual reality world – with emails, texts and phone calls every day. She guessed this must be how it was for film stars. She used to read that actors complained break-ups occurred because of work. Perhaps it was true. Meanwhile there was the move to Chelsea to organise, and as the freebie pile of goodies grew, Sharon was faced with clearing out skipfuls of old crap.

As she started the painful process, she unearthed an album from underneath layers of school reports and certificates. Inside, there were pictures of her mother, her father and herself. Sharon realised that actually she had been quite a normal, rounded child. She had felt fat since she could remember, but maybe she'd got it wrong. Maybe the weight hadn't started piling on until after her mother had died.

She decided to try her father again and, steeling herself to speak to her stepmother, she waited patiently while he came to the phone. It was then he gave her the news of his tests.

'Darling, you know I've not been able to eat much recently? Well, it's a problem with the oesophagus. Don't be upset, but I'm afraid it's cancer.'

The word hung in the air, like a poisonous gas, a powerful word that clutched at her heart with giant, crab-like pincers. 'How bad?' she croaked.

'Pretty bad, darling. In fact, very. No hope, I'm afraid. They've said it's terminal.'

The floor dipped under her, and her legs gave way. She stumbled backwards and dropped on to the sofa. This couldn't be happening. Not to him. Not to her. 'I'll come right away,' she said, tears pricking her eyes as she thought of her dad. She needed a hug to get over the shock – to make it not real. To make everything all right again.

'Er … I'd better check with Carolyn. Just a minute. Carolyn dear, can Sharon come down?'

Sharon felt a flicker of anger that he had to ask at this time in his life. It burst into a searing flame when she heard the woman's heartless response: 'Well, we've people coming over to see you later, and I don't want her to come if she has a cold or anything.'

'Darling …' said her father, weakly.

'I don't have a cold,' snapped Sharon. 'Do you want me to come?'

'Of *course* I do.'

'Then I'll be there.'

'Better make it the weekend, darling. Could you come then?'

Sharon agreed, not wanting to upset him, but she was boiling with rage at being sidelined now. As she hung up, she reached for a box of chocolates, and sobbed into her glass of milk.

That Saturday, the drive through Bournemouth to her father's home was agony, a trip that took her down Memory Lane at every road she took.

Sharon looked to the left, peering down a cul-de-sac. There was the school where her daddy used to drop her off. To her right was the restaurant he had taken her to on her ninth birthday. And as she rounded the corner, she braced herself to see the rink where he had taught her to skate. She remembered the first time. Oh, how nervous she had been … yet her daddy had held her hand and she had never fallen over, not once. Her mummy had watched from the side, clapping, wrapped in a fur-edged coat, holding her hands out to hug them both. As the ghosts of her childhood cried out from every street corner, her eyes filled with tears. She longed for good times gone. Times that would never come again. Those days were lost forever. The skating rink was now a duplex cinema.

She drove through the town centre engulfed in loneliness, knowing the memories would be even more poignant and hard to deal with in just a few months' time. Or would it be weeks? Maybe days, even.

Finally, she knocked on the door – dreading Carolyn's icy greeting. Their house. No longer her home. As usual, her heart pounded at the thought of having to face her stepmother, which would be a thousand times worse now because of her father's illness, and the reality of dealing with eternal goodbyes.

Even though he was expecting her, the cluttered living room was full of Carolyn's relatives, including Sharon's stepsister, Esme, who sat there with her fiancé, and Sharon's half-brother, Damien. Everyone was engrossed in watching tennis on TV. Sharon took in the array of antiques and photos crowding the room: pictures of Carolyn's children receiving degrees, getting engaged, laughing, having fun. There wasn't a single one of Sharon.

On the sofa opposite, looking somewhat lost, her father had visibly shrunk and his jowls were a ghostly grey. Sharon smiled at Damien – assuming the boy *was* her half-brother: he hadn't even been born the night Sharon was dismissed from the family home. She had asked her dad many times about him, wondering if he ever talked about his big half-sister, but he had admitted that Carolyn was determined to keep him away from Sharon. He didn't know why, he'd said sadly.

Her father was blind. Sharon suspected the reason was very simple. His wife didn't want her son to know how cruel she could be to another woman's child. Maybe one day, when the boy was grown-up, she would have a chance to tell him the truth. But that was a long way off.

She stared at the green-eyed, dark-haired youth. Same eyes. This was her flesh-and-blood brother. She didn't know the first thing about him, but now was too tragic a time to start trying to find out.

Carolyn, true to form, was busy putting on a show of the good wife, making a real fuss of her father. It seemed to Sharon she was trying to claim her role as his loving, caring partner. It looked a bit staged. 'Joe, would you like some more tea? Soup? You must eat that up – it's so good for you.'

Her father told her the latest medical situation. It was awful. The tumour now blocked his throat, and all he could eat was liquefied food. He wasn't hungry, but he was basically starving to death. He had to eat something to stay alive, but all he could swallow was baby goo. As Carolyn tucked a napkin over him, Sharon thought how weird old age was: in life you went in a complete circle from helplessness to helplessness.

Conversation was stilted because her estranged family sat there the whole time listening to every word Sharon and her dad exchanged. She couldn't believe their insensitivity. She'd driven for hours to sit with her father – who had just told his daughter he was going to die. His *real* daughter. His only daughter. And there she was, trying to make final memories with her dad while her stepsister and some strangers chatted and watched the telly.

Worse, she knew she'd have only a little time with him – no more than twenty minutes because of his tiredness. Yet Esme and the others sat there, refusing to move. Sharon fought the urge to scream at them to get out. But years of abuse and fear of Carolyn's temper cowed her. Was it deliberate? Esme lived around the corner, and had all the time in the world to spend with her stepfather: why on earth were she and her boyfriend insisting on being there now?

When Sharon nipped off to the loo, she overheard the truth.

'Don't worry, Mum, I'm making her feel uncomfortable,' Esme said to her mother, as she brought more tea in from the kitchen.

So, that was it. A ploy to wind her up. She tried not to let it get to her: Esme had been brainwashed by Carolyn.

Then her mind drifted back to when her stepmother had thrown her out – on the 'night of a thousand daggers', as Sharon called it. She had been sixteen, Esme fourteen and Mona seventeen. That night, Carolyn had come home from dinner with her father in a foul mood, no doubt aggravated by her pregnancy. She had stalked into the living room, and Sharon had looked up nervously, knocking over a glass of water on the table. The woman had gone mad. Her face had darkened and she had screamed at Sharon's clumsiness. It was the final straw: Sharon was getting older, and she was finally building up the courage to answer back. As Carolyn culminated in a screech that Sharon was the disgusting spawn of her mother, she had retaliated, 'I hate you!' then run to the safety of her room.

Carolyn had ordered Esme and Mona into her own bedroom. Sharon could only guess at what lies they were being told about her.

When they emerged, they had entered Sharon's room, her private sanctuary. Esme stood hugging her mother's side as she ordered Sharon to leave the house, while Mona screamed, 'Fuck off!' They had snarled at her like a pack of she-wolves.

Cornered at the far end of her room, Sharon had looked to her father to stop them. But his anguished face just peered around the door and his shoulders shrugged helplessly. As the screaming increased, Sharon had felt her body leave the scene and float above, removed. No mother to protect her. Betrayed by her father. Hated by her stepfamily. The hurt was too much to bear, and her mind had taken its own steps to save her. As the screaming around her continued, she packed a case and her father drove her to the station. He put her on a train to London with the address of an old friend of her mother. It was ten p.m. and it was raining. But the drops pounding on the train windows were as nothing compared to the tears tumbling down her cheeks.

Now, forcing away the images of that night, she tried to concentrate on talking to her dad, ignoring the others in the room. Giving her a big smile, he put his skinny arm around her, and she laid her head on his chest. They chatted quietly about the old days while the step-throng around them continued to talk and watch TV. The situation was totally surreal, and Sharon was torn. Did she stay, drinking in every feature, every gesture her father made, committing it to memory, fearing this would be the last time she'd ever see him alive? Or should she leave, escape the awful atmosphere and regain her sanity?

Carolyn brought in mushy peas and some substance that looked like gruel, and Sharon watched in pain as her father tried to swallow. The irony stuck in her throat even harder than the food in his. For there she was, obsessed with her appearance, trying to gain weight, and there was her father starving to death. Gain weight, lose weight, right weight, wrong weight: in the end, none of it mattered, not when it came down to this.

'Darling, I'm not afraid of death, you know … never have been.'

That was one of the many things she loved about her father. 'How long do you think it … How much time did they …?'

'Oh, well played!' said Esme's fiancé loudly, to the TV.

'Don't know, darling. It might be six months.' Looking at his shrunken form, she doubted he was telling her the truth, but it was a comfort.

Finally, biting back the tears, she hugged her dad and said goodbye, she would see him again very soon. As he hobbled to the door like Yoda, a fraction of his normal size, she stared at his face and tried to freeze-frame it. A sweet man she loved, who had failed to protect her. Now he never would.

She turned to Esme and, in an attempt to rewrite the terrible history of their youth, asked her if she would let her know how her dad was doing. Her stepsister replied noncommittally, 'Someone will.' She had spoken in Carolyn's exact tones.

Sharon sighed. As she walked towards her car she felt that the wicked stepmother had won. And, unlike Cinderella, she would never have a happy ending.

Driving along the motorway it hit her that, even though he was still alive, her father's life had now reached its conclusion. His tale was told. As she sobbed all the way home, she had never felt so alone.

Back at the flat, she realised the opposite. With a growing pack of paparazzi at the door, the chances were that she would never be alone again. And, as the première neared, interest in her continued to grow, fuelled by the announcement of her fashion deal with Bessie B's, and screen test for *The Banquet*. Actually, she'd found out about the latter from the press, along with everyone else. She had laughed, thinking it was a joke. But it was a clever publicity-generating move by Selsick, who had deliberately leaked the story before he had mentioned it to her agent. That way, even if she said no, the story had made column inches.

The official offer was confirmed two days later by her model agency, and by then Sharon had decided: What the hell? Why not?

In truth, the idea of acting had terrified her ever since she'd screwed up her role as a bush in the school nativity play. (Her branch had poked Mary in the eye and the little girl had cried louder than Baby Jesus.) Still, she was heading out to LA for Brett's première, so she might as well give it a shot. In for a penny, in for the big green bucks!

This time, when she arrived at the Beverly Hills Hotel, she was shown straight to the Presidential Suite, where she fell into Brett's arms. He seemed delighted to see her and, after a screenworthy passionate kiss, hugged her close to his chest.

She told him how she'd missed him, and how much she wished

he'd been there when she'd found out about her dad. He fell silent, stroking her hair. Then he stroked her back, encircling her waist. Sharon felt comforted. The silence continued. Until she felt uncomfortable. 'What's up?' she said. 'Are you okay?'

'Actually I was wondering if you were. You've lost so much weight.'

Sharon stood back, not sure if he was genuinely concerned or just worried about her as his arm candy. 'I'm going through a lot at the moment,' she countered defensively.

'I know that, and I'm here for you. But still, at our level, we have to exercise some control.' Sharon was speechless and burst into tears.

'Look, forgive me. I'm a prick. An absolute prick. I'm sure it's just what you're going through, with your dad and all that. Come on, babe, make yourself beautiful and let's go see a movie!'

Sharon disappeared into the pink granite bathroom to shower and repair the damage. Three hours later, following a visit from the hair artiste, the makeup artiste and the nail artiste, she was ready for her first public première. But as she slipped on Max's black creation, she was horrified to discover that it was loose. Well, more than loose: it gaped under her arms, and bagged around her buttocks. She gingerly stepped on the hotel scales, keeping on rings, shoes and diamond necklace.

She'd dropped another eight pounds. Fear gripped her. Was she sick like her dad? Was something seriously wrong? In panic, she even considered stuffing her bra and pants with toilet paper for extra padding, but the horrifying image of her trailing white loo roll down the red carpet put a stop to that idea.

Pale, she walked into the living room, wrapping the stole around her body to hide her disappearing curves.

'Are you okay?' asked Brett, concerned. He was impeccable in an Armani black suit and tie, like a classic Hollywood leading man.

He led his lady out to the limo, and she chattered nervously, trying to hide her sudden body insecurity. She was quaking at the thought of the public scrutiny she knew lay ahead.

Timed to perfection for maximum impact, their car swung down Sunset Boulevard towards Grauman's Chinese Theater. The crowds roared as it pulled up, and Sharon squeezed Brett's hand for good luck. He smiled. 'Nothing to worry about. It's showtime.' With that, he stepped out of the car, and waved like an old pro, his switched-on mega-watt smile more dazzling than the searchlights that swivelled over the throng.

Sharon got out, and went towards the red carpet. Security men in black were all around her, urging her to join Brett. She held one end of her long stole, but suddenly, she couldn't find the other! Surreptitiously groping behind her, she smiled for the crowds, the cameras flashed and thousands stared. She was faced with a choice: to make an inelegant turn and stoop, which would show off the looseness of the dress, or trail the stole dramatically behind her, like a catwalk model. She chose the latter.

The crowds roared again as she took her place next to him, he smiled at her, and arm in arm they walked towards the magnificent piece of kitsch – a green Chinese pagoda – that marked the entrance to the historic cinema. The flash bulbs were so intense that spots danced before her eyes. As Brett stopped to sign autograph books, and shake hands, Sharon posed on the carpet, a giant circular bank of photographers crying out her name from all directions. It was wild!

Brett took her hand and they posed together,

'Kiss! Kiss!' chanted the crowds. He looked into her green eyes, and smiled enigmatically. They didn't kiss. Instead they waved and walked into the buzzing foyer to be greeted by the microphones and booms of various TV crews keen to hear Brett's thoughts on America's stance in its foreign policy.

He rose to the occasion with passion and belief. Sharon was impressed: this was his big break from being a pretty boy, and she knew how much it meant to him.

As for her, she was asked more important life-affecting questions, such as 'What designer are you wearing?'; 'Whose shoes are those?'; 'Which is your favourite lip gloss?' The attention was overwhelming, and she was having a blast. They took their seats in the auditorium, and as the lights dimmed, she detected a nervous twitch on Brett's fine-boned cheek – the first symptom of anxiety in him that she'd ever seen.

The film began with explosions, death and destruction. Brett was playing a cool CIA agent who finally let his principles rule his head. A lot of Muslims died, and a lot of Americans. It was depressing, heavy and meaningful. Sharon was unsure if it was bloody brilliant or bloody awful. The only thing that moved her was the odd sensation that the giant face on the screen was right next to hers; the hand brandishing a Kalashnikov was the hand that caressed her thigh.

Afterwards applause filled the cinema, and they swept out with the producers and headed off to Spago for a celebratory dinner.

Sharon was deeply conscious of her figure and anxiety dulled her appetite. As they sat at their table, she felt her dress ride up under her armpits – there was no flesh to keep it in its rightful place. Yanking it down, she quietly asked a waiter to get her some safety pins.

Everyone was congratulating Brett, shaking hands, back-clapping, laughing and joking. Two producers asked him to come to their offices next week to discuss a couple of projects they thought he might like to direct. It was looking good.

Sharon, meanwhile, was looking in the sparkling goody-bag hooked on the back of her chair. It was astounding. Inside there was a crystal Swarovski bikini, a diamond-studded eye mask, a new perfume called Flesh encased in a sculpted bottle of a large woman reclining, a four-foot adjustable tummy chain from Gucci, and some Godiva chocolates. For a film that had been so meaningful, the goodies were outrageously meaningless. That was Hollywood, she guessed, irked by the tummy chain – she could probably fold it in half and still wear it.

That night they returned to their suite, and had a wicked time. But Brett made a couple of comments that jarred: 'Eat some more cheese,' he'd insisted, while they had their alcoholic nightcap. 'It's wonderfully fattening – you don't want to let yourself go now, do you?' Worse, as they curled up together, he placed his hand on her hip, but withdrew it a few seconds later.

'Something wrong?' asked Sharon.

'Your hip just felt a bit … bony, that's all. No worries, Shaz – go to sleep.' And he kissed her shoulder softly.

But she couldn't sleep. She tossed and turned, knowing this man was used to utter perfection, and she was no longer the ultimate.

The next morning the papers were hand delivered by his producer. And Sharon's life fell apart.

Twenty-four

FILM FLOPS MORE THAN DATE'S DRESS!

Brett Stone's directorial début, a mish-mash of meaningless drivel designed to whip up anti-American sentiment, was bad enough, but his girlfriend, Shaz, a multi-million-dollar international model, known for her taste, wore a dress by up-and-coming British designer Maxine Du Pré that looked two sizes too big …

Underneath the article there was a shot of Sharon leaning forward: the dress was so loose that her left breast was falling out. Worse, you could even see the clear shape of a collar-bone.

'THE DESCENDANT? STONE'S FILM – OR SHAZ'S DRESS?'

Another paper pictured her hiking up the bodice. 'After last night's première, both were on their way down …' it continued mercilessly.

'Oh, God, I'm so sorry,' said Sharon, burying her face in her hands. The embarrassment that he had been shamed even more by having her as his date was unbearable.

Brett sighed long and hard, like a condemned man. 'It's okay. It seems the film would have been panned either way. You've just given them fodder for a funny headline. They'd have found others, I'm sure.'

'It's not all bad,' said his producer, handing him the *Washington Post*: 'Brett's attempt to wake up America put most of us to sleep. However, there were moments of sheer genius.'

'Sheer *genius*, Brett. That's good enough to get you another film, my son!' said his producer, desperate to find something to redeem the situation.

Brett snatched the paper eagerly: 'However, there were moments of sheer genius. Just not nearly enough.' He tossed it on to the sofa in disgust. 'They just don't get my work,' he snarled sullenly.

Sharon looked at the photo accompanying the story. Her dress bagged and drooped around her body like a black bin-liner. How apt. She certainly looked a pile of rubbish, she thought.

At the bottom of the piece there was more: 'Supermodel Shaz famous for the Descent perfume campaign, draped her stole in imitation of a vintage movie star outside Grauman's famous Chinese Theater – but without the voluptuous curves to back it up, the flaunting descended into a joke.'

What? It was so unjust! She wanted to scream – to explain to each and every one of the readers that the stole was ridiculously long, she'd simply dropped the end and was too nervous to pick it up. But there was nothing she could do.

Brett's producer left them alone with a servile bow, and they sat in silence, picking at the stack of waffles, French toast and bacon.

Half an hour later, the phone rang for Sharon. It was Quinton Selsick's assistant, confirming the time of the screen test. Knowing she was a total novice, Brett was kind, telling her the whole thing would be a cinch. But her confidence was badly shaken.

She dressed carefully in a voluminous white blouse, with pleated tennis skirt for added fullness. She judged her legs in the mirror – the calves and thighs were still nicely plumped – but was a concave curve appearing at the top? No, it only seemed to show when she flexed her ankle and lifted her leg.

On her flaxen head, she popped an Alice band, leaving her hair to cascade loose. It was very Californian preppy, in the style of the 'victim' part she was up for.

Brett kissed her good luck on her perfect little nose and, settling down at the bureau in the suite's living room, said he had loads to sort, but would be waiting for her to come back so he could find out how it had gone.

The studios were only round the corner from the hotel, and she arrived at the giant hangar far sooner than she would have liked. As she tried to go over the script, she was clucked and fluffed by a batch of 'mother hens', making concentration impossible. When her hair and makeup were perfect, an assistant led her out to the floor. Quinton came over and gave her a hug, like a long-lost brother – then steered her to an actor, who was holding a script.

'This is Luke, he's going to read the part of the killer, your boyfriend. You've just found your friend's boiled head in the kitchen. Now I know this is in at the deep end for you, but I have to be sure you can handle the script. Come the real thing, we'll have plenty more time to develop the scene, so for now, just give it what you can, okay?'

Sharon nodded fearfully. So many people standing around, all scrutinising her from head to toe. The script had been sent to her in England, but try as she might to remember the lines she'd learned on the flight over, her mind was a complete blank – she couldn't even remember her surname.

The back lot darkened, and three spotlights were trained on the set of a Martha Stewart-style country kitchen.

'So, you think you know me, do you?' said the actor, narrowing his eyes wickedly.

The words and direction clicked into place.

'Not really. There are times when I haven't got a clue who I'm with.' She edged towards the knife in the drawer.

'Does that worry you?' asked the boyfriend/killer, menacingly.

'No ...' wavering tremulously '... I – I like a bit of mystery. Really. I do ...'

'Did you see me in the woods with Nikki yesterday? I sensed you were following me.'

'No. No, of course not. I was in town all day, shopping. I saw a dress I really liked ...' Wide-eyed innocence as she groped behind her for a knife.

'Liar. You've been watching me. Like I've been watching you. Every moment.' He was walking slowly towards her.

'I didn't see anything. Please, Luke ... please. You're scaring me – please, back off ...' She was biting her lips in fear, a bead of sweat trickling down her forehead. 'I want to go home, it's getting late.'

'I love the smell of fear ... makes me hungry, Lucy. You're so tasty ...' sniffing her neck like a dog '... I could eat you up.' He went to kiss her, then yanked her by a handful of her hair, grabbed her hand and twisted it.

'Aaaaagh!' Ear-piercing scream. She dropped the knife to the floor.

'What's this, my little love? A knife? And just what were you going to do with that?' Long pause. Very long pause.

Shaz's mind blanked again. No idea of the next words.

'Er, peel the potatoes?' she offered, desperately.

'CUT!'

After screwing up the last line, Sharon expected to be thrown off the set, but Quinton was striding towards her, grinning like a cat who'd just downed a gallon of cream. 'I love you, you're brilliant!' The people on the set burst into applause. Sharon was stunned – although, to be fair, she had really 'felt' the part as she acted it.

'You were so good you passed the ol' Jonesy test.' He beckoned to a set painter smoking a fag in a corner of the room. 'The hairs on the back of his arms prickled when you screamed – isn't that so, Jonesy?' The old man nodded, proudly showing off his arm.

'We'll be in touch, Shaz. There's a couple of … minor things worrying me, but other than that, the part is yours.'

'Oh, what kind of things?' said Sharon, deflated.

'Oh, you know what Hollywood can be like! A bitch dominatrix that rules us all! But nothing that can't be sorted, I'm sure. I'll talk to your agent. How about a spot of lunch?' Sharon declined, innocently thinking it was more important to get back to see Brett than to lunch with the producer.

By the time she drew up at the Pink Palace, she was feeling high and low about the audition. Keen to ask Brett for his advice, she bounced into their suite, but he wasn't there. Instead, a note was propped on the antique mahogany table.

Sorry, Shaz – had to go to an emergency meeting, not sure what time I'll be back. May not be able to take you to the airport, but my driver is at your beck and call – ring front desk.

Love, Brett

She sank on to the sofa in despair. She knew he was losing interest, and why. She glanced into the mirror – even the new outfit she'd worn for the screen test was a little loose. Sharon reached for a chocolate from the elaborate box of truffles on the table. But somehow the stress of it all had taken away her appetite.

Back home, the papers were cruel. The British press had a reputation for building up and pulling down, and Sharon's star was certainly 'On The Descendant'. At least, that was the lousy pun three papers used – complete with visual of Brett's film logo.

Worse, the waiter she'd asked for a couple of safety pins had sold his story to the scummiest Sunday tabloid. The article was entitled:

SHAZ'S SAFETY PIN SHAME

The bastards ran a front-page story on how he'd 'found her crying in the toilets and she'd begged for my help'.

A few days later she got 'papped' and more was to come: a picture of Shaz getting out of a car and accidentally flashing her slimmer thighs. Placed next to an image of her original poster for Descent, the headline ran 'GOING DOWN!' with a big circle ringing her smooth, cellulite-free legs. The same shameful story ran in three supermarket rags.

Her heart was plummeting with her weight, and the latter truly did seem to be falling. Two days after bingeing on Chinese takeaways and thick stuffed crust pizza she braved her scales again. This time, the needle stopped at 160 pounds – eleven stone four. At this rate, she was hurtling towards being an English size twelve! As for her body mass index, she suspected it was around twenty-three – although maths had never been her strong point.

This was bad – really bad. She couldn't even face the castings lined up on her answerphone. She'd also started sleeping badly, weight paranoia gripping her at three in the morning, and holding her in its tight grasp until daybreak.

Debbie headed over, armed with the latest books and a diet disc to help her put on weight. 'This is the biz!' she announced, heading towards the hi-fi. She read from the back cover: "'INNERSPEAK – using subconscious techniques of self-hypnosis and affirmations, we guarantee the pounds will pile on in days. Just believe in what your mind can achieve, and your body will follow."

Okay, you ready?' she asked, having made Sharon comfortable on the sofa, feet up.

Sharon studied Debbie's figure as she fussed around her. 'Actually, Debbie, you look like you've put on a few.'

'I have! This tape is fantastic. Trust me, it'll work. You just have to play it every day in the background and repeat the affirmations.'

The disc began with the sound of waves breaking on the shore, followed by whispering.

'I can't hear a thing! How the hell is this going to work?' asked Sharon.

'It's sinking in subconsciously. Say these words.' Debbie handed her the cover of the CD. Inside was a long list of affirmations.

My body is feeling warm and rested.
I feel fat cells growing on my thighs.
I feel large, lumpy and tired.
I am always hungry. I need food to survive.
My body wants regular meals.
I care about myself, and reward myself often.
My body needs snacks.
Sugar is good for me.
I need to rest lots, and often.
I nourish my body with the treats it deserves.
Every day and in every way I'm a winner.

'Oh, for fuck's sake' said Sharon. 'Next it's going to say, "My body is a temple."'

'It does, further down. And it is,' said Debbie, hurt.

'Well, its worshippers are deserting in droves,' sighed Sharon. However, desperation meant she persevered, listening to the thirty-minute tape three times in a row.

'Promise me you'll play it every day, any time you can, okay?' said

Debbie, beginning to sound like Jules D.

'I promise. What else have you got?'

'Lots of books. Bestsellers,' said Debbie, brightly, holding *Eat Yourself Fat* in one hand, and *Fat is a Fabulous Issue* in the other.

Sharon flipped through the pile, picking out the ones that appealed, and settled on *The Re-tox Plan* and *Think Big For A Better You*.

'Jules is also on her way over,' said Debbie, looking at Sharon, clearly concerned.

A flash of irritation crossed Sharon's mind. Was it because they were true friends that they cared or because she was the cash cow?

'Darling, I came as quick as I could. Is it true?' said Jules D, in hushed tones, as if visiting a sick patient.

'It is,' confirmed Debbie, ushering her through the door.

'Well, I've never heard of anyone dropping two dress sizes in two weeks. Let me have a look at you, darling.'

Sharon stood up, turned around, and held out her loose waistband.

Jules D gasped. 'It's not great. But it can be sorted. I've got these wonderful vitamins and fattening pills. It's going to be fine, okay?' she said, delving into a large, very expensive crocodile bag.

As often as not, Jules D ended her sentences with 'okay?'. It was always so comforting. It was one of the idiosyncrasies Sharon loved about her friend. The other was her endless supply of croissants and champagne. Always adorably generous, she never came empty-handed; this morning she had surpassed herself with a supply that would have sated the five thousand.

'Almond, chocolate, pistachio, marzipan … Oh, and I've also got healthy peach – that's the flavour of the champagne.' Raising a toast to the girls, she added, 'It's just a blip, darling, okay?' smiling warmly at Sharon.

Sharon asked Jules meekly what she intended to say to Z&ZaK. 'It's a little tricky, sweetheart – there's the weight clause in your contract. I think I'll have to be unavailable for a few days. As for Glacé Inc., why don't you avoid going in for a while, and tell that bitch Kristin you're off to a health hydro? If you can drop two sizes in two weeks, I'm sure we can help you gain the same. Now, tuck in.'

As Sharon nibbled slowly, her eyes glazed over with a faraway look. Jules D lowered her voice, and took a deep breath as she touched on a subject that Sharon seemed loath to talk about. 'Obviously, there's the trauma of your dad's illness, which must be affecting you far more than you think. I can easily put out a press release about it. It'll explain a lot, and take the heat off you. People will sympathise, be much more forgiving.'

Sharon didn't doubt they would. But the truth was, she was eating more than ever. It wasn't a question of lost appetite. Her father's diagnosis had only a little to do with her dramatic weight loss. The pounds had been falling off since the Crystal Ball. Tempting as it was to play the 'dying father' card, it would be tasteless and immoral. She shook her head adamantly.

'Sharon, maybe it's not related, but why won't you at least talk to us about your dad?' said Jules D, softly.

'If I don't talk about it, it isn't real,' said Sharon. She took a giant bite of croissant, and closed the subject.

Luckily, the *INNERSPEAK* affirmations and her increased food intake seemed to work. Sharon put on three pounds in three days, and felt a little happier.

During this time Simon called often to see how she was. Despite the hoo-hah in the press, and the fact she was now dating a film star, he was incredibly kind and understanding about her dad's illness, not shying away from the fact that he was dying, and asking her exactly how she felt.

He usually rang her at night, and she opened up to him about her past in a way she never had with anyone before. They spent hours talking, Sharon curled up on her pink pastel duvet responding to his velvet voice, like a lover of classical music. Simon had the perfect nickname for Carolyn: 'The Wicked Witch of the West'. It made them both laugh at a time when Sharon felt like crying.

But whenever Simon wanted to arrange for her to meet him face to face, she would make excuses, deeply insecure about the way her life was plummeting, in more ways than one. Finally she agreed to brunch round the corner, and wore the loosest top she could find, adding a padded money belt around her middle for extra bulk.

'Who cares about weight?' he said, when she told him the press were making her feel suicidal. 'Look at me! I'm probably one of the leanest men you'll ever meet! Most women love a big guy.' He was definitely lean, but now that Sharon was shrinking, he didn't seem half as slim as he had the last time they'd met. She guessed it was all relative.

'Listen, Sharon, an experiment was done a long time ago called Brown Eyes/Blue Eyes – you can look it up on the Net. A brilliant teacher tried to show her kids the dangers of racism. She told the class that there had been some amazing scientific research that pronounced all the children with blue eyes intellectually and physically superior to those with brown eyes. Thing was, within a day, the blue eyes were lording it over the brown-eyed kids, and the brown-eyed kids let them, feeling ashamed of their eyes.'

'The next day, the teacher came in and reversed the situation, telling her class she'd got it totally wrong, and actually it was the *brown*-eyed kids who were superior. Vindicated, they turned even more viciously on their friends with blue eyes, who suddenly felt totally inferior.'

'Thing is, neither attitude made the slightest sense.'

'You're saying it's the same with body image?' asked Sharon, trying hard to concentrate on Simon's theory, and not his own beautifully intelligent eyes.

'Absolutely. I'm a photographer and, believe me, I know fashion changes all the time. One minute, velvet knickerbockers look cute as hell, the next they look sillier than Novice Nun Barbie. Same with shape. As long as you're healthy, there is no better or worse size. It's only what the media convinces us looks good. Or bad. Attractive or ugly.'

Sharon loved conversing with Simon. He was bright, funny, and effortless company. 'Tell me, what did Max say about the dress? I feel awful. It was a great number, you know – just not great on me. My fault.'

'Ah, don't worry about Madame Du Pré. You got her name known all over the world. She said to say, "All publicity, *c'est fantastique publicité*, daaarling!"' He had caught her French accent perfectly. 'So, anyway, how's the film star you accessorised it with?'

He had finally asked the question she'd dreaded. 'Brill.' She hadn't heard from him in three days.

Simon laughed. 'I just don't get what you see in him.'

Sharon giggled, remembering the conversation she'd had with Simon over Jaz.

'Well, he was so … so keen. And I was flattered!' she repeated. Once again avoiding the word 'gorgeous'.

'And universally famous?' joked Simon.

'Well, there *is* that!' They fell about.

Mascara stinging her watering eyes, Sharon headed to the Ladies for a makeup check, but when she came back, she saw Simon had picked up her mobile and taken a call from Kristen. He held out the phone to her and she grimaced.

'Shaz, I've had Quinton Selsick on the phone. He thinks your acting is excellent.' From her disbelieving tone, Sharon could tell the woman thought she must have slept with him to get such a good review. 'However, I'm not going to mince my words. He says you're too skinny.' There was a silence as it sank in.

'So that's it?' asked Sharon.

'No, not exactly. He says he hears it's to do with family stress, and if you can show you're sorting yourself out in the next couple of weeks, the part is yours. But you need to gain at least two stone before the studio will sign you.'

'Oh, well, no problem, then.'

'You tell *me*, Shaz. You've been avoiding all our calls, and we haven't seen you since you came back from your last LA trip.' She sounded more cold and uptight than a penguin's arse. 'I suggest you book into a Thin Farm ASAP. If you get this role, it's worth half a million pounds for four weeks' work. Not to mention the launch of a whole new career. Is that incentive enough for you?' The disdain in her voice was almost tangible.

'Sure,' said Sharon. 'I'm sorry.'

'Meanwhile,' added Kristen, 'for the sake of your reputation, I'm holding all bookings and go-sees until you've sorted yourself out. So concentrate on it.' The phone clicked.

'Another drink?' asked Simon, seeing her crestfallen face.

'Pint of Guinness, packet of peanuts and two bags of crisps,' answered Sharon, with determination.

Lose a pound. Stabilise for a couple of days. Gain one or two, lose four. By the end of the following week, despite gargantuan efforts, she had dropped a further five pounds. Sharon had gone to her GP for help. He immediately sent her to a hospital consultant specialising in size dysfunction. After she had undergone more tests than a laboratory mouse, everything came up negative. In poor comfort, the only thing her doctor could finally offer was a dizzy concoction of tranquillisers and sleeping pills.

That was when she knew she *had* to visit Dr Marvel again. She'd been trying to get through to him for days but, worryingly, the telephone number Doctor Marvel had given her was 'temporarily out of order'. She was faced with no choice but to turn up on his doorstep. *En route* to Riversal Road in a taxi, she looked at the throngs in the West End streets. In the shop windows there were Tent Dresses, Tatters Dresses and Greek Widow Dresses. But, sadly, no Droopy Première Dresses, she mused.

'What number, love?'

'A hundred and fifty,' said Sharon. He pulled over at 148.

'That's odd. Can't find it,' he muttered, scratching his head. 'Are you sure you've got the right address?'

'Yes.' She handed him the paper.

'Well, that's what it says.' He was puzzled. 'Sorry I can't help you. Dunno where a hundred and fifty is. Bloody weird. However, I can tell you it's not called that.'

'What do you mean?' asked Sharon, handing him a fat tip.

'Well, y'know. It's like the way Cadogan Square looks like Cad-o-gan. It's actually pronounced Ca-dug-an. Same with Riversal Road. It's not River-sal. It's called River*sal* – as in "reverse".'

Sharon stood there. Digested the fact. And froze.

'Ta-ta, luv. Can't wait to tell the missus I had you in the car, so to speak. Cheers!' The taxi drove off.

Riversal Road. It had been exactly 150 days since she'd visited 150 Riversal Road. Dr Marvel's Miracle? Her throat constricted in fear. What had they done to her? Why had the magic reversed? She ran up and down the road, eyes filling with tears of panic, desperate to find the clinic.

Then she remembered how she'd spotted it the first time: through an old mirror two workmen were carrying across the road. And it all fell into place. There had been something odd about the first sighting, and now she knew exactly what it was. It was the name of the clinic: all the other shop names had been *reversed*. Dr

Marvel's Miracle Weight Clinic should have read backwards, like the others. The hairs on her arms stood on end. Cold fear clutched at her throat, like the clammy hands of a witch.

She grabbed the arms of passers-by, interrogated shop owners and begged traffic wardens, but an hour later she had to concede. The clinic was not there. It was gone. It might never have been there. It would probably never be there again. She was alone in this world. Alone with her dilemma. She was fighting unknown magic – magic probably more powerful than anything her willpower could ever control.

Twenty-five

'Sure I'll come with you,' smiled Debbie. 'I still want to put on some weight myself.' Sharon studied the thin farm brochure Kristen had ordered Zara to bike over. 'CHOMPERS – THE RIGHT WAY TO GAIN,' claimed the front page, showing an elegant fortress set in magnificent grounds.

'Okay, well, the deal is you make sure I do *whatever* they demand, okay? Mind you, it's damned expensive – about a hundred pounds for every pound I want to put on,' sniffed Sharon.

'Ah, but think what else you'll gain! Five hundred grand! A Hollywood contract. You've *got* to do it.'

Of course Sharon would do it, and pay for her assistant to come with her. She only hoped the £4,500-a-week price tag meant that the spa worked.

'The thing is, Debbie, I'm scared they won't be able to help. The doctors say they can do nothing, and I'm eating more than I ever used to.'

'But what are you actually eating? It's vital. Think about it,' urged Debbie, handing her a Diet Plan notepad and a pen.

Sharon looked at the catchy slogan on the cover: 'What You Eat Should Be A Big Deal'. 'Okay, let me think …' She'd had her usual two bowls of cereal and cream for breakfast, and the two chocolate bars with her morning coffee that she'd had ever since Jules D had given her an article from the *Lancet* that showed how milk chocolate prevented osteoporosis.

Lunch? No problem. She always started with two bread rolls and butter wherever she dined, and tended to stick with courses that involved thick, cheesy sauces. When she had dinner at home, she was careful to order thick-crust pizzas or Chinese – and always with either fudge cake or banana toffee fritters. Nope, she really didn't think she was slipping up at all.

But then she reluctantly allowed herself to remember the fruit stall on the way home. Such a friendly chap. They'd started chatting, and it had seemed only polite to buy his fruit. Such a delicious display of shiny red apples and plump green grapes. How could she resist?

Guiltily, she recalled buying a half-pound of each. So what? So, she'd eaten an apple. Well, two, if she was honest with herself. No harm in that. But there was. She had to admit it had filled her up more than she'd expected, and she'd missed her usual afternoon tea and cake.

The grapes had spoiled her appetite just before dinner – and there had been that banana. She'd eaten the lot.

'Any fruit or veg?' asked Debbie, with the uncanny perception of a mind reader.

'Just a couple of apples,' Sharon answered, innocently.

Her friend took a judgemental intake of breath. 'Go on, I bet that filled you up!'

'Well, I guess so. But I still managed two puddings after dinner,' she added proudly. She didn't want Debbie to think she was a sad, skinny bird.

'Sharon, this is the kind of stuff you've got to watch out for,' warned Debbie, stretching her sinewy body. 'Trust me, you don't want to end up looking like me.'

A week later, the two girls stared up at the high, ivy-clad stone walls of CHOMPERS Health Club.

'Looks just like a prison,' shivered Debbie, nervous at the prospect of being force-fed.

Sharon felt a little more confident. After all, she was practically normal. At least, she was nowhere near as skinny as Debbie.

The towering medieval doors groaned with exclusivity and torture. 'After you, my lady.' Debbie curtsied.

Was that a bud of sarcasm? Sharon suspected that Debbie's attitude was increasing in ratio to her boss's decreasing girth. Or was she just being paranoid? Whatever. Sharon's fragile new confidence felt a little tremble as she entered the high hallway. What if she failed *here*? She would be stuffed. This was the Last Chance Saloon.

Their footsteps echoed on the cold flagstones. Sharon's stilettos, reinforced for her struts on the catwalk, clipped so loudly that she tried to tiptoe up to the reception desk. Behind it, an auburn haired, rosy-cheeked doctor in a white coat signed them in.

'Woah,' whispered Debbie to Sharon. 'If I come out with a figure anything like hers, it'll be worth the agony ... and your money.'

Sharon clocked the woman. The white cloak clung to her perfectly proportioned fulsome shape, and although she was clearly middle-aged, she had the irresistible appearance of a mouth-watering treacle dumpling.

'Hello, Sharon, Debbie. My name is Dr Honey Battenburg. I'll be assigned to you for the entire week. Any problems, come to me. In moments of weakness, girls, remember – I'm only a buzzer away.' She smiled kindly. 'It's a battle to achieve perfection, and I'm on your side. This way.' She gave a smile that advertised expensive cosmetic dentistry and led them to a sterile white room. Sharon sniffed enviously. Even the woman's name oozed extra inches.

She handed them thick towelling robes, told them to strip to their undies and left them alone. By the time she returned, the two girls were huddled together like Romanian refugees.

'Who's first on?' asked Dr Battenburg. Seeing Sharon wasn't going to budge, Debbie reluctantly volunteered, and stepped cautiously on to the scales.

'Drop your gown, dear,' the doctor instructed her gently.

Standing there almost naked, Sharon had to admit Debbie's figure had been steadily improving since she had first visited her after their row. She could see the way her bottom had started to spread and dimple prettily. Sweet crinkly wrinkles poked from underneath the rotund cheeks. Her thighs had also filled out: curvaceously convex at the side, instead of muscular and concave.

'Um ... not too bad.' Dr Battenburg slid the weights along the top of the professional scales, chewed the end of her pen and did some quick calculations. 'Okay, we need to get your body mass index up quite a lot, and ideally you should aim to put on between twenty-five and thirty-five pounds – a nice size eighteen.

'And now you, Sharon. Please, let me take your dressing gown for you.' Aware she was dealing with a celebrity, Dr Battenburg's tone was far more obsequious.

'Let's see, here we go ... a hundred and forty-five pounds. About size ten. Hmm. I think we can do a lot better than that, can't we, dear?'

'WHAT? No! No – that's impossible!' Sharon grabbed the woman's arm. 'Do it again! These scales are wrong! *DO IT AGAIN!*' she screamed.

Dr Battenburg backed away, her hand searching nervously for the emergency button that would bring the men in white coats running. 'I'm terribly sorry, my dear. These are state-of-the-art scales, accurate to the nearest milligram. Calm down, Miss Plunkett, please. I know it's sometimes a bit of a shock to be faced with the truth, but we have to know these things, don't we?'

Glancing round in wild panic, Sharon noted the sympathy in Debbie's eyes – and hated her for it.

'Listen, my little love. You've nothing to worry about,' soothed Dr Battenburg, as if she was talking to a frightened toddler. It had the right effect: Sharon sobbed quietly as the doctor patted her hand. 'Here's your activity and health programmes for the next forty-eight hours. You'll be monitored carefully. Be strict with yourselves and you'll definitely see results in the end.'

With a reassuring, motherly smile, which made Sharon want to throw herself into the woman's dumpling squashy bosoms, she led them to their sleeping quarters.

The room was luxurious beyond belief. Fur bedspread, deep pile carpets. Log fire and, on the mahogany table, a bunch of pink chrysanthemums with a card saying, 'To one of the world's most beautiful flowers! Good luck, Jules D.' It was so, so typical of her, and so sweet, but Sharon was momentarily deflated. Until she'd read the card, she'd thought maybe Brett had sent them.

'I love it here! I thought we were heading into a monastery cell, but this is truly the Kingdom of Heaven! Look, television, DVD, bar and fully stocked fridge,' said Debbie, clapping her hands in glee and opening the door. 'Oh, look at that,' she quavered. Alongside milkshakes of every flavour, there were designer chocolate bars, cashew nuts, fudge, crisps, and pretzels – each separated and labelled Monday, Tuesday, et cetera. A red sign stated, 'Minimum required daily intake'.

A sight that would once have made Sharon think she had died and gone to Heaven now made her feel like Hell. All she wanted was a glass of iced water. Sharon had kept it secret, but she had begun to hate the taste of junk food. It was weird, but anything too sweet, creamy, sugary or savoury sometimes made her feel sick. On the other hand, she often craved fruit and vegetables, like a ravished rabbit. But, of course, they wouldn't help her bulk up.

'There's no way I can go through with this.' She quailed, glancing at the fire escape.

'Don't be so pathetic,' chided Debbie, irritated. 'Look, silly, it's simple.' She opened a peanut crunch bar, and ate it in three bites.

Sharon calmed down, and lay on the bed sucking a finger of fudge. On Debbie's advice, she kept still and saved calories as she watched her friend unpack their bags.

Later that afternoon, while Debbie headed off for an unenergetic game of tiddlywinks in the sports arena, Sharon stretched out for a relaxing massage. As the Swedish therapist kneaded her flesh, she imagined it was being stretched and expanded.

Stretched, expanded … and filled.

'And this oil contains factor twenty-two,' grinned the handsome blond Viking. 'After all, you don't want to get a suntan, do you? It always amazes me how it makes women look so much slimmer and smooth-skinned. A disaster.'

Sharon peered down at his hands rippling over the tops of her thighs. Over the last few weeks, the grapefruit peel had vanished. Now it looked more like orange peel. Nope. Sharon had to face it. More like a slightly bumpy apricot. Talking of which, for some unknown reason she really fancied one right now. Oh, how she craved that tart, fresh taste. Tangy, fruity and light.

By night, both girls had retired for a cosy night with the stack of DVDs. Sharon had become nervous of being seen by the other guests – she had recognised a famous footballer's wife with a well-known eating disorder in the room next to her.

'I don't understand why you want to hide,' said Debbie, desperately keen to star spot. 'There's no shame in being here – it's almost a status symbol.'

'No, it's not, Debbie. You're confusing it with rehab. The press are never so kind about this sort of thing.' Sharon, of course, was right.

And her face was well known to all. Anyone could spot her and tell the papers. Even the staff. Could she trust Viking Boy? Could she even trust Dr Battenburg not to talk in return for a down payment on her retirement?

For the tenth time that night she checked her text messages. Finally there was one from Brett. She replied by pressing the call button.

'Hi, babe, how's it going?' said the famous voice at the other end.

'Not so great. I feel miserable. I haven't heard from my father — I have a feeling the messages aren't being passed on. And I hate it here. I just want to go home,' she bleated.

'Now, come on, Shaz, what's happened to that voluptuous big woman I kissed at the ball?'

'She's just thrown up three packets of crisps and a Twix,' wailed Sharon.

'Stick at it, sweetheart. I know you can do it.' And the phone went dead.

'Well, that's incredible,' trilled Debbie. 'I can't believe the difference.' She had just undergone two hours in a herbal water-retention tank to plump up her fat cells.

Looking at Debbie's pink, glowing, fertile-fleshy body, Sharon nodded morosely. Unlike Debbie, who had gained three-quarters of a stone, she had lost a further fourteen pounds. A steady two pounds a day. At this rate, she had sixty-three days to live before she vanished. At six feet tall and only nine stone two, she was now nearing size eight.

'There is, of course, surgery,' advised Dr Battenburg, deeply perplexed and worried that a client as high profile as Shaz would leave the premises weighing less than she had when she entered.

Considerably less. There was no question: the sacred reputation of CHOMPERS was dangerously at stake.

'What does that involve?'

'Well, lipo-addition. It's painful, I won't deny it. And a fairly new procedure. We use a harmless silicone fat substance that is then siphoned into your buttocks and stomach. I'm not sure with such continuing and dramatic weight loss that it's the right course for you, though. We need to stabilise you first.'

'So what do we do until then?' asked Sharon, helplessly.

'Therapy. That's what we need to try next, my dear.' She checked a clipboard of notes. 'We've run every test imaginable. Your problem is clearly not medical, and according to our monitoring, you're not breaking the rules. Sometimes the mind is stronger than any of us gives it credit for. It's time to meet Dr Grotemaster. He has his own slightly *eccentric* methods, but he gets marvellous results. Come with me,' said Dr Battenburg, leading Sharon way down into the bowels of the gargantuan building.

'Dr Grotemaster, meet Miss Sharon Plunkett. You have her notes.'

Sharon looked at the other people sitting in the semi-circle around the room. Most hung their heads pathetically. All were slim. Hideously slim. English size eight and below.

'You look shocked, Sharon,' said Dr Grotemaster. 'Ve 'ave here American size zero and in some cases – stand up, Stacy – size double zero.' Stacy, all hair extensions and spoiled pout, was dressed in designer tracksuit and trainers, but you could still see her bones. 'Tell our new friend Sharon how we are all united on one thing. We are, aren't we, class? Tell us what it is.' He thwacked a ruler against his thigh, like a Nazi SS officer flicking a whip.

'*Gaining weight*, Dr Grotemaster,' they chimed as one.

'Sit down, Sharon. Over there,' he ordered, in a thick guttural accent. His balding head and half-moon glasses, mean lips and sharp nose made him cold and intimidating.

Sharon turned with pleading eyes to Dr Battenburg, but she simply pointed at the chair too. 'Go on, dear. Do as the good doctor says.'

Dr Grotemaster continued, 'Now, I vant you all to think "fat". Do you understand?' He put on music – an old vinyl record on a vintage gramophone. It scratched out the Pastoral Symphony.

'Ludwig van Beethoven ... a master. Like *you* are all masters. Masters of your own minds. Now,' he smacked the ruler down hard on a tabletop, 'I vant you to imagine "fat". Do you understand? Close your eyes and imagine your body growing. *See* it growing. How do you look? Turn around in the mirror of your mind. Now, *feel* it growing. *Sense* it growing. *You* can make it happen. It *vill* happen. Repeat: "I CAN MAKE IT HAPPEN ... I CAN MAKE IT HAPPEN!"'

Three days later, it hadn't happened. Three pounds lighter, she lay on the floor with the other losers. Soft, tinkling music played in the background, as Dr Grotemaster tried variations on a theme.

'*Feel* those dimples on your thighs. Imagine your skin bubbling,' he urged.

Sharon imagined her thighs. But it was useless. She knew the truth: her unique, lumpy, soft, watercolour skin was turning into a blank, boring canvas. Her hand snuck down to feel it. Smooth, unblemished in texture. Taut and sleek as the flank of a thoroughbred. How her heart cried.

Later that night, it was to cry some more. After days of silence and unreturned calls, she had a text from Brett. Excitedly she pressed the open button. But it simply read:

```
Sorry Shaz - not going to work out. Brett.
```

That was it. Seven words. Seven short, shitty little words. Sharon threw the phone from her in anger. 'That bastard! I'm not going to let him finish with me like that!' she railed. 'I can't believe it – by text!'

'Oh, no, that's so *mean*,' said Debbie, sympathetically – though she'd done the same thing many times.

'Look at that! The prick couldn't even be fagged to type in the word "it's" – as in "it's not going to fucking work out"!' cried Sharon. 'Bastard! I'm going to tell him exactly what I think!'

'Please, Sharon, don't do it. He's so not worth it. Let it go.' Debbie tried to stop her dialling with a rugby lunge, but Sharon still had enough strength to shove her friend off.

Trouble was, Sharon had experienced too much pain recently to just 'let things go'. 'Hi, it's me. Thanks, Brett. I got your sweet text. Tell me something, how does a man who pays more than a quarter of a million dollars for a kiss just walk away like this? What happened?'

There was a silence. Then: 'Shaz, it was easy. Now leave me alone.'

'Just answer the question.'

'Okay, if you insist, I will. First, look in the mirror. Word has it you're losing even more weight, and you're as skinny as a sparrow. I don't like slim women, okay? They turn me off. And, second, if you must ask, that quarter of a million was well-spent PR. Amazing coverage. I got it all back on tax, okay? I have to add, though, it was a great kiss. Unexpected bonus. Take care now. 'Bye.'

Sharon looked at the silent phone, and felt the same dark helplessness she'd experienced as a little girl. Unable to answer back. Unable to defend herself. She howled and rocked like a baby as Debbie held her in her arms. As she tried to sleep, despair kept her tossing and turning for the tenth night in a row. Once again, the dark bowl of night made her a murky soup of fear.

*

She'd asked her father to walk her down the aisle; she'd thrown her bouquet to Jules D and the waiting crowds, waved to the paparazzi, and sailed off with her actor in a golden hot-air balloon.

'You're too light!' he yelled at her, as the balloon rose higher and higher. Then a scrawny bird flew by and burst it with its beak.

She tumbled down, down, down. Down to her death.

The next day, Dr Grotemaster had a breakthrough as he tried to break her down. But it wasn't what he expected. His methods had changed. Now he was getting his class to group-cradle each other and talk about their generally troubled childhoods, though some had suffered more than others.

'Very good, Stacy. So, your brother flirted with your best friend, and they ignored you. Very good. Now, Sharon, let's hear from you.'

Sharon made no move to lie in the centre of the group. They all held their hands out for her, their faces warm and shiny. Sharon felt ridiculously touched, but resisted the naff horror of the idea.

'Trust me, it vill vork. Ve've had many famous clients here – people you'd never have guessed needed our help. You do as I say. You need to open up. Discretion is my middle name.'

What's your first and last? thought Sharon, bitterly. Hitler and Goebbels?

Half an hour later, Sharon was still talking, her face drenched with tears as she described her mother.

'Vas she slim, your mother, or fat?' asked Dr Grotemaster.

'Oh, model slim,' said Sharon, proudly. The class and the doctor looked puzzled, but Sharon was now drifting into her own past world.

'And vot happened ven your father remarried? How did your new family make you feel?'

'Lonely. An outsider. An outcast. Unwanted, worthless.'

'And vhy do you think that vas?'

The people in her group held her close, stroking her hair as she choked out the answer.

'My stepmother was full of hatred for my mother. My father never got over her death. He never loved his new wife as much, and I think she knew it. I was so like my mother – everyone used to say so … and when they did, I would catch Carolyn looking at me with such bitterness. I think she – she wanted me to disappear.'

'So, how did you cope? Vot did you do?' he said, polishing his round-rimmed glasses fervently.

'I don't know …'

'Yes, you do. Picture your life back then, Sharon. There you were, all alone …'

Sharon shifted uncomfortably, hating the feelings that rose up from her gut, like the arms of a strangling octopus. She remembered the constant rows. Her stepmother screaming at her because she'd left a drawer open. Her stepmother storming into the sanctuary of her bedroom brandishing a plate she'd forgotten to wash up. Her father doing nothing to protect her. Her stepsisters quietly smug, watching her get into trouble again and again. Esme and Mona … Esmeralda and Desdemona. Good grief, she'd never noticed that before: their names would have been perfect for the Ugly Sisters …

'Concentrate, Sharon. Follow through the visualisation. What did you do after a row?'

Sharon allowed herself to picture one. The row in the kitchen when she'd spilled the gravy. She remembered crawling back to her room with a packet of biscuits. The time she'd left the door unlocked? She'd taken the telling-off, then hidden in the garden. She'd sobbed for hours – but at least she'd had that yummy coffee cake to comfort her.

A pattern was emerging …

'Go on, Sharon, ve are getting somevhere, go on … you ate.

Good. How did you see yourself vhen you looked in the mirror?'

Dr Grotemaster's excitement was mounting, his magnified eyes peering at her as if she was a slithery specimen on a Petri dish.

Sharon pictured herself in her little bedroom. The full-length mirror hanging on the inside of her cupboard door. She remembered the hours and hours she would stand there, staring at her face, tears streaming down her slim cheeks, hands tearing at her young, slender body.

'I – I looked just like my mother. But *she* hated my mother. I didn't want to look like Mummy … It hurt too much. It really hurt.'

'Oh, God, I wanted to be loved again. That was all I wanted. I thought if I didn't remind her of Mummy, she would care for me.' Sharon let out an almighty, shuddering sob and continued, talking to herself almost in a trance. 'Stupid, stupid. If I don't look like Mummy, you'll like me better. *She*'d like me better. I'd like me better. So … so I ate. I ate and ate. I ate until I got huge. Until I looked nothing like my mummy, nothing like my old self. I felt better … I felt worse.'

The room fell silent in sympathy, as Sharon digested the revelation.

She looked up at Dr Grotemaster, then at her companions, who were wide-eyed and stunned.

'Oh, my God, I *ate*. Non-stop. *That* was why! So I wouldn't look like my mother!'

It was as if a light bulb had been switched on. No, that was a cliché, and the moment deserved so much more than that. It was a sudden realisation that burned brighter than the Blackpool Illuminations, the Northern Lights and the Millennium Fireworks against one very dark night sky.

Sharon cried out in anguish, memory … and relief, as she forgave herself for all the years of loathing her body and her lack of willpower.

'Right, so ve have to stay vith zis feeling of wanting to eat, live zis moment again,' snapped Dr Grotemaster. But it was too much for Sharon: she apologised, hugged the group and disappeared to her room to make an urgent call.

Twenty-six

Dialling Bournemouth for the third time, she left a message asking someone, anyone, to call. Her dad had only spoken to her once since her last visit, and it had been heated. She hated going into the house – because of all the old wounds it opened up – so she had asked if she could take him out for tea at a little hotel only fifty yards from where he lived.

'Yes, dear. That would be lovely, really lovely,' he agreed happily. Sharon was thrilled at the idea of sitting in the pretty courtyard and having some private time with him. At this stage, every moment with him was precious.

Ten minutes later, he rang back. 'Why are you asking me to do this? I'm a sick man,' he stated accusingly, as if Sharon had invited him to dance naked on hot coals.

Sharon was dumbstruck. It had seemed perfectly reasonable to her. Even though he was ill, she knew he often went out with his wife to catch the fresh sea air. Indeed, he'd told her she couldn't see him the day before because he was going to Esme's house for lunch.

What had happened in the ten minutes since he had been so excited about going out with her? Sharon knew exactly what had happened. She could just imagine Carolyn's shrill, nagging voice when her father had said he was going out for tea.

'Joe, you're a sick man. You know that. How can you think of going out for tea? I have all your medicines. What if something goes wrong? I'm not taking the responsibility, Joe – after all, I'm the one looking after you …' The manipulation of his wife was so obvious to Sharon, why not to him? It was as transparent as an oxygen mask what she was up to. The woman was determined to make Sharon's last few hours with her father as uncomfortable as possible. If nothing else, Carolyn was consistent.

Compromising, Sharon told him she would come down to see him if he could make sure that they could be alone – no TV on, no step-relatives in the room. He'd said he'd organise it, and call her back. Two weeks had passed, and she was still waiting.

A couple of hours later Debbie joined her in the room, and was surprised to find Sharon standing stock still, staring at her slim form in the mirror, eyes distant.

'You know what?' said Debbie, oblivious to the drama going on in Sharon's head. 'Perhaps the answer is not to move so much.' She was towelling her hair from the Jacuzzi she'd been soaking in, and insisted they both try the Stomach Exercise Room.

'Come on,' Debbie cajoled. 'You never know, you might enjoy it.'

Very slowly, as if guiding a sick patient, she led her friend along the meandering corridors until they reached a glass door. Sharon looked inside the large, wood-floored hall. It was too much and she turned away. Debbie pushed her through the door. Dressed in fluffy white robes, about twenty guests lay on white leather *chaises-longues*, like a school of stranded walruses. A corpulent customer shifted his weight and clicked his fingers at the staff. Worried at his exertion, one of the attendants immediately ran over and handed him the remote control panel for his personal TV system. They lifted the headphones on to his ears, and he grunted a perfunctory 'Thank you.'

The table beside each lounger was laden with goodies. Popcorn, flapjacks, marshmallows, boiled sweets. Without taking his eyes off the screen, the man opened his jaws, allowing the attendant to pop in three pink marshmallows dipped in chocolate.

'Take a lounger,' insisted a plump young male trainer, wearing a white tracksuit embroidered with the CHOMPERS emblem in gold.

Sharon stretched out, the leather-cushioned base hard under her bony frame. It reminded her suddenly of the *chaise-longue* in Dr Marvel's waiting room.

'What would you like to watch? Modern, musical or old classics?'

'I don't know. I don't even care. Maybe an old classic?'

He plumped a cushion behind her back, put a DVD in the side of the TV and pulled it across her on a swing arm. 'How about this? *The Mirror Crack'd* with Rock Hudson and Elizabeth Taylor?'

Sharon was annoyed at his choice. Was he being subversively rude? Then she sat up with interest. 'Stick it on,' she demanded.

She waited for the appearance of Liz – an old film. Would it show her as slim or fat? She sometimes thought she'd dreamed a world in which women were idolised for being skin and bone. But when Taylor made her appearance, it told her absolutely nothing. She was simply plump and middle-aged. Despondent, Sharon flopped back weakly and, believing she had acquiesced, an assistant immediately stepped forward to spoon-feed her some cake. She took the first mouthful, which tasted unbearably sweet. She craved some fresh juice or fruit.

'Come on, just one more,' coaxed the trainer, firmly.

'Please, no,' she begged, crumbs of chocolate cake making a dark moustache around her mouth.

Looking around the room at the others chomping away, Sharon's stomach turned. She was going to be sick.

While she was crying and puking into the toilet, the door suddenly swung open. 'You naughty, naughty girl!' scolded Dr Grotemaster. 'You're doing that on purpose.'

*

'Ve *vill* get to the bottom of zis ... I believe ze vay forward is hypnosis. It vill unleash the corners of your mind.'

He was beginning to take her failure personally, and he scared her. Certainly, a private session with the Nazi was so not what Sharon wanted, but she'd just received a phone call from Kristen: 'Michael Grey wants to meet with you as soon as you're released – I mean when you come home. So be quick, and be fit – if you know what I mean. Size eighteen, nothing less.'

Sharon was so far from that target, she didn't even have the energy to reply. The moment Michael Grey saw her, the contract would disappear faster than her skinny butt. But it did spur her on to sort out the rest of her life before it was too late.

'Now go back, Sharon – go back to when you first felt unhappy about your weight.' Grotemaster had her stretched out on a soft couch in his office. Books were neatly stacked two feet high on his desk. The walls were covered with packed shelves, apart from one, which proudly displayed obscure certificates from universities and conferences all over the globe.

The lights were lowered, the blinds drawn. Suddenly she felt very, very sleepy. His voice drifted in and out, in and out ... All she wanted to do was go to sleep, and for his voice to go away. But every now and then she heard a question, and found herself answering heavily, exhaustedly, in the hope he'd be satisfied and drift away. Far, far away.

'... and so, you say, you took this ... magic pill. What happened next?'

Sleepily Sharon described the hope she had felt on the day she had gone shopping for something new – a wardrobe of clothes to suit how she was going to look. 'It said I couldn't eat anything for two hours ... so I just shopped and shopped. Bliss.'

His voice seemed even more distant ... she could barely hear it.

But he prodded her to speak some more. She floated in and out of consciousness.

'I saw this beautiful yellow dress, tiny blue flowers ...' Off she drifted again, like a boat softly bobbing on a long mooring rope.

He hauled her back a little. 'You say you were in a cubicle, and the dress vas too small? How did zat make you feel, Sharon?'

'Bad ... really, really bad. I couldn't get the dress off. I remember ...'

There was a long, long pause.

'Remember what?'

'I remember falling to the floor, sobbing. I was hot, suffocating in there ... miserable. Hated myself. So sad ... so lonely. So ugly. And then, I ... I saw my bag.'

She stopped.

'What was inside, Sharon? Go on.'

'Inside was a piece of cake ... a fairy cake I had left over from earlier. I reached for it and – OH, GOD!' Like a drowning bug fighting a whirlpool, she forced herself fully awake and sat suddenly upright, dizzy. 'OH, MY GOD! OH, MY GOD!' She grabbed his collar with both hands. 'Dr Grotemaster, YOU'VE GOT TO HELP ME!' I *ate* it. I ATE! I didn't wait the *two hours* on the instructions! I ruined the spell. I ruined it! Do you understand now?'

Peeling her hands off his white coat and trying hard to hide his disgust at their boniness, Dr Grotemaster looked at her resignedly. He didn't understand, not at all. And, despite all his professional experience, he didn't think there was any hope that he ever would.

Twenty-seven

Sharon stood in the shop doorway as the day darkened. Above, a monstrously bulbous cloud filled the skies, stretched its pregnant belly and released a heavy gush as its waters finally broke. Her phone rang. It was Jules D, calling her back.

'I got expelled,' said Sharon, ashamed. 'They asked me to leave.'

'Oh, my poor love, I know. I read all about it.'

'What's been happening in the outside world? Go on, tell me your worst.' Sharon wiped raindrops off her face.

Jules D took a deep breath, ready to use years of honed diplomatic skills. 'Okay. Well, Z&ZaK have cancelled the contract for the time being. Thing is, Shaz, it's a really sophisticated brand. They were a tiny bit disheartened when you got mobile-phone papped at CHOMPERS.' That was a Jules D understatement of the highest order.

The front pages had run a sneaked-out shot of Sharon in a screaming match with a bald-headed doctor, shoving a giant cake into his bespectacled face. ZaK's actual words had been 'Fire the skinny bitch!'

'Urban Cool has, er, cooled off a little too. Slight problem there, from what I hear.'

'But they never put a weight clause in because they were mainly shooting my face. Even though they've dropped me, surely they can't ask for any money back.'

'Um, well, you may have noticed half the name of the product is, unfortunately, "Cool" – and there is a clause about behaviour. Alas, food fights at a thin farm aren't quite street cred at the moment … although maybe I could put a spin on that,' she added hopefully.

'Don't bother. What else?'

'Remember that cover shoot you did for *Rich Recipes* magazine just before you flew out for the première?'

'Yes, in my bikini eating a pavlova.'

'Well, some bastard from the photography studio sold a story to the tabloids that he spent six hours retouching your image to make it look fatter. Big storm. Readers screaming they were being fooled, and all that.'

'I had nothing to do with it! That's not fair! Christ, how much did he retouch?'

'Oh, I don't know. The usual they always do, probably. You know, teeth, hair. But I think he also shortened the shot to make you look more rotund … and maybe added an unnecessary bump or two. They do it to cover shots all the time. It's just that people don't realise it. Bad luck, sweetie, that's all.'

'Anything else I should know about?'

'Damn – other phone's going. Sorry, darling, I've got to go. Call you later, okay?'

Sharon put the phone down, feeling more alone than ever. She felt Jules D had lost interest professionally and as a friend. She was more washed up than the wrappers in the fast-filling gutters that gurgled at her feet.

Sharon walked along the windswept streets, a shadow flitting between the big, the bold and the beautiful. With so many pounds lost, her walk felt airy and light, almost as if she was floating. It increased her feeling of invisibility. She spotted a Minus Miss Shop, selling size twelve and below for skinnies. Wandering in, she looked at the other women, heads down, sorting through the drab, uninspiring clothes to find something, anything, that would flatter them and make them look a size larger. The shop girls employed were minus sizes, to make the customers feel more normal. Sharon eyed the minuscule American double-zero assistant behind the counter, and knew she wasn't that far off. Whatever, at six foot tall, everything hung on her willowy frame like damp rags on a scarecrow.

She aimlessly wandered out, not caring to buy anything, not caring whether she ate or drank, not caring whether she lived or died.

At first, there had been a plethora of break-up articles in the press – bitchy features with titles like 'SKINNY SHAZ STONE-WALLED BY BRETT'. But now they concentrated purely on her weight, with features like, 'SKELETAL SHAZ SHEDS STONES!' accompanied by pictures of her tiny frame, hand held in front of her face, hiding from the camera lens. It was utterly insane. How could the number of pounds a girl weighed *rate* such coverage? How had it ever come to this? But there she was, on front pages alongside global warming, war and world peace.

Luckily enough, Sharon's trademark eyes and hair could be easily disguised with a hat and dark glasses. In the streets, it seemed no one had a clue who she was. Or maybe they just didn't expect to see someone so well known walking around like any other shopper.

As she braced against the wind to head home, she heard a tiny *ting*. She thought she might have imagined it. When she checked she saw she had a message from her father's home number. She clicked, and read with horror: 'Your father's condition has dramatically worsened. Call if you want to see him.'

Shaking, she dialled immediately, and Esme answered the phone. 'Yes, well, he had a bad night. Don't think he's going to hang on for long. Come now if you want to see him.'

She couldn't drive after such a shock, she thought. She didn't know what the hell to do. Distraught, she rang Debbie, but then remembered she was still at CHOMPERS, finishing the third week. She rang Simon's studio, but was told by one of his gang that they thought he was out of town on a shoot.

Somehow, three hours later, blinded by tears and the harsh hammering rain, she found herself standing outside her father's house. Hands trembling after the hellish drive, she stood there for ten minutes, trying to compose herself, feeling a churning wave of anger, betrayal, hatred and love.

Finally she plucked up the courage, and knocked.

A nurse opened the door and showed her into her father's bedroom. Like a wizened old warlock who had snuck into a giant's bed, he lay asleep, propped up with a couple of pillows.

Sharon gasped, desolation sweeping through her with an icy chill. The final days of illness had left him almost unrecognisable. And, no, he wasn't asleep. He was in a coma. She was too late. In shock, she thought of all the things she had wanted to say to him, the words she'd been formulating on the way down. But it was all too late.

'When did he fall into this state?' she asked Esme, who suddenly looked uncomfortable.

'Well, he's been getting worse day by day. But he went into the coma yesterday morning.'

Sharon realised that they hadn't texted her until after he was unconscious, robbing her of any chance to talk to him. No question that was deliberate. She fought back the bitter words she longed to say, and turned her attention to the frail shell that barely breathed in front of her.

'I'll leave you alone. Take your time,' said Esme.

Sharon stared at her father, and touched his hand. It was warm, alive. He was so motionless that she had almost expected it to be cold.

'Dad ... Dad? Can you hear me?' Nothing. 'Dad, it's me, Sharon. I'm here.' No response. Sharon noticed his walking stick propped up against the flowered wallpaper, and tears fell as she realised he'd never use it again. She tried to wrap his limp arm around her, feeling like a lost little girl and knowing it would be the last time she'd ever have a hug from her daddy. But there was hardly any room to curl up next to him. She laid it down gently.

Whispering, 'Dad,' over and over again, Sharon thought back to the old days when he had occasionally visited her in Kingston. He'd always tried to excuse Carolyn's behaviour. 'Sweetheart, I know you two don't get on, but she looks after me.' It had been his mantra for years. Funnily enough, he had never said to Sharon, 'I love her,' about his second wife, which would have been easier to take. Just 'She looks after me well.' That had always hurt, especially when Sharon was a young girl. After all, *he* was the parent. It was selfish. What he meant was: 'Sorry, darling, she's really nice to me, even though I know she's horrible to you. If you love me, you should be happy for me.'

Whatever. That Carolyn's behaviour had made it difficult for Sharon to see much of her father in later years was his bad karma. The price *he* had paid. Never having stood up to her, had he finally felt trapped at the end? Maybe.

She tried to push away the negative thoughts, and looking at her father now, she just wanted to tell him how many memories she would carry of him. How she would always remember him with love. Would he look out for her on the other side?

His breathing was laboured and irregular.

She had started to speak softly to him when Esme unexpectedly came back into the room. Remembering their brief time as kids together, Sharon felt a fragile bond between them now. 'Is this normal? How long has he been breathing like this?' she asked quietly. Her father would take a deep breath, then stop for a while, then breathe again. Each breath, she thought, might be his last.

'Since he went into the coma. I'll get my mother to come in again.'

No! thought Sharon, experiencing the queasy fear Carolyn's presence always made her feel.

But Esme had left the room, and Sharon panicked. When she had arrived, she had thought they would at least give her twenty minutes but now that was to be snatched from her. She hadn't said anything she had wanted to say – she hadn't told him she loved him. Hadn't kissed him goodbye. Before she could gather her thoughts, Carolyn flounced in, and draped herself across the bed.

'Please just give me two minutes to say goodbye,' said Sharon, wanting precious seconds alone with her dad for the last time.

'I'm his wife. I deserve to be here. He might die at any minute.'

Sharon was horrified. This woman had had many weeks to say her goodbyes, many days and hours when her father had been capable of responding. Now she wanted to steal the little time Sharon had too. The woman's selfishness was indescribable. Shocking. Despite a three-hour dash through the storm, Sharon was going to be left with no tender farewells, nothing. The cuckoos were once again taking everything they could from her.

'I'm his daughter!' Sharon snapped. 'I'm only asking for two minutes.' At the very least, Carolyn could have chosen to wait by the door for a few moments. But, no, she refused to leave, settling herself even closer to Joe in a pathetic act of possessiveness. Sharon stood back, disgusted. 'You really are an *evil* woman!' she cried, in anguish. Words she should have said long ago. Shakily, she stood to leave the room and her stepmother forever.

Unmoved, Carolyn pursed her lips self-righteously and raised an over-plucked eyebrow. She looked just like the wicked stepmother in *Cinderella*. Cruel.

A small, rattling sigh escaped her father's lips. Startled, both women turned hopefully to the bed. Sharon paled at the thought that the last words her dad would hear were hers cursing his wife. 'They say the last thing to go is hearing,' said Carolyn, relishing the unexpected weapon of revenge Sharon had just handed her. With a thin smile, she plunged it straight at her stepdaughter's heart. 'What have you *done* to him?' she cried, fluttering her hands, waving Sharon out of the room immediately. 'You've killed him! Nurse!' she screeched, eyes not leaving Joe's face. His body lay still.

The seconds hung in the air, like hovering angels of death. Sharon could almost feel the beat of their wings against her cheek. Then he sighed again. More like a whisper. Both women bent their heads nearer. He whispered again: 'My Gizelle …'

It was Sharon's mother's name. It hadn't been mentioned in the house for years. Carolyn had banned it. And now it rested flagrantly on his lips, soft and warm, treasured and loved. 'Gizelle …' He drifted far, far away. His breathing returned to a deep, coma-rasp.

Full of longing and love, it was the most beautiful, heart-wrenching sound Sharon had ever heard, a gift to her. She knew it was the perfect time for her to go. Looking at her father for the very last time, she stroked his forehead, then swept out with new dignity. On the way, she glanced at Carolyn's distraught face, features frozen, like a gargoyle's. Sharon smiled sweetly at her. The irony. With just a single word, she had irrefutably won. Somehow both women knew it would be the last word he ever spoke. Neither would forget it. And no one, not even Carolyn, had the power to take that priceless moment away.

Her father died twenty hours later. The nurse sent the date of the funeral by text.

Twenty-eight

It was dark outside. Sharon lay curled in a ball, eyes staring at the tissue-strewn floor. Weeks had passed. Or was it a day? Maybe it was just an hour. Sharon had lost all track of time. The loneliness and the knowledge that she'd never see her father again came sporadically and often. A sudden memory surfacing would create a wave that would rise, then crash over her, leaving her sitting in a sea of salty tears. She'd had a few phone calls from Debbie, Jules D and Simon, but didn't have the energy to reply. What the hell? None of them really cared anyway.

At random intervals she had dragged herself up to the scales and stepped on. It seemed her weight had finally settled at 114 pounds, just over eight stone. At nearly six feet tall, the falling elevator had juddered to a halt, leaving her an American size zero. The magical 'dream weight' she had once longed for, in a galaxy far away ... Well, at least she wasn't going to disappear, she surmised miserably. But how had she ever thought this look was stunning? To Sharon, now used to thinking big was beautiful, her head seemed too large for her body, a little alien in appearance, while her sad shoulders jutted sharper than a wire coat hanger. She was so gaunt she could fit into children's clothes. *Infants'* clothes, at that.

The thought that equally tortured her was her lack of willpower, the fame and beauty she had lost because of it. She couldn't forget the scene in the cubicle, berating herself again and again for eating the fairy cake. How could she have not lasted *two* pathetic little hours? Regardless of her mixed-up life as a kid, she was now an adult. There was *no* excuse: she should have had more control. But instead she had been a deliberate back-seat passenger as she drove along the highway of self-destruction – and it had taken this to see it.

Whatever. One thing was for certain: she had thrown away her big chance, destroyed the one miracle that had truly changed her life.

Well done, Sharon. She took a swig of wine.

On the occasions she could raise herself up, she trawled the Internet in a desperate fervour. Dr Marvel or his Miracle Weight Clinic were nowhere to be found. But she did find sites dedicated to stars' weight: whether up or down, every pound was monitored. The truly-obsessed fan could even receive emails announcing if their idol had lost or gained a quarter of a pound. It was sicker than her own body, thought Sharon.

She lay there trying to think of one good reason to live. But it was hard. She now had no family. No one to care about her. No one to call on Christmas Day. Or to call her.

She also had no work. She had been dropped from Glacé Inc. like a melting dollop from an ice-cream cone. Splat. Contracts cancelled and money owed back. To add to her woes, she was due to move out of her home and sanctuary in just two days' time. Not only had she so far failed to pack a nail file, she was moving to a strange new place with a staggering £600,000-plus mortgage. And since she wasn't working, she'd probably have to use the last of her money to pay it off. What would she live on then?

But, worst of all, the papers and magazines had continued their merciless onslaught. She couldn't pass a newsagent's rack without seeing 'Skinny Shaz – Shock Snaps' splashed all over the covers.

She was everyone's figure of fun. All she wanted to do was crawl out of sight, like a wounded bear. No, she was flattering herself. That animal was warm, big and cuddly. She was a starved little mouse. A measly little wounded mouse that had scabby fleas. Or was that fleas and scabs? Whatever...

If only she could hide somewhere for*ever*. Move away. As she thought about it, the idea grew more and more appealing. Who the hell would miss her? Not Jules D. She just saw her as a client. Not Debbie. Instead of best friend, Sharon was just her boss and a passport to a glamorous life. A life Debbie was already experiencing with John ... Joe ... Jack? What's-his-name. A life Sharon was never going to experience again. Then there was Simon. Gorgeous, funny, witty Simon. He'd never fancy her now. Oh, get real, face it: he never had fancied her. Sharon groaned. If only she could stop the hurt. If only ...

Then she realised she could go away forever. The drawer in her bathroom contained the answer. A supply of sedatives that would send her to dreamy sleepy bye-byes, and all her problems would fade away. Just like her. What a great idea! A feast of barbiturates.

She wrapped her old fluffy dressing gown round her almost twice, and made her way slowly to the vanity unit. Her long legs shook with what she knew she wanted to do. She reached inside, took out two bottles of dainty white pills and carried them back to her messy nest-bed.

She swallowed a couple with a third glass of wine and laid her head back.

She rang Debbie.

'Hi, Sharon! Long time no speak! How are you coping?'

'Not great. Not great at all. Oh, Debbie ... I feel so alone.'

'Sorry, speak up, kiddo. What did you say? You feel you want to own ...?'

'I feel so ... Can't you hear me?'

'Not too well. You're rerouting to my mobile. Hey, guess what! Remember that crappy Saturday job we had at the Cut Above? Well, I'm *there*! They're having a launch party. Can you believe this? They want *me*, as your assistant, to open their new salon two doors down. I'm *so* excited! *Me*, a celebrity! They're actually paying me. What a hoot! Have to go over and cut a ribbon – I just heard that cow manageress saying she hopes I can do it better than I cut anyone's hair!'

'Sounds fun. Hope you have a really good time,' said Sharon, weakly.

'You okay?'

'Sure. I'm fine. 'Bye. Have fun now. Have a good time for me.'

She was feeling drowsy. She had to make the decision to go for it or not. She held up the pills in the bottles and shook them as if they were carnival maracas.

'All I wanted was to enjoy life a tiny little bit more. To fit in. That's all,' she murmured. What to do, what to do? She held a bottle outstretched in an upturned palm. '"To be or not to be, that is the question."' She struggled to remember her classroom Shakespeare lessons. 'To be fat, or to be thin? "Whether 'tis nobler in the mind to suffer the slings and arrows of outrageous fortune" … each has brought with it? "Or to take skinny arms against a sea of troubles … To die: to sleep …"' she finished dramatically, pleased with the Sharonspeare version.

There was no one to hear her performance. She sobbed with loneliness, slugging back a fourth glass of wine in despair. Did she really want to do this to herself? Could she do this? No.

She decided to ring Jules D.

'Darling, how are you?'

'Okay,' said Sharon, sadly.

'Okay? Not by the sound of it. Look, I can't talk – I'm with a client right now. I'll call you back, okay?'

'No, no, don't worry. Don't. It doesn't matter. You stay with your client. I'm fine. Really fine. See ya. Must have lunch. 'Bye ...' Sharon hung up, tears making her sore eyes even redder. She felt so let down. So alone.

All she knew was that she didn't want to feel anything anymore. Ever.

Maybe that meant she had to die. Hopefully Heaven was a place where people didn't have bodies so nobody was judged. Maybe everyone's soul just floated around, like a swarm of happy atoms.

Her mind was rambling as her eyes felt heavier. She tried to pour another glass but, hands unsteady, spilled the wine over herself. Grabbing the bottle, she tossed back a gulp, then took a long, hard look at her body in the full-length mirror at the end of her bed.

Ironic. She was exactly as she had once dreamed she wanted to be, all those weeks ago in life before the Pill.

You did it, Sharon! She sighed with disgust. So there she finally was. Size 0. A great big nothing. An empty hole she'd fallen into. No, make that slipped. An oval mouth that gaped ready to swallow what was still left of her.

At only twenty-one, the elasticity of her skin meant it shrink-wrapped her bones now, leaving her taut and firm. But now that just seemed bland. Boring and bland. Not a pretty wrinkle, dimple or roll to be seen. Tears silently falling, she looked at her back view with a hand mirror. The gap between her stick thin thighs gave her legs the emaciated look of a famine-struck African infant, her protruding ribcage the carcass of an antelope. It was horrible! She smashed the hand mirror against the wall, shattering its glass across the wooden floor. Wobbling now, as the drink and drugs took effect, Sharon sank to her knees, rocking herself back and forth. She rocked incessantly, silently, like an orphaned cot baby that would never be picked up. Being slim, being fat ... It didn't matter. All she had ever wanted was to be normal, to be loved.

330

The papers now said she was a skinny freak. She picked up what was left of the mirror, and stared at her reflection, distorted in the shards. She hated what she saw: the pain in her eyes frightened her. Forget the pills – they took too long. She could end it now. A couple of slices on the flesh … Quick and easy. She picked up a large, vicious fragment that had skittered behind her, her green eyes reflected back, a dull, muddy sludge. Then, with her other hand, she reached for the pill bottle.

'To be or not to be?' Which to use, which to do? The irony was so heavy, she gave a bitter laugh. The mirror had ruled her life. A pill had changed it. How about both? she thought cleverly.

She downed another swig of wine, popped another pill, and poised the sliver of glass. 'Ouch!' It was a superficial cut, so not a lot happened. She was doing this all wrong. Pathetic, pathetic, pathetic. Maybe the Grecians had got it right: a nice hot bath, cut the wrists and take the pills. Or maybe take the pills and cut the wrists. Either, both … or none?

Slowly, she crawled towards the bath like a poisoned slug and turned on the taps. She pulled herself up and over the side, settling into the cold walls as warm comforting water embraced her body. She was a baby in a wonderful white cot …. It rocked. … It was a cradle. It was a 'coffin'. Her mind drifted along on the tide.

She didn't care. Not long now before I can just switch off … Peaceful, lovely … loooovely sleep.

Somebody was banging at the door.

How irritating, thought Sharon, eyes shut, head rocking.

'Go away! I'm too tired,' she shouted. But it came out as a whisper.

Keys jangled, and the voice of Mrs Lucas, her landlady, could be heard. And a man's.

But Sharon had slipped into blissful oblivion.

Twenty-nine

'Dong!'

The sound of a gong reverberated in the air, its echo mixing with the incessant wail of an emergency siren. Head thudding, Sharon felt the wheels of the ambulance bounce and ricochet over speed bumps, her body jerking like a rag doll against the stretcher restraints.

'Dong!' She opened one eye groggily.

'Doctor, she's comin' to … Hello, darlin'! Welcome back,' said the stunning blonde in a white mini skirt and cheeky nurse's hat.

Oh, God, thought Sharon. I'm hallucinating. Leaning over her, velvet-soft bosoms protruding like a pair of puppies, the sexy nurse from Dr Marvel's clinic snapped the elastic of the oxygen mask as she removed it from Sharon's face. Behind her swayed Dr Marvel, head to toe in green paramedic robes, banging a gong with a dainty silver hammer.

'Ah, Sharon, my dear girl, how are you feeling?' Dr Marvel tossed aside the gong and took hold of her wrist in a caring-consultant manner.

Sharon tried to speak, but her mouth wouldn't move. It felt frozen shut, as if she'd had a block anaesthetic from the Marathon Man's dentist.

'Um.' He sighed theatrically. 'Barely a heartbeat. Nearly stopped. Not good. Not good at all. Still, we've been expecting this.' He checked her pulse against his Mickey Mouse wristwatch.

'Then it's time to ask our patient the question, Docter,' urged the nurse, in a Southern belle drawl. 'Time is a-runnin' out.' She grinned, holding up a giant green egg-timer. 'Ah think she's ready.'

Sharon looked wildly around her for help, but there was no one in the ambulance except the two mad medics and herself. The vehicle rattled with oxygen tanks, tubes, dials, yellow webbing and, in the corner, giant red scales. The same old-fashioned type she'd seen in Dr Marvel's clinic. He took out a torch and shone it mercilessly into her eyes while the nurse unravelled rolls of trauma bandages.

As the doctor peered into her face, fairground music crackled out of the walkie-talkie dangling from a strap behind him. With humungous effort, Sharon leaned forward and grabbed his lapels. 'Whothehell*are*you?' she managed.

'Okay, dear child. I suspect you might be a tiny bit annoyed at how things have turned out. But, really, you should have read the instructions.'

'You shnould have gwarned me' she drug-slurred. Despite his best efforts to shake her off, Sharon clung onto his gown like a pesky little stick insect.

'Relax, my dear, relax. We can help. We just need you to answer a little question. A squillion-dollar question, in fact – the fast buck, the quick cent … the silver dollar,' he pronounced, suddenly slipping into corny game-show rhetoric.

Sharon tried to protest. She was the one with questions, she thought angrily. Who the hell *were* they? Where had their clinic vanished to? How had they … ?

But before she could utter a clear word, he had peeled her hands off him and a lollipop-shaped thermometer was thrust under her tongue.

'You tricked me with your advert!' she managed to convey,

helped by the psycho-Bates look in her eyes.

'Now, that's a little harsh, Sharon. We never said we had a pill that would make you lose weight.'

'The doctor's right. We never misled you. All we promised was "a magic chance to change your life".'

'ALL!' squeaked Sharon, now sounding like an emasculated mouse due to the obstruction of the thermometer, which, she thought, tasted appropriately of humbug.

'Often in life you get what you wish for, if not in the way you thought,' sighed the nurse, gazing longingly at the doctor.

Sharon tried to argue.

'No talking now.' The nurse shook her head. 'Honey, jus' relax and listen to the doctor. He has somethin' real important to ask you …'

A firm hand was placed on her shoulder, pinning her back as the vehicle veered dangerously to the right. 'Okay, Sharon. Here it is. When you first came to visit us, I know you were desperate to be hip, fashionable and cool. More than that you said you were "dying to be slim". And look at you. You finally made it. Of course, sadly, you made it *here* … in a literal sense. And in this little parallel world.'

'So it *is* a parallel world?' she managed to mumble.

'One of many.'

'I don't understand…'

'Sharon, have you not heard the irritating new-age maxim "Ask the Universe and it will provide"?' Well, it will. It's a fantastic, infinitely massive, sprawling, evolving force, and in some really deserving cases, it does provide. And we are the Earth's guardians of this little-known law of physics. Or, in your particular case of reversal, perhaps we should call it "physical law"!' He chuckled, amused at his wit.

He looked proudly at his nurse, who pinched his bottom.

'All highly complicated astrophysics, but I'll try and explain,' he continued. 'Take Einstein's conversion of mass to energy, add it to V=RY – as you know, that's Ohm's Law – then divide by Velocity = DT – that's speed, and I don't mean the drug because, as you probably know, that's 1-phenylpropan-2-amine. But I digress … Compare it to the Apparent Stellar Magnitude M=25log to the power of 10, I + K. Next, multiply it by the fundamental *pi*, subtract the mystical number seven from the equation and – well, you get the drift.'

Sharon didn't. The only word she had understood was 'pie'.

'However, there are always conditions that can dramatically alter the result, as you have unfortunately found out. In truth, I've been feeling a little bad at how things have turned out for you, my dear.'

'Bad, my poor darlin', real bad.' The nurse smiled, stroking Dr Marvel's hair comfortingly.

Sharon's irritation was growing. '*You* feel bad!' She snorted.

Turning to pick up the magnifying glass behind him, Dr Marvel peered at her closely, his eye enlarging to a giant saucer. She recalled their first meeting – she had arrived at his clinic full of hope and despair.

'Now … here's the good bit,' he went on. 'I've been working twenty-four/seven on your case. I need your answer. We can send you back, reverse the formula and deliver you to your first world, no problem. A world where slim is in, remember? Better than that, you can return to it exactly as you are. Imagine, you'll be a celebrity size, itty-bitty-sexy-skinny-minny, boringly referred to as size zero.'

'I'm not sure I want to go back,' she replied, thinking of her old flat, her boring job and the aching loneliness waiting for her there.

'Or you could simply stay here as you are. Or we could send you back as you were. The choice is yours. Whichever you prefer. Hurry up, we're almost there – and you still need to answer the squillion-dollar question.'

Stunned, Sharon tried to comprehend the offers. 'What if I don't answer you?' she muttered, still muffled by the thermometer.

'Tut, tut. Don't spoil our game.' The doctor smiled.

'One or the other, darlin', one or the other,' chimed the nurse, holding up four exquisite fairy cakes, one pink, one purple, one lilac, one blue. On top of each lay a matching Smartie. Only it wasn't a Smartie, Sharon realised, it was a pill.

She looked down at her scrawny frame, taking in the jutting lines of her elbows, the gristly sinews snaking down her arms. She tried to remember why she had yearned to be thin. She had once thought it so desirable. She envisaged herself trotting down Bond Street in her old world, lanky racehorse legs striding, head held high. But the thought of it just made her feel exhausted, frail, ugly. No, there was no way she wanted to remain as she was. No way, no matter what world she was in. She had grown to love her soft curves and yearned to have some back. But she had grown to hate the press scrutiny of having a famous body. Then she thought of Simon … Debbie … Jules D. And something important that had just occurred back at her flat. Something good. What was it? It was all a weird blur, but she knew she wanted to see each one of them again, as soon as she could …

The nurse leaned over close to hear her answer, removing the strange thermometer with a flourish. Sharon found she could suddenly talk perfectly. Her mind was as clear and sharp as glass. 'The thing is, I love it *here*,' she announced, as realisation dawned. Her head swam again … fat, thin, skinny, plump, old world, new … Confusion overwhelmed her. 'Can't I just stay here? Please, help me. Please … I don't really care how I look. I just want to feel content. Feel good. Oh, God, what a choice. Help me, please. Isn't there a happy medium?'

Dr Marvel gave her a joyous, maniacal grin. Like Batman's 'The Joker' after a big fat joint.

'DONG!'

He banged the gong more ferociously than ever.

'THAT IS THE RIGHT ANSWER!' bellowed the nurse and Dr Marvel in unison, the reverberations of the gong numbing Sharon's ears.

A game-show sting blasted out of a hanging walkie talkie adding to the deafening noise. Beaming triumphantly, the nurse kissed her on both cheeks, then joined the doctor in a triumphant high five. 'We did it!'

What answer? She hadn't given them one. They hadn't even asked the question. As Sharon looked at them, bewildered, the nurse whipped out yet another fairy cake, this time a vanilla one with rainbow sprinkles and a white pill, and told her to take a big bite out of it, ensuring she ate the sweetie on top.

Losing the will to care, Sharon did as she was told. It was utterly delicious. Intoxicating. The icing melted over her taste buds, releasing a lavender scent that reminded her of a violet-cream chocolate on a sunny spring day. As she licked her lips to savour the last morsel, the straps were released on her bed, and she attempted a wobbling stand, helped at either side by the doctor and nurse. At that moment, the ambulance screeched to a juddering halt. The doors were flung open, and blinding white rays of light poured in. All three let go of each other to save themselves falling over. Silence at last. Shielding her eyes, Sharon took a tiny step towards the light … For just a second she thought she saw her father smiling, arms outstretched. Had she died? She concluded that she had. The bright light welcomed her closer, like the soft, enclosing wings of an angel.

Thirty

The hospital room was deathly quiet. Outside an approaching siren wailed. Simon sat on the bed's hard edge, his head in his hands. He shuddered at the sound of the siren, as if he was being shaken awake. His head was throbbing, and the noise made it worse. Then it faded away.

'Why?' he asked aloud. No one was there to answer him.

The landlady had let him into Sharon's flat, but that was all she could have done. That was all anyone could do now.

'Why did she do it?' he asked himself. If only she'd talked to him more. 'Oh, Sharon, why?'

He felt a hand on his shoulder, and looked up to see a familiar, equally distraught face. 'It's all right,' said Debbie, looking down at him, with a shaky smile. 'I'm here.'

'I just don't understand,' he said. 'I don't get it.'

'There's nothing to understand.' Debbie sighed, feeling the pain of guilt and sadness. 'Poor Sharon, she was going through so much. We should have seen it coming. I think she just felt she had nothing to live for.'

'But she had *us*,' he said, eyes welling.

'I don't think she knew that,' said Debbie, sitting down next to him. 'She was always so insecure. Ever since her mum died. It didn't help that her dad remarried so fast, and to such a nasty piece of work. Poor thing felt so rejected, she just never believed she was worth loving.'

'Oh, Sharon … you silly, sweet girl. You were always so lovable. I was falling in love with her, you know. I should have told her earlier.'

In love with her?

The voices were floating in the air, disembodied.

I'm dreaming, thought Sharon.

No, it wasn't a dream. The last moments were coming back to her.

I'm in Heaven! she thought, relieved she'd made it over to the other side. And someone's saying they love me. Somebody actually loves me … What a heavenly place this is. She sighed, her body bobbing lightly on a soft, fluffy cloud.

The voice sounded deliciously familiar. It was Simon's. What was he doing up here?

Wait, it's coming from far away … Well, of course. Obviously, in Heaven you can hear those on Earth whom you care about. She loved Heaven. It seemed she'd be able to see as much of Simon as she wanted. It was good being a free spirit. But it was surprisingly dark. She couldn't see a thing. Nothing. Where were the bloody lights that were supposed to guide you? She had walked out to look for her dad. Where had he gone? Shouldn't he be waiting for her, hands outstretched, at the end of a tunnel or something?

Sorry, but it really was too bloody dark. Must find an angel to complain to. She strained to see in the pitch black.

Her eyes flicked open.

'Great,' said Debbie. 'Simon! She's coming round again!'

'Sharon, you're going to be okay. We're here,' said Simon.

Sharon looked into his eyes, and breathed a deep sigh. She was alive.

She was lying in a hospital bed. The damp tendrils of her hair spread over the pillow. She tried to lift her hand to his, but it was leaden and heavy. Then she noticed that her wrist was bandaged.

'Do you remember what happened? How many pills you took?'

Sharon squeezed her mind hard to concentrate.

Not many – two, maybe three.

'Debbie, show her the bottles.' There were two, completely empty. Crumbs, thought Sharon. No wonder they were freaked. Then she was shaking – the shock of what she'd nearly done.

'Things would have been far worse if the second bottle had been sleeping pills instead of vitamin C!' Simon grinned. 'And, don't worry, they've pumped your stomach out,' he added.

'You're going to be fine. Your tummy's empty,' said a comely nurse behind him.

Oh, God, had Simon seen all that? Sharon was mortified.

'What else do you remember?' the nurse encouraged her.

Had she puked *on* him? She tried to recall …

There was Simon turning off the bath taps. What had happened? Like steam clearing from a bathroom mirror, the scene in her memory slowly unravelled …

She remembered the banging on the door, and then his voice: 'Sharon, speak to me. It's me, Simon.'

'Oh, God, no – I look like crap.'

He'd sighed. 'Great! You're still with us! What the hell do you think you're doing?'

'I – I don't know. I just want to sleep. Please, I really need to sleep.' There had been a splintering noise and the door had opened. She had tried to curl into the foetal position, but Simon had bent into the water, lifted her light frame up into his arms and cradled her, like a precious child. There was water all over the floor.

'Sharon, come on. Wake up,' he had said, as they headed towards her bedroom.

'What are you doing here?' she'd tried to ask him, but her mouth was working strangely.

'Debbie rang me from Croydon – Jules too. You hadn't spoken to any of us for three days, and then you called us in one go. And you sounded terrible.'

'You rang me before?' Sharon had been confused.

'Many times.'

She had looked at him through half-closed eyes. She had felt so drunk, so floaty, and so sure she was going to die. She remembered feeling she had nothing to lose. Not a jot.

'*Soooo*, tell me, Simon, what do you really think of me … really think?' she had slurred, as the room swam around her. 'Am I cute?'

'What do I think? I think … You want the truth? Okay, why not? Hang in there, and you'll get it.' He'd flopped her on to the bed, bound her wrist with a twisted towel, made an urgent call, then wiped her face with an ice-cold flannel. Sharon had forced herself to wait, fighting the urge to roll into a ball.

It had been ages before he spoke again. 'Here it comes, then. You always make me laugh. I love being with you. You're great. Very cute. More than cute … In fact, oh, God… you might as well know … I probably love you. There, now I've said it. What the hell? I'm crazy about you. Adore you. Always thought you were gorgeous as hell. Now, start talking back, don't fall asleep.' At this point he had crouched over her, rechecking her arm, ripping something up and tightening it around her wrist. His cool, practical manner and controlled emotion were so attractive.

'What – me? You love me? Always thought I was lovely? Fat or thin?'

'Both. Sure. Why not? I've told you it's all in the mind, anyway. Keep trying to tell you that. And, hey, I'm not exactly built like a caveman!' he had added modestly. 'Though now I think of it, they had some good ideas. Let me take you for a drag.' He had thrown her arm over his shoulders and forced her to keep moving.

She had thought he was the most beautiful caveman in the universe. And when her drowsy mind had finally registered the meaning of his words, it was the best morsel of news she'd ever had. And then she remembered more. The best bit. As he'd propped her against a wall for a rest, he'd bent his head and brushed his lips across her forehead. She had responded automatically, throwing her head up to his. He had pulled back, a little surprised. Then he'd leaned down and softly kissed her lips. Twice. Each time causing a tingling sensation all over her body. His mouth had tasted sweet, like strawberries and clotted cream … like almond crème brûlée … like coconut cookie ice cream … Yes, she was finally getting her just deserts! But he had made her hunger for so much more. Sharon knew she had managed a smile before she had closed her eyes, desperate to sleep.

As it all flooded back she suddenly wanted to live – life was good! She looked longingly at Simon, standing over her like a ridiculously handsome, concerned medical student, then at Debbie. Even though she was dressed in her finest designer suit, her lipstick and mascara were smudged. And her face was extraordinarily pale. It's Coco Chanel the Clown, Sharon thought, with naughty irreverence. She closed her eyes, and tried to remember what had happened next.

The sound of clattering stilettos on wooden floors, and Sharon saw Debbie's chubby legs stalking into the bedroom, her feet clad in a high pair of red fake Louboutins.

'I got here as soon as I – Oh, my God! I'm too late!'

Through half-closed eyes Sharon had seen Debbie throw her hands to her mouth in diva hysterics.

Simon had calmed her. 'I know there's a lot of blood, but it's just a superficial cut. I think she's going to be fine,' he'd said, turning back to pull Sharon close, wiping the damp hair off her forehead tenderly.

'Debbie, you came too?' Sharon had said, struggling to open her eyes and focus. 'I thought you were busy…'

'Of course I came, you silly cow. Missed my big moment too! You had me so worried, Sharon. Really worried. I love you, you know. You're my oldest mate.'

'And now your skinniest!' Sharon recalled smiling soppily.

They told her the paramedics were on their way. The room had gone dark again.

Then they had arrived. 'You go downstairs, let them in. I'll stay with her,' Debbie had said, as she slipped under Sharon's arm to take her weight.

'No, you go,' said Simon, worried. 'I don't want to leave her. I don't think I ever want to leave her,' he had added quietly, this time looking directly into Sharon's sleepy green eyes.

Below the window she had heard the siren howl …

And finally she remembered what had happened inside the ambulance. Had she been hallucinating? As the blanks in her memory tussled to fill themselves, she thought she could hear the distant fairground music of Dr Marvel. It was coming from the hospital radio. Following her gaze, the nurse clicked it off and left the room. Debbie called after her, getting directions to the canteen.

'What do you fancy?' she asked Simon. He didn't need to answer.

As he reached for her friend's hand, Debbie smiled and discreetly left the room. Sharon felt a sudden shock of excitement as his fingers made contact with hers. And the fluttering of her heart was nothing to do with the electrodes wired to her pulse. What had the gypsy said? 'I see a man involved in pictures.' It wasn't Brett. Of course it bloody wasn't. Simon touched her cheek and caught a tear on his finger. Sharon looked at it, confused. For the first time in her life, she had shed a happy one.

She'd ask her father to walk her down the aisle; she'd throw her bouquet to

Jules D and the waiting crowds … and …

And then the image faded. Nothing came to mind. Nothing filled her imagination.

What type of wedding? She couldn't picture it. But it was not to do with the sleeping pills or the wrong man. She didn't want to think about it this time. Sod it.

He deserved more than a stupid fantasy because he was different. This was real. And she would take it one step at a time. Right there and then, she knew the only thing that mattered was that he really, really cared about her – fat or thin.

And they were finally going to get it together.

Epilogue

Eighteen months later

The studio lights shone in her face, the music blared, and Sharon watched a young minus-size model toss her golden hair in the wind machine, her long limbs, slender torso and tiny bottom disguised in baggy white jeans and a loose T-shirt. She felt a little sympathy for the girl … it wasn't easy to be so slim in a world that celebrated curves.

'Love it. Perfect. Give your hair another shake,' said the famous photographer, running his hands through his own floppy hair with a disarming smile.

As the girl worked in front of the lights, the rest of the team buzzed around Sharon like busy worker bees attending to their queen. Should the model wear this top or that one? More eye makeup? Less lippy? Would Sharon like her hair up, down, straightened, curled, or cut? Sharon knew she could say, 'Shaved,' and it would happen.

She was so happy! She imagined the swarm carrying little placards, saying, 'Sharon Rules Okay!'

Clear green eyes, glossy locks and glowing skin, Sharon had never looked healthier. Wearing a floaty top and marabou-trimmed skating skirt from Maxine Du Pré's latest collection, she swanned over to Simon to ruffle his hair.

'God, you look fantastic. I love you, kiddo,' said Simon, glancing up from behind the tripod.

'Love you too,' she trilled, with no fear of rejection.

'Darlings, isn't it time for a break?' said Jules D, coming out of the studio kitchen with a tray of champagne flutes and *pains au chocolat*. Max was at her side, laughing at some private joke between them.

As Sharon took a mouthful of the delicious home-baked pastry she gave Jules D a giant hug. 'I owe you so much, Jules, thank you.'

'Really? I think the croissants might be a little stale,' smiled Jules D.

'You know *exactly* what I'm talking about!' insisted Sharon.

'Ah, you must mean my dinner with Mr Grey. Marvellous man. Mar-vell-ous. There I was, eating and drinking with him, while you were popping pills and slitting your wrists. Silly girl.'

'Had I known at the time you'd set up a meeting with him, I might have given that bit a miss!' said Sharon.

'You'd had so many knocks that I didn't want to give you false hope. But maybe I should have. I knew I could pull it off. More champagne?'

'Make that a coffee,' said Debbie, protectively, emerging from the dressing room with a grin.

Armed with a stack of clothes in one hand and a pot of coffee in the other, she clip-clopped over in a pair of purple velvet shorts and thigh-high pink suede boots that made her chubby legs seem even more curvaceous. These days, Debbie was thrilled with her plump figure, but in a grateful, self-deprecating way, not at all smug.

As Sharon poured herself a steaming, aromatic cup, she recalled the moment when she had found out that her life would change yet again.

It was when Jules D had visited her in hospital later that awful night …

'Is she okay?' she had asked, rushing into the room.

'She's going to be fine,' Simon had replied, sitting at the side of the bed, stroking Sharon's arm softly.

Sharon had opened her tired eyes to see Jules D, normally so together and controlled, now looking shaky and ashen-faced.

'Thank God!' she had said.

Sharon saw shock on her friend's face when she noticed her bandaged wrist. 'I'm sorry,' she had apologised lamely. 'So very sorry. I just didn't think anyone cared. Gosh, you left a client for me!'

Jules D had knelt down and hugged her. Sharon had felt a warmth sweep over her, a feeling of protection she hadn't felt since her mother died.

'Of course I did, you sounded so strange. Darling, you're one of the funniest, most lovable women I know, but you're also the most desperately insecure. Listen to me, Sharon. I know you think you're not worth loving, and I also know exactly why you think that. But, believe me, you are, okay? I'm going to have to get you a pile of those self-esteem books … and a free consultation with one of my clients. He's a top therapist, okay?'

'Okay,' Sharon had agreed meekly. 'In fact, it seems my life is always okay when you're around,' she whispered.

As Sharon had closed her eyes, Jules D softly placed her hand against her cheek and let out an unaccustomed sob. 'We've had such a fright. Why did you do it, Sharon?' asked Jules D trying to compose herself.

'Tell us why? I know things were bad, but you've got lots to live for.'

Sharon had struggled for words, embarrassed. 'At the time, it didn't seem that way … no family … no work. I was a failure. Nothing lined up.'

'Not true, Shaz. For a start, you've got us. And as for work, darling, things can always change. As it is, I've got some amazing news to tell you, but I don't think now's the time. Wait until you're feeling stronger.'

'Oh, please,' Sharon had begged. 'Please? I'd love to hear some good news. Go on.'

'Okay – if you're sure? … Well, when you rang, I wasn't really with a client, I was having dinner with Michael Grey.'

Still groggy, Sharon had struggled to remember a face to go with the familiar name.

'Darling, the man who wanted you to design a range for Bessie B's?' Jules D gently prompted.

'Why were you with him?' Sharon had asked, unclear what Jules D was leading up to. Was she dating him?

'My poor darling, you were so miserable, so distraught with all the horrible things happening to you, I wanted to see if I could salvage anything for you. And guess what? He told me he still thinks you have amazing style, fat or thin. He told me that when he met you, he was completely knocked out by you. So, I made a suggestion. And he thought it was brilliant. He wants you to be the figurehead of his Minus Miss chain for slim women. How about that? And it's going to be near enough the same mega-deal as he offered you for Bessie B's!'

'Really?' Unreal! Sharon had thought to herself.

Life had a funny way of reversing when you least expected it.

At that point Debbie had come in, carrying a tray of hot coffee and a plate of canteen doughnuts. Shrieking with delight at seeing Jules D, she had shoved the tray down and they'd flown into each other's arms. Then they had turned to look at Sharon.

This was her family. Sharon had an overwhelming urge to hug them all. 'Thank you, all of you, for saving my life. And I don't just mean today.' She'd held out her arms.

The four had clasped each other tightly, and a blissful surge of belonging had coursed through Sharon for the very first time. The outsider was now on the inside.

So here she was. The third shoot for Minus Miss was going brilliantly. Sales had increased dramatically, Michael Grey was thrilled, and she was now in charge of the collections. Sharon stretched her legs under the table. They were long, curvaceous and saucily dimpled at the thigh.

She sighed with pleasure: they looked so utterly feminine. The incredible thing was that, over the months, she had slowly and steadily put on weight. She was now too big to model for the Minus Miss range, but not big enough to be a gorgeous Glacé Inc. model again. Oddly, she had stuck at around size fourteen. She didn't care – she felt fantastic. Indeed, she was what you could call a happy medium! *Exactly* what the doctor had ordered.

Luckily, Mr Moneybags Michael Grey said it didn't matter either. Skinny girls everywhere knew she could identify with them. And they with her. After all, they had seen her fall from grace. No question in their minds that Shaz understood the hell of being unhappy with your weight – being laughed at. Being considered 'uncool'. She had been one of them and they would never forget it.

As everyone stopped work to hit the champagne and croissants, Sharon looked fondly at *her* gang, smiling as they teased and chatted with each other, and once again felt a great sense of wellbeing.

She no longer felt alone. Ever.

And it was great.

She took another sip of coffee and watched the model laughing in the corner of the studio as she tried on a wacky hat. Sharon admired her confidence. The minus-size world of modelling was a tricky one. You had to have a really stunning face, like this girl. Sharon had thought of using a size six or even a size zero girl for her shoots, but to make the clothes look good it was safer to choose a size ten or twelve. The fashion world was so damn 'lookist' – even a standard agency minus-size model wasn't really that minus.

As the coffee taste tingled on her tongue, a thought began to percolate …

She had a formidable team around her, right under her nose.

With Simon doing the photography, Max designing, Debbie

organising admin, and Jules D in charge of marketing and PR, she had a feeling they could make Minus Miss a major global brand.

They would be bold, not apologetic, make the customers feel truly good about themselves, not ashamed. They had to make them believe there was nothing wrong with being skinny. Instead of resorting to baggy styles and white garments to accentuate their customers' curves, they should design clothes in far brighter colours. And maybe tighter – or even in slimming *black*. Now, there was an idea! With Maxine's clever designs they could make a statement, and do an *entire collection* for Minus Miss in black. Why not? It would be great to make these women feel proud about the shape and definition of their bony bodies. That would get fantastic PR too.

In fact, with the right advertising, promotion and press coverage, maybe there was a way they could actually make it in for women to be thin.

Sharon smiled secretively at the challenge. Of course, she knew both sides of the looking-glass, from every angle and every pain. And that was a huge advantage.

First, there would need to be a drastic shift in the public mindset led by the media. A prolonged and extensive campaign to redefine conventional attractiveness. That was the key. Sharon knew she had unique experience in this field – an idea of how it could be done, which no one else could touch. She was also very famous. Indeed, when she weighed it up, she believed there was every chance she could make Minus Miss big.

Very big.

The real squillion-dollar question was … should she do it?

If you enjoyed the book…

I'm often asked what gave me the inspiration. Well, I can pinpoint it exactly. It was when I got on the scales one morning and realized that yet again I'd put on a few pounds. I thought how much I hated my figure and wished I were in a world where I would be celebrating this news, instead of looking at my body in disgust.

Lack of self-esteem is a problem that affects practically all of us, and I feel concern for the generations to come. Below is a true incident that tells me there is a strong message to get out there:

Over coffee with a gang of school mothers, one of the group told us how the day before a girl in her child's class had lined up all the others in weight order! She then flounced down the line proclaiming 'you're okay', 'you're plump', 'you're fat!' As she was the coolest, prettiest, slimmest girl in the year, they were all hoping for her approval.

Horrified, I asked the mother what words of wisdom she had offered her daughter and she sheepishly confessed the first thing she had said to her child was: 'Where did you come in the line up?'

The children in that class were only ten years old.

What's happening to create this extreme body consciousness? Media manipulation of what is now considered to be ideal is warping our perspective. The evolution of cheap photo retouching means elongated and flattering images are literally everywhere, and it has become an ever-present advertising technique. No wonder so many of us feel despondent with the reality.

Those of us who remember Twiggy, will recall she was named as such because she was exceptionally skinny. Check out her old photos and compare her to today's catwalk models. She'd be the 'norm'.

I want to stress that the message of *Making it Big* is NOT about being fat versus slim. I am just attempting to expose the machinery and madness of being a model or a celebrity today, and the insane pressure of that world, that filters down to all of us.

It is about extremes on both sides. Neither is healthy.

More than anything, it is an attempt, however small to help women reclaim their right to be content with the way their body naturally looks.

The fact is our mindsets can be easily altered to view beauty in a different way.

The truth is, there is no 'perfect size'. Just a happy, healthy size.

If you want to get involved or feel the same way here's some ideas to inspire you in return.

a) Support this campaign at http://www.realwomen.org.uk/

b) Check out this video:
http://www.campaignforrealbeauty.com.au/dove-self-esteem-fund/evolution-ad.asp

c) Have a look at these gorgeous curvy women:
www.judgmentofparis.com

I'm always keen to hear your views on my Twitter page:
@LyndsayRussell or facebook:
http://www.facebook.com/pages/Making-It-Big/211788495512450

Best wishes,

Lyndsay

http://www.lrussell.com